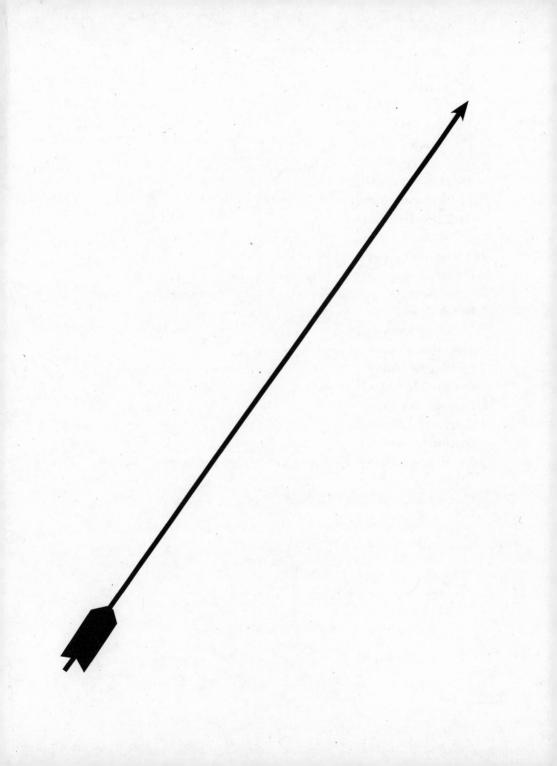

ALSO BY JOHN L'HEUREUX

The Medici Boy
The Miracle
Having Everything
The Handmaid of Desire
The Shrine at Altamira
An Honorable Profession
Comedians
A Woman Run Mad
Desires
Jessica Fayer
Family Affairs
The Clang Birds
Tight White Collar
No Place for Hiding
One Eye and a Measuring Rod
Picnic in Babylon
Rubrics for a Revolution
Quick as Dandelions
*The Uncommon Touch: Fiction and Poetry from the Stanford Writing
    Workshop*, ed.
Conversations with John L'Heureux

THE HEART IS A FULL-WILD BEAST

THE

HEART

IS A FULL-WILD BEAST

And Maketh Many Wild Leaps

NEW AND SELECTED STORIES

JOHN L'HEUREUX

A PUBLIC SPACE BOOKS

A Public Space Books
323 Dean Street
Brooklyn, NY 11217

Stories from this collection appeared, in earlier forms, in *The Comedians* (Viking), *Family Affairs* (Doubleday), and *Desires* (Holt, Rinehart, & Winston) as well as the following magazines:
"The Torturer's Assistant" in *Story*
"The Handmaid" in *Catholic World*
"On Garby Road" in *Epoch*
"Communion" in *Sequoia*
"Clothing" in *Tendril*
"The Rise and Rise of Annie Clark," "The Long Black Line," and "Three Short Moments in a Long Life" in the *New Yorker*

Significant support for A Public Space Books has been provided by the Drue and H. J. Heinz II Charitable Trust and the Chisholm Foundation. This publication is also made possible, in part, through a grant from the National Endowment for the Arts, and generous contributions from the Amazon Literary Partnership, the New York State Council on the Arts, and other corporations, foundations, and individuals. We are grateful to all of them.

Library of Congress Control Number: 2019939458
ISBN 978-0-9982675-7-9
eISBN 978-0-9982675-9-3
Distributed by Publishers Group West

www.apublicspace.org

9 8 7 6 5 4 3 2 1

Like everything I write, this book

—a poor thing, but mine own—

I dedicate to

JOAN POLSTON L'HEUREUX,

my wife, my life,

my love

The heart is a full-wild beast

and maketh many wild leaps.

—*Ancrene Riwle* (c. 1230)

CONTENTS

MYSTERIES

MARRIAGES

DOUBTS

CERTAINTIES

MYSTERIES

THE COMEDIAN

Corinne hasn't planned to have a baby. She is thirty-eight and happy and she wants to get on with it. She is a stand-up comedian with a husband, her second, with no thought of a child, and what she wants out of life now is a lot of laughs. To give them, and especially to get them. And here she is, by accident, pregnant.

The doctor sees her chagrin and is surprised, because he thinks of her as a competent and sturdy woman. But that's how things are these days, and so he suggests an abortion. Corinne says she'll let him know; she has to do some thinking. A baby.

"That's great," Russ says. "If you want it, I mean. I want it. I mean, I want it if you do. It's up to you, though. You know what I mean?"

And so they decide that of course they will have the baby, of course they want the baby, the baby is exactly what they need.

In the bathroom mirror that night, Russ looks through his eyes into his cranium for a long time. Finally he sees his mind. As he watches, it knots like a fist. And he continues to watch, glad, as that fist beats the new baby flat and thin, a dead slick silverfish.

Mother. Mother and baby. A little baby. A big baby. Bouncing babies. At once Corinne sees twenty babies, twenty pink basketball babies, bouncing down the court and then up into the air and—whoosh—they swish neatly through the net. Babies.

Baby is its own excuse for being. Or is it? Well, Corinne was a Catholic right up until the end of her first marriage, so she thinks maybe it is. One thing is sure: the only subject you can't make a good joke about is abortion.

Yes, they will have the baby. Yes, she will be the mother. Yes.

But the next morning, while Russ is at work, Corinne turns off the television and sits on the edge of the couch. She squeezes her thighs together, tight; she contracts her stomach; she arches her back. This is no joke. This is the real thing. By an act of will, she is going to expel this baby, this invader, this insidious little murderer. She pushes and pushes and nothing happens. She pushes again, hard. And once more she pushes. Finally she gives up and lies back against the sofa, resting.

After a while she puts her hand on her belly, and as she does, she is astonished to hear singing.

It is the baby. It has a soft reedy voice and it sings slightly off-key. Corinne listens to the words: "Some of these days, you'll miss me, honey…"

Corinne faints then, and it is quite some time before she wakes up.

When she wakes, she opens her eyes only a slit and looks carefully from left to right. She sits on the couch, vigilant, listening, but she hears nothing. After a while she says three Hail Marys and an Act of Contrition, and then, confused and a little embarrassed, she does the laundry.

She does not tell Russ about this.

Well, it's a time of strain, Corinne tells herself, even though in California there isn't supposed to be any strain. Just surfing and tans and divorce and a lot of interfacing. No strain and no babies.

Corinne thinks for a second about interfacing babies, but she forces the thought from her mind and goes back to thinking about her act. Sometimes she does a very funny set on interfacing, but only if the audience is middle-aged. The younger ones don't seem to know that interfacing is laughable. Come to think of it, nobody laughs much in California. Everybody smiles, but who laughs?

Laughs: that's something she can use. She does Garbo's laugh: "I am so hap-py." What was that movie? "I am so hap-py." She does the Garbo laugh again. Not bad. Who else laughs? Joe E. Brown.

The Wicked Witch of the West. Who was she? Somebody Hamilton. Will anybody remember these people? Ruth Buzzi? Goldie Hawn? Yes, that great giggle. Of course, the best giggle is Burt Reynolds's. High and fey. Why does he do that? Is he sending up his own image?

Corinne is thinking of images, Burt Reynolds's and Tom Selleck's, when she hears singing: "Cal-i-for-nia, here I come, right back where I started from…" Corinne stops pacing and stands in the doorway to the kitchen—as if I'm waiting for the earthquake, she thinks. But there is no earthquake; there is only the thin sweet voice, singing.

Corinne leans against the doorframe and listens. She closes her eyes. At once it is Easter, and she is a child again at Sacred Heart Grammar School, and the thirty-five members of the children's choir, earnest and angelic, look out at her from where they stand, massed about the altar. They wear red cassocks and white surplices, starched, and they seem to have descended from heaven for this one occasion. Their voices are pure, high, untouched by adolescence or by pain; and, with a conviction born of absolute innocence, they sing to God and to Corinne, "Cal-i-for-nia, here I come."

Corinne leans against the doorframe and listens truly now. Imagination aside, drama aside—she listens. It is a single voice she hears, thin and reedy. So, she did not imagine it the first time. It is true. The baby sings.

That night when Russ comes home, he takes his shower, and they settle in with their first martini, and everything is cozy.

Corinne asks him about his day, and he tells her. It was a lousy day. Russ started his own construction company a year ago just as the bottom fell out of the building business, and now there are no jobs to speak of. Just renovation stuff. Cleanup after fires. Sometimes Victorian restorations down in the Castro District. But that's about it. So whatever comes his way is bound to be lousy. This is Russ's second marriage, though, so he knows not to go too far with a lousy day. Who needs it?

"But I've got you, babe," he says and pulls her toward him and kisses her.

"We've got each other," Corinne says and kisses him back. "And the baby," she says.

He holds her close then, so that she can't see his face. She makes big eyes like an actor in a bad comedy—she doesn't know why; she just always sees the absurd in everything. After a while they pull away, smiling, secret, and sip their martinis.

"Do you know something?" she says. "Can I tell you something?"

"What?" he says. "Tell me."

"You won't laugh?"

"No," he says, laughing. "I'm sorry. No, I won't laugh."

"Okay," she says. "Here goes."

There is a long silence, and then he says, "Well?"

"It sings."

"It sings?"

"The baby. The fetus. It sings."

Russ is stalled, but only for a second. Then he says, "Rock and roll? Or plainchant?" He begins to laugh, and he laughs so hard that he chokes and sloshes martini onto the couch. "You're wonderful," he says. "You're really a funny, funny girl. Woman." He laughs some more. "Is that for your act? I love it."

"I'm serious," she says. "I mean it."

"Well, it's great," he says. "They'll love it."

Corinne puts her hand on her stomach and thinks she has never been so alone in her life. She looks at Russ, with his big square jaw and all those white teeth and his green eyes so trusting and innocent, and she realizes for one second how corrupt she is, how lost, how deserving of a baby who sings; and then she pulls herself together because real life has to go on.

"Let's eat out," she says. "Spaghetti. It's cheap." She kisses him gently on his left eyelid, on his right. She gazes into his eyes and smiles, so that he will not guess she is thinking: Who is this man? Who am I?

Corinne has a job, Fridays and Saturdays for the next three weeks, at the Ironworks. It's not the Comedy Shop, but it's a legitimate gig, and the money is good. Moreover, it will give her something to think about besides whether or not she should go through with the abortion. She and Russ have put that on hold.

She is well into her third month, but she isn't showing yet, so she figures she can handle the three weekends easily. She wishes, in a way, that she were showing. As it is, she only looks... She searches for the word, but not for long. The word is *fat*. She looks fat.

She could do fat-girl jokes, but she hates jokes that put down women. And she hates jokes that are blue. Jokes that ridicule husbands. Jokes that ridicule the joker's looks. Jokes about nationalities. Jokes that play into audience prejudice. Jokes about the terrible small town you came from. Jokes about how poor you were, how ugly, how unpopular. Phyllis Diller jokes. Joan Rivers jokes. Jokes about small boobs, wrinkles, sexual inadequacy. Why is she in this business, she wonders. She hates jokes.

She thinks she hears herself praying: Please, please. What should she do at the Ironworks? What should she do about the baby? What should she do? The baby is the only one who's decided what to do. The baby sings.

Its voice is filling out nicely and it has enlarged its repertoire considerably. It sings a lot of classical melodies Corinne thinks she remembers from somewhere, churchy stuff, but it also favors golden oldies from the forties and fifties, with a few real old-timers thrown in when they seem appropriate. Once, right at the beginning, for instance, after Corinne and Russ had quarreled, Corinne locked herself in the bathroom to sulk and after a while was surprised, and then grateful, to hear the baby crooning, "Oh, my man, I love him so." It struck Corinne a day or so later that this could be a baby that would sell out for any one-liner... if indeed she decides to have the baby... and so she was relieved when the baby turned to more classical pieces.

The baby sings only now and then, and it sings better at some times than at others, but Corinne is convinced it sings best on weekend evenings when she is preparing for her gig. Before she leaves home, Corinne always has a long hot soak in the tub. She lies in the suds with her little orange bath pillow at her head and, as she runs through the night's possibilities, preparing ad-libs, heckler put-downs, segues, the baby sings to her.

There is some connection, she is sure, between her work and the baby's singing, but she can't guess what it is. It doesn't matter. She loves this: just she and the baby, together, in song.

Thank you, thank you, she prays.

The Ironworks gig goes extremely well. It is a young crowd, mostly, and so Corinne sticks to her young jokes: life in California, diets, dating, school. The audience laughs, and Russ says she is better than ever, but at the end of the three weeks the manager tells her, "You got it, honey. You got all the moves. You really make them laugh, you know? But they laugh from here only"—he taps his head—"not from the gut. You gotta get gut. You know? Like feeling."

So now the gig is over and Corinne lies in her tub trying to think of gut. She's gotta get gut, she's gotta get feeling. Has she ever felt? Well, she feels for Russ; she loves him. She felt for Alan, that bastard; well, maybe he wasn't so bad; maybe he just wasn't ready for marriage, any more than she was. Maybe it's California; maybe nobody can feel in California.

Enough about feeling, already. Deliberately, she puts feeling out of her mind and calls up babies instead. A happy baby, she thinks, and at once the bathroom is crowded with laughing babies, each one roaring and carrying on like Ed McMahon. A fat baby, and she sees a Shelley Winters baby, an Elizabeth Taylor baby, an Orson Welles baby. An active baby: a mile of trampolines and babies doing quadruple somersaults, backflips, high dives. A healthy baby: babies lifting weights, swimming the channel. Babies.

But abortion is the issue, not babies. Should she have it, or not?

At once she sees a bloody mess, a crushed-looking thing, half-animal, half-human. Its hands open and close. She gasps. "No," she says aloud, and shakes her head to get rid of the awful picture. "No," and covers her face.

Gradually she realizes that she has been listening to humming, and now the humming turns to song—"It ain't necessarily so," sung in a good clear mezzo.

Her eyes hurt and she has a headache. In fact, her eyes hurt all the time.

Corinne has finally convinced Russ that she hears the baby singing. Actually, he is convinced that Corinne is halfway around the bend with worry, and he is surprised, when he thinks about it, to find that he loves her anyway, crazy or not. He tells her that, as much as he hates the idea, maybe she ought to think about having an abortion.

"I've actually gotten to like the singing," she says.

"Corinne," he says.

"It's the things I see that scare me to death."

"What things? What do you see?"

At once she sees a little crimson baby. It has been squashed into a mason jar. The tiny eyes almost disappear into the puffed cheeks, the cheeks into the neck, the neck into the torso. It is a pickled baby, ancient, preserved.

"Tell me," he says.

"Nothing," she says. "It's just that my eyes hurt."

It's getting late for an abortion, the doctor says, but she can still have one safely. He's known her for twenty years, all through the first marriage and now through this one, and he's puzzled that a funny and sensible girl like Corinne should be having such a tough time with pregnancy. He had recommended abortion right from the start, because she didn't seem to want the baby and because she was almost forty, but he hadn't really expected her to take him up on it. Looking at her now, though, it is clear to him that she'll never make it. She'll be wacko—if not during the pregnancy, then sure as hell afterward.

So what does she think? What does Russ think?

Well, first, she explains in her new, sort of wandering way, there's something else she wants to ask about; not really important, she supposes, but just something, well, kind of different she probably should mention. It's the old problem of the baby... well, um, singing.

"Singing?" he asks.

"Singing?" he asks again.

"And humming," Corinne says.

They sit in silence for a minute, the doctor trying to decide whether or not this is a joke. She's got this great poker face. She really is a good comic. So after a while he laughs, and then when she laughs, he knows he's done the right thing. But what a crazy sense of humor!

"You're terrific," he says. "Anything else? How's Russ? How was the Ironworks job?"

"My eyes hurt," she says. "I have headaches."

And so they discuss her vision for a while, and stand-up comedy, and she makes him laugh. And that's that. At the door he says to her, "Have an abortion, Corinne. Now, before it's too late."

They have just made love and now Russ turns off the light and they lie together in the dark, his hand on her belly.

"Listen," he says. "I want to say something. I've been thinking about what the doctor said, about an abortion. I hate it, I hate the whole idea, but you know, we've got to think of you. And I think this baby is too much for you, I think maybe that's why you've been having those headaches and stuff. Don't you think?"

Corinne puts her hand on his hand and says nothing. After a long while Russ speaks again, into the darkness.

"I've been a lousy father. Two sons I never see. I never see them. The stepfather's good to them, though; he's a good father. I thought maybe I'd have another chance at it, do it right this time, like the marriage. Besides, business isn't always going to be this bad, you know; I'll get jobs; I'll get money. We could afford it, you know? A son. A daughter. It would be nice. But what I mean is, we've got to take other things into consideration, we've got to consider your health. You're not strong enough, I guess. I always think of you as strong, because you do those gigs and you're funny and all but, I mean, you're almost forty and the doctor thinks that maybe an abortion is the way to go, and what do I know. I don't know. The singing. The headaches. I don't know."

Russ looks into the dark, seeing nothing. "I worry about you, you want to know the truth. I do. Corinne?"

Corinne lies beside him, listening to him, refusing to listen to the baby, who all this time has been singing. Russ is as alone as she is, even more alone. She is dumbfounded. She is speechless with love. If he were a whirlpool, she thinks, she would fling herself into it. If he were... but he is who he is, and she loves only him, and she makes her decision.

"You think I'm losing my mind," she says.

Silence.

"Yes."

More silence.

"Well, I'm not. Headaches are a normal part of lots of pregnancies, the doctor told me, and the singing doesn't mean anything at all. He explained what was really going on, why I thought I heard it sing. You see," Corinne says, improvising freely now, making it all up, for him, her gift to him, "you see, when you get somebody as high-strung as me and you add pregnancy right at the time I'm about to make it big as a stand-up, then the pressures get to be so much that sometimes the imagination can take over, the doctor said, and when you tune in to the normal sounds of your body, you hear them really loud, as if they were amplified by a three-thousand-watt PA system, and it can sound like singing. See?"

Russ says nothing.

"So you see, it all makes sense, really. You don't have to worry about me."

"Come on," Russ says. "Do you mean to tell me you never heard the baby singing?"

"Well, I heard it, sort of, you know? It was really all in my mind. I mean, the sound was in my body physiologically, but my hearing it as singing was just..."

"Just your imagination."

Corinne does not answer.

"Well?"

"Right," she says, making the total gift. "It was just my imagination."

And the baby—who has not stopped singing all this time, love songs mostly—stops singing now, and does not sing again until the day scheduled for the abortion.

The baby has not sung in three weeks. It is Corinne's fifth month now, and at last they have been able to do an amniocentesis. The news is bad. One of the baby's chromosomes does not match up to anything in hers, anything in Russ's. What this means, they tell her, is that the baby is not normal. It will be deformed in some way; in what way, they have no idea.

Corinne and Russ decide on abortion.

They talk very little about their decision now that they have made it. In fact, they talk very little about anything. Corinne's face grows daily more haggard, and she avoids Russ's eyes. She is silent much of the time, thinking. The baby is silent all the time.

The abortion will be by hypertonic saline injection, a simple procedure complicated only by the fact that Corinne has waited so long. She has been given a booklet to read and she has listened to a tape, and so she knows about the injection of the saline solution, she knows about the contractions that will begin slowly and then get more and more frequent, and she knows about the dangers of infection and excessive bleeding.

She knows, moreover, that it will be a formed fetus she will expel.

Russ has come with her to the hospital and is outside in the waiting room. Corinne thinks of him, of how she loves him, of how their lives will be better, safer, without this baby who sings. This deformed baby. Who sings. If only she could hear the singing once more, just once.

Corinne lies on the table with her legs in the stirrups, and one of the nurses drapes the examining sheet over and around her. The other nurse, or someone—Corinne is getting confused; her eyesight seems fuzzy—takes her pulse and her blood pressure. She feels someone washing her, the careful hands, the warm fluid. So, it is beginning.

Corinne closes her eyes and tries to make her mind a blank. Dark, she thinks. Dark. She squeezes her eyes tight against the light, she wants to remain in this cool darkness forever, she wants to cease being. And then, amazingly, the dark does close in on her. Though she opens her eyes, she sees nothing. She can remain this way forever if she wills it. The dark is cool to the touch, and it is comforting, somehow; it invites her in. She can lean into it, give herself up to it, and be safe, alone, forever.

She tries to sit up. She will enter this dark. She will do it. Please, please, she hears herself say. And then all at once she thinks of Russ and the baby, and instead of surrendering to the dark, she pushes it away.

With one sweep of her hand she pushes the sheet from her and flings it to the floor. She pulls her legs from the stirrups and manages to sit up, blinded still, but fighting.

"Here now," a nurse says, caught off guard, unsure what to do. "Hold on now. It's all right. It's fine."

"Easy now. Easy," the doctor says, thinking, Yes, here it is, what else is new.

Together the nurses and the doctor make an effort to stop her, but they are too late, because by this time Corinne has fought free of any restraints. She is off the examination table and, naked, huddles in the corner of the small room.

"No!" she shouts. "I want the baby. I want the baby." And later, when she has stopped shouting, when she has stopped crying, still she clutches her knees to her chest and whispers over and over, "I want the baby."

So there is no abortion after all.

By the time she is discharged, Corinne's vision has returned, dimly. Moreover, though she tells nobody, she has heard humming, and once or twice a whole line of music. The baby has begun to sing again.

Corinne has more offers than she wants: the hungry i, the Purple Onion, the Comedy Store. Suddenly everybody decides it's time to take a look at her, but she is in no shape to be looked at, so she signs for two weeks at My Uncle's Bureau and lets it go at that.

She is only marginally pretty now, she is six months pregnant, and she is carrying a deformed child. Furthermore, she can see very little, and what she does see, she often sees double.

Her humor, therefore, is spare and grim, but audiences love it. She begins slow: "When I was a girl, I always wanted to look like Elizabeth Taylor," she says and glances down at her swollen belly. Two beats. "And now I do." They laugh with her and applaud. Now she can quicken the pace, sharpen the humor. They follow her; they are completely captivated.

She has found some new way of holding her body—tipping her head, thrusting out her belly—and instead of putting off her audience or embarrassing them, it charms them. The laughter is with her, the applause for her. She could do anything out there and get away with it. And she knows it. They simply love her.

In her dressing room after the show she tells herself that somehow, magically, she's learned to work from the heart instead of just from the head. She's got gut. She's got feeling. But she knows it's something more than that. By the end of the two weeks she is convinced that the successful new element in her act is the baby. This deformed baby, the abnormal baby she tried to get rid of. And what interests her most is that she no longer cares about success as a stand-up.

Corinne falls asleep that night to the sound of the baby's crooning. She is trying to pray, Please, please, but with Russ's snoring and the baby's lullaby, they all get mixed up together in her mind—God, Russ, the baby—and she forgets to whom she is praying or why. She sleeps.

The baby sings all the time now. It starts first thing in the morning with a nice soft piece by Telemann or Brahms; there are assorted lullabies at bedtime; and throughout the day it is bop, opera, ragtime, blues, a little rock and roll, big-band stuff. The baby never tires.

Corinne tells no one about this, not even Russ.

She and Russ talk about almost everything now: their love for each other, their hopes for the baby, their plans. They have lots of plans. Russ has assured Corinne that whatever happens, he's ready for it. Corinne is his whole life, and no matter how badly the baby is deformed, they'll manage. They'll do the right thing. They'll survive.

They talk about almost everything, but they do not talk about the baby's singing.

For Corinne the singing is secret, mysterious. It contains some revelation, of course, but she does not want to know what that revelation might be.

The singing is somehow tied up with her work; but more than that, with her life. It is part of her fate. It is inescapable. And she is perfectly content to wait.

Corinne has been in labor for three hours, and the baby has been singing the whole time. The doctor has administered a mild anesthetic, and a nurse remains at her bedside, but the birth does not seem imminent, and so for Corinne it is a period of pain and waiting. And for the baby, singing.

"These lights are so strong," Corinne says, or thinks she says. "The lights are blinding."

The nurse looks at her for a moment and then goes back to the letter she is writing.

"Please," Corinne says, "thank you."

She is unconscious, she supposes; she is imagining the lights. Or perhaps the lights are indeed bright and she sees them as they really are because she is unconscious. Or perhaps her sight has come back, as strong as it used to be. Whatever the case, she doesn't want to think about it right now. Besides, for some reason or other, even though the lights are blinding, they are not blinding her. They do not even bother her. It is as if light is her natural element.

"Thank you," she says. To someone.

The singing is wonderful, a cappella things Corinne recognizes as Brahms, Mozart, Bach. The baby's voice can assume any dimension it wants now, swelling from a single thin note to choir volume; it can take on the tone and resonance of musical instruments, violin, viola, flute; it can become all sounds; it enchants.

The contractions are more frequent; even unconscious, Corinne can tell that. Good. Soon the waiting will be over and she will have her wonderful baby, her perfect baby. But at once she realizes hers will not be a perfect baby; it will be deformed. "Please," she says, "please," as if prayer can keep Russ from being told—as he will be soon after the birth—that his baby has been born dumb. Russ, who has never understood comedians.

But now the singing has begun to swell in volume. It is as if the baby has become a full choir, with many voices, with great strength.

The baby will be fine however it is, she thinks. She thinks of Russ, worried half to death. She is no longer worried. She accepts what will be.

The contractions are very frequent now, and the light is much brighter. She knows the doctor has come into the room, because she hears his voice. There is another nurse too. And soon there will be the baby.

The light is so bright that she can see none of them. She can see into the light, it is true; she can see the soft fleecy nimbus glowing beyond the light, but she can see nothing in the room.

The singing. The singing and the light. It is Palestrina she hears, in polyphony, each voice lambent. The light envelops her, catches her up from this table where the doctor bends over her and where already can be seen the shimmering yellow hair of the baby. The light lifts her, and the singing lifts her, and she says, "Yes," she says, "thank you."

She accepts what will be. She accepts what is.

The room is filled with singing and with light, and the singing is transformed into light, more light, more lucency, and still she says, "Yes," until she cannot bear it, and she reaches up and tears the light aside. And sees.

MUTTI

The eight o'clock bell had already rung, but Anton stood on the footbridge anyway, watching the dark water. The bridge was off-limits during school hours, but nobody was around to see him now, and Anton liked the feeling he got, leaning over the bridge, and so he stood there, waiting. It was cold, and getting colder, but there was no ice on the stream yet. There would be ice on the way home though.

A boy in the lower school had drowned in the stream a year ago; that was why the bridge was off-limits. Anton watched a patch of leaves pull away from the bank and eddy out into the middle of the stream. He squinted, turning the leaves into a brown jacket, his own, floating toward him as he stood above, watching. There was a small rock directly beneath where he stood. If he could make the leaves float toward the rock, touch it, he would have the picture of his own dead body, facedown, floating there beneath him. Drowned. He concentrated hard, willing the patch of leaves to drift toward him. But the leaves caught for a moment against a branch and spun in a full circle, trailing behind them a dark green patch, slimy, changing the shape of everything. Then suddenly, for no reason, the leaves broke free of the branch and came to rest against a rock. Anton smiled. Perfect. The back of his head was just visible above the water, the dark brown jacket moved in the stream, washed by it, softly, easily, and Anton inhaled the cold water deeply. Drowned. Dead.

He could not leave the bridge so long as his body lay there in the stream.

It was getting late. He always missed the eight o'clock bell, but he did not want to miss the 8:10 and the end of homeroom period. It was Friday, and if Mr. Hollister were to call him in again, it would be today. If he called him in, he would skip gym. If he called him in, he would get through the morning all right, and then maybe the afternoon. And then there would be the stones, and his mother, and all Saturday and Sunday with nothing to be afraid of.

Move, then, he wanted to say to the body beneath the bridge. At once the leaves broke away from the rock. Again Anton smiled. It was going to be a safe day.

In the corridor outside homeroom everything was silent. He peeked through the little glass window and saw Miss Kelly pacing up and down in front of the room. She was wearing her Friday sweater, green-blue and baggy, and she was mopping her nose with a tissue. She always had a cold.

The principal was making the morning announcements and his muffled voice came in little spurts through the heavy door: PTA, cheerleading, speech club. Anton opened his locker and put away all his books except American history; he would need that for first period. He hung up his coat, his cap, his scarf. He looked both ways for a moment and then quickly, in a single hurried motion, he took off his face and hung it on the side hook, so that only his profile showed. And then he slammed the locker door, ready, as the 8:10 bell rang for first period.

"You're late, Anton," Miss Kelly said at the classroom door. "Go to the office and get a pass. Oh, and here's a note. Mr. Hollister wants to see you in the guidance office during your first free period. So please don't be late for him. You're always late, Anton. I don't know why that has to be." Miss Kelly hugged herself in her green-blue sweater. "Can you tell me why that has to be? That you're always late?"

Anton said nothing.

"Well, I've had a little talk with Mr. Hollister about you. I've told him you're doing very well in English, your written work, but you don't talk enough. You don't contribute. Don't you think you could contribute more?"

Students had begun to drift in for Miss Kelly's English class and some of them were listening, Anton knew.

"We both like you, Anton. Mr. Hollister and I, both. I want you to understand that. We're just concerned about you. You're just so…"

But Anton was not listening to her. He was listening to the fat girl in the front row, who was saying to her girlfriend, "We're concerned about you, Anton. We love you, Anton. We adore you. Oh, Anton!"

"Very well," Miss Kelly said, seeing that he was not listening to her, seeing his face redden. "Please see Mr. Hollister during study. And please be on time."

Brisk now, all business, she said to the class, "All right, people, please settle down. We are still on Chaucer and it is already December and we are a full century behind."

Miss Kelly was in love with Mr. Hollister, Anton knew, and he knew too that Mr. Hollister would never return her love. Mr. Hollister loved him.

He got through American history and algebra and art without having to say anything. As always, he knew the answers, but he kept silent even when he was called on. He preferred that the others think him stupid and just ignore him. He didn't want them to look at him or talk to him or even talk about him. He wanted not to exist. Or to be invisible. To escape. So he waited.

Even in art class he waited. Art was an elective and Miss Belekis had seen at once that he had a real gift for draftsmanship, so she had loaned him books on anatomy and told him to draw whatever he wanted. She had praised his first drawings—fat peasant women knitting or praying or peeling apples, imitative stuff—and he had liked her praise, but he saw the danger of being noticed. And so for Miss Belekis he drew the same peasant women again and again, trying to make the drawings seem less finished each time, trying to conceal his growing mastery of craft. After a while, he just gave her the same old drawings.

She stopped commenting, but she continued to loan him the books.

Years later, as a famous sculptor working in marble and stone, he would remain just as secretive, a mystery to his agent and the galleries where he showed. He was a recluse. He saw almost nobody. And though he always sculpted from life and, in time, went through three wives and a mistress, he claimed he just didn't like people. He merely sculpted them from stone.

But now, in high school, he had no choice. He was forced to see people. Still, he could keep them from seeing him. And so, though he continued to take home the books that Miss Belekis loaned him, he showed her only the same old pictures of peasant women. Meanwhile, at nights and on weekends, he made good progress with the human figure, drawing it over and over in every imaginable posture, and always nude. This did not embarrass him. This was art, and it had nothing to do with life.

In life, he was terrified at the idea of a nude body. This was why he cut gym class repeatedly. All the boys taking off their clothes in front of one another, looking, some of them even wanting to be looked at. And Coach Landry encouraging it all. It made him want to run and hide. And they looked at him, too.

Only last night he had been drying himself after his shower when he noticed a few dark brown hairs, down there, and he realized he would never be safe again. He squatted on the bath mat and covered himself with both hands, squeezing tight, and praying, "Oh no, God, please don't let me get big there, and have hair that shows, and be like the others. Please don't let me ever be a man." But even as he prayed, he knew it was hopeless. He took his hands away and the dark hairs were still there. It would happen to him, too. Nothing would stop it. Not prayer. Not anything.

"Anton, my friend. Come right in," Mr. Hollister said. "Have a seat. Go on, sit down. Now, tell me. How are things going? Things going okay?"

"Yes." Anton looked down. Mr. Hollister was wearing his red turtleneck. His blond hair was long and floppy. He crossed his legs wrong.

"Good. Good. So how are you doing? Oh, well, we've done that, haven't we. What I really mean, Anton, is that as your guidance counselor, I'm concerned about you. I mean, you're a really bright young man, but you're always late for everything, and your teachers say you don't contribute in class, and, gosh, I've noticed myself that you're, well, you're... let's say independent. Some might say a loner. Some might even say antisocial. But I understand that. I do. I was a private kid myself. Like you, in a way. You know?"

Anton looked up at him and resolved to tell him nothing. He would break in. He would destroy. "You're thin, Anton. Do you eat enough? I mean, do you have a good appetite?"

"Yes."

"Good. Good. Well, frankly, what I really want to ask about, express my concern about is... the bruises. The cuts on your hands, your face sometimes, that broken wrist you had. I mean, Anton, how do you have so many accidents, for instance? I wonder if you could tell me about that."

"I'm clumsy. I'm not careful."

"Well, Anton, I was wondering about your folks. Your mom and dad. Do you get along with them okay? I mean, they never hit you or anything, do they?"

"No."

"I mean, those bruises aren't from them. Your father doesn't hit you or anything? Even once in a while? You could tell me, you know. I could make sure he'd never hurt you again."

"No."

"No, of course not. We just have to check, you know. And your mother, neither? No?"

"They never hit me."

"Well, let's see. I know quite a lot about you," Mr. Hollister said, and flipped open a manila folder on his desk. "We know quite a lot about each other, I mean." He leafed through several sheets of paper.

What he knew was that Anton was fourteen, an only child, male. He was born an American citizen, of Russian and German parents.

His father was a translator of Slavic literature. His mother was a housewife. They had lived in this small Massachusetts town for less than a year. What he knew was that Anton was alone.

"Don't we," Mr. Hollister said.

"Don't we what?"

"We know quite a lot about each other, I mean."

Anton waited for a moment and then looked him full in the eyes. "Yes," he said.

Mr. Hollister cleared his throat and uncrossed his legs and looked again at the sheets of paper in the folder. Slowly his face began to color. When he raised his eyes, he found Anton still looking at him, waiting. He lowered them again.

"Well, any time you want to talk, Anton, you feel free to just come in here and see me." His voice was different now. "I'm concerned about you, as you know; about all the kids. So you just come ahead anytime. Okay?"

"Thank you," Anton said. He lowered his eyes finally, and then he stood up to go.

"Anytime," Mr. Hollister said.

Mr. Hollister and Coach Landry were prefecting at the west end stairs when the crowd started down to the lunchroom. Seeing Anton approach, Mr. Hollister said, intending to be heard, "I'm concerned about that Anton fellow. He's a fine young man, I think." And Coach Landry, not intending to be heard, but heard nonetheless, said to him, "Just keep it in your pants, Hollister."

Anton drifted with the crowd downstairs to the lunchroom, and then slowly, almost aimlessly, walked on past it and, once out of sight, moved quickly down the corridor to the gymnasium area and the boiler room. Nobody ever came here except to get to the gym.

Anton ate his lunch in a stall in the men's room, or rather, he ate the apple, having thrown away the sandwich and the cake as soon as he had left home that morning. He was safe here. The walls and the cement floor were painted dark green and the massive stalls were made of oak and coated with many layers of varnish. There were no windows and only a single small bulb lit the room. It smelled like church. There was a new men's room on the far side of the gym, with white walls and tan metal stalls and lots of light. The boys used that place all the time, but nobody ever came here. Anton sat on the high toilet in the abandoned men's room and ate his apple.

So, it was almost over. And he had made it this far. Only two more classes. Tomorrow he would spend all day drawing. And Sunday too, if he wanted. He finished the apple and continued to sit there, his hands folded in his lap, waiting.

The rest of the afternoon passed slowly. He was called on three times in French class and twice he gave the answer quickly, almost eagerly. The third time, though, he caught himself and pretended he didn't know the answer.

He had slipped earlier today with Mr. Hollister, coming out from behind his school face to look at him, and he had almost done it again in French. He would have to be more careful. He could see Miss Pratt looking at him the way she looked at the others, encouraging him to risk an answer, right or wrong, enticing him out. He thought of his real face hanging downstairs in the green locker. When Miss Pratt called on him again, she would find he was not even there. The bell rang. Only one more class to go.

Miss Kelly was crazier than usual today. She kept sniffing and mopping at her nose and hugging herself, but at least she did not call on him. She seemed, in fact, to be deliberately avoiding him. "The Prioress's Tale," she was saying, raised the most interesting problems of anti-Semitism in Chaucer's Middle Ages. The Jews of course had been driven out of England in 1290. Which meant that Chaucer was probably writing about Jews, and about anti-Semitism, from an accepted tradition rather than from any actual experience of his own. Did they see what this implied about the Christian worldview of that time? Somebody raised his hand to contribute. Anton turned and saw that it was Kevin Delaney, who said that he used to live in Bridgeport and he knew some Jewish kids there and they were just like anybody else; they weren't like New York Jews at all. This got Miss Kelly all upset, though she pretended that he had made an interesting contribution, and then she tried to get them to talk about prejudices and stereotypes in their own lives. Everybody had something to say about this, and they all began to talk at the same time. Anton smiled to himself; they'd do anything rather than read Chaucer. Finally the bell rang and Miss Kelly thanked everyone for an interesting and profitable discussion. In three minutes he would be free.

But instead of just piling her books and papers while they waited for the final bell, Miss Kelly signaled him to the front of the room. She turned her back to the class and edged him around so that nobody would hear her. There was that interested silence. "You can talk quietly, class," she said loudly, and when finally there was a whisper or two, she said, "I hope you found that discussion period helpful, Anton. You see, we all have strange notions about other people sometimes, and sometimes all of us feel that we are outsiders. Do you see? I hope you see that."

Anton began to blush. What a fool the woman was. They were all looking at him, every one of them. He wanted to kill her; she was killing him. But he only stood there, his eyes lowered.

"I had a little talk with Mr. Hollister, you see." She paused for a moment, but Anton said nothing. "Did you have a good talk with Mr. Hollister? Mr. Hollister is a very unusual man. He has the ability to care. He is a feeling person who feels for others. Mr. Hollister…"

She wasn't talking to him. She was just talking.

Anton raised his eyes and stared at her. He was thinking he could say simply, "He doesn't love you. He will never love you," and she would die, right there, in front of the classroom.

Suddenly Miss Kelly stopped talking and looked at him. "What?" she said. "What is it?"

Anton said nothing.

"Why are you looking at me that way?" she said. "Stop that. You stop that right now."

It seemed hours before the bell finally rang.

Anton braced his books under his left arm and walked across the footbridge without looking at the water on either side. There would be ice on the stream by now, at least along the edges. And there would be ice at the clay bank. He walked with purpose, but not too fast. He didn't want the others to walk with him or to offer him a ride—not that anyone ever had. But he was careful just the same.

After a half mile, Anton turned off High Street onto Putnam Road and he was completely safe at last. He had a two-mile walk down Putnam, past the woods and the old mill and the clay bank, and then another half mile and he would be home. His mother would be in the kitchen, watching television and sipping her muscatel; his father would be out in the cabin working on Gorky. He would show her the bruises and cuts and she would console him, and at night he would lock his bedroom door and draw the things he had felt while she cradled him in her arms. And then he would fall asleep and dream of dying.

He broke a branch and used it as a walking stick. He was an old man taking little steps, propped up by a cane that bent beneath his weight. He walked this way up to the twenty-fifth tree. For the next twenty-five he walked like his mother. And for the next, like his father. He hugged himself, sniffing, and said, in Miss Kelly's voice, "I had a little talk with Mr. Hollister today, Anton." And then for a long time he walked like himself, thinking of Mr. Hollister and how he crossed his legs wrong, and of Miss Kelly. Both of them had seen him with his real face. It was getting harder to hide. He wanted to say real things. He wanted to refuse. But mostly he wanted not to be noticed. And now he was getting hair down there, and he would get big like all the others, and he would be like them in every way except inside, where he could be just himself, and terrified.

He thought of that picture of the old woman on a bridge, screaming. It was called *The Scream*, he thought. He saw the blackness of her open mouth, and he shaped his own mouth like hers, and in a moment he heard the long high wail coming and it would not stop. But finally it did stop. He was dizzy then and black spots sparkled behind his eyes, but he had done it and he felt good. And he had passed the old mill without looking at it once. In a minute he would be at the clay bank.

He rounded a turn in the road and there it was, a cliff of clay thirty or forty feet high, half of it chewed away by some huge machine so that you could see the layers and layers of red and brown and gold and blue gray. You could spend hours staring at it and never succeed in counting all the colors.

He would never paint in color until he could paint this, he thought. He would never risk it. But then what was he thinking, since he knew he would never paint at all.

There were ice patches here and there, and frozen chunks of clay, and some good patches of shale. Anton took off his mittens and quickly, expertly, slashed at the knuckles of each hand with a small slab of stone. The blood came slowly but he was patient and waited before slashing again. He did not want to go too deep.

And then, somewhere inside, he heard himself think, But what if I don't die. "What if?" he said aloud, and at once he saw himself naked, walking down the school corridor. He was big and hard and he had hair down there. Miss Kelly and Mr. Hollister turned away from him in disgust, and the others all laughed at him, but he did not care. He walked through the corridor and out the front door and down the hill to the little footbridge. He looked back at the school, but nobody had followed him, nobody cared anymore. Without a pause, naked in the cold, he dove into the icy water and swam.

No, he could not let it happen that way. The old way was better. Death would happen if he just waited.

He looked down at his hand and saw that the blood had begun to flow nicely. He made a quick slash vertically across the back of it and then he was done.

On the edge of an ice puddle he found the right piece of frozen clay. It was a silver blue, the color and weight of steel, and it fitted his palm perfectly. He tossed it in his right hand a few times, got the feel of his fingers around it, and then gathered his books for the short walk home.

He thought of the picture he would draw tonight. A naked man, old, emaciated, tied to something—a dog, a horse, something dead—and out of his mouth small birds come flying.

And as he walked, making up his picture, he beat his right cheek with the frozen piece of clay. He beat it slowly, rhythmically, making the cold flesh swell a little, making the bruise settle into the skin. His cheek grew red and redder, veins surfacing slowly and breaking, preparing the flesh for the purple and black that would follow later.

Anton closed the kitchen door and stood there waiting for his mother to notice. But there was no need to wait; she seemed to have expected it.

"No, oh no," she said, crying. "They've beaten you again, my poor Anton, my poor baby." She held out her arms and he came to her. She cradled him in her lap, whispering over and over, "This is a terrible place, a terrible place. But Anton, my baby, Antosha, you've got your *Mutti*. You'll always have your *Mutti*. Your *Mutti* loves you."

He could smell the sweet wine on her breath and feel her strong arms around him and her soft breasts warming, protecting him. He abandoned himself to the luxury of her grief.

WITNESS

Morgan Childs was a born manager. By the age of forty she had managed her way into a marriage, a son, a divorce, and a tenured professorship of statistics at a major West Coast university. She had a reputation as a model California woman—that is, one who could independently raise a child, chair a university department, and conduct a love affair with flamboyance and with style. She managed always to initiate the affairs and, when the time seemed right, to terminate them. Afterward she kept her lovers as friends.

Morgan Childs and Jamie O'Hara met for the first time when he was tending bar at a faculty Christmas party. He was only twenty-six and looked even younger, but Morgan asked him if he liked women who were forty, and he said yes. And what else? Well, he had been a seminarian for three years, he was now a graduate student in psychology, and, desperate for money, he tended bar at faculty parties. Like now. She said that was nice because she needed a drink and there was a high degree of probability she would need another, tomorrow afternoon, at three. And so they met the next afternoon at her place, and they had another drink, and then they went to bed. The affair lasted from Christmas till Easter. It was early in Lent—Lent bothered him, he said—that Jamie first told Morgan he wanted to break it off.

"You're jumpy," he said. "And you make me jumpy."

"I'm usually the one who ends these things," Morgan said.

"And then there's my wife. And the kid."

"I'm not sure I'm ready to break it off."

"Not to mention your kid."

"There's the matter of my wrists, after all."

"And most of all my religion. It's all right for you, maybe, but I can't do it during Lent."

"Lent? You give up sex for Lent?"

"Catholics can't. At least I can't."

"It makes me glad I'm a Jew. Half-Jew. Non-practicing."

"Well, it's over. Period."

And so at Easter Jamie left her and went back to his religion and his wife and the kid. Morgan had no family to go back to; her divorced husband was off somewhere in Israel plotting against Arabs and her son Julian had left three years earlier for Choate and came home now only for summer break. Of course, even if she had a family to turn to, she wouldn't have. What could a family tell her about this sickness, this disgrace? What could anyone? Because, by the end of their affair, Morgan bore upon her elegant Jewish wrists the bloody wounds of her new and inexplicable condition.

The pain in her wrists had begun a full month before the wounds actually appeared. She had just finished her afternoon class in applied multivariate analysis, and she was driving back to her apartment to meet Jamie for a quick one before he would rush off to his family and she would rush off to the ballet. She stopped for the long light at Page Mill Road and, though she had resolved to quit, she said what the hell and reached for a cigarette. She was thinking about Jamie and his hard little behind and about not being late for him when, with no warning at all, the cigarettes flew from her hands and a pain shot through her left wrist so hot that tears sprang from her eyes, and her hand flapped wildly in the air as if caught in some terrible machine. She screamed once, a high light sound, and pitched forward onto the steering wheel, her right hand clutching her left wrist, her face twisted in agony. And then the pain struck her right wrist as well.

She was completely conscious. She was aware of her foot pressed hard on the brake and she was aware that the light must have changed because cars were speeding by her on both sides, and behind her someone was honking a horn. She was aware of all this, but for a long minute she could do nothing about it. It was as if only the pain existed. It spread from her wrists up her arms and out, to fill her whole body. It possessed her. Her own existence had ceased altogether.

And then some man was shouting at her, rapping at the window. "Are you all right?" she heard him say. And then there were two men, rapping, staring in at her. "I'm all right now," she said. "I can manage." Somehow she pushed herself back in the seat and, with her dead hands clinging to the wheel, she steered the car forward until she was able to get into the right lane and finally pull to the curb, where she turned off the ignition and waited to pass out. But nothing happened. The pain in her wrists—incredibly—was gone. Her head was aching, her breath was coming in short heavy gasps, but there was no pain at all in her wrists.

Had she imagined it? No. There was no mark of any kind, no cut, no burn. She could believe—she could prove—it had never happened, except for the certain evidence: the cigarettes had flown from her hands and were scattered on the seat and on the floor. And that pain. That pain was its own evidence.

She shook her head. She was forty and getting a little crazy. She was working too hard. What she needed was Jamie O'Hara's good hard body. She drove home fast and, without a word about what had happened, she took him straight to bed.

A week later it happened again. This time she was alone in her office. She had been preparing a lecture on Hotelling's T^2 statistic when it struck: the same sudden pain, the same wild flapping of the hands, the scream, the tears, and then nothing, nothing at all. Afterward, when she came to herself, she discovered that she had snapped her pencil in half and scattered her notes and papers everywhere. Her desk was a shambles.

It had happened in the car while driving, it had happened now in her office; it could have happened anywhere, even in the middle of a lecture. A lecture. She imagined those 120 faces turned up to her in disbelief as she broke off talking about the organization of data and began to scream and flap her hands in the air and roll her head back and forth with the terrible pain. No, she couldn't risk having that happen. Something had to be done, and now.

She strode from her office and out to the parking lot and from there directly to the emergency room of the university hospital.

"You'll have to be more specific," the doctor said, frowning.

"It's happened twice," Morgan said. "Once at the intersection of Page Mill and El Camino Real about a week ago. Exactly a week ago. And again today in my office, perhaps half an hour ago. Or thirty-five minutes." He looked at her in a funny way but said nothing. "The pain is hot and sharp. Like a needle, a heated needle, something larger than a size-seven knitting needle. And it strikes here. Exactly here."

The doctor took her left wrist in his hands and pressed the spot she indicated. And then her right wrist. "But it doesn't hurt now?"

"No."

"Here?"

"No."

"How about here?"

"I showed you where it was. You've moved a full inch away."

He sat back in his chair and looked at her. "There's no sign of anything. No sign of an injury. No sign. Do you use your hands a lot?" He gave her that funny look again.

She checked the name tag on his lapel. Underhill. She didn't know any Underhill. And yet he looked at her as if she should, as if they were in collusion about something.

"Manual labor, I mean? Gardening? Some sport?" He gave her half a smile.

"I use them," she said. "But not in a way that would explain that pain."

"All right," he said, "very good," and stood up as if he had settled everything. "We'll have you x-rayed and see what turns up."

She was already at the door when he said, "You really don't remember me, do you?"

"Underhill?" she said. "How do I know you?"

"Think."

"Doctor, I have no time for games."

"Not even underwater games? In honor of Saint Patrick?"

At once it came back to her. Every year the Callahans held a Saint Patrick's Day party to which they invited absolutely everybody they knew. It discharged their entertainment obligations for the entire year and it broke up the spring semester perfectly, and just about everybody went. The Callahans had a heated pool and last year, late in the party, Morgan had gone swimming in the buff with a nice young man with remarkable ability to perform sexually even underwater. That nice young man, she realized now, was Dr. Underhill.

"I'm sorry," Morgan said. "I *am* sorry." She smiled at him as if he were Jamie. He winked; or, it seemed to her that he winked. "I think at a moment like this, the socially correct thing to do is go straight on to x-rays."

The x-rays, however, showed nothing except the finely articulated bones of her elegant Jewish wrists. Dr. Underhill studied the x-rays carefully, examined her wrists once more, and returned again to the x-rays. It was a fluke, he said, it would probably never happen again. She could relax. It was mysterious but not meaningful. And, he assured her with that half smile, he looked forward to seeing her again at the pool.

It might happen again and it might not. But Morgan taught statistics, and she knew the odds and she was determined that if it did happen again, it would not happen in public. And so the next Friday she took the precaution of canceling her class and staying home in her apartment. She would get through this thing, if she must, by herself.

She drew the curtains and put *Parsifal* on the stereo and settled in for a pleasant day of total distraction. But for the first time those long thin opening strains failed to draw her along with them; instead she caught herself lightly rubbing her left wrist with her right index finger. And then her right wrist with her left index finger. She found she could locate the precise point of... of what? Of entry, she was thinking, as if she had been violated somehow. Raped. And yet there wasn't a mark, not even a shadow. She held her wrists up to the light as if she expected somehow to see into them, to see something lodged there, something growing that would eventually burst through the skin. But nothing was there, and meanwhile Gurnemanz was leading his young squires in prayer and she hadn't paid any attention at all.

She snapped off the stereo and picked up the new Harold Robbins. She didn't bother with the titles; they were all the same, trash. But trash gave her what she was looking for in fiction: human psychology at its most uncomplicated. The good and the bad. The right and the wrong. Problems of human behavior presented, jazzed up, resolved. Robbins was very satisfying, with just enough sex thrown in to make it read easily. But this one didn't hold her and after four or five pages, four and a half, to be exact, she realized that she hadn't been reading at all. She had been mentally counting her pulsebeat, her attention given over to the soft throbbing in her wrist. "Damn," she said aloud. "This is hopeless."

She phoned the psychology department to leave a message for Jamie, but when the secretary answered, Morgan thought better of it and hung up. She must get through this day alone. She must reassure herself that the pain was a fluke and that young Dr. Underhill—that underwater surprise—was indeed right, that she had nothing to worry about. And so she baked a streusel swirl cake for her son, Julian. She would package it and mail it off to him at Choate. Very maternal, that. And then she repotted three philodendrons, the only kind of plant she had any luck with. Then she took a long bath. But still the day dragged on. It was only two o'clock. She wondered if Jamie would phone. No. He'd drop by her office or phone her there, but he wouldn't guess she'd be at home. She turned on the television and looked at *One Life to Live*. It was so slow, so boring. How did women watch these things? The heroism it must take to be a housewife. She flipped through a number of channels; it was the same sort of crap on all of them. On

The Doctors an intern who looked very much like Jamie was trying to get out of a relationship with Clarissa or Helena or somebody. He had no reason, he just wanted out. Very much like Jamie. *The Doctors* ended and *Another World* came on. God, how could she get through this? She sat in the darkened room staring at the flickering images on the television, the blond heads, the perfect teeth, all those confused faces, but she thought only of the pain she was expecting. She was waiting for it, she wanted it over and done with. She flicked off the television set and closed her eyes. "When it comes, I'll be ready," she said.

But she was not ready. At exactly 3:18—she had just opened her eyes to check the time—the pain struck so hot and sharp that she was lifted from her chair, writhing, shaking, until she slipped to the floor on her knees. The agony of it. She lay there for almost an hour, gasping, with terrible lights shooting behind her eyes.

It stopped finally and she sat up and examined her wrists; there was a small bruise the size of a nickel on the inside of each. Dizzy, drunk almost, she staggered to the telephone and called the psychology department to leave a message for Jamie.

"He's right here," the secretary said, covering the mouthpiece but not well enough. "It's her," she said. Morgan heard the telling giggle.

When Jamie took the phone, Morgan asked him in her new jumpy way—as he called it—to come over at once. He had to get home, he said, he had to babysit while the wife went to the Stations, he had to…

"Come now or don't ever come again, you bastard," she said, and he heard something in her voice that he had never heard there before. He was at her apartment in less than twenty minutes.

They sat in silence, neither of them knowing what to say. A cup of tea was set before Jamie; Morgan sipped brandy from an outsize snifter. After a while she put the snifter down and began, slowly, to tell him everything. She recited the previous incidents in meticulous detail, she described the pain, she showed him the bruises on her wrists. When she finished, she sat back and waited for his reaction. And Jamie, the fool, looked her straight in the face and laughed.

"In the seminary we'd have said you were a stigmatic. You know, like Therese Neumann."

"A what?"

"A stigmatic. One of those saints that have the wounds of the nails in their hands." Morgan merely stared at him, expressionless. "From when they nailed Christ to the cross, you know…"

"I know what a stigmatic is," she said. "I'm trying to…"

But Jamie was enjoying this and would not be stopped. "I mean, Jesus has these wounds here and here, and some saints get them too. It's all very mystical. Maybe you're one of the chosen."

Morgan struck him then. She slapped him hard on the side of his face and, as he sat there astounded, she slapped him twice more. Then she leaned back in her chair and reached for the brandy snifter. "I'm dead serious," she said, "and you're playing the Catholic fool."

There was silence between them for a long time.

"We're going to have to break this off," he said finally.

"Because I slapped you?" She was still angry, but holding it in.

"Because it's against my religion. I should be with my wife at the Stations, not screwing you in the middle of a Friday afternoon. It's wrong, Morgan, it's just wrong."

"I might point out that you are not screwing me, and what on earth station are you talking about?"

"The Stations," he said. "The Stations of the Cross. During Lent…"

"I don't want to know," she said, furious all over again. "I detest that religion. I detest Catholics and everything they stand for. It's sick, what they say and do. It's demeaning. It's dehumanizing. Catholicism is not the opiate of the people, it's the lobotomy of the people. It's, it's…" and her rushing voice cracked and she lowered her head and began to cry quietly.

Jamie rose and placed his hands on her shoulders. She threw her arms around his waist and hugged him to her.

"Come to bed," she said. "I want you."

He sighed and continued to stroke her hair.

"I need you," she said, something he had never heard her say before.

"What?" he asked.

She pulled away from him and smiled crookedly. "I need you. I'm that desperate, that I'd say it."

Jamie laughed softly, but she ignored him. She began to knead his small behind and as he leaned into her, she pressed her face against him. She unbuckled his belt. "Like a whore," she said, smiling up into his face, but it was unlike any smile he had ever seen.

Frightened and strangely aroused, he lifted her from the chair and carried her into the bedroom.

Morgan resolved never to see Jamie O'Hara again. She would do what she had always done when she broke up an affair: start a new one. And so on Sunday, though she had intended to skip the Callahans' annual Saint Patrick's Day party, she went, and almost the first person she ran into was the one she was looking for, young Dr. Underhill from the emergency room.

"Well, look who," Morgan said. "We meet once a year, it seems."

"Except for medical emergencies," he said. "How's that wrist?"

"Well, it doesn't keep me from using my hands."

He gave her that funny look of his and she was ready with her own. "Let me get you a drink," he said. He was gone for a while and Morgan took in the pool and the garden and the people milling about, the same old people telling the same old stories. It was depressing. "Dissidents? Dissidents?" she heard someone say. "I can tell you about dissidents. I've been a prisoner of conscience for most of my life." It was worse than depressing. Morgan's forced high spirits were deserting her rapidly. She thought she might just leave. But by then Underhill was back with her drink.

"To our annual swim," he said, clinking his glass to hers. But as she drank, he said to her, pointing, "That's a mean-looking bruise you've got there. Let me take a look at it."

"No," she said and pulled away. "Don't touch that." Her voice was high and sharp and people turned to look. "Sorry," she said. "I mean it's just a silly bruise. It doesn't even hurt."

"Your other wrist has one too. What have you been doing, pounding nails with your hands?"

Her face twisted suddenly. "Why don't you go for a long swim!" she said. "Why don't you go drown." She handed him her glass. Then she left him and the party and went home.

She poured herself a glass of brandy and drank it pacing up and down the living room, through the bedrooms, in and out the bath. She tried to make her mind a blank, to obliterate by the power of her will Jamie and Underhill and those damned bruises on her wrists. She finished the brandy and poured another. She sat down to write a long chatty letter to Julian. "Dear Julian," she wrote. "I'm sorry as hell you've decided not to come home for Easter, but you can be sure we'll make your summer break a very special one. I miss you, Juli, more than I ever have." And then, though she had intended to write about campus gossip, something he always enjoyed, she found herself writing, "I have this pain in my wrists that is worrying me sick." She stopped writing and stared at the paper. She stared at her wrists. She was becoming obsessed. She was half-mad. She poured herself another drink, then tore up the paper and drove back to the Callahans' party.

She got herself a drink and moped around the edges of conversation groups, trying to look absorbed. The party was reaching its final phase; people were passing a cigarette from hand to hand, inhaling deeply, seriously, and then exhaling the thin silver smoke slowly, waiting. The crowd had thinned and was thinning even more. There were four people in the pool, all in bathing suits, and as Morgan watched, they came out and toweled themselves off by the bug lights, laughing, shivering at the sudden cool.

"We've got to stop meeting this way," Dr. Underhill said from behind her. "You've come back?"

"To say I'm sorry. And to get a drink." She held out her empty glass.

"I'll get you a drink."

"Do."

He came back with the drink. "I get a second chance?" he asked. "Shall we start over?"

"Let's."

"Okay. That's a mean-looking bruise on your wrist. I've been thinking about it."

"Not that. Forget about the damned bruise."

He smiled that half smile but said nothing.

"You're quite a swimmer, I recall," she said.

"I'm best underwater," he said.

"Promises, promises." She downed her drink and held out the empty glass.

"Are you *trying* to get drunk?"

"One more. And then we'll stroll to the dark end of the pool and in no time it'll be our time to swim." But she had two more drinks before the party had thinned enough for nude swimming.

Three or four people were stretched out in lawn chairs, smoking good Colombian and half-sleeping, half-listening to the reggae that still came from somewhere inside the house. Morgan and Underhill were alone in a corner of the pool.

"Jesus, look at you," Underhill said, and he slid his hands from her waist up to her breasts and around behind her shoulders. "You've got a fantastic body."

"Enjoy it," she said.

"I will," he said. "Slowly and thoroughly and, believe me, this time you'll remember who I am." She laughed and led him on, playing with him the way she knew men liked. They were all the same and she was an expert at this sort of thing. And so when he entered her, she was more than ready, and she threw back her head until it rested on the tile border of the pool. Her hands lay lightly on his shoulders.

He was caressing her, supporting her. And then she became aware that, even as he was thrusting slowly back and forth, his hands had moved from her buttocks to her breasts and then to her arms. He ran his hands to her elbows, to her wrists. In the dark, feeling his way surely and finally, he found the bruises on her wrists and began to press them with his thumbs.

"Is this how you like it?" he whispered to her. "Is this how he does it?"

The water churned slowly as he continued to thrust, but Morgan was aware only of the strange feeling at her wrists.

"No," she said, but he only pressed harder.

"Do you like it?" he said. "Do you want it?" as the dull hard pain he was causing pressed into her wrists and into her consciousness. She raised her head from the tile, fully aware now of what he was doing, and desperate to stop him. She shouted something unintelligible and tried to strike him but he held her hands tight in his own. She sank her teeth, hard, into his shoulder and as he pulled away from her she tore her wrists free. At once she lunged at him. In charge now, and with a kind of preternatural strength, she drove him deep beneath the water. Her hands were at his throat, and she pressed down on him until she felt his head strike the cement at the bottom of the pool. He was struggling fiercely, pushing against her, his arms and legs flailing the water, but he was unable to break free. And then, suddenly, he stopped fighting her because her hands came loose from his throat and his body rose, sodden, to the surface of the water. He stood, gasping and choking, and braced himself against the side of the pool. He spit out some water, gagged, and threw up. He tried to call for help but no sound came out. He looked down at Morgan, who was lying on the surface of the water, facedown, her long hair spread in an aureole about her head. He grasped her shoulder and turned her over on her back. Her eyes were open. Jesus, what a mess, he thought. He called for help, but whoever it was in the lawn chairs at the other end of the pool was beyond hearing.

He dragged her out of the pool and kneaded her abdomen with his fists until water shot in small jets from her mouth, and she threw up, and finally came conscious. They lay sprawled side by side in silence, the only sound their labored breathing. After a long time, he propped himself up on an elbow and studied her face.

"You play rough," he said.

"I'm crazy," she said.

"Who'd have guessed it. A little S and M underwater. I can dig it. I like it. But you could have warned me."

"Take me home? Please?"

"I'm up for it."

"Please."

He took her home. When she woke the next morning, her back and her behind were covered with welts. A man's leather belt lay on the floor next to the bed and pieces of her torn clothes were scattered everywhere. The silk cord from her robe was still knotted around the bedpost. Morgan turned her head toward the wall, and pulling her knees to her chest, she began to shake soundlessly.

So this is madness, she thought, this is what it means to be insane. She lay in bed the entire day, reduced to a kind of stupor. She would never leave this room again. She would die here.

By Tuesday morning she decided that this was insanity indeed, to lie in bed and let one awful night overwhelm you. She got out of bed determined to take control of her life and put it in definitive order. She resolved to stop smoking and drinking. She did the laundry. She cleaned the bathroom. She went to her office and caught up on paperwork. When Jamie phoned and left a message, she did not phone back. Her life was her own, by God, and she was going to keep it that way.

That afternoon she lectured on design of experiments. Wednesday afternoon she lectured on discrete censored data. Wednesday evening she broke down and had a pack of cigarettes and several drinks. Thursday she saw the psychiatrist.

"I was lecturing on psychological data and factor analysis, Dr. Sloss, when suddenly it occurred to me that perhaps I'm imagining this pain in my wrists."

"Imagined pain can be real pain."

"It is real, that's what I mean. But I wonder if thinking about it, being obsessed by it, could bring it on."

Dr. Sloss leaned forward in his chair and fixed her with his milky blue eyes. "It's none the less real for being obsessive."

"I mean it's not a physical thing. There's nothing here you

can point to and say, 'It's a broken bone, it's a strained tendon, it's arthritis.' It's nothing like that. So if it's not physiological, it must be psychological. There has to be some logical explanation. I myself must be the cause of it. Do you see?"

"You would make a very good psychiatrist. You see things very clearly."

"But if I am the cause, then what do I do about it? How do I stop myself imagining it?"

"You go so far and then you stop."

"What do you mean?"

"Well, it's obvious, isn't it? Just think for a moment."

"Think of what? There are facts, hard data, to consider here. Facts have explanations. Facts can be dealt with, even psychological facts. Fact: I must be causing this. Response: how do I stop it?"

Dr. Sloss smiled at her and said nothing.

"Well?"

"I am amused at how you've passed over the obvious. If you are the cause, as you say, of these bizarre pains in your wrists, if you are imagining these pains, as you say, the question is not how do you stop it, but why are you imagining it. Don't you agree? The question is why do you want this pain? Why do you need it?"

Morgan's face went red.

"When you can tell yourself why you need it, you may find it disappears like magic."

Morgan stood up and moved toward the door.

"Tell me about your childhood," he said, but she had already left the room.

He shrugged and buzzed his secretary. "Make an appointment for Mrs. Childs a week from today. She'll want to see me again."

Back in her office Morgan found a note from Jamie saying he had broken off with her; he had to go back to his family and his religion: it was all over. "So go," she wrote on the bottom of his note and walked over to the psychology building to leave it in his box. But there at the door were Jamie and the department secretary talking and smiling, leaning into one another in that way Morgan knew so well. "Another fact," she said to nobody and crumpled up the note. Underhill and Sloss and Jamie O'Hara. And her wrists, of course, she mustn't forget her wrists. All facts. If she could say why she needed any of them, maybe they would all disappear like magic.

She returned to her office and told the secretary to cancel her Friday class.

"But there is no class," the woman said. "It's Good Friday."

"Good Friday," Morgan said. "I'd forgotten."

"Well, of course, they're your holy days too, aren't they."

"No. Yes."

"Well, anyhow, Catholic or Jew, it's a day off, right? And we can all thank God for that."

Morgan went home to wait.

Magic. There were no probabilities to magic. Given enough skill, every trick was guaranteed. And here was the solution to her problem: sleight of hand. On Friday morning she drove to Dalton's and bought three books on magic and for the next several hours she practiced making a large linen handkerchief assume the shape of a duck, a rabbit, a mule. She practiced making a nickel disappear, making it turn into four nickels, making it come out of her ear. She was clumsy and none of the tricks really worked, but the practice was time-consuming and required intense concentration and, for a while at least, she was able to put the idea of the pain out of her mind. She had a long lunch in town and returned home at quarter of two, determined to practice her magic and outwit that damned pain. There was something right, something mathematically perfect, about using sleight of hand—gross magic—to outwit this thing. She was convinced that if she could keep her mind completely distracted at three o'clock, she would escape the pain this time, and forever. Like magic.

But precisely at 2:00, as she twisted her handkerchief into a nearly perfect rabbit, the pain struck, and her hands seemed to be wrenched free of her wrists. She threw back her head and waited and waited.

When finally she looked down, she saw a small rivulet of blood trickling from the wrist into the palm of each hand, and the foolish handkerchief was spattered with bright crimson spots. "No!" she screamed. "No." But the blood continued to trickle from her wrists into her palms and onto that handkerchief. She stared, sullen, at the awful sight. "It means nothing," she said. "Nothing at all." She crumpled the handkerchief and flung it from her. But the blood fell, a tiny drop at a time, to the dull gold carpet at her feet.

Morgan dreamed that night that Jamie O'Hara had tied her to a cross and was hammering nails into her wrists. "You're a stigmatic," he said. "You're the real thing." And he hammered and hammered. "You've been chosen, Morgan. You have no choice in the matter." She woke up with a terrible thirst and a headache and a pain in her side. "God damn you, Jamie O'Hara," she said. "God damn you to hell."

But in the afternoon she went to the reference library and looked up stigmata in all the encyclopedias. "Stigmata are the signs of the wounds Jesus sustained in his crucifixion or the pain associated with such wounds that have appeared in some of his followers who have had ecstatic experiences." She raced down the page, reading carelessly, jumbling facts and dates. The first well-known stigmatic is Saint Francis of Assisi (about 1181–1226)… Saint Catherine of Siena… Saint Teresa of Ávila… no two cases are alike… modern examples are Therese Neumann (1898–1962) and Padre Pio (1887–1969), who were examined medically and shown to have signs of wounds…, no evident reason to suppose that the production of the stigmata surpasses the power of nature… the most common feature is the stigmatic's consciousness of being identified with the suffering of Christ.

She read all the encyclopedia accounts, short and repetitious, and she checked the card files under *stigmata, the preternatural, the supernatural*. She found a book by René Biot called *The Enigma of the Stigmata* and read it through, going back and back again to passages that seemed to describe her own case. But when the library closed and Morgan went home, what she took with her was one sentence:

"There is no evident reason to suppose that the production of the stigmata surpasses the power of nature."

Dr. Aaronson had won a Nobel Prize for his work in hematology when he was still a very young professor in Munich. But pressured by hospital authorities to engage in genetic research on what they referred to as "expendable" patients—some Jews but mostly just idiots—he fled Germany in 1935 and ever since then had taught and studied in the university hospital. Morgan chose him as her last resort. He was old, and she wanted somebody old, and he was certainly not a fool. If Aaronson couldn't help her, nobody could. She had phoned him the night before and said she realized he no longer saw patients, she realized he had only emeritus affiliation with the med center, but would he see her as a service to science? She had a problem that so far defied rational explanation, it defied pure reason.

"For you, my dear, no. For pure reason, yes. Come at eight tomorrow morning."

And so on Monday morning, Morgan sat in his office waiting for his verdict. Dr. Aaronson had examined her and found nothing; he questioned her about specifics of time and place and the variability of the pain's intensity. He sat back for a long while, looking at her in silence. He had deep-set brown eyes and heavy white eyebrows that half-concealed them. His heavy German accent made everything he said seem portentous, but something in the timbre of his voice today made him sound bemused.

"Are you a hysteric, Mrs. Childs? No, I think."

"Rarely," she said. "No."

"No, I thought not." He sat in silence again, and then he said, "From the phenomena you describe, from the absence of any physical or psychological explanation, I have to conclude that, unless new data present themselves, that you have been—how shall I put it—'blessed' with the stigmata. I am very glad I agreed to see you. You are familiar with the stigmata? Yes?"

"I am a Jew, Doctor. Nonpracticing. I do not believe in God. I hate religion of any kind because of the superstition it breeds and the harm it does to believers."

"Yes?"

"I have no aspirations to sanctity or indeed to any kind of singularity arising from belief in God, especially belief in a Catholic God."

"Yes?"

"Furthermore I am what people call *promiscuous*. Very promiscuous. I find it hard to imagine that the God of Roman Catholics has singled me out as the right person to carry around with her the wounds of Jesus Christ. No. There is another explanation, a scientific one, and that's what I've come to you to get."

"Of course, of course," Dr. Aaronson said. "And we'll get to that. Together. So come to me on Friday and let me study the phenomena as they occur." He smiled and put his hands together as if in prayer.

"Not if you insist that this is the stigmata."

"Does calling it one thing or another change the nature of it? It is what it is by any other name."

"But what is it?"

"Let us call it a scientific curiosity," he said. "Come on Friday."

On Friday Morgan spent the day with Dr. Aaronson and he observed the phenomena as they occurred and he concluded that, call it what she would, it was remarkably like the stigmata.

"But I am a Jew," she said.

"So am I," he said. "This must be studied. This must be watched. This is very exciting."

"Exciting for you, perhaps. For me it is terrifying. I feel as if I am haunted, possessed, as if there's some other life in me."

"Ah," he said. "That may well be," and he raised his bushy eyebrows and smiled.

The next Friday there was no pain and no mark upon her wrists, but the Friday after that the wounds bled once again. Morgan was prepared now for any eventuality. She had bought several new dresses—Friday dresses, she considered them—with long sleeves ending in ruffles which half-concealed her hands. Around her wrists she wore her tennis sweatbands to catch any blood that might flow. She was ready. She would ask for help now from no one. She was not going to be somebody's terrified lover and she was not going to be a spiritual guinea pig either. She was in this alone.

The time she used to spend on pleasure—on Jamie and on all the others—she now spent on books. In class she was lecturing on tests of significance and, though the material was highly complex, her presentation was lucid. Theorem, proof, example. Theorem, proof, example. Her mind clicked over like a computer and her tongue found all the right words. They were good lectures: everything accounted for and explained.

But she had not accounted for or explained the marks on her wrists. Sometimes she bled, sometimes she had only the pain, sometimes there was nothing. She could no longer predict what would happen, or even when. She had bled once on a Thursday evening, and then again early Friday morning; on another Friday she had torn off the sweatbands to staunch the flow of blood only to find there was no blood at all, only a small whitish star on her flesh.

Dr. Aaronson phoned. "Has it happened again?" he asked. "The scientific curiosity? Yes? Both the wounds and the bleeding?"

"Sometimes both, sometimes just the pain."

"It's as I said. The stigmata."

And he called back the next week and the week after that. "It's the stigmata," he said. "Why don't you let me study this? You could make a gift to science, yes? Let me study you."

"I'm studying it," she said. "I'm making progress."

But in fact she was making very little progress. She had studied the bone, nerve, blood system of the hand and arm. She had studied normal and abnormal cuts, wounds, abscesses. She had studied medical oddities of every kind. In desperation she had even statistically calculated the probability of having a disease never before isolated in medical history. The probability was infinitesimal.

Unwillingly, therefore, but determined to resolve this contradiction in logic, she took from the library everything she could find on the subject of stigmata. Most of what she found was hagiography, accounts by blindly credulous old priests of saints—women usually—who went for years without a bite of food, who prayed day and night, in and out of ecstasy, and whose principal reason for existing seemed to be to pour out buckets of blood from wounds in their hands or feet or sometimes both. Any account was like every other: heroic sanctity right from the cradle was rewarded in later life by these bloody testimonials to God's favor. Terrific.

She went back to Biot's *Enigma of the Stigmata*, which she had raced through months ago when all of this began. She liked the title. An enigma was a puzzle, a problem, a set of facts. Enigmas could be understood, resolved, and finally dismissed. But what she found in the book failed to resolve the enigma; rather, it compounded the problem. Case histories succeeded each other in a dizzying display of unreason, impossibility, contradiction. But Biot's approach was scientific, suggesting possible origins of the stigmata in hysteria, neurosis, even psychosis. He gave his closest attention to modern cases where there was verifiable medical evidence. He was detached, concerned with hard facts. But what struck Morgan in every one of Biot's accounts—and how was it possible she had missed this before?—was his insistence that no stigmatic had ever claimed personal sanctity.

So she could be... it was possible... granting, of course, that there is a God.

No. There was another, an obvious alternative. Like those poor lunatics in the saint books she had been reading, she might simply be mad.

And, it struck her, she really was mad. She began to peer at herself in mirrors and store windows to see if she could catch herself off guard, to see if she could see what others saw. She still looked like a well-kept forty-year-old woman who had her life perfectly in control, but she knew otherwise. Her life was out of control, her mind was out of control. And then the pain came, and sometimes the blood, and she would hug her wrists to her chest, cradling the madness against her. Like Lucia, she thought, or like some poor crazy witch they hung in

Salem. It was not God or the devil, it was simply madness.

She had nightmares every night now and they carried over sometimes into the day. She found herself one morning in her office staring at a piece of graph paper, mentally filling in the little squares to form the image of a body stretched upon a cross. Suppose these wounds, these mental lapses, were from some spirit—God, say— how would you fight it? Or them? She took a pen and began filling in every other square of the graph paper, but in her mind she was in a singles bar, picking up a man, any man at all, taking him home, taking home two at a time. She lay in bed, letting them use her, letting them invent new ways to grind pleasure out of her body, and at the moment of climax she shouted, This is for you, God, how do you like it? I'll beat you at this yet.

She ground her teeth and continued to fill in the squares. She could call Underhill and have him bring his sex toys, tie her to the bed. But of course it was stupid to think of using sex against God. Only Christians and Jews thought sex had a moral dimension. Certainly God didn't.

She caught herself then, thinking dangerously. Assuming his existence.

She kept a bottle of vodka in the bottom drawer of her desk for emergencies like this, and she poured herself a stiff shot. If there is a God, she thought, why is he doing this to me?

She was still filling in squares when a student knocked and came in and saw Professor Childs drinking vodka and filling in little squares on graph paper.

"I'm sorry to come here outside of office hours," the girl said, "but I've got a class, like, during your hours."

"I've been thinking about God," Morgan said. "What do you think about God?"

"Well, I really don't know," the girl said. "I'm not really that much of a Jesus freak."

Morgan laughed and said, "Jesus freak; a happy combination."

"What I came in for, actually, was to ask if I can take your course for a pass instead of a grade? Even though it's, like, past the deadline to let you know? I mean, I wonder if you'd let me?"

"Do you think God would let you?"

"Actually, I don't know. I think so though."

"Well, then, you may. I want to be at least as generous as God."

"Oh thanks. I mean, really. You've like saved my life," the girl said, backing to the door. And outside she said to her boyfriend, who was waiting for her, "You wouldn't believe it, Childs is drunk out of her mind," and they went off together to smoke a joint and celebrate the good life.

Morgan was drinking herself to sleep these days and sleeping badly at night and then drinking a little more to get herself going in the morning. "I can't help it," she said to the mirror, "this is just what mad people do." And she looked at her wrists, bruised today, a sign that she might bleed in the afternoon. Probably.

She did bleed, as it happened, but she went to the end-of-year party anyway. It was not actually the end of the school year since there were lectures scheduled for Monday and Tuesday, and then there were final exams, but it was close enough and everybody needed a party. So Morgan put on a Friday dress and her sweatbands and went.

Jamie O'Hara was tending bar and so Morgan kept away until late in the evening when she had had enough to drink not to care anymore.

"And how is my favorite seminarian?" she said.

"I've missed you," he said. "I've seen you at the parties I've tended, but I guess you didn't see me."

Morgan gave him her ironic smile.

"I guess you did see me and didn't want to."

"Ah," she said.

"Well, how've you been, Morgan?" He said her name in that way of his, and smiled.

Morgan thought for a moment of his cute little buns and what fun he could be and then she decided in favor of sex.

"I've been mad," she said. "Crazy." She did that thing with her eyes.

"I'll bet," he said, returning the eyes.

"To madness."

As she lifted her drink to toast him, the ruffle at her wrist fell back and Jamie looked from her drink to the white sweatband.

"I see you've still got your stigmata," he said. "It's a great grace."

"Well, I've earned it, don't you think? With my clever hands."

"Your theology is weak, Morgan. You can't earn grace." And as she leaned forward to caress the hair at his wrist, he added, "You can't escape it either."

She pulled her hand away as if she had been stung.

"I'll escape," she said. "You little Catholic bastard."

She went home alone.

Morgan slept all day Saturday and at night, still sick and dizzy from the evening before, she dressed and made up and went off to Gatsby's, a singles bar where the young bachelor types and a few of the more affluent graduate students hung out. Faculty never went there and so she knew she could pick somebody up in relative privacy. Not that she cared much about privacy. Right away she met someone from the business school—a student she had run into once, somewhere— and he bought her a drink. Then she bought him a drink. Already she was drunk. One more drink and she was only partially conscious. The student drove her home, found her key, and laid her on the sofa. She came awake then and, drunken and desperate, grasped his hand. She began to cry softly, still holding on to him. After a long time she stopped. "I can't escape, can I?" she said. "I can't escape." And he, not knowing what to say, wishing only to get away from this crazy woman, agreed with her. "No," he said sadly, "nobody escapes."

On Sunday she awoke calm, perfectly composed. She lay on the sofa, still in her dress and heels, and said to the empty room, "I have the stigmata. I am a stigmatic. There is no escape, no place to hide." She smiled slightly and rolled over and went back to sleep.

Much later in the day she went for a long walk through the campus and thought about what it meant to be who she was. Nothing had changed, she discovered. She was still Morgan Childs, a PhD in mathematics, a mother, a good teacher, a good lover. She could just relax into this new role and, as she had managed everything in her life, she could manage this too. Morgan Childs, stigmatic.

She had a bottle of wine with dinner, and then poured herself a brandy and settled down with the telephone. "Julian?" she said. "How are you, Son? How is school?"

"Okay and okay," he said.

"I know," she said. "Julian, you'll be coming home in a couple weeks, Julian, and there's something you should know."

"Uh-oh," he said. "A live-in boyfriend?"

"No, nothing like that. Nothing. It's that I've discovered that, in a way it's impossible to explain, I've become a stigmatic."

"A what?"

"A stigmatic, Juli. It's someone who—"

"You need glasses?"

"Julian, it's somebody who has the wounds of Christ in the hands and feet."

"Oh."

"I only have them in the wrists."

"Ma, are you drinking?"

"Julian. The thing is, they sometimes bleed on Friday."

"That's cool, Ma. I'm on your side."

"It's true, Julian. There's no escape from it."

"You take care, Ma. See you soon."

She held the dead telephone in her hand for a moment and then put it down and picked up her brandy. She would make another attempt. This was, she was certain, the right, the necessary thing to do. She would phone Dr. Underhill, with his watery expertise and his kinky sex games. He answered on the second ring.

"This is Morgan Childs," she said. "Do you remember?"

"Ready for more?" he said.

"Those pains," she said, "in my wrists. Do you remember I saw you about them?"

"What pains?" he said. "What is this?"

"Well, it's the stigmata. I thought you should know."

"When do you want me? I'm ready anytime."

She phoned Jamie O'Hara. "You were right," she said. "It is the stigmata. And there is no escape."

"Are you all right?" he said. "What's the matter with you?"

"I'm fine," she said. "At last I'm fine."

"You'd better slow down on the booze, lady," Jamie said, but Morgan had already put the receiver down.

She phoned Dr. Sloss, the psychiatrist.

"Some data for you," she said. "That pain was real. It was the stigmata."

"Real pain, imagined pain, it is all one. The question is why you wanted it, why you needed it."

"No, the question is how do you get away from it."

"Yes? And the answer?"

"There's no getting away from it. There's no escape."

"I've kept your appointment open. You'll want to come back."

"Not now. Not now that I know it's just the stigmata."

"You'll be back. Just try to keep an open mind."

She poured herself another brandy and made one last phone call. She phoned Dr. Aaronson.

"You were right," she said. "It was the stigmata."

"Come and see me, Mrs. Childs. Let me examine your wrists, yes? We will study this?"

"It's nothing," she said. "I can live with this. I can manage."

On Monday she was to give her last lecture of the school year. She awoke and stretched and thought, Well, I've made it through safely. Nobody knows. Except, of course, the ones she had called, the ones she had had to tell to discharge that obligation. Why had she told them? It had seemed right. They had to know. But at once another thought came to her. What if it should happen during the lecture: the pain, the flailing hands, the blood? No, it was Monday. It could not possibly happen on a Monday. Nonetheless, at breakfast she poured a good shot of vodka in her orange juice, just for courage.

By late morning she had become totally preoccupied with the idea that she would suffer an attack during the lecture. She wore a Friday dress, just in case, and now she put on her sweatbands. She would get through it somehow. She had a small vodka, freshened her lipstick, and walked to the lecture hall.

It was a windup class, pulling everything together and pointing it all toward the practical, the pragmatic. She had done it often before.

"Everything comes back to facts," she was saying. "There is nothing that cannot be explained once we have a sufficiency of information. The first and final function, then, of a course in statistical analysis is to explain, within a specified field of reference, the likelihood and in some isolated cases the necessity…"

And as she had feared, the pain clutched at her wrists and shook her with such violence that the papers flew from her grasp. Her hands, flapping, clattered against the lectern. Her head went back and she gave a terrible groan and then pitched forward. Somebody from the front row jumped up and ran to her. She could hear him saying, "Are you all right, Professor Childs? Shall I get somebody? Are you all right?"

Morgan waved him away finally and sat in silence behind the lectern. She was only vaguely aware of the 120 students who sat, silent, motionless, waiting for whatever would happen next. "She's drunk," somebody said. "Or crazy." She heard other comments, remotely; they did not apply to her any longer. She was another person, one none of them knew. Beneath the hot pain she could feel the blood gathering. It would trickle down her palms, were it not for the sweatbands she had put on. Blood dripping from her wrists to her palms, from her palms to the floor. It would be the ultimate humiliation. Morgan looked out at the faces swimming before her; they were smug, assured; they could explain everything this life would bring them. What they needed was their own assault by the stigmata. And then she thought, I can save them from themselves, I can give them mine. And at once it was clear to her why she had made those phone calls the previous night, why the blood had begun to flow in the middle of her lecture. She would be a witness.

"I must explain," she said, and returned to the podium. "We presume, perhaps rightly, that anything can be explained once we have all the facts. But of course there remains a mystery to fact, to some facts. Take, for example, the fact of the stigmata."

She clutched her hands to her chest as she was assaulted by another wave of pain. She went on and students began to whisper to one another, to shift uneasily in their seats.

"By *the stigmata* I refer of course to that phenomenon in which certain people throughout history have borne upon their hands and feet, and sometimes in the left side, the wounds of Christ upon the cross. It is a fact that these wounds appear without warning and disappear sometimes without a trace. They bleed real blood, they are extraordinarily painful, they are often accompanied by a kind of ecstasy. It is important to note about the stigmata this further fact: It can happen to anyone, a believer or a nonbeliever. No spiritual or mental or physical superiority is implied. The stigmata is a fact, an assault by the mystery of fact... which some call God."

Morgan paused and then turned back the long cuffs of her sleeves and held out her arms to them. "I myself am a stigmatic," she said, and they could see that on each wrist she wore a sweatband, a three-inch absorbent bandage. "Look," she said, and in a final gesture of self-sacrifice, she tore the sweatband from her right wrist and then from her left. "See," she said, extending her wrists to them, her face turned away, her eyes closed. Let them stare at the blood, let them stare at the possibilities ahead of them.

There was silence in the room, and then after a while some whispering, and then she opened her eyes and looked. The sweatbands shone glistening white and her wrists, turned out and displayed for the students, were smooth and unmarked. And yet the pain continued to burn there like some unearthly fire.

———

Morgan did not attend graduation. She received many letters of condolence, get-well cards, even bouquets of flowers. Word of her nervous breakdown swept through the campus: delusions of grandeur, religious fanaticism, advanced alcoholism. A major collapse. She was the talk of the university, for over two weeks.

By the beginning of fall semester, however, her collapse seemed nearly forgotten. Morgan was back from a summer's rest in Italy, she had lost a great deal of weight, and she seemed pretty much her old self. So perhaps it had been a minor collapse after all. Everything gets exaggerated in academe.

And yet there was something decidedly different about her. She was ironic now in everything she said, she was teaching less well, she continued to lose weight. But there was something else; she seemed only partly there. In a month or so Morgan was in the hospital with trouble that looked like leukemia but wasn't.

Old Dr. Aaronson came to visit her and was shocked by what he saw. Morgan was hooked up to a number of tubes that fed her and drained her and fortified her blood; but what shocked him most was her face. She looked dead. The skin was pulled tight across the bones and her eyes rested in their hollows as if they had been set in stone. When she smiled at him, her lips were thin and bloodless.

"The stigmata?" he said.

"A disease of the blood."

"You still bleed? You still have the wounds? Yes?"

"Not since that time in class." She turned her wrists toward him; they were smooth and white, with only a tiny white mark on each; an ancient scar or even a skin discoloration, that was all. But no stigmata.

"You should have let me study," he said. "We have missed our great opportunity. Yes?"

Morgan smiled. "There is no escape," she said.

She died a week later, on a Friday. Julian was there, and so was Jamie O'Hara and Dr. Aaronson. Morgan had been unconscious for some time and the three men were standing by her bedside talking about the weather and then the World Series.

Suddenly Morgan was sitting up. Her eyes were open, staring at something above and in front of her. "Oh," she said, and again, with a kind of longing in her voice, "Oh."

And then her hands flew from her sides, shaking furiously, and her whole body convulsed, pulling the tubes from her arms and toppling the IV unit. The glass shattered as it hit the floor and a nurse came running in, but nobody else moved. They watched Morgan, who had fallen back against the pillow and was gasping for breath. Her back arched and her head turned upward as if she was leaning eagerly into a long and smothering embrace.

They watched while she held that position for a full minute and part of another. Finally the tension began to drain from her body, slowly at first, and then more completely until at last she lay motionless, her head to one side on the pillow. The nurse moved forward, her hand on Morgan's wrist, feeling for a pulse.

"I can manage now," Morgan said with what seemed to be a smile.

Under *cause of death* they wrote: disease of the blood; and under *other significant conditions* they wrote: none.

THE TORTURER'S ASSISTANT

I am the torturer's assistant. I am not in training to be a torturer, nor do I aspire to any other position—horizontally, vertically—in the same line of work, nor am I any longer embarrassed by the inferiority implicit in being called *assistant*. I am the assistant. To the torturer. That is my job title and my vocation.

Be at ease. I am not going to detail for you what goes on in our workplace. You, I presume, are like everyone else. You know about torture, you are ashamed of it, you try not to be interested in it. I am the same, though I have no choice when it comes to knowing about it. I know a great deal, and I am expert at handling all the devices of torture. I work quickly, efficiently, with a minimum of fuss, and I never call attention to myself. I am only a functionary. I am not the star. It is important in torture to keep to your place.

I did not choose this job, I was chosen for it. At eighteen, in the military, I was singled out because of my attention to detail, the fastidiousness of my bunk and locker, my strength and endurance. But chiefly because I talked, when we were allowed to talk, about my dog Patch. You will remember that at just about this time the Department of Special Information was looking for a new breed of torturers, men with wit and intelligence and feeling. Feeling especially. Several of us were chosen as potential torturers and each was given an individualized test. They began by having me shoot a dog. It was a sick dog, dying anyway, and I was to put it out of its misery. Then we moved on to a stray dog. Then a camp dog that was everybody's friend. (I should make clear from the start that they never said I must shoot the dog or they would shoot me. It was not that simple. But it was implied, strongly. Furthermore, from time to time, an example was made of torturer washouts; their military careers were terminated; some were disappeared.) I shot the dog. Then there was knifing, hanging, strangling with bare hands; first small animals, then larger ones, etcetera, etcetera. I did it all. In the end, however, I was lucky because my superiors felt I lacked the initiative or perhaps the imagination to become a torturer of the first rank. So they assigned me to be a torturer's assistant.

It is the custom today for the torturer to decide what is good and necessary, but sometimes a Director of Torture will take over and may even participate in the conduct of the operation. These are usually directors who have had a personal relationship with the patient to be examined or who themselves—one must face the sad fact—have an unfortunate sexual problem. (I must be particularly unobtrusive at times like these.) It is my job to prep the patient, stripping him, setting the blades or electrodes or clamps in place, getting him in position for whatever the torturer—or the director, if that is the case—decides to do to him. You notice I say *him* even when the patient is a woman or a child. It is our way of achieving the necessary distance that makes torture possible. The work is bad, no one denies that, but I do what I can.

I give comfort, I give love. That is how I justify my job.

I have promised not to burden or offend by giving you details of life, and sometimes death, in our workplace. And I will not. But to explain the peculiar nature of my vocation—for it is that, a vocation—I must say a word about the history and nature of torture itself. I will be brief, very brief, proceeding chronologically.

There are the classical methods involving pointed instruments, heated irons, fire, and the rack. (The rack, contrary to popular belief, is very ancient.) Then neoclassical, with their improved methods of stretching, breaking, piercing, mutilating, and the many uses of barbed hooks. Renaissance, with new suspension devices, disemboweling and drilling and drowning, fire of course, the pendulum, the boot, the narrow bore—a homocentric universe of pain. Romantic: chiefly blades, knives, axes, starvation, deprivation of light and water; all of it designed to simulate a literary notion of hell. Modern and postmodern: we move into psychology, the exploitation of dark and unnameable fears, the application of electricity and other shocking forms of heat and cold, the centrifuge, the yoga cage, the needle, the slice. Modern was the ripest period for torture because so much was permitted, and indeed approved, by so many. Possibilities were limitless, patients were in good supply, and the medical field often lent its special expertise. Postmodern torture is more refined, more sophisticated, but the actual practice of torture has become rarefied because of official, though not actual, disapproval. (Political pressures explain this apparent contradiction.) There are only so many methods of torture and these are a few of the most popular, not including variations. The main thing in torture, naturally, is the patient himself and his most fragile, most vulnerable, most accessible parts; in short, his afflictive potential. Eyes, ears, the mouth—including lips, tongue, teeth. The armpits, the fingernails, the soles of the feet. The anus: certain torturers, especially certain Directors of Torture, specialize in the anus. And finally, and always, the genitals. Throughout history, these are the patient areas that have most interested torturers, with the genitals, of course, at the top of their list. (One historical note: at the beginning torture was used not to elicit information but merely to exacerbate the pains of death, but with the rise of more refined civilizations, torture has been used almost exclusively to obtain information.)

Now that is the end of that and I can get on to the important part.

Called to this job, obliged to survive mentally and spiritually in spite of what I do for a living, I have found a way of making my work meaningful and rewarding.

This is what I do. In the workplace we often use an ancient dentist's chair; the patient brings ready-made fears to it, which is useful, and for the torturer there is the advantage of the chair's mobility, putting the patient and any particular part of the patient's anatomy within easy access of even the clumsiest instruments. When I get the patient properly seated, I tip him back so the light shines directly in his eyes—soon he sees nothing but white light, which is the exact color of pain—and I strap him down lightly or firmly, whatever is required, and set in place the particular instruments of torture.

But while I am settling the patient, moving quickly and efficiently about my business, I touch him, I say things to him, I prepare him for what must follow. The touch is, in my experience, the most reassuring thing I offer. Firmness is everything. I place my hand firmly on the upper arm, just below the muscle, and I squeeze hard enough so the patient knows I am there and he can rest secure in my care. I let him pour his fears and his tensions into my hand, I support him, I enclose him. "Good," I say, "you're doing good." I don't move my hand about, I don't rub or massage; the patient could not endure that. I always choose the location for touch with the greatest care. The arm is good, and the thigh, but midthigh only, never near the groin. The best position, as you would imagine, is the shoulder, with the thumb at the front of the throat and the hand splayed firmly against the hard muscles behind the neck. This position is always successful. The right word, combined with this gesture, can be a kind of salvation. "Are you all right?" I ask, "Are you doing all right?" and though he never answers—he cannot, he is sealed in a carapace of terror—I respond for him, "I know," I say, "I know." I attach the instruments and softly, in a lover's whisper, I say, "This pain will be sharp and long. It's going to really hurt, but I'll be right here with you"—a touch on the arm or the thigh, or if the genitals are involved, the touch of a single finger just above the area, never on it, never—"it won't be much longer" or "it will last a lot longer, so try to hold on, try not to fight the pain, just let it happen," and I place my hand on his shoulder, firmly, saying, "you're doing good, you're doing very well."

I have a wife, like you, and a son and a daughter. We live out beyond the city in a small housing development with a little plot of land. Even torturers' assistants have a life outside the workplace.

We have a goat and a few chickens, but we don't have a dog. My son wants to be a geographer when he grows up, my daughter wants to be a nurse. My ducklings, I call them, my chickabiddies. I tuck them in at night, I touch their small bodies gently, gently, because I know what can be done to them. No, mine is not a life I would have chosen in every respect, but whose is?

"This will be a short, sharp pain and it will leave a taste in your mouth. A bad taste like copper filings. And you'll smell the burned flesh for quite a while. Are you ready? Are you okay?" and I lean against him, lightly, so that he is not a body alone in space, in pain, but part of the general mess of things. "Okay," I say, very softly, lovingly, and before I signal the torturer to begin, I say to the patient, "You're doing a good job, you're doing very well," and I touch his chest with my fingertips, lightly, the tiniest reassurance.

Mostly they do not die. That usually comes as a surprise to everybody: the director, the torturer, the patient. Mostly they live, broken, deformed, yes, but it is life and not death. Their families prefer life—life, in the abstract—though in fact the families are the last to know whether the patient is alive or dead. But for me, the assistant (and for the patient, of course), there is nothing abstract about the life of torture.

"Okay?" I say, and I let him feel my breath upon his cheek, I look into his eyes, I smile the merest fraction of a smile. "Don't fight the pain," I say, "give in to it, surrender, become one with the pain, until you don't know what is you and what is the pain because it's all one and you are merely existing, waiting for it to end. And it will end." I tell them this, and it is true, because it does end eventually. The torturer tires. The director ejaculates, if he is one of those. Everybody eventually wants to get to bed. And despite what you hear, all-night torture is quite rare.

Most do not die, as I have said. But for those who do, I am there in a special way. This is the most personally satisfying part of my job. At the end what they know is only my touch, my soft voice, my encouragement, and, I like to think, my love. "This pain will be a long one, it will be hot and searing, give yourself over to it, let it become who you are." And as they prepare to surrender, I say, whispering, "Love, it is all love at the end. I love you, remember that, you are wholly loved," and then I press my hand firmly on an arm, letting them feel they are embraced, they are held up in the fire of the electric shock, they cannot fall, they cannot fail. I caress them with my voice, I murmur to them. They surrender, knowing they are loved, and there is nothing more to worry them, forever.

Then I signal the torturer.

They let me do all this, the torturers. I don't know why.

I am aware, of course, that when this government falls and the investigations are made and the corruption exposed, I will be the first to go. (Not by torture, however; my death will be humane.) Then the torturers. Then the prison guards, etcetera, etcetera. But not the Director of Torture. He will be away, on holiday, and when he returns he will hold high office in the new government. That is how things are. There is little hate in any of it. There is absence only.

Yesterday morning at Mass the priest read the Gospel about the raising of Lazarus. "Jesus called him from the dead back to life," the priest said. "Ask yourselves, my people, whom have you called back to life?" He said a lot more, because he had to explain the metaphor, but I stopped listening there, for shame of my work and of my life. I have called no one back to life, I have hastened them on their way, though I have given what comfort and love I can. But the priest was right, of course, what I do is bad, and the good I do is not enough. (I think, why did Jesus allow Lazarus to die in the first place? But that is merely defensive thinking, since I know it is the fate of all of us to die and Jesus can't take the blame for everything.) Thoughts of death and dying were in my mind all day.

In the afternoon a terminal patient placed his broken hand upon my wrist and turned his eyes toward me, grateful, and died. We do what we must here and we remain as kind as we are able. Nevertheless, sometimes I feel I can't go on.

Then last night around two in the morning I was awakened by

a terrible cry. In the deep dark, still not sure I was awake, I thought it must be the scream of a patient and that my mind had wandered, I had committed some crucial error. But no, almost at once, I realized I was home, in my bed, beside my sleeping wife, and in the blue trees outside in the garden it was mating season and some great raucous bird was calling to another, who answered—fierce, demanding—and their cries went on and on. They were hoarse, barbaric cries, human almost.

My wife woke up and said, "What? What is it?"

"It's just a bird," I said. "Two birds. It's mating season."

She fell off to sleep at once.

I lay there listening to the birds, the invocation and response, and after a while the bitterness of their calls turned sweet—how could that be?—and the harshness took on the rhythm of some rough music. It was a sound completely physical, completely mysterious. I listened and I felt myself dissolve into the sound. There were no boundaries between me and it. I became, for one salvific moment, that hard music. And for no reason at all I began to cry. And then slowly, slowly, my heart filled with a gladness I could not explain, and I was at peace, and though I could not understand it, I knew that, despite everything, life is good.

THE HANDMAID

I will tell you the worst right away, and then after that you can see how all this has come about. You will not have to worry that there is something unspeakable to follow. I am telling you the unspeakable now.

The soldiers have raped me and cut off my breasts and slit my throat. They have done other things with a knife: one of them made a star shape down there around my sex, another one carved the shape of a cross on my face. They have left me for dead, these four soldiers of the military police. And of course I will be dead, in minutes.

So that is the worst. Now you have nothing else to fear.

My name is Maria Luz Buenvida. I am the daughter of Jorge Buenvida, the filmmaker, and of Helena Curtin, who is American. My brother, Miguel, is one year older than me, and I am eighteen. That is my family. Like me, they are all dead or dying.

Until a year ago we were very wealthy; we were one of the privileged families in our country. We had a large apartment in the city and, though we almost never went there, we also had a ranch in the hills. I attended the convent school taught by the French nuns, and Miguel was enrolled in the university. My father made films. My mother supervised the housekeeper and the parties and played with Mimi, her miniature poodle. We were very happy; and we were safe, we thought.

You must understand that we did not live like most people in the capital. My father's films meant that he had all kinds of friends and business acquaintances: actors, painters, poets, screenwriters, shipping people, even high officers in the army. Most of his friends, of course, were from our own country, but he had others who were American, Greek, French, Italian, and he spoke their languages. Mostly we spoke English at home, at first because my mother was uncomfortable speaking Spanish and later because all my father's friends seemed to prefer it. English was chic. At parties—and we had large parties in those days, almost every weekend—there would be a lot of drinking and loud conversation and everyone would be speaking English with a different accent, calling my father George and my brother Mikey, Americanizing every name. It was at one such party, I suppose, that it all began.

"Your father's films. Do you understand them?" It was Colonel Garcia, old and fat and a little drunk. He was flanked, as always, by two soldiers of the *guardia*, the military police. He spoke to me in Spanish. "Do you?"

"I like them," I said. "Spanish, please," he said, and so I repeated, "I like them" in Spanish.

"Are you ashamed to speak Spanish?" he asked, smiling. "Is it because of your American mother?"

Guests, even military guests, do not talk this way to their hosts unless they have a reason. Behind his smile there was some kind of threat. Though the Buenvida money and prestige had always kept us outside the reach of the military, I was careful how I answered.

"Colonel," I said, "you misunderstand. I am proud to speak Spanish. In fact, my English and my French are very weak. It is just that film people, sometimes, like to speak English."

"Your father's films. I do not understand them."

"He is a poet, my father."

"They are never contemporary; always they are set in some time long past. Why is that, do you suppose? A man like your father is a man of our times, not of yesterday. And yet, he is not a political man, your father. Is he?"

"No," I said. "Not political."

"Sometimes..." He stood silently, examining the olive in his glass. After a moment he picked up the olive between his thumb and his forefinger, held it toward me, and—with no trace of any emotion— he squeezed the pimento from the heart of the olive into my glass. "Sometimes, one must be."

Later that night, of course, I told my father everything that had happened, everything except what Colonel Garcia had done with the olive.

"Garcia's a drunk," my father said. "He can't touch us." He thought for a while. "No," he said, "he has no power over us. Just forget about him. And don't mention this to your mother."

Naturally I would not have mentioned it to my mother.

She was a woman who lived in constant terror: of sickness, of revolution, of investigation. And so she drank. But as an American, she was quite safe. We were all quite safe.

In a week or two, I forgot about Colonel Garcia, or at least I succeeded in putting him out of my conscious mind. My father had completed his new film, *Ifigenia*, and was busy editing it. Our long school holiday had begun and so I was able to go with him, sit in the editing room, and watch how he worked. He liked having me with him. During those weeks I learned—though I did not understand until much later—what a good filmmaker my father was, and what a great man.

It is true, as Garcia said, that my father has never made a contemporary film. He cannot. He cannot indict the military and the aristocracy and, yes, the clergy, except under the cloak of ancient history. And to that history, which he cannot alter, he brings his own mystical belief: that from all this suffering there must eventually come some kind of redemption. And so his films seem to be mythological— even fantastic—to some critics. But always they are a metaphor for our lives today. My father was very much a political man.

We gave no parties during these weeks and my father, who spent all day at the studio and all evening planning the next day's work, made it clear he wanted Miguel and me out of the house in the evenings. He said it was not good for young people to mope about as we did, that we ought to be with people our own age, that we ought to get out and have fun.

"Le Disco," Miguel said. "That's where I always go."

Actually, my father did not want us to see my mother pour herself a new drink each hour, growing calm around ten o'clock, and at midnight resigned—for the next few hours—to her life in exile. That is how she thought of her life here, as exile. Because even if she had been brave enough to return to the States, she had nobody to return to. Her parents were dead. No brothers or sisters. She had only us. And she was drifting away from us much faster than my father knew. She did not understand that Miguel and I are of this country, that we love it, that we do not want to run away. By this time she had given up trying to convince me to go to college in the States; she had long since given up on Miguel; she clung only to Mimi, her little white poodle, who sat in her lap and slept on her bed and, no matter what the occasion, was never allowed out of her sight.

And so, to please my father, Miguel and I went dancing at Le Disco. I hated it. The boys in their tight jeans and their hundred-dollar silk shirts. The girls waiting, teasing. Everyone desperately having fun, dancing and shrieking so as not to think of what lay out there in the darkened streets: the national police, the army police, the treasury police, the secret police, the *guardia*, the steel-plated Toyotas circling the block, the small black cars driven by men who concealed their faces beneath military caps and sunglasses, all the trappings of terror. And inside, the noise and the light. Strobe lights in all the colors of blood. Metal clashing on metal. The smell of perfume and sweat. Only the occasional disfigurement warned of the world outside Le Disco. A slashed ear, a long scar on one side of the nose, the whitened burn mark from cheek to chin: these were the victims of interrogation, dangerous to be seen with, untouchables.

It was my fault that one of these, Virgilio Bellorin, a photographer for *La prensa*, was put through a second interrogation. Miguel was dancing with some girl from the university and I was standing against a wall, thinking of my mother and how she was moving deeper into drink. I found myself staring, without realizing it, at a young man who looked almost exactly like Miguel. He had the same thin face and the same anxious eyes, but wore his hair long, almost to his shoulders. This gave him a soft look, almost feminine, and it struck me suddenly that he looked more like me than like Miguel. And because at that moment the gods who manipulate our lives willed that he come over and stand next to me, I turned to him and said, "We could be twins."

He smiled at me, his lips parting slowly over his perfect white teeth, and he said, "Well, I would like that." There has never been a smile more beautiful.

And so I fell in love with him, at that moment, forever, and with only nine words spoken between us.

He was looking at me, and I returned his look, but I could think of nothing to say. I had been so forward. I was confused. And he said nothing.

But then he pushed back his hair from his left cheek, exposing a long thick scar, and said simply, "But there is this."

Before I could realize what he was telling me, he turned abruptly and left. At once Miguel appeared at my side and said, "Are you crazy? Have you lost your mind? We've got to get out of here," and took my arm and rushed me to the door. "*Guardia*," he said, indicating with a jerk of his head the military police standing by the entrance. "They may have seen you." And of course they had.

We came out the door of Le Disco just as two of the *guardia* were pushing Virgilio into a small black Datsun; they climbed into the car and roared away before they had even closed the doors. But by this time two others had taken me by the arms and lifted me from the stairs. I heard Miguel shouting and someone pushed from behind and one of the soldiers let me go. I tried to break free and run, but the other soldier pushed me hard against the car, my hands behind my back. I could see nothing, but I heard cursing and the sound of fists against flesh. Someone groaned in pain, a body hit the pavement, people were running. And then my head was pounded hard against the car door and when I woke I was in a tiny interrogation room.

Someone was asking me over and over how long I had known Virgilio Bellorin, what was my relationship with him, did I know he was a subversive.

"My name is Buenvida," I said finally. "I am the daughter of Jorge Buenvida, the filmmaker. And of Helena Curtin, who is an American citizen."

"We know quite well who you are, senorita. We have been through your purse and all your cards of identity. But things are not now for you and your family what they once were. Do you understand that? You are now just another suspect being interviewed. Please notice, interviewed; not interrogated. Now let us try again. How long have you known Virgilio Bellorin?" No one touched me. No one interrogated me.

After an hour or more they let me go. My father was in the waiting room, furious but strangely quiet. He had asked to see Colonel Garcia but was told the colonel could not be disturbed except on important matters. He had made demands, issued threats, promised reprisal, but he had gotten nowhere. He had decided then to get me free first of all, and only afterward get revenge.

"You see, senor?" the soldier said as he led me into the room. "Here is your daughter, safe and sound. Our little interview is finished."

I walked slowly to my father's side. There was no embrace. "Miguel?" I whispered. My father nodded.

"And you, senor? You are calmer now. That is good. Because things have changed for you here. As you see."

Things had changed more than we knew. A realignment in the government, a shift in military power, a payoff, a betrayal, a murder: who could guess what really had happened? But Colonel Garcia was now a powerful man and he was convinced that my father was a threat to him.

A long time passed, a month, two months, and nothing happened to us. My father was finishing the editing of *Ifigenia* with the meticulous care he brought to all his films, frame by frame, image by image, and I sat next to him the whole time, learning how to conspire for freedom.

Miguel had survived his fight with the *guardia* with only a broken rib and a great number of bruises. It was he who insisted that we go back now and then to Le Disco and it was there that I again saw, but did not speak to, Virgilio Bellorin. "Don't!" Miguel said as I moved, appalled, toward Virgilio, and later, on the dance floor, Miguel said, "Don't you see I am one of them?" Le Disco was where they set up their meetings and passed on messages. But I could not think what it meant that my brother was a revolutionary; I could think only of Virgilio's face, his mouth scarred, his beautiful smile shattered. It seemed to me at that moment that our country's freedom came at too high a cost.

Our family's freedom ended the following day. I was sitting on one side of my father, his assistant on the other, as we watched him study the movement of Ifigenia's hand in a series of ten frames. The gesture must appear to be ultimate resignation, he said, and everything depended on the length of time the gesture took. Fewer frames or more?

"Notice the difference it makes," he said, but he never finished his sentence, because at that moment the door burst open and the room filled with military police, rifles cocked and pointed, and someone said softly, almost sweetly, "You are under arrest." In no more than a minute my father was handcuffed and taken away, and in a few minutes more they had gathered every reel of film in the room and taken that away too. A single soldier remained. I was crouched in a corner, my hands at my face, and this soldier came to me and helped me to my feet. And then lightly, as if it were an accident, he touched me between my legs and said, "Perhaps you will be next." He smiled at me and left.

Miguel and I spent the rest of the day at the prison trying to get some information about Father. They would tell us nothing. We asked to see Colonel Garcia but we were told the colonel could not be disturbed except on important matters. Go home and wait, they told us, and finally, at six o'clock, they turned us out.

We had decided not to tell Mother, but when we got home, she already knew. "What has happened to your father?" she said. "They've taken him, haven't they? They've arrested him." And then she told us about the telephone call. Military police had seized our ranch in the hills, confiscated the cattle and all movables, and burned the buildings to the ground. They claimed that the ranch was a safe house for revolutionaries. No charge had yet been brought, nor had any official contacted her; the telephone call was anonymous, from a friend.

We lit candles at the cathedral that night, and prayed, and then we sat in the living room in silence, Bach and then Telemann playing in the background, until at last we could say it was time to go to bed. My mother had nothing to drink.

The next morning, early, Miguel went to keep vigil at the police station; my mother and I went to the American embassy. The former ambassador and his wife had been to our parties often, had even requested private screenings of my father's films, but several months ago a new ambassador had been appointed. We did not know him. He was more aloof than his predecessor, spent more time within his compound than outside it, and had turned the embassy itself into a fortress. He represented, so *La prensa* said, the increased hostility of the new American administration.

My mother and I were admitted to the embassy and were told we would have to wait. An armed guard took us to a small sitting room and left us there, and after an hour or so an old woman in a maid's uniform brought us coffee. My mother asked her when someone would finally see us, but the woman only shook her head and said nothing. My mother paced the room, her hands trembling. I sat and thought of my father, and of Miguel, and of Virgilio. How had any of this happened? And why? After another hour, my mother was asked to step into the next room. There she was allowed to tell her story to a secretary, and afterward to an assistant, and after that to another assistant, who took notes. I waited, my hands knotted in my lap, sure we were being betrayed. At the end the American ambassador himself spoke with her, listened, and then rose to dismiss her. "We will do whatever we can," he said. "It is not easy."

At home, my mother took Mimi from the arms of the housekeeper and clutched the little dog to her breast. "I'll never see Jorge again," she said. "They'll murder him. We'll all be murdered in this terrible place." But again, she did not drink.

Miguel had news, and not good news. My father was accused of crimes against the republic: giving arms and a safe house to revolutionaries, financing the vigilante movement, seeking to overthrow the legitimate government. These charges were not yet public; it was not clear whether they would even bother with charges at this point; there was plenty of time, now. Colonel Garcia himself had passed on this news to Miguel, taking care to add that the principal charge against my father was his revolutionary propaganda—namely, the film *Ifigenia*. "Tell your sister," he said, "that I understand your father's films quite well now."

And so we concluded that my father must still be alive. Imprisoned, certainly. Tortured, we had no doubt. But still alive, and still able someday to return home. Others had returned. He might. And so, for the moment, we had hope.

Despite our hope, or to sustain it, we took the precaution of going each day to the cathedral, evidently to light a candle for Father, but actually so that we could pass through the cathedral cloister to the archbishop's palace where, in a waiting room, outside the scrutiny of the police, we examined the photos of the disappeared.

Virgilio, Miguel told me, was one of the photographers responsible for these photos. Every day he risked his life taking these photographs and doubled the risk by getting them seen. Some he was able to place in *La prensa* as news items. "Woman and two daughters killed; assailants unknown. Bodies of three men discovered in a suburban *barraca*; headless, castrated; assailants unknown. Two nuns raped and murdered; bodies discovered in an alley; assailants unknown." Some of these photos were printed on broadsides and, under cover of night, hung up in shopping malls, in movie theaters, in streetcars. But the archbishop's palace was the main clearinghouse for these photographs.

The five heavy picture albums were bound in white plastic, their covers decorated with pastel scenes from American cigarette advertisements: a young woman in a filmy dress, a handsome man, a stream, a weeping willow. And inside were pictures of missing people, the disappeared. The whole world has seen newspaper photographs of the body dumps at El Playón, but in our country—officially—El Playón does not exist. Nonetheless Virgilio and others have photographed the dead, the evidence of torture and mutilation still fresh on their bodies. Cigarette burns on the breasts of young girls. Hands and feet lopped off with blunt knives. A severed head, its eyes gouged out. And, always, young men who have been castrated, their genitals stuffed in their mouths.

Miguel and I sat together, turning page after page of the most recent photographs. When we finished, sick, nearly dumb, I asked Miguel, "Did Father know this?" Miguel nodded. "This is what all his films are about," he said.

Things went on in this way for some time. Each day my mother would put Mimi into the arms of the housekeeper and then go to the American embassy and ask for help. Miguel and I would check the newest photographs and afterward, still hoping, we would go to the nearest police station and ask to see my father. At night the three of us would have dinner together, pretend to listen to music, and then go to bed. During this time we knew, of course, that our house was watched, and that we were followed in the street. A long black car with smoked-glass windows was stationed day and night across the street from our apartment building; one man in front, two in back, ready. Nonetheless at least once a week Miguel would slip out in the middle of the night to rendezvous with the Student Liberation Front. He gave me a number I could telephone, a code I could use to identify myself and to ask about him, just in case some morning he did not return at dawn. He would not give me the code for Virgilio.

Then one morning Miguel did not come home. I told my mother he was sleeping late, he had a headache, he was worn out, and so she left for the embassy suspecting nothing. Every second hour that day I called the number Miguel had given me and I used the code: I was a

Marx Brothers fan and could someone tell me at what time *A Night at the Opera* was playing. "Wrong number," a man said and hung up. If there was news, he would have called back immediately. No one called.

That night, with no Miguel, with no telephone call from an anonymous friend, I had to tell Mother he was missing.

At first she was very calm. "This is the end," she said and rocked Mimi in her arms. "This is how it all ends." But after a while she began to sob, and she did not stop. I tried to comfort her, I brought her a glass of water, but her sobbing became wild, she began to scratch her face and claw at her hair. She was hysterical. I stood there, helpless, useless, and then I thought of my father and my brother, and I slapped her, hard. After a moment I got her a cold cloth for her face. "Try to remember who you are," I said to her. She lay down in her bedroom then; she did not want dinner. She wanted nothing, she said, except to forget. At midnight, hearing her at the liquor cabinet, I got up, put on my robe, and went out to her. "Please," I said. "Not now." She looked at me as if she hated me, and then she poured herself another tumbler of brandy. "Mother," I said, but it was too late.

Virgilio Bellorin came to my bed that night. He was suddenly there at the door to my room; I had not heard a sound; I was not afraid.

"Miguel is all right," he said. "There was a shooting. Two police were killed. The *guardia* didn't get him, but he may have been recognized."

I wanted to ask, Where is he? And where is my father? And how did you get in here? And what is happening to all of us? Instead I asked only, "Is he all right?"

"You should know nothing. If you are interrogated, it is better that you know nothing. He is all right."

"Sit here," I said, touching the side of the bed. I put a finger on the left side of his mouth. "They have hurt you," I said. "You have a scar." I traced his lips with my finger, and he licked my finger with his tongue, and I raised my head to kiss him on the mouth. He kissed me back and then pulled away.

"Not from pity," he said.

"From love," I said.

And so we made love until nearly dawn and during that time I forgot my father and my mother and my brother. I gave myself up to myself.

The next morning, my mother was awake before I was. Sick from drink but desperate and determined, she announced she was going to accompany me to the police station and she was going to make demands. One last attempt, she said.

"Miguel is safe," I said, but when she asked me how I knew, I only shrugged and said I just felt sure that he was.

At the police station she demanded to see Colonel Garcia. She demanded to see her husband. She demanded information about her son. She looked fierce, and beautiful, and I thought, Perhaps she is not yet lost to us, perhaps she will be the savior of us all. The captain ignored her at first, but then he had an assistant make a telephone call, and in a short time armed police began to come and go, briskly, with purpose, and suddenly my mother was told to come this way.

Colonel Garcia was smoking a cigar, his feet propped up on an open desk drawer. He did not rise and he did not offer her a seat. "What a noisy American woman you are," he said. "You must stop bothering my friend the ambassador. You must stop demanding information on your husband and your son. You are making a great nuisance of yourself." He pushed back in his chair and flicked the ash from his cigar. "This is a republic of law, senora. If you obey the law, you have nothing to fear. Yes, this is so. Your husband is simply a traitor to our state. And we have reason to believe that your son, he too is a traitor. But they must be investigated. They must, as we say, be detained." He paused a moment and then drew heavily on his cigar. "You must learn a little patience, senora. Patience is a great virtue." He dismissed her. Furious, frightened, she went straight to the American embassy, where, just as she had begun to fear, no one was willing to see her.

That night my mother and I made no pretense of eating. She went to her bedroom with a bottle of brandy; I sat in the living room, listening to music but thinking only of Virgilio.

I thought first of all the distinctions I had been taught by the nuns—love and lust, premarital and postmarital sex, mortal and venial sin, culpability for sin, the malice of sin, sins of commission, of omission, of desire. And then I thought—and realized it was true—that there had been no sin at all between me and Virgilio. We were two people huddling together against the dark and the danger. We were, for one brief second, holding back death.

And I saw then, as if in a vision, that my own death would be long and terrible and triumphant.

Sometime after midnight my mother's door opened and she came into the living room. She blinked against the light for a moment and then she spoke to me, her voice broken, her speech slurred. "Come with me," she said. "We'll leave this place. You and me and Mimi. Jorge is dead; they've killed him; they've tortured him and killed him. And your brother…" She broke down and sobbed for a minute. But then she went to the liquor cabinet and poured herself another drink and, as if she had returned to good sense, she began again, "Come with me, Maria. They've killed your father and your brother and they'll kill us too. There is a curse on this place, there is a curse on us." But finally she saw the coldness in my eyes and the anger in my face, and she stopped. She took her drink to her bedroom and after a while I could hear her packing things in a suitcase. "My jewelry," I heard her say, "and cash, and…" I went to my room.

The next morning, incredibly, she was sober and full of purpose. "I am going to the American embassy," she said, "and then to the police station. If they will not see me and if they will not tell me about Jorge and Miguel, I am coming back here for my suitcase and passport and for you. I will fly to Washington. I want you to come with me. But with you or without you, Maria, I am going." The housekeeper arrived then and my mother, without another word, put Mimi into her arms and left.

That was this morning. And on this one day, the gods who decide our fates decided mine and Virgilio's and Miguel's.

An hour after my mother left the house, the *guardia* arrived. From where I stood in the living room, I saw them push past the housekeeper and, though I wanted to run, I went toward them. "You have no right to be in this house," I said. "Your presence here is strictly illegal."

"Search the place," the lieutenant said, ignoring me. And to the housekeeper, he said, "Save yourself trouble, old woman. Go home." And then he sat on my mother's watered-silk sofa and put his feet up on the coffee table. He lit a cigar. "It's your brother we are interested in," he said finally. "Not you."

From the bedrooms I could hear furniture being banged and pushed, drawers torn open and slammed shut, laughter. Mimi had crawled into my arms and was snuggled against me, whimpering softly. "Make that Yankee dog stop that," the lieutenant said. "It is a very annoying dog. Things that weak and whimpering have no right to live. Don't you agree, senorita? The weak should be stomped out."

The soldiers had finished their search and they had not found Miguel. "Take her in for questioning," the lieutenant said. "I myself will have a look."

The interrogation was like the previous one, only much longer. Where was my brother hiding, and why? Who was Virgilio Bellorin? Why did I go each day to the cathedral? For whose photograph was I looking? And again, where was my brother hiding, and why? The soldiers took turns questioning me, and near the end Colonel Garcia looked in, smiled, and said, "Your father sends his best wishes." Shortly afterward, I was released and allowed to return home.

I knew what I would find there and I thought I would not be able to bear it. But we can bear anything, if we must.

My mother's room was chaos. Her twin lamps had been broken and drawers had been turned out onto the floor and the entire room was strewn with her clothes, but the bed was neat, the spread smooth, and where the pillow should have been there was her suitcase. Inside the suitcase, of course, was Mimi's body. Her throat had been slit and her fur was matted with blood. I think it was then that I saw how inevitable my own fate was. I closed the suitcase and put it under the bed.

I telephoned the embassy. No, they had no news of my mother.

Yes, she did say she was returning to the States. No, they did not know if she had actually left. I telephoned the airport, but they could not release passenger lists. I paced from room to room for nearly an hour and then I telephoned the number Miguel had given to me. "I am desperate to see a Marx Brothers movie," I said. "I am dying to see one, any one; it does not have to be *A Night at the Opera*. Do you understand?" They understood, but said nonetheless I had the wrong number. And then, in minutes, a woman called and said, did I know that Hitchcock's *Vertigo* was playing at the Cid. If I hurried, I could make the eight o'clock showing. I prayed all the way to the theater. The cab was slow and the driver insisted upon talking and I kept saying, "Hurry, hurry, please. If I am late, if I am late…" but I could not imagine what would happen if I was late.

I bought my ticket and was standing in the dark at the head of the aisle, letting my eyes adjust, hoping Miguel would appear, when suddenly there was a scuffle in the row to my right: the sound of a punch and then a gasp and feet kicking against the floor. Two *guardia* yanked the body of a young man out of the row of seats and into the light of the lobby. His face was bloody, his jacket torn. Miguel, I said to myself, sick with fear. But it was not Miguel; it was Virgilio. I watched as they threw him into a red Toyota van and then, stupid, stunned, I went back inside and waited through *Vertigo*, praying for the dead and dying.

It is almost over. I walked home through streets where no one walks. A car would slow and follow me for a block and then turn away. And then another car. And another. Police cars. *Guardia* cars. Assassination cars. And I walked. At home I let myself into the darkened apartment and sat by the window looking out on the street. It was some time before I realized that the long black car that had been stationed there was at last gone. Why? Because we no longer mattered to them? Who could say?

I must have fallen asleep because all at once Miguel was in the room with me. I cried in his arms, and he let me cry, and after a long time, he said, "It is not over yet. Father, Mother, Virgilio. We will be next." I stopped crying then and I kissed him. I clung to him, pressed myself against him. "Yes, yes," I said. He held me; he held me back. "All right," he said at last, and we made love, my brother and I, as if we could somehow crush ourselves into just one person, become one body, one soul.

Afterward he asked me if I had done this with Virgilio.

"Yes," I said. "I loved him."

"Good," he said, and after a moment, "he was my lover too."

The police, when they came, found us in the kitchen having tea. They put Miguel in one car, me in another, and drove off in different directions. They brought me to this leafy hill and did these things to me. The first one who raped me started to slice off my left breast, but the others wanted to have me while I still had my breasts, so they made him wait until they were all finished. And then they cut the star around my sex. And the cross on my face. They must do these things for courage, to be able to go on. Always they violate sex. Always they put the sign of the cross on their murders. Always they silence the dead mouth.

But mine they will not silence, for I have seen my fate. I will rise from this leafy hill, I will ascend from this body, and I will soar above them like some terrible bird of night.

I will not be a picture in the archbishop's palace, not another faceless one. I will be virgin once again. Cleansed in my own blood, my breasts lucent, and in my throat a triumphant cry, I will sprout wings of bronze and I will course through the night; at dawn I will hover above them, the murdered, the defiled, the dying; I will draw them to me; and I will draw the evil and the sick and the depraved and I will assume them, in my breast, in my loins, in the star they carved on me and in the cross upon my face; I will take them into myself and they will be transformed, made whole, all one.

And at the last all will be well.

A FEW NECESSARY QUESTIONS

"Your name?"

"Paul Gregoire."

"Address?"

"I, well, I'm staying at a hotel until I can find a place... a flat."

"A hotel?" She didn't believe him.

"It's an inexpensive hotel."

"Phone number?"

"I don't know. Oh, here it is: 373-2455. But..."

"I have what I need, then, Mr. Gregory. But we cannot be of help to you over the phone, Mr. Gregory, unless you come into the office. We only do business in the office."

"Yes, of course."

"All right, then, Mr. Gregory. Cheerio."

She hung up. Paul Gregoire looked into the dead phone for a minute—he hadn't thought people actually said "cheerio"—and then he too hung up. He had spent four days walking through Kensington and Chelsea looking for a flat, and he had found nothing. The hotel clerk, who was anxious to be rid of him, suggested he try an agency, Wasps or London Flats. He did, and now he stared at the phone and once again began to cry.

He cried almost soundlessly—the hotel walls were so thin—and rocked back and forth hugging his knees. He was crying because he had learned only recently that you are either living or dead, and he knew he had a choice to make. In less than an hour he stopped crying and walked down the corridor to the bathroom, where he sank to his knees and threw up. He washed and went off to London Flats on Gloucester Road.

Pudding, someone said.

Paul Gregoire studied the stitching on his shoe and tried not to frame a response.

Bread pudding.

Chocolate pudding.

Rice pudding.

Plum pudding, but that was something different, a cake.

Figgy pudding. Somewhere crippled children were singing, "We all love a figgy pudding," stridently, relentlessly. How could they do this, make themselves a parody of happiness, a Christmas joke? He wanted them to stop. It was unspeakable to allow innocence to mock itself this way. He wanted to hit them, to twist their stunted arms and make them stop. "We all love a figgy pu-u-dding." A child reached out to him. He snatched the arm and twisted it hard, but it was so thin and fragile in his grip that he grew frightened and dropped it. His fingerprints were seared into the flesh. The child looked up at him, waiting for whatever would come next. "So bring some right now."

He rested, leaning against the wall that surrounds the Brompton Oratory. And then he slammed his right hand against the stones until it was puffy and blood ran freely from the broken flesh of the knuckles.

That night at the hotel he wrote on the back of a paper bag. *London Flats on Gloucester Road is a long dark closet with three desks, each overseen by an angry young woman. The first looks like Princess Anne but with even less chin; the second never appears except in a shiny black dress—her name is Avril and from the way the others refer problems to her she appears to have seniority or at least depositary rights over the more attractive apartments; the third is a milk-white, fluffy blond who looks as if she is starving herself into another Twiggy. We sit on a bench along the wall: teenage boys with hair to their shoulders; blushing young secretaries who want a bedsitter for five pounds a week; widows on pensions hoping for a single room with a heating coil; four or five Indians (there are Indians everywhere in London; every occupied phone booth contains at least one Indian); two uncomfortable gays looking for a convenient pied-à-terre; and I, Paul Gregoire, American, nearly ex-priest, waiting, studying the stitching on my shoe.*

He folded the bag so that Boots the Chemist faced up, and then he slipped it between his shirts in the bureau drawer, where the cleaning woman found it the next morning on her appointed rounds.

"And so you entered to save your soul."

"Yes, Father."

"And the souls of others."

"Yes."

"In short, to save the world."

"Father, I never had such…"

"Yes or no."

"I can't say."

"You must say. These things have to be simplified. Matters of the soul are complex beyond all human understanding, and the particular distinctions that one priest wants to make in discussing the nature of his vocation, and his fall from it, have to be reduced to the realizable, the comprehensible. Rome is patient, but you must answer. Now, yes or no."

"Yes."

"So you entered to save the world and found yourself pitying it." The old priest waited. "That is what your story seems to imply."

"Yes. I don't know. Yes."

"And then fearing it."

"Yes."

"You feared what you came to save."

"Yes, but I don't mean pity the way it comes out when you say whatever you said, and what I fear isn't something frightening, it's the stark madness of good people doing evil and not realizing, it's…"

"My son, my good man, you are not on trial. We imply no value judgments here. The facts are all we want. You desire to leave the priesthood, to be reduced to the lay state, and I am here to examine your case. Only facts. Thus far I see no cause. Now we will go back. You entered to save your soul."

Father McDonnell's room is a coffin stood on end, Paul Gregoire wrote. *I began to sweat and then to shake. I don't think he realized I was crying.* He drew a line beneath this and wrote, *Was there not even one priest at Dachau?* And then another line and, *I must stop listening to what is not being said.*

Reading this the next morning, the cleaning woman concluded that he was too strange, even for an American.

Avril Smythe had dismissed the Indians and, with a new cigarette in hand, fumbled through her packet of soiled cards, muttering quietly and puffing. "Next," she called without bothering to look up. "Next, please, next."

Paul Gregoire approached her desk and sat down on a very old kitchen chair, which at once gave way beneath him.

Avril looked up sharply and frowned. "Careful," she said, "the leg isn't on proper. Bring that chair from over there." And frowning still, she reached into her dress and gave a firm tug to a strap. Then with a little arch of her back, she slung her breasts across the desk as if she expected him to do something with them or at least comment on them. It was, he would discover, merely her way, part of a separate performance played out for each customer. It had nothing to do with him personally.

"Name."

"Paul Gregoire."

She recognized his voice from the phone. And he was good looking. She inhaled deeply and leaned back, studying his suit, his tie, his coarse American accent. He could afford sixteen pounds at least. "You're looking for what, then, Mr. Gregory?"

"Well, actually, what I'd like is a place with one bedroom, perhaps in Kensington."

"How much?"

"I thought perhaps twelve or fifteen pounds a week."

"Impossible," she said, "out of the question."

"I see. Well, what do they rent for?"

She hadn't heard. She was not going to hear.

"Around here?" she said, "twelve or fifteen pounds a week around here?" She waved her hand grandly, and he realized that with that gesture she had made the Underground station across the street, the Wimpy Bar next door, the unspeakably shabby office in which they sat—she had made all of them disappear and they were, Paul Gregoire and Avril Smythe, at tea in Kensington Gardens. He sat silent while she looked at the grand scene she had created and then, abruptly, she descended to this scruffy little office where they sat. In a chummy manner she said, "You've got to go up to sixteen. Fifteen won't ever do it. Never. Sixteen is good; and eighteen." She stopped speaking and her eyes emptied out and she seemed to choke back a sob. She couldn't go on. "But don't do more than eighteen. It's not worth it, not around here."

"Are you or are you not?"

"But what? I don't know what you want to know."

"Are you or are you not a Jew?"

"But I'm a Catholic priest. You know that. Of course I'm not a Jew."

"We thought you'd say that."

"I'm not."

"Why do you keep protesting? Do you hate the Jews?"

"No. I like them."

"'Some of my best friends are Jews.' Is that what you're saying? Why do you condescend to them? Is it a cover-up?"

"I don't know what you want from me."

"You are a Jew, aren't you. You're a Jew who thinks he's God."

"I am only…"

"You're a Jew," they said, closing in on him.

"Yes, I *am* a Jew." He could hear his voice rising, strong above the other noises. They were getting a needle ready, preparing the injection. Two of them wrestled him to the floor, and another tore off his trousers. "I am, I am a Jew!" he shouted.

He felt the sharp jab of the needle in his left buttock, and then someone turned him over on his back.

"Now we can go to work on him," a voice said.

For over an hour he cried soundlessly, hugging his knees, rocking back and forth. And for another hour he stared at the Boots bag. Then he wrote.

Avril Smythe is a hastily assembled mobile of fruits and vegetables. Her mouth is a badly puckered crab apple, her breasts are cantaloupes. And when she walks, her buttocks are watermelons. He paused for a moment and then continued. *She is hanging on the way you grip the window ledge in nightmares just before you wake up.* There was no more room to write.

The cleaning woman took the shirts out of their plastic wrappers. They were new shirts, neither had yet been worn, and she removed the pins with elaborate care. Unfolding the shirts on the bed, she admired the material for a moment, caressing it, and then, with a quick glance over her shoulder, she slit the two shirts from the hem of the tail to the little collar button in back. She folded them, replacing the pins and the cardboard stiffener exactly as they had been. She put them back in the bureau drawer, with the Boots bag just as she had found it.

At half past ten in the morning Mrs. Rivers had already had her elevenses: gin and a piece of toast. She leaned against the doorway, one hand on her hip, the other at her throat. She blinked into the sunlight and tried to focus.

"Miss Smythe sent me," he said. "From London Flats."

"You're Mr. Gregory?"

"Gregoire, actually. It's a French name."

"Oh God, French! Well, it's not your fault."

"No."

"You're younger than I expected. I expected someone not so young. She said on the phone that you write for *Life* magazine. I thought you'd be older."

Paul Gregoire had once written a review of a book by Teilhard de Chardin but, although *Life* paid him for it, they had never printed it. Pressed by Avril Smythe for his present occupation (none) and his previous occupations (also none), he had lamely admitted that he had once done a review for *Life*.

"It was only a review, actually," he said now.

"Well, if you work for *Life*, you must know me."

"Oh, are you connected with *Life*?"

"You ought to know, if you work for them. *Life* did a perfectly enormous story about us maybe ten years ago. Back in the fifties. The Riverses. We were the last of the White Rajahs. That's what this is." She jabbed him with her pointed fingers, on one of which glittered a very large diamond. "That's a reward for twenty-five years of living with wogs."

"Wogs?"

"Oh Christ, Africa! We were the last of the White Rajahs!"

"I see."

"Look, do you want to see the flat or don't you?"

She pushed ahead of him and with surprising agility led him down a narrow flight of outdoor stairs. They descended in a heavy mist of gin and perfume.

She was talking, endlessly talking. Paul Gregoire looked at the wiry hair, the deep furrows in her brow, her cheeks caked with powder that had begun to crack. What was she saying? If only she'd stop. Just stop. "We were something in India. We mattered then. Not like now with those Beatles and all the foreigners." Her lashes were heavy with mascara, and in the corner of one of her dim gray eyes, pus had gathered. She must be eighty, pickled in alcohol. Now she was talking about the previous occupant, a French girl—"from France, if you believed her"—who had a froggy lover, and what a mess they had left the flat in.

He was not listening, and he was only faintly aware of the apartment; it was small and cold and musty, a tomb for the last of the White Rajahs.

"Well?" she said.

"I'm sorry, what were you saying?"

"I said eighteen pounds a week, take it or leave it."

"Eighteen pounds." He could hear Avril Smythe, *Ridiculous, it's not worth ten.* "Eighteen pounds," he said, "that sounds all right. That's good. I'll take it."

"Payment in advance," she said.

He took out his wallet and handed her the money.

"I won't be moving in until next week," he said.

He could not look at her as she kneaded his shoulder and the tightened planes of her face cracked in a smile. "You're a godsend," she said. "Come upstairs and have a drink."

He had handed her salvation at a bargain price. It had been so easy.

He had a new Boots bag, a smaller one; it had contained tranquilizers. He smoothed it out tenderly. *Pity and even compassion can destroy. Empty hearts do not count; we have always had them. Only the full ones matter.* Who said that? Somebody.

He got up and, for no reason other than that he did these things, he went to the bureau and took out his new shirts. Rapidly he tore away the plastic bags, the pins, the cardboard. The shirts were ruined.

Later he wrote simply, *Do you see?*

"Now, Father Gregory, you are an American?"

"Gregoire, Father. Yes, American."

"I see. Well, how does it happen that you have come to England to apply for laicization? You ought to have done this in America. The paperwork is horrific." He belched, apologized, and pushed away his glass of wine. "For my stomach. Paul recommended it to Timothy, unless I'm mistaken."

"About the papers, Father. I came to England. Then I decided."

"So much the worse. You know, of course, that Father McDonnell has sent you to see me because your testimony was not satisfactory. He sees no grounds on which you might be granted a decree of laicization. You have been, it seems, an adequate priest, if a bit overly zealous. Seems you are unwilling to accept your human limitations. That sounds to me like spiritual pride. Not good. Not healthy." He consulted his notes. "He says you cry." He suppressed a smile. "You cry?"

Paul Gregoire, holding back tears, said nothing.

"Very well, I think we can work this out. Your name?"

"Poor John."

"Poor Elspeth, you mean."

They left then, two elderly ladies, beautifully dressed, who had spent the evening sipping vintage port at Yates's Wine Lodge in the Strand. Paul Gregoire, who had been eavesdropping, paid for his sherry and followed them. They were old and they were giddy, so he had to pace himself carefully, dallying behind them and then catching up and passing. Take out the Underground map, examine it until they catch up, let them pass, and then follow once more. He had been doing this sort of thing for weeks now. It was the only contact he had with the living.

"But poor John, with that nose."

"What about the nose?"

"My dear, it's so big and long."

"John has a long nose, and flat, like a duck's bill."

"Exactly it, long and flat like a duck's bill."

They stopped to laugh and to hold each other up. Paul Gregoire passed them. In a minute he would stop to study his map. "And his eyes. Poor John. Some men have nice eyes and that makes up, but not John."

"Not John. John has shockin' eyes."

"John has shockin' eyes and a nose like a duck's bill. Poor John."

Two drunken old ladies, laughing and laughing, and here am I, he thought, what?

John has shockin' eyes, he wrote on a laundry ticket and put it in his wallet. He smiled. It was something to smile about.

"You mustn't be discouraged, Mr. Gregory, it's very hard to find a place in London." Avril Smythe pulled hard on her cigarette and sent a steady stream of smoke into his eyes.

"But I've taken a place. That's what I'm telling you. In Kensington."

"For how much, Mr. Gregory?"

"Well..."

"How much?"

"Eighteen pounds a week."

"Where in Kensington."

"Just off the Gloucester Road. Near the hospital."

"Not Mrs. Rivers. Not the White Rajah."

"I'm afraid it is."

"Well, God help you, that's all I can say."

He could think of nothing to say in reply.

She gave him a throwaway ballpoint pen with London Flats on it. "To keep us in mind for your next move."

Dear Father Gregoire: I have been in AA now for over a year and I want you to know that I owe it all to you. I could never of done it without you. To me you are a saint of God and I mention you every meeting at the AA. You have brought me back to life. Thank you very much. Sincerely, Ralph B. Otter

Paul Gregoire stood on Waterloo Bridge turning the letter over and over in his hands. After a long time, a very long time, he came to a decision, and it was the letter that fluttered from the rail to the dark waters beneath.

"Guilty or not guilty?"

"Guilty."

"Avril?"

"Smythe."

"Tears?"

"None."

"Pudding?"

"Pudding?"

"Again: pudding?"

"Oh, yes. Figgy."

"Pity?"

"Sentiment."

"Again: pity?"

"Sentimentality."

"The White Rajahs?"

"I can't…"

"Yes or no?"

"Yes."

Time passed and more time passed.

A year passed.

Time wasted and not wasted.

God changed. He became an immanence, unnamable, unknowable.

"The waste remains, the waste remains and kills."—Empson. He wrote this on the flap of his airplane ticket.

"Your name?"

"Paul Gregoire."

"This your passport?"

"Yes."

The customs inspector called a police officer. "He says this is his passport." They both studied the photo and then the man. The policeman shrugged.

"Nothing to declare?"

"No."

"Nothing?"

"Nothing."

"Open that."

Paul Gregoire opened the suitcase, and the customs official rooted among the T-shirts, the socks, the soiled evidence of three years in England. He ignored the two torn shirts.

"What's this?"

"Those are tranquilizers. I don't use them any longer."

"Well, well, well. We'll just hold on to these if you don't mind."

"I don't use them anymore. It doesn't matter."

"And this?" It was the London Flats ballpoint pen. He thought of Avril Smythe, dead now in Kensington. Suicide.

"And what's this thing?"

"It's a miniature elephant. It's ivory."

He whistled again, studied the little ivory carving with care, and placed it apart with the tranquilizers. After half an hour everything in the suitcase had been examined, and a neat pile of evidence lay to one side.

"Step behind that screen."

Behind the screen three men watched while Paul Gregoire removed his clothing. They picked up each item, pulled at the seams of his shirt, felt his trouser cuffs. They made him stoop over, made him raise his arms. Finally they had checked everything, looked into his mouth, searched beneath his arms, spread his legs, and examined his crotch. They had found nothing.

He could feel the violence in the air.

Sweating with frustration, furious, one of them punched him lightly but repeatedly in the ribs. "Okay," he said, "okay, what are you hiding?"

"Nothing," Paul Gregoire said, naked, but suddenly invulnerable.

The punch came harder. "Open up, you bastard, what are you hiding?"

A long silence. The man raised his fist, waiting.

Paul Gregoire had reached the crossroads of fear and understanding. "God." He said it simply, as if it were true. He did not smile.

They let him go then, realizing he wasn't dangerous after all, just another nut.

ANSWERED PRAYERS

1.   When he died, he was ready for it, more or less.

He was pulling out of a side street, thinking about God, when he realized the car approaching on his left was not going to stop, not even slow down. It struck him broadside doing sixty. He felt his own car rise in the air, twisting, and he caught a glimpse of the astounded face of the other driver, and he said to himself, Now I'm dead. Then he heard a tearing sound as his car fishtailed into a chain-link fence, and he said to himself, Well, I mustn't be dead after all. What luck. But he was dead by the time the ambulance came.

His name was Donovan Enright and he had been a Jesuit priest, with a lot of Jesuit ideas. They buried him with a guitar Mass and an upbeat homily.

2.   Donovan Enright had nothing in common with Gene Sullivan, the man who killed him, except that they both were Catholics and they both were forty-five.

Donovan had been a Jesuit for twenty-seven years and a priest for fourteen of those years. He had kept his vows as well as any priest and better than most. Which is to say, as Donovan himself had said more than once, "You can spend a little money and still be poor, and you can do what you want to and still be obedient, but you can't fuck around and still be chaste." That was one of his Jesuit ideas. Mostly, Donovan kept his vows by keeping to himself. He had trouble making friends, and most of the Jesuits he knew best were too intellectual for that sort of thing anyhow. And besides, life was a lot less complicated if you stuck to your own room and just thought. Once, during the religion craze of the sixties, he had put some of his ideas on paper and published a book about the Death of God theologians. He didn't think much of them and the Jesuits didn't think much of his book. So he went back to teaching theology and sitting in his room with his ideas until one night Gene Sullivan killed him and his life was different forever.

Gene Sullivan's only vows were his marriage vows and he kept them as well as most men. In his late thirties he had had a steady mistress, but when he turned forty he decided to play the field. He was a cop and so had opportunities. He hung out with his police buddies at the Up Front Café, which featured a topless hostess and a girl who wore white boots and half a bikini. The girl in the boots was Needa Mann and she worked out on a little platform way in the back, snapping her fingers and moving around in time to the music. Gene had made it with Needa, as all the other cops had before him, and she was good. Even just watching her snap her fingers and roll that sweet butt could take his mind off of home. At home was his wife, Jayne, who always had big pink rollers in her hair, and his daughter, Sheree, and his son, Kevin. After night duty the guys all got together at the Up Front and had a few beers. One night Gene left the bar early and cruised the combat zone until he found a girl he had picked up twice before on lewd and lascivious. She saw he was out of uniform and knew what the deal was, so she got into the car and gave it to him parked in the A&P delivery dock. He went back to the Up Front then, feeling shitty, and had a couple belts and then a couple more. He was mad, at himself, at his whole goddamn life. There was no way out of anything. Life was a trap.

He was thinking this while he drove home to Jayne and, preoccupied, did not stop, did not even slow down, until his car struck Father Donovan Enright's car. His life was different after that.

3. "We've been on this subject for a week now, Father, and I'm still not sure what you hold. Are you saying that there is, or there is not, life after death?"

    Father Enright was still alive at the time, so he pushed his glasses back on his nose and leaned into the question. "That's a rather simplistic formulation of the problem, wouldn't you say?"

    "Yes, it is. Can you answer, please?"

    Students turned around to get a look at the questioner.

    "Simplistically, yes, there is life after death. But immediately the question arises, what do you mean by 'life'? Or, for that matter, by 'death'? What would be wrong, say, about the rather Protestant notion that we live after death in the memories of those we have known, of those who care about us? Just as, for example, Lincoln or Gandhi or even Jesus live in our memories."

    "But aren't most people, after a short time, not remembered at all? What about their eternal life?"

    Father Enright pounced. "Ah, you see? Democracy of the spirit. The life of the soul, Mr., ah—Mr. Smith, is it?—the life of the soul is rooted in mystery. It has no room for democracy. We did not elect God, we are not all equal. Why should not each of us, therefore, enjoy an eternity proper to himself? A life perfectly fitted to the life we led on earth?"

    And then he went off onto his other favorite ideas and everyone relaxed because none of that would be covered in the final exam.

4. Gene Sullivan took one look at the body in the car and knew it was all over for that poor bastard. He checked the area, the skid marks, the position of the two cars. By the time police arrived he had a plausible story ready, one that would stand up in court, so long as nobody measured the skids, etcetera. The guy must have been drinking, he said. He came shooting out of that side street like a bat out of hell, never stopped at the sign, must have been drunk, he said. By the time the ambulance came, it was clear the guy was dead.

    Somebody found his wallet and it turned out he was a priest.

That was good in a way. No lawsuit. No family. But, Christ, a priest!

Chico Mulligan drove Gene home and had a drink with him.

"Don't worry," Mulligan said. "I'll fill out the report myself. Maybe he was drinking, maybe he was speeding. I'll take care of it. We're buddies, right? You'd do the same for me, right? All right, so don't worry!"

After Mulligan left, Gene poured himself a tumbler of Four Roses. Then he woke Jayne and told her how he was almost killed, how the other guy was dead. She kissed him and hugged him and then poured him another drink.

"Come on," she said, "come on, baby," and she led him off to the bedroom, where for a whole bunch of reasons he couldn't do anything. "Forget about what happened," she said, her hand busy beneath the sheet. "Put him out of your mind."

Finally he fell asleep and then she fell asleep. But even in his dreams, Gene kept seeing the dead priest's face.

For Donovan Enright, the dead priest, it was the first of many unusual nights.

5.   So this was it, Donovan thought, I'm gonna be summoned every goddamn time! At first he couldn't figure it out, but after the third time he realized it fitted perfectly with everything he had thought about an ironic God.

It went this way. The cop would be doing his stupid police work and minding his own business and then all of a sudden he'd stop and think of that priest he had killed, and once he thought of him he couldn't get him out of his mind. That was Donovan's signal. He had to drop everything and live locked in that mind until the cop forgot about him. Tough shit that, for Donovan, life might be going along nice and peaceful, his ideas on heaven and hell and eternity clicking by with smoothness and precision; as soon as Gene thought of him— whammo—it was all over.

Some eternity. Some joke. It had been going on for months now and Donovan was beginning to get fed up.

6.   "As to the question of eternal reward—or, as you have just formulated it: is there a heaven and a hell?—I would say yes, there is a heaven and a hell. God rewards us by giving us whatever it is we have always wanted."

He had paused then, and even the dullest of them had looked up. Father Enright was known to be peculiar, but surely he was not actually proposing a pie-in-the-sky heaven.

"That is to say, if you have put yourself first in all things, then that is what you'll get: you'll spend eternity looking in, contemplating yourself. But if, on the other hand, you have lived for other people—for God, if you wish—then you will spend eternity looking out. Looking out at what, I would not care to say."

They had continued to stare up at him, perhaps imagining him dead. A vein throbbed in his temple and he had looked severely at the thirty-some expectant faces as he said, "Those who are determined to be damned will find, I think, that their peculiar prayers are answered."

The next week he was killed in that fishy car crash.

7.   At first, Donovan hadn't minded much. It wasn't like being dead at all, this summons to somebody else's life.

"Come on, baby," Jayne had said, and then she had taken her husband to bed and fooled around with him. Donovan hadn't gone along at first, in and out of Gene's mind as he was, but as Gene got excited, the thought of the priest returned more and more strongly to his mind, and so Donovan had no choice. Poor, obedient, and chaste, Donovan wrestled in that bed, his heart racing and his body pumping wildly right up to the moment of release. He gasped along with Gene, flopped over on his side, and waited till his heart slowed down. Donovan was just about to submerge beneath a tidal wave of self-disgust, when Gene suddenly forgot about him and fell asleep. Donovan was finished with and went back to his old thinking.

Gene made love to his wife often now, and sometime during the event invariably called up that damned priest. After a few of these times, Donovan came to realize that this was his afterlife, it was God's will, and he began to surrender to it. Who was he, after all, to pick a quarrel with God? The sex was terrific, and the complexity of the emotions that went along with sex was a revelation. Sometimes while Donovan writhed in what he continued to think of as the act of love, he would shudder with a surge of undiluted hatred, and then he thrust hard and his chest expanded with the feel of punishing and he thought, Good, good. And sometimes when they were having dinner, he would look at the cop's daughter—because Gene would look—and think of the things he could do to her, how it would feel, how it would teach her what was what. Donovan even found himself once—when Gene was shaving and his son came in to take a shower—he found himself thinking about the kid. My God, the kid? But Gene cut himself then, maybe deliberately, and so the priest went straight out of his thoughts.

That kind of variety kept Donovan in a continual state of wonder. Life had never seemed like that. No such thoughts had ever crossed his mind while he was alive. Or had they? No. He had never even made friends with Jesuits, let alone with women. It was too much of a risk. He had wondered once, in his late twenties, if maybe he was queer. He had wondered for quite a while, and had even thought of seeing a shrink, but decided finally that if your car was up on blocks, it didn't really matter whether it was manual shift or automatic drive. And then in his early thirties he decided he wasn't queer anyhow. And now all this desire: the wife, the daughter, even the son.

A few months passed and the summonses became more frequent. Donovan was beginning to get fed up.

8.   The summonses became more frequent and more boring: while Gene was on duty in the prowl car, while he sat swilling beer in the Up Front, while he—God help us—sat on the toilet fiddling with himself. Every few hours his mind would slip from whatever he was doing and sure enough that damned priest would be back. Gene became jumpy and irritable, not just at home, but everywhere. He was not sleeping nights. He was never relaxed. He could not keep the face of that dead priest out of his mind.

Gene couldn't figure out why. He had killed guys before, two of them. Some kid in a stolen car had pulled a gun on him and he had had to shoot it out. And he had killed another guy, a Puerto Rican who had gone nuts and was holding his own kids hostage. Gene had killed both of them and never thought about it for a minute. But this priest here, he couldn't get out of his head.

And then one night when he and Chico Mulligan were on duty in the wagon, they got a 10-13 to West Roxbury. It turned out not to be a 10-13 at all, just a couple of kids who broke the window of a liquor store. One of them they'd picked up before, Jesus Sanchez, a punchy bastard who was always looking for real trouble and someday would find it. Sanchez had a bottle of Canadian Club in his hand, and as the two policemen came at him, he broke it off at the neck and made a lunge at Mulligan's face. Mulligan used his leather sap and decked Sanchez with one tremendous blow to the side of his head. "Humane," Mulligan said, letting Sanchez lie there while they frisked the other kid and then hustled him into the wagon. Then they got Sanchez by the hands and feet and tossed him into the wagon too. But as Mulligan was about to slam the door, Sanchez kicked out with a pointed shoe and caught Mulligan flat in the chest.

In seconds the two cops were inside the wagon. Gene held Sanchez from behind while Mulligan worked him over. Sanchez went limp and Gene dropped him to the floor, but Mulligan was not done. He kicked the body up against the wall and then worked up and down, getting him in the shins, the knees, the crotch, the chest, using his sap on the back of the head.

"Christ," Gene said, "you're gonna kill him," but Mulligan didn't stop. And then there was a siren from a squad car, and then another, and Gene pulled Mulligan off Sanchez.

"Resisting arrest," Mulligan said. "You saw him."

"Right," Gene said.

But before they brought him into the station, Mulligan took the precaution of slipping some uppers into Sanchez's pocket. Gene filled out the report the way Mulligan wanted; it was what you did for a buddy.

But the next day, when Sanchez died without ever regaining consciousness, Gene thought of the priest he had killed—he couldn't tell why—and from then on the priest was constantly in his mind.

Donovan had to relive the beating the two cops had given Sanchez. But now it was he who held the struggling Sanchez. And it was he who—along with Chico now—swung his foot at the shins, the knees, the defenseless crotch. After a while Donovan realized he almost liked the feeling as his foot crunched against the yielding flesh. Yes, he liked it.

It was then that Donovan began to wonder if he had gone to heaven or to hell.

9.   In an afterword to his book on the Death of God theologians, Father Enright had recorded various unconnected thoughts about the mysterious nature of sin and punishment.

"The God they say is dead is actually the democratic God of their own fabrication. The true God, the God of justice and of irony, lives forever."

"Sin is behovely. Therefore, irony is behovely. How else explain Julian of Norwich, among other wonders."

"It would seem that God allows pride and arrogance to go unpunished. He does not. It is only that some sins cannot be punished except by other sins. Thus the man of pride is often allowed to slip into sins of the flesh. Sometimes we cannot find ourselves until we are wholly lost."

A lot of crazy ideas, his fellow Jesuits said. They felt he did too much thinking, alone in that room.

10.   The day after Sanchez died, two things happened.

The first was that Gene Sullivan went to confession. He didn't know why he went, and he didn't want to go, but he ended up inside the confessional anyhow. It was as if he'd been dragged there, with no power to resist. He told the priest that a while back, he had been in an accident. He had had a few drinks, he said, and maybe he was a little under the influence because he really hadn't seen the other driver and, anyways, he had killed him. The priest asked a lot of questions, like was there a family left behind and all that, and Gene said no, no, nothing like that, and after a while the priest gave him absolution. But as soon as he came out of the confessional, it started in all over again. He hadn't admitted that the guy he killed was a priest or that Chico Mulligan had filed a false report saying the priest had been drinking, so he figured the confession was no good and the sacrament wouldn't take. He was right back where he had started. He stood for a minute on the church steps wondering if he should go back and tell the rest. "*O bone Jesu, exaudi me.*" He looked around to see who was talking, but nobody was there. Jesus, he said to himself, and all the way down to the station he played rock music really loud, but he kept on hearing that smooth voice saying, "*Exaudi me.*"

The second thing happened down at the station. Chico Mulligan came up to him and said he had to talk, so they got into Mulligan's car and drove out toward Brookline.

"I gotta get this card for my wife's anniversary, see. We'll go to this place where Reilly's girl works, the House of Cards, wait'll you get a look at her tits. Out to here."

Gene's mind was still on confession; the voice he had heard had to be that dead priest's voice. The thought made all his teeth ache.

"Tits out to here," Mulligan was saying.

Disgusting, Gene thought. And to Mulligan he said, "Look, Chico, I got a lot on my mind. I don't give two shits for Reilly's girl's tits." He was trying to get that priest out of his head.

"Hey, that's a song, practically," Chico said. And in a deep bass, to the tune of "On Top of Old Smokey," he roared out, "He don't give two shi-its, for Reilly's girl's tits, de-da-da-da-da-dum, de-da-da-da-dum."

"Come on, for Chrissake, Chico! Don't you ever get serious?"

"I been serious." Mulligan gave him a sideways smile. "I was serious the night you killed the priest. Yeah, I been serious. I was serious all right when I filled out that report. 'Tread marks, none. Alcohol consumption… '"

"All right! All right! Forget I said anything. Just forget it."

"I can forget, Gene, old buddy. Old Chico, he can forget. By the way, how's *your* memory?" he said, as he parked the car. He slammed the door on Gene's answer.

In the House of Cards, Mulligan was feeding Reilly's girl a whole string of double-meaning gags, so Gene pretended he was looking at cards. He picked one up and opened it as if he were reading, but he could hear the sex in Mulligan's voice, and he shook his head. Goddamn pig, he thought, and took a quick look at Mulligan and the poor girl. "Better a millstone be put around his neck," Gene said aloud, and the girl looked over at him, smiling, and then back to Mulligan.

"Jeez, I like your tits," Mulligan said. "I mean, your cards. Your cards, I mean."

Mulligan and Reilly's girl laughed it up then, but Gene left the House of Cards and sat waiting in the car. He couldn't figure out what was the matter with him. It must be the confession, he figured.

In a minute Mulligan came out of the store, laughing, but when he got in the car he was all business. "It's about Sanchez," he said.

The kid they had brought in with Sanchez had got word out to some smart-ass reporter that Sanchez had been beaten to death. There was going to be an investigation. Gene Sullivan would have to testify.

"What about Sanchez?" Gene said.

"He was resisting arrest, you remember that. He was crazy with drugs, so I had to subdue him. I hit him twice. You remember that."

"Yeah, I know that."

"I remember how it was with your priest. You remember how it was with my spic. Right?"

"Right."

"Right. So just don't change your mind when the heat gets on."

They drove back to the station, Chico Mulligan singing his song about Reilly's girl's tits, Gene Sullivan wondering why he kept thinking the things he was thinking.

His mind was no longer his own. He began to wonder if he was losing it.

11.   The smart-ass reporter had really started something with his story about the death of Jesus Sanchez. There were riots in Roxbury, minor ones, but they got a lot of press coverage. The hotshot social scientists started coming out of the woodwork, writing editorials in the Sunday paper and demanding police reform. Chico Mulligan was investigated for police brutality and, although a lot of stuff surfaced about his beating kids and fags and spics, there was no hard-core proof. But then every other day there were stories about graft and police rip-offs and insurance to small businesses, until finally the word came down from city hall to pick a couple of guys and kick them off the force. With plenty of publicity. So Chico Mulligan was on his way out and Gene Sullivan was under investigation.

Jayne was crying every day now at breakfast, just sitting there sucking on her bad teeth. And his own kids looked at him like he was shit. Gene spent a lot of time at the Up Front and a lot of time just driving through the dark streets. Donovan Enright had become his constant companion. The dead priest's thoughts filtered through Gene's mind so that Gene never knew anymore what he was thinking and what was being thought for him.

As for Donovan, he was tired as hell of all this and was going to end it even if it killed him.

Gene had resisted the temptation to go to confession again and this time tell everything. And he took desperate steps to maintain control over his own mind. He had thought about it plenty and finally came to the conclusion that the only way to get a priest out of your head is by a lot of drinking and screwing and taking chances. So when he got off duty, he'd go straight to the Up Front. After a few drinks, he'd cruise around in his car and pick up a hooker, twenty minutes with her and then back again to the Up Front. Then he'd drive the turnpike, getting the speed up to eighty, ninety, seeing how close he could come to an abutment before he'd chicken and swing the car back onto the lane. He was crazy, he knew it, but he would do anything to get away from that voice inside his head.

Finally he'd go home, drunk, and collapse in bed next to Jayne, who lay staring at the ceiling. Next morning she'd be crying at breakfast. Gene didn't know where it would end.

Donovan knew.

12.   "O Lord, we commend to you the soul of your servant, Donovan, that, having departed from this world, he may live with you. And by the grace of your merciful love, wash away the sins that in human frailty he has committed in the conduct of his life. Through Christ our Lord. Amen."

Then the singing:

> Day of wrath! O day of mourning!
> See fulfilled the prophets' warning,
> Heav'n and earth in ashes burning!

And a whole lot more. It was a nice service, really, if you got rid of those damned guitars. Donovan was looking forward to it, again.

13.   On the last night of his life, Gene got the word that he would be temporarily relieved of duty until the investigation on him was complete. Seems they had turned up some hard evidence about payoffs and falsified reports, and they were looking into his involvement with the numbers. No sweat, Gene said, and took off for the Up Front.

Needa Mann was strolling to the music, snapping her long fingers, when he came in and took a seat up close to the stage. He had a beer. After that he had some John Jameson and a beer for a chaser. Needa twitched her butt at him and he gave her what he hoped was a hungry look.

"When you're hot, you're hot," somebody said to him. It was Reilly, drinking a beer.

"He who lives by the sword, dies by the sword," Gene said to Reilly, and thought, Jesus, this is really it, this is really the end.

Gene and Reilly had a few more beers. Donovan let the liquor settle in, waiting for his chance.

After a while Gene went to take a leak. There was nobody in the men's room and Gene stood in front of the mirror for a long time, looking at his face. Then he took out his pistol and put the barrel in his mouth. He looked at himself like that and after a minute turned in profile to see another view. He could blow his head off. All he'd have to do was just release the safety and press the trigger. Then it would be all over—the life, the wife, the whole shitty deal.

The door slammed open and he pulled the barrel out of his mouth quickly.

"Thought you fell in," Reilly said.

"Up yours, Reilly." Gene put the pistol into his holster and went to get another drink. But Donovan had had enough of the Up Front and was eager to get on with life. And so Gene ordered the drink but didn't wait long enough to drink it. Before he knew where he was, or why he was there, he was in his car heading home.

It was after midnight and he sat in the kitchen waiting for somebody to keep him from what he was going to do. He had placed the pistol on the table in front of him. He wouldn't use it… unless. He got a bottle of Four Roses and a soup bowl full of ice. He filled a tumbler with ice and booze and drank it slowly. After a long while, he got up and walked down the hall to the bedroom. Jayne was asleep, the big pink rollers in her hair. He went back to the kitchen and waited. He fiddled with the pistol for a while and then poured another tumbler of Four Roses.

He was dozing, his head on his arms, when he heard Kevin saying, "You drunken pig." Gene looked up and saw his son, so young, so defenseless. He wanted to protect him.

"You are," Kevin said. "A drunken pig."

Gene stood up woozily. He put his arms around the boy, hugging him, trying to find the words to tell him how things were. "You don't know," he said, slobbering.

Kevin pushed with both hands against his father's chest and Gene was flung against the wall. His head snapped back hard and, sobered a little, he slipped to a fighting crouch, ready to take the boy on. But

Kevin had left, and Gene stood with fists clenched, facing an empty doorway. He picked up the pistol, turned it over in his hand a couple of times, and jammed it into his holster. Then he was slamming the door hard and the car wheels were churning gravel on the driveway and he was out of it, once and for all.

He was not thinking now, it was too late for thought. He was in the car, driving down to the combat zone. But he passed through the zone without even checking out the girls. At the Hancock building he stopped the car long enough to toss his belt and holster into the back seat and slip his pistol into the door clip next to the driver's seat. Then he drove directly to the meat rack. He'd pick one up, a butch one, and he'd beat the shit out of him. He'd dump him in the A&P lot. It didn't matter why. He'd do it.

He cruised slowly around the block twice, slowing down to check out what was for sale. He stopped at a big muscular kid with white pants and shaggy blond hair. Gene blinked the caution lights and the kid ambled over to the car.

"Hi, guy," he said, putting his head in the window.

"Get in," Gene said.

The boy tipped his head from side to side, checking Gene's face and build. "Hmm," he said.

"Get in."

"Regular or special?"

"Regular."

"How much?"

"Ten."

"Ten?" He pulled away from the window.

"All right, twenty." The boy got in then, and they drove around making small talk about the weather.

"What's your name?" Gene said.

The boy laughed. "Smith," he said. "What's yours?"

"Jones."

"What else? Say, tiger, can we get this over with? I don't feel like driving around all night."

Gene pulled onto a side street, and down an alley, and finally he parked behind an apartment building. He tried to work up some anger at this fag he was going to beat the shit out of. He tried to recall why he had to do this, but Donovan was lodged firmly in his mind, and Gene could feel nothing. But he had to. He had to mangle this kid. That was why he had come down here. That was why he had picked the kid up, why...

And then suddenly, with the force of revelation, he knew exactly why he was here. Leaning his head against the steering wheel, he gave way to long racking sobs that shook his entire body. He cried as if he intended never to stop.

After a long while Gene felt a hand move on his back and shoulder. "That's okay, that's okay," he heard the boy saying. "Coming out is hard at first."

"You don't know," he said. "You don't know what any of this is like."

The boy only tipped his head to one side and pursed his lips.

Gene felt the boy's hand move on his leg. He shook off the hand and drew a long, deep breath. Then, his mind on nothing but the dead priest, Gene backed out of the parking space and pulled out of the alley and eventually onto the turnpike. The car accelerated to fifty, then sixty.

The boy next to Gene gave him an anxious look and moved away from him. "You're driving crazy," he said. "I want to get out."

Gene took the pistol from the door clip and pointed it at the boy's head. "I'm a cop," he said, "and if you touch that door handle, they'll have to pick you up with blotting paper. You're coming with me." With the boy beside him cringing against the door, Gene lowered the pistol and pressed harder on the accelerator.

He drove straight into the deep night, of one mind about life and death, as the speedometer hit eighty, ninety. The abutment loomed before them and Gene kept his hands firmly on the wheel. There was a roaring sound inside his head and then, for the life of him, he could not recall anything about why he was doing this. But at the very moment of impact, the priest's astounded face flew up suddenly before his own, and he heard someone say, "Now I'm dead," and could not tell if the voice was his own or the priest's.

And what happens now? Gene thought, or maybe it was Donovan.

14.   Miraculously, the boy survived. He was thrown free of the wreckage and was found unconscious in the middle of the speed lane. He had two broken arms and a slight concussion, but no permanent injuries.

He was out of the hospital and back on the job in only a few months, but it took him just about forever to get that damned cop out of his mind.

MARRIAGES

THE ANATOMY OF BLISS

THE PROBLEM

The problem, so the shrink says, is whether Calder is willing to put up with his wife's idiosyncrasies. Is he willing? Does he want to? Yes or no.

The problem, as Calder sees it, is the handwriting on the wall.

THE WIFE

The wife's name is Honey-Mae and Calder hates it. Almost any other name is better than Honey-Mae. It sounds trivial. It sounds as if she wears bobbed hair and red circles on her cheeks. As if she speaks with a lisp and sucks pralines all day. Calder hates her name. And she—so Calder tells the shrink—hates him.

THE MAN SHE HATES

Calder. This man is not the hateful sort. He smokes pipes, of course, because he's an academic, and he asks how things are going at the shop, are the orders coming in okay, ahem, and whether or not she remembers to take her One A Days. But deep down he is not hateful. No.

He had a vicious streak once, but not anymore. During his childhood he had, with all the other kids, doused a cat with gasoline and then set it on fire. And he had stripped his little sister so that everybody could look. And he did other things.

But when he grew up, he did mostly responsible things and the vicious streak just dried up.

He went to war.

He went to graduate school.

He learned five languages and became a promising assistant professor of comparative literature.

And now he is a dutiful citizen and a loving husband with tenure not far off. So he is, naturally, outraged by the handwriting on the wall.

THE CHILD

There isn't any child. Either they can't have one or they haven't hit the right combination yet. Sometimes Honey-Mae mopes around the house and he wonders if that's what it is.

"Is it a child? Is that why you… you know?"

"It isn't a child," she says.

"Then what is it? Why do you do it?"

By now it is clear where the scene is going. At the end she says, "I love you," and she cries and this time, again, he does not leave her.

MONEY

It can't be money, because they have as much as they need.

WORK

Honey-Mae never misses a day of work. She chooses material for drapes and sofas and chairs, and her choices are always right. Her clients say there is nobody like Honey-Mae for the perfect decorating touch. So? What is it then?

HOW IT ALL GOT STARTED

"What's this?" Calder said.

"What's what?"

"This, under the hook."

Honey-Mae started out of the room.

"It's writing," he said. "It's three words here under the hook."

"I'm taking a bath."

Calder stood outside the bathroom door, suddenly angry. "Honey-

Mae," he said, "I'm talking to you. I said what is that writing?"

"I'm taking a bath."

He heard her begin to hum.

Calder had been hanging up his study corduroys on the hook just inside the closet door when he saw what looked like a bug. It was on the wall under the clothes hook and it wasn't moving. He shifted the corduroys to his other hand and gave the bug a quick hard swat. Then he squinted and adjusted his glasses. It wasn't a bug after all. It was handwriting. The writing was very small but the letters were perfectly formed, a little column of three words. He guessed they were words, some kind of words, though they certainly weren't in any of the languages he knew. "What's this?" he had said then to Honey-Mae, but she was having none of it and was sitting in the bath now, humming, while he stood outside the door feeling angry and wondering why.

He went back to the bedroom and finished undressing. He stood before the full-length mirror and looked at himself in profile. He was getting a pot. He sucked in his stomach and watched the bulge disappear. "It's no good," he said to the mirror. "You can't go through life holding your breath." He reached into the closet for his pajamas and threw a quick glance at the corduroy pants. He pushed them tentatively with a finger. The writing was still there. He found himself getting angry again, and feeling foolish too.

Honey-Mae came trailing steam and perfume from the bath and, laughing, she flung herself on top of him.

"Num, num," she said.

"Listen," he said, "what's that writing in the closet?"

"I don't know about any writing," she said, her decorator's hands busy with his pajama tops. "I'll make little patterns on your chest," she said.

He made a mental note to show her the writing in the closet, afterward, but Honey-Mae was playing tiger lady right now, and what the hell.

"You're so good," she said, her voice gone velvet.

"Mmmm," he said.

The next day the writing was still there. He shrugged and made another mental note to ask her about it and then forgot.

A week later there was a fourth word and then a fifth. He was sure there had been only three. Honey-Mae was getting her robe from the closet just then, and he took her arm and turned her, saying, "Lookit. What's this?"

And that was how it all got started.

THE WRITING

The writing is small, in a cursive hand, made by a blue ballpoint pen, fine tipped. The words are of varying length, but they spell nothing.

Calder has copied out the words in his most careful hand. He has consulted his dictionaries and his texts on dialectic and grammar. He has even consulted the awful T. D. Wood, who knows everything. But the words spell nothing.

It must be a code of some kind. Calder is at work studying books on code when suddenly two more words appear. This is it. This calls for scrupulous scientific analysis. While Honey-Mae is at the shop, he sets up special lights and he photographs the words exactly as they appear beneath the hook in his closet. He has the prints blown up to five times their size. He compares; he isolates; he grinds his teeth in frustration. He feeds the words into a computer—forward, then backward, then any old way. It is hopeless. It isn't a code. Or perhaps the code is incomplete.

Calder has begun gaining weight. He eats absentmindedly, but all the time, and he has begun dreaming that threats are being made on his life. But all the threats are in code. He tells Honey-Mae none of this. He is determined she must not know, though he can't say why. But who can be writing these words? Who is doing it?

THE PROBLEM

"Well, if you're not doing it, who is? Somebody's doing it."

"Why are you so angry?" Her reasonable voice. "It's only a little writing on the closet wall. Nobody's ever going to see it."

"Maybe it's Amber. It must be Amber."

"Get dressed, Calder. You're going to be late."

"But why would Amber want to write on the closet wall?"

AMBER

Amber has cleaned house in this neighborhood for the past fifteen years. During that time professors or their wives have accused her of hitting the dog, spoiling the children, drinking the liquor, smoking the grass (Professor Wood, the accuser), and sitting down on the job. She has never been accused of writing on the wall. She quits.

THE MAN SHE LOVES

There are ten words now. Now there are fifteen. Now twenty. Calder has no control over it. He wishes they were not there. He wills them not to be there. But there they are, tiny irregular scratches descending in a perfect row beneath the hook in the closet. Words. In no language he knows. He says nothing more about it to Honey-Mae. They pretend to each other that the words are not there.

But now they have made love, and it is good, and they are lying against each other, counting breaths. He kisses her wet forehead. She sighs and nuzzles him. And then he says it.

"It is you, isn't it. Making those marks."

"Marks?"

"Marks. On the wall. In the closet."

"No."

"It is."

"No, Calder. I swear it isn't."

They lie together, silent. Honey-Mae moves her shoulder against him, but he does not respond.

"You do believe me, don't you? Calder?"

"Yes. I want to. Yes, I do."

"I love you," she says.

In the morning he is full of energy and when she comes out of the bathroom, brisk, ready for work, he mentions almost casually, "You know, it's the damnedest thing. Where do you suppose those words are coming from?"

And just as casually, she says, "I wrote them." Calder stares at her, a pain in his chest. "You? But you told me…"

"Oh, for God's sake, Calder, don't make such a big thing out of everything." And then she is off to work.

THE SHOP

Mrs. Fischer is leafing through a book of sample brocades. Each time she turns a heavy page, she fingers it and checks Honey-Mae's reaction. The tiniest frown, the tilt of the head in a question, the pursed lip. Mrs. Fischer has not yet made the right choice.

Honey-Mae is sitting at her little antique desk helping Mrs. Fischer select the fabric for a Queen Anne wing chair. Honey-Mae is wearing her oyster pantsuit with the beige silk blouse. She is short and shouldn't be able to get away with a pantsuit, but somehow she does. Her blond hair, clipped close to her head, emphasizes her delicate features. She uses no makeup except a gray pencil above her lashes. Her eyes are large and silver. Sitting there, expectant, encouraging, she is herself the most impressive sample of her art.

Honey-Mae smiles gently as Mrs. Fischer touches for a second time the melon and gold brocade that is perfect for her wing chair.

"This one, I think," Mrs. Fischer says.

"Perfect," Honey-Mae says.

Perfection. The brocade is perfect, and so is the shop, and so is Honey-Mae. Yet, in less than a quarter hour Honey-Mae is on the telephone to Calder, sobbing over and over, "Forgive me, forgive me."

CELEBRATION

Calder has been voted tenure and so they are going to dinner at the Silly Goose to celebrate. "Life is good sometimes," Calder says. He reaches into the closet for his dark blue suit and checks the wall beneath the coat hook. Smooth, white, unspotted. He shouldn't have checked, but he can't help himself. After their last fight Honey-Mae had scrubbed the wall with Bon Ami and most of the writing had come out. Later he thought he saw signs that new words had been written and then erased, but he couldn't be sure. Anyway, no words are there now, and he shouldn't be checking.

The celebration is perfect. A tenderloin of lamb and a Nuits-Saint-Georges and, before bed, there will be some very good brandy. And the two of them together, in love, with no writing on the wall.

She is in the bath now and Calder carries the little silver tray with the two snifters into the bedroom and puts it on her bureau. Perfect.

Suddenly he thinks how he can surprise her. He goes to her side of the closet and looks for the lace negligee he bought her on their honeymoon in Florence. White chiffon. Where is it? His fingers flick through her dresses, but there is no negligee. Just as he decides that it must be in the bureau, his eye catches the long skirt through a transparent plastic cover, way in the back, against the wall. He takes it out carefully, making sure it does not catch on anything. And then he gasps, holding the gown crumpled against him. He stares straight ahead at the wall, the white wall, covered from top to bottom in minute handwriting, words, words in long columns, in perfect lines. Words covering the entire wall.

Honey-Mae is standing behind him, naked and perfumed. She looks at him with disgust, with hatred. She turns and walks, wooden, to the bed.

Calder takes the brandy to his study. He sits in his big leather chair, gazing helplessly at the books everywhere around him. He drinks the brandy, and keeps on drinking until he is drunk.

THE PROBLEM
"Why?" he says. He is begging her. "Please. Just tell me. I want to understand. Why do you do it?"

"What does it matter?" Honey-Mae says, surly, not herself. "You've never loved me anyway."

THE LOVERS
Calder and Honey-Mae have decided on a frank talk. The morning

light streams through the blinds and a frank talk seems the sensible way to begin the day, to begin a new life.

"I just want you to be happy," Calder says.

"I know. I know that." Honey-Mae burrows into his chest.

"No, I don't want you to burrow now. I want us to have a frank talk. Will you do that for me?"

Honey-Mae sits up, all business.

"I just want you to be happy," he starts again.

"I know that."

"And if you're writing on the walls like this, something must be the matter."

She says nothing.

"Right?"

"I'm not writing on the walls."

He says nothing.

"Suppose I did?" she says suddenly. "Suppose I threw shit all over the walls? So what? You've done worse."

"Me! I! What have I ever done?"

"Well, I'm not writing on the walls."

"This is hopeless. There's no sense trying to have a frank talk with you. Nothing ever follows in logical order. There's never any sequence. It's just denial and accusation. I thought we were friends. I thought we loved each other." He says the last part bitterly and pushes his way out of bed.

"Calder?" Honey-Mae tugs at his sleeve as he sits at the edge of the bed fishing for his slippers. "Calder, I'm sorry. I'll try. I'm trying my best."

Honey-Mae hides her face in the pillow and begins to cry. Calder bends over her, smoothing her shoulders and back. He kisses the nape of her neck, slowly, lovingly. She turns and pulls him down on top of her.

And then he asks, "But what are you writing? Or what do you think you're writing?"

"I just do it," she says, her face turned away now.

"But why? Words have to mean something. Why?"

"Why can't you be with me?"

"But I am with you."

They are silent for a while: he staring at her profile, she with her face to the wall. Finally she speaks, her voice shattered.

"You understand nothing," she says. "Nothing."

THE SHRINK

Dr. Rampersad practices at the university medical health center but he takes some private patients too. The problems are always the same, variations on a theme.

"She writes on the walls?" he says, with only half a smile.

"The closet walls, only."

"Do you know why she does this?"

"No. That's the problem. That's why I'm here."

"And how do you feel about it?"

Calder gives a very long, very clear explanation of how he feels about Honey-Mae's writing on the walls and when he finishes, Dr. Rampersad is silent.

"The Goldberg Variations," Dr. Rampersad says finally.

"Pardon me?"

"Or *The Art of Fugue*."

"Bach?" Calder says.

"Tell me about you. Tell me what you want out of life."

SURPRISE

In class Calder lectures on the mythic elements common to Don Juan, Don Quixote, and Faust. He is happy. He forgets what awaits him at home. As he crosses the campus to his car, however, the tension begins and by the time he reaches home, he is covered in sweat. How can this be happening? Is he losing his mind? He pauses at the front door and pretends to examine the lawn. Everybody in this town is crazy on the subject of crabgrass, so nobody is going to care if he stands there for an hour staring at the ground. Finally, sick, he puts his key in the door and goes inside.

"Honey-Mae?" There is no answer. "Honey-Mae?" he calls again, a new sound in his voice.

Honey-Mae is working only half-time these days and if she does not answer, it means only one thing. Calder squares his shoulders and walks down the corridor into the sunlit bedroom. Honey-Mae is lying unconscious on the bed, but Calder only glances at her as he strides across the room. The closet door is open and the floor is heaped with clothes.

The walls are covered with writing.

THE MONTH

For one whole month everything has been perfect. Honey-Mae has painted the closet and she has not gone near a pen or a pencil. Calder brings her flowers every other day, they dine out on the weekends, they are friends.

"What do you suppose it was?" he asks her.

That look comes over Honey-Mae's face and, as it does, he feels something tighten in his chest.

"I mean, do you think it was tension, or overwork, or something? Maybe you were worried for me, that I wouldn't get tenure. I mean, it has to have some logical explanation."

"Why do you have to bring it up?" she says. "Do you like to humiliate me? Don't you think I'm disgraced enough?"

"You?" he says. "You! That makes me laugh. What about me? Do you have any idea what it's like to live with a crazy woman? Do you have any idea what it's like to be at school, talking about Don Juan and the perfection of unattainable ideals, and be thinking, Yes, by now she's finished one wall and is moving on to the next one? She wants to have the whole closet finished by the time I get home. For a surprise. For a treat. And meanwhile the kids are looking at one another, figuring I'm losing my mind. Christ, it's out of *Jane Eyre*, the loony in the attic. You make me sick. You disgust me. I wish to God I'd never laid eyes on you."

Later, much later, he wakes her up and says he is sorry.

"I've got a vicious streak in me, I guess."

"It's my fault."

"It's mine too."

"Will you hold me?" she says.

She is shivering and when he takes her in his arms, she clutches at him, pressing her body into his. "Make love to me, please. Please." And he does, frightened, because he is making love to a stranger.

THE HANDWRITING ON THE WALL

Honey-Mae is writing on the walls every day now and she makes no secret of it. She goes to the shop in the morning where she sees customers and puts in orders for fabric and furniture and accessories. She does her work well. By noon she is back at home and she writes without stopping until she collapses or until she hears Calder at the front door. He comes in and stares at the writing and stares at her. Sometimes he tells her he loathes her. Sometimes he tells her she needs help. But mostly he tells her that unless she stops, and stops now, he will leave her. She says nothing. She turns to the wall, covered with her tiny script, and she sleeps.

THE PROBLEM

Calder stops suddenly in the middle of his lecture comparing the poetic vision of Saint John of the Cross to the mystic vision of Cervantes. It has just struck him that he has no idea what he is talking about. After a minute he goes on anyway.

THE PROBLEM

Honey-Mae wakes him in the middle of the night and says, "I love you, Calder. You are the only one. I love you. I love you."

Calder lies there with his eyes closed, his hand dutifully caressing her back.

DATA

"I've had it. I'm done with her. I want out." Dr. Rampersad raises his eyebrows one-sixteenth of an inch.

"I know how that sounds, but I want out."

"Well, that's a choice you have to make."

"I don't want to leave her, but I've got to. I can't take any more. I'm not sleeping, my work is going to pot, I look like hell. She looks like hell too, for that matter. I've done everything I can think of. I've begged her to stop. I've pleaded. I've tried to be understanding. I've been a bastard, too, I can't help it. I've got this vicious streak and she brings it out in me. You should see the walls. It's unbelievable. It's a crazy house. The bedroom, the bathroom, the kitchen. She's even started now on the living room. She's left my study alone, that's the only place. I go in there and get drunk."

"She's left your study alone."

"Oh, she'd never write in there."

"Why is that?"

"She just wouldn't. It's where I, you know, do everything. My writing, my books. She wouldn't."

"And you get drunk there."

"Well, only sometimes."

"And why do you get drunk?"

"To escape. You know, just to get away from it."

"And do you?"

Calder looks at the shrink. Forty dollars an hour for this.

"I come back to the study," Dr. Rampersad says. "Why do you suppose she leaves that, of all the other rooms, untouched? What do you suppose it represents to her?"

"It's where I work. It's… oh God… it's…"

"It's where you go to escape, you said. It's where you do everything, you said. Your writing, your books."

"Yes?"

"That's what you said."

"Yes."

"Is she trying to tell you something? This Honey-Mae? Is she trying to make you notice her? And even while she's doing it, protecting your most secret place? What if she should invade that place? What would that mean to you?"

"She wouldn't."

"But if she did?" The shrink is wearing his little half smile.

"She wouldn't."

"She may." Pause. Tick, tick, tick. "She will."

"I love her. She's crazy, but I love her."

"You have to decide what you want," the shrink says.

"What I want."

"And then get it."

THE WOMAN HE LOVES

Honey-Mae has put on the weight she lost and she is back at work. She has painted the walls of every room except Calder's study. She never goes in there.

She does not write on the walls.

She is the perfect wife.

THE WOMAN HE HATES

Honey-Mae has done it again. But only a little bit. In the bedroom closet.

Calder flings his glass across the room, almost at her but not quite, and then he slams out of the house. In a minute he is back, with a purpose.

He goes to his study and comes back with a marking pen. In huge black script he writes "I hate you" across the bedroom wall. He writes it three more times and then he turns to face her. She is slumped against the door, her head bowed. Her small body shakes as she cries silently.

THE SHRINK

Honey-Mae has agreed to see Dr. Rampersad. Calder waits in the reception room until she comes out, pale, smiling faintly.

"What did he say?" Calder asks as soon as they are in the car.

"He says I am unhappy."

"But why do you write? Did he say? Does he know?"

"He said it sounds to him that I do it because I'm unhappy."

"Unhappy?"

"I'm sorry." She covers her face with her hands.

"What's the use," he says. "What's the use of anything."

RESOLUTIONS

Calder is in his office listening to a student talk about the subtle connection between Saint Teresa's *Interior Castle* and Franz Kafka's *The Castle* when Calder suddenly realizes something and blurts out, "She is unhappy."

"What?"

"Can we talk tomorrow?" Calder is all action now, gathering books, throwing papers into his satchel. "Let's talk tomorrow. I have to get home."

"Who's unhappy?" the student says.

"I have to go."

Calder tosses the satchel into a corner and makes a break for the door, leaving the student behind. "Unhappy," he says. He knows what he will find when he gets home, but it doesn't matter.

He runs a yellow light at Fifth and Bryant and another one at the corner of his own street, but he knows he won't get caught. Not now. Not today. "She is unhappy," he says aloud, to nobody. "Unhappy." His heart races because it may be too late. He bounds up the walk, into the house, straight to his study.

Honey-Mae is on her knees, so engrossed in her work that she does not even turn at the sound of his steps.

Beside her and behind her rise long shelves of books, some with torn jackets, some with notepaper sticking out of them. She has pushed aside the heavy desk, loaded with his papers, notes for lectures, outlines for articles he will write.

She kneels before the wall, which had been white this morning, and which now is covered with words. But not columns of words this time, not random scratchings. No, the words grow from the baseboard and rise up the long length of white wall into airy patterns of trees and flowers and animals. The words are all in different colors, written close together, so that you do not see *happy unhappy happy*, you see only the flowering tree the words have formed, and on the tip of the longest thinnest branch the delicate shining blossom that says *bliss*, over and over.

Honey-Mae kneels before her work, before this blessed jungle, creating words, oblivious.

"It's all right," he says.

At the sound of his voice she crouches and hides her face. He has never actually seen her writing before. He kneels beside her, carefully, and strokes her hair.

"It's all right," he says very softly. "I know. I know."

She lifts her face to him and he kisses her, first on the brow and then, almost formally, on the lips.

"I understand," he says. She turns to face him and he watches, astounded, as slowly, slowly, the madness drains from her eyes.

They sink to the floor and lie there in each other's arms, not making love, only looking. Above them are his books and his papers and the flowers and trees full of happiness, unhappiness, happiness they have finally made. It is bliss.

But he and she do not look at the wall; they lie next to it and stare into each other; looking, and looking.

BENJAMIN

A month after his father died, Julian began to feel constant pain beneath his left arm. He was short of breath, and often during the night he ran a fever. Heart trouble, the doctor said, and sent him to a specialist, who ran an impressive battery of tests, all of which proved negative. By this time Julian had begun having stomach pains and occasional nausea, so the heart specialist sent him to another specialist, this one in internal medicine. Again a battery of tests proved negative. Julian was a young man, a lawyer in his midtwenties, with no history of illness and no obvious psychological problems; the three doctors concluded he was suffering from nerves. They gave him tranquilizers and pronounced him well.

To Julian's surprise, the tranquilizers seemed to work; the pains subsided, and the nausea went away altogether. He was surprised because he suspected there was a great deal wrong with him other than nerves. His suspicion ripened into certainty until finally, without telling Anne, he went to a psychiatrist and told him what he had told none of the other doctors: that ever since his father's death, he had had a horror of making love.

The psychiatrist smiled and nodded his head.

Julian was unable to explain what he meant by *horror*. He wanted to make love, he said, but he was afraid. But *afraid* wasn't the right word either. He felt a terrific revulsion, he said, as if death were in the room, as if he were holding death in his arms. Immediately he began to protest that he loved his wife, that their sex life was very good, that he had begun to feel this way only recently. And even now he didn't feel this way all the time. When they made love during the day, it was fine. It was only at night that he had this horror, this... and he shook his head, unable to describe what he felt.

Julian saw the psychiatrist through June and July, tracing his family history and his own many times over. He related grim memories and happy ones in greater detail each time, but he came no closer to an understanding of what his horror of lovemaking really meant. He was thinking of giving up therapy altogether when August came and the psychiatrist went on vacation. Freed from chasing after his secret self, Julian felt expansive, and proposed to Anne that they go back to London to see Benjamin.

Two years earlier on their first trip to London, neither of them had liked cats and so, apart from feeding him a tin of Sainsbury's every day, they had paid no attention to Benjamin. They were on their honeymoon and noticed nothing except each other. Then one morning they woke and made love and Anne said that while he took his bath she would go downstairs and start breakfast. Benjamin was asleep outside the door and when she opened it, he stretched luxuriously, rolling over on his back, curling in a ball, and sitting up finally with one paw over an eye.

"Poor thing," Anne said, "with nobody to love you." She bent to pat his head and Benjamin arched his back, rubbing against her and purring. "Come on, I'll feed you," she said, and started down the stairs.

Julian heard her laughter and came out on the landing.

"Look at this," Anne said. "She thinks she's a dog."

"He."

"Look."

Benjamin stood on the carpeted stairs, his body across Anne's foot, and whenever Anne forced her way down to the next step, the cat turned on his back and slid head downward to the step below. And then he would stand, purring, and throw his body against her foot once more. When they reached the bottom, he streaked across the tile floor to the kitchen. It was the beginning of their love affair with Benjamin.

And now after two years of marriage they were going back to London to find once more in London a civilized way of life, and to get a rest, and to see Benjamin. Most of all to see Benjamin.

They opened the door, and there he was. Before Anne could get in the house, Benjamin was rubbing his head and back against her legs, flopping on his side and wriggling, purring all the while.

"Sweet kitty," she said, and stroked his back over and over. "She's been waiting at the door for two years now, haven't you, poor Benjy?"

"Hullo, catty," Julian said, becoming British. Benjamin allowed himself to be patted by Julian and then went back to rubbing against Anne.

"You're hungry, aren't you, Benj? Well, I'm going to give you some lovely food. Come on."

At the word *food*, Benjamin padded away to the kitchen and took up his station at the refrigerator. Anne was emptying the tin of cat food into the blue ceramic dish when she heard Julian calling from the bedroom above.

"The Hills left a note, hon. They say that he's to have only half a tin a day. He's on a desperate diet."

"I've already given her a whole one."

"Mrs. Hill says the vet says it's imperative. Imperative. She's got it underlined."

"Well..."

He couldn't hear the rest.

"What?"

"I said Benjy's on vacation too. He's celebrating our anniversary."

"Come on up here and we'll celebrate."

"Why don't you go to bed? You should go to bed, your famous nerves and all."

"Come up here."

She came into the hall from the kitchen and saw him standing naked on the lower landing.

"Julian, for God's sake, people can see you through that window."

"I can't keep this up forever."

"Pig. I married a pig," she said.

"It's your big chance. Ta-ra!"

"Honestly, why are you so perverse? You never want to have sex under the most normal conditions, but when we get off the plane and we're both dying of jet lag you decide it's the time to get cute." She had meant to joke, but the words came out serious.

"Nine, eight, seven..."

"Get away from that window," she said, and ran up the stairs.

After they had made love, they lay side by side looking at the ceiling. For a long time neither said anything.

"It's going to be a good trip, isn't it," she said.

"Yes, I'm really going to try."

"If you can just put your worries out of your mind, you know? It's because you're always thinking about them."

"What do you mean, worries?"

"Well, you know. Your pains in the chest and then the stomach trouble. The doctors said there's nothing wrong with you."

"Maybe it's up here," he said, tapping his forehead. He wanted to tell her about seeing the psychiatrist.

"No, it's just your nerves. What you need is some sleep instead of getting up and reading half the night."

"Maybe I should see a shrink."

"That's ridiculous. People like us don't go to shrinks. We see what has to be done and we do it. Period. Shrinks are for people who live miserable lives because they're afraid to hurt anybody."

"Where'd you get all that?"

"Partly I thought it and partly I got it from Bill."

Bill was Anne's brother, a priest.

"Yeah, well, Bill needs one."

"He goes to one."

"He should."

"He does. But you're not like him. Neither am I. As soon as you decide to stop worrying that you're dying, the pains will go away. You're probably identifying with your father."

"Bullshit."

They rolled over and lay back to back.

"I'm sorry I mentioned your father. I apologize."

"It doesn't matter."

"Are you mad?"

"Well, what the hell do you know about my feelings for my father? He had good points and bad points, and he's dead. And I am not identifying with him."

"I know it. That was stupid of me."

"Let's not fight. We're just beginning a vacation."

They rolled over and lay face to face.

"I love you," she said, nuzzling him.

She was just beginning to fall asleep when Julian said, "I'm going down to sit in the sunroom and read for a while. Okay?"

She would have said no, but jet lag had set in for real and at the moment she felt she was on the defensive.

"I'll get up too."

"No," he said, bending over to kiss her. "You sleep."

"Do you mind?" Her eyes were closed, her lips barely moved.

"Sleep."

At the door he turned and looked at her. He thought of waking her, of making love again right away, or in the sunroom maybe, on the floor. But no, she needed sleep after the flight.

We see what has to be done and we do it, he said to himself as he went down the stairs.

He sat in the wicker basket chair staring out into the garden. It was a beautiful garden, typically English. A square of thick green grass was bordered by sweet peas and geraniums. Some purple flowers with long thick petals tangled with the roses and hollyhocks that clung against the walls enclosing the garden. A huge tree stood to the right, its branches weighted with hundreds of hard green pears. Small birds rustled in the bushes and the sun poured into the garden and into the little room where he sat.

Next door a gang of boys were playing some kind of noisy game that involved throwing or kicking a soccer ball against one of the garden walls. He could hear their shouts, could tell they were very young.

He felt cozy. He felt at home.

This was his favorite room in the house, though certainly it was the strangest, with modern glass doors that ran from floor to ceiling. The other rooms were crammed with antiques, Victorian stuff mostly, chairs of fruitwood and prickly mohair, small round tables and heavy ornamented cabinets, tiny paintings, massive frames. But the sunroom was from another age entirely. The walls were stark white, and cold. A small piano stood in one corner, a stack of sheet music piled on the floor next to it. A packing crate held some tattered paperback books and a clay cat one of the children had made. Toys were everywhere. They had thought at first it was a playroom until they realized that the large pine table flanked on either side by long benches was the only dining table in the house. There was no other furniture in the room, except the basket chair, wicker, with no cushion. The room was at once modern and barbaric.

He began to feel drowsy in the warm sun. He shifted lower in the chair, propping his head against the hard wooden frame. Benjamin appeared outside the glass doors, curled up on the step, changed his mind, and moved to the stone slab that served as a potting bench. Despite his diet, the cat was still very fat. Watching him, Julian said aloud, "Oh blessed Benjamin, no tranquilizers for you." He continued to gaze out at the garden. If it weren't for the intermittent shouts of the boys next door, he might fall asleep himself, he thought. He was still thinking this an hour later when he woke.

He was chilly. The long shadow of the pear tree had fallen across the glass doors, and he shivered in the cool room. He rubbed his neck and then the sore spot at the back of his skull where it had rested on the hard wood. He leaned forward, about to stand up, when suddenly something large and gray fell into the center of the green lawn. It was a pigeon, so large that Julian laughed aloud when he realized what it was. Another pigeon joined the first. They seemed to drop from the sky, plummeting into the garden as if their weight were too much for wings to sustain.

Julian was watching the pigeons attack the fallen pears, plunging their beaks deep into the rotting fruit and tearing, when suddenly he saw Benjamin slink from the stone slab to the step and across the grass in one swift, fluid motion. He would not have thought Benjamin could move like that. He laughed again; the picture was preposterous. The pigeons were as big as the cat, could perhaps topple him with one bat of their wings, and there was Benjy sneaking up on them, the jungle hunter ready to do battle for his dinner. Julian was enjoying the scene, wishing Anne were with him to enjoy it too, when suddenly he heard a loud, "Scat! Get away then." A small fat boy stood on top of the stone wall, stamping his foot loudly and shouting at the cat. The pigeons flew off, beating their heavy wings, and Benjamin came out of his hunting pose and darted into the rosebushes.

Julian studied the boy. His face was completely round and pasty white, and his head sprouted thick tufts of fiery hair. He had on short pants that were green and a strange kind of white shirt with little puffs at the shoulders. He looked like a troll in rolling breeches. Quickly he let himself down from the wall onto a compost pile and from there down into the garden. He moved around, kicking at the flowers, and then scooped up a large white soccer ball. Julian smiled at the thought of such a fat little thing playing soccer. With the ball under his arm, the boy began to call, "Here, kitty, kitty. Come on, cat." He crouched, waiting. He was very patient.

Benjamin moved from the cover of the rosebushes and settled among the sweet peas at the edge of the grass. "Here, kitty, kitty," the boy called again and again, but the cat was having none of it. Slowly the boy moved across the lawn, talking softly to the cat, nice kitty, pretty cat, until he was no more than a few feet away. Benjamin poked his nose out from among the flowers, and then his whole head. One foot was just beginning to emerge when suddenly the boy raised the soccer ball high in the air and with both hands brought it down hard on the cat. The ball struck him at the base of the skull and for a moment he sprawled, both front legs flattened out on either side of his head. And then with a terrified scream he dashed from among the flowers, tore across the lawn, and disappeared into the roses on the other side of the garden.

Julian leaped to his feet and shook the glass doors, trying to get them open. They were locked, and though he twisted the key furiously back and forth, he could not open them. He ran into the kitchen and out the back door, his face burning. He wanted to get his hands on that damned little troll, he wanted to take him by the neck and thrash the life out of him.

But the garden was empty. There was no sign of the boy or the ball or the cat.

Julian went inside and poured himself a large drink. He concentrated on being calm. It's silly, he told himself, to fly into a rage over some perverse little kid. But then the picture came back to him, the boy with his hands above his head bringing the ball down on Benjy's head, the cat sprawled and terrified, and himself unable to open the glass doors to the garden. Julian began to get furious all over again. He sipped the drink slowly, forcing himself to think of the warm track it made through his chest into his stomach.

Later he told Anne what had happened, and she said she understood. But she did not understand. Why should a grown man, a lawyer furthermore, come apart because a kid was mean to a cat? It made no sense. It was precisely to escape that sort of insanity that they had come to London in the first place. Well, they were off to a great start. Later still, when they were in bed and she put her hand on his chest and he moved away from her, Anne said once again that she understood. And, rejected, she promised herself that if they ever made love again it would not be until Julian had become his old self once more and was desperate for it.

By the beginning of the second week things were no better. Everything had gone wrong from the start. There was the kid with the soccer ball. And then food poisoning in an Indian restaurant in Soho.

Julian with a fever, Anne vomiting. Anne with a fever, Julian vomiting. Things couldn't be worse, Anne said. And then Walpurgisnacht.

They were getting dressed to go out for dinner when the doorbell rang. Julian answered it, still buttoning his shirt.

"Excuse me, sir. Might we fetch our ball from your garden?"

There were three of them, about ten years old, and with that ruddy complexion and open stare that Julian liked to think typical of English children. One was considerably taller than the other two and acted as their spokesman. Julian liked the looks of them.

"Just don't pester the cat," he said, and held the door for them to come through.

"Over the wall is easiest, sir," the leader said. "That is, if you don't mind."

"Sure," Julian said. "Sure." He was charmed. They had called him sir.

He watched from the kitchen window while the boy got the ball and climbed back over the wall. He poured himself a Coke, thinking how nice English kids were, thinking he'd like to raise his own children in England.

The ball came flying over the wall. In a moment the tall boy came over after it and stood examining the windows of the house. When finally he saw Julian in the kitchen, he pointed at a pear, questioning. Julian nodded. The boy picked a pear and put it in his pocket, picked two more, and then disappeared over the wall. Almost immediately the ball was thrown into the center of the garden. Oh no, Julian said to himself. At once the three boys were in the garden. Then five of them. Julian went upstairs where Anne was just finishing her makeup.

"Oh my God," he said, "I don't know what I've done."

She closed her eyes in exasperation. Again, she thought.

"What do you mean?" she said.

"Look!"

There were seven or eight of them now going wild in the garden. One had a stick and was beating pears off the branches. They were shrieking and throwing the pears into the tree and over the garden walls.

"They're just going a little berserk. That's how kids are," she said, smiling. She taught fifth grade and knew. "They'll stop in a minute." She went back to the mirror.

"But, my God, they're really doing damage to that tree. Look, there are broken branches all over the lawn."

"They'll stop," she said. "Why don't you stop looking, for heaven's sake. You seem to want to make yourself frantic. Make us a drink, why don't you, before we go out."

He followed her down the stairs.

"There's nothing worse than a grown man trying to control a crowd of kids," he said. "But what'll we tell the Hills if they wreck the garden?"

"They won't," she said. "You worry too much."

He looked out the kitchen window, though he had promised himself he would not. The garden was littered with pears and broken branches, but the boys had stopped their screaming and were gathered in one corner of the lawn. One of them held a dead tree branch over his shoulder, and at the same moment that Julian realized he was the red-haired troll, the boys all shouted, "There he is, get him!" and the boy with the branch brought it down like a club on something in the flowers. Benjamin sprang from among the hollyhocks and streaked toward the back door.

Julian ran outside. "Are you crazy?" he shouted at them. "You might have killed that cat. Now get the hell out of here and stay out."

"He's a killer, that cat is. He kills," the red-haired boy said.

"I told you to get out of here. Now get."

The gang of boys moved to the wall and slowly climbed over it, looking behind them all the while, whispering to one another.

Anne was waiting for her drink.

Julian, still trembling with rage, was taking ice from the tray when the first pear hit the house. He thought perhaps it fell from the tree. But then there was a volley of pears. One splattered against the glass doors of the sunroom where Anne was sitting. The doors rattled but did not break.

"Julian, you'd better do something," Anne said softly.

He dashed through the back door and was immediately hit by a pear. "Hey," he shouted, "hey, you kids, cut it out!" Sticks began coming over the wall, followed by rocks and empty tin cans. And then there was the shattering of glass as a stone went through the upstairs bedroom window, and a tinkling sound as fragments of the windowpane fell to the stone steps outside the sunroom.

Julian rushed through the house, out the front door, and around to the other side of the garden wall, where he caught the boys still laughing and screaming and throwing things.

"All right, you little bastards. What the hell do you think you're doing?"

"We're only playing," one said.

"Took a pear or two."

"Didn't do nothing, actually."

"You. What's your name?" Julian grabbed the shoulder of the tall boy who had so charmed him a short while earlier.

"David."

"David what?"

"I didn't do nothing. It was Hughey tried to get the cat." He pointed to Hughey, the fat boy with red hair.

"Answer me. I said David what?"

"Agnatelli."

"All right, David Agnatelli, you take me straight to your father."

The boys fell silent at this and Julian moved in for the kill.

"Do you know what I am?" he said, addressing the court. "I'm a lawyer. What you call a barrister. Do you know what that means?"

They knew it meant trouble.

"Now you take me straight to your father."

"He's not in. He won't be in for another hour."

Oh God, Julian thought, now what do I do?

"I'll see him in an hour. I have your name." And then inspiration struck him. "Meanwhile, you've got a cleanup job to do. You, you, and you. Climb over that wall and pick up every last scrap of rubbish you threw there."

"But we didn't do nothing," Hughey said.

"Not you. I don't want you in that garden at all. Understand? But you, you, and you. Now!"

He watched with relief as they obediently climbed the wall.

"I'll take care of you later," he said to Hughey and walked away, trying to look dignified.

Anne met him at the front door:

"They're cleaning the place up," she said. "I can't believe it."

"They'd better," he said, striding straight through the house to the garden.

"I'm really surprised at you," he said to David. "I thought you were much nicer boys than that," and he went on and on about what he had expected of them and how there was never an excuse for deliberate cruelty and about the damage they had done to someone else's property. By the time they had finished cleaning up, Julian had thoroughly intimidated them, and he came into the house feeling a little proud of himself and a little foolish for feeling proud.

"My brave man," Anne said, and the words hung between them like an accusation. "Well, I had to," he said after a moment, feeling only foolish now. "For the cat."

"I know you did," she said. "I know."

Late that night as they lay in bed, Julian nuzzled her cheek and shoulder and finally whispered, half confession, half apology, "I felt like such a fool trying to bully a bunch of kids as if I were the warden of a reform school."

"I know," she said, "but you had to. It was out of control. They might have killed poor Benjy." Automatically, despite her resolution, she put her hand on his stomach and moved it tentatively to his hip. She could feel the resistance and withdrew her hand.

"I'm going to read for a while," he said, and got out of bed.

"Whatever you want," she said.

She pretended to be asleep when he came to bed an hour later.

It was a beautiful morning, still cool but with a strong sun that promised perfect walking weather. He put a pot of coffee on the stove and stood looking at it. He stretched, bent over to touch his toes. He did a push-up and decided that was enough exercise for now. He was barefoot, but he opened the back door and stepped outside onto the wet grass.

"Hey, cat!" he called, but Benjamin at the end of the garden paid no attention. He crouched, head pulled in, one paw slightly raised. "Benjy!" Julian called again. The cat continued to crouch, patient, motionless. And then, so swiftly that Julian wasn't sure he had seen it, Benjamin sprang at something, flailing with his paw, and then leaped back as if he were afraid. Julian frowned and started to cross the garden to see what Benjamin was hunting, but the grass was long and slimy and his feet began to feel cold. "To hell with it," he said and turned back. He was pouring coffee when Benjamin came through the cat port and took up his stance at the refrigerator.

"Well, how's the old hunter?" Julian said, kneeling to pet the cat. He knew Benjamin endured the petting for the sake of the food, and he took advantage of the cat's hunger to get in several more strokes. "Nice old Benjy. Catch a pigeon, Benj? Hmm? Hmm?"

Benjamin meowed and rubbed his head against Julian's ankle.

"Bought love is better than none, Benj."

Julian spooned a quarter tin of Sainsbury's onto the blue plate; Anne could give him the rest later. He was beginning to feel good. He cut two slices of bread, threw the stale one in the garbage, and spread butter thickly on the other. He hummed as he moved around the kitchen. "I'm going to invest in life," he said to the cat. "I'm going to bask in the sun with English bread and butter. That's what I have to do, and I'm going to do it. What do you think of that, fat Benjamin?"

The cat meowed for more food.

"Not on your life."

Benjamin waited until Julian went into the sunroom, and then he gave up and went back to the garden to hunt.

Julian was sitting in the wicker chair with his second cup of coffee when he spotted the toad under the bench. Good God, he thought, if I'd sat on the bench I'd have stepped on that thing barefoot. He got up and looked at it. Why on earth would anybody buy kids a rubber toad, he wondered. It was a perfect replica, actually. Too perfect to be real. Perhaps one of the kids bought it himself, to scare somebody. The thought crossed his mind that he was afraid to touch it, but that was silly.

He made breakfast for Anne and went upstairs to wake her. He kissed her, and then they wrestled in the bed. He thought of making love and to hell with breakfast. He would let her decide.

"I made your breakfast. It's all ready. What do you say?" And Anne, recalling his rejecting her only hours before, said, "Yummy, yummy," and slipped out of bed.

They were carrying plates of eggs and bacon into the sunroom when Julian said, "Oh, don't be scared of the rubber toad underneath your bench. The cat must have been playing with it."

Anne looked at it for a moment. "It looks real," she said, stooping to pick it up. "Yuck, it is real," and she pulled her hand away.

"It can't be real. It's too perfect. Look at the way the legs go out."

"Legs or no legs, that damned thing is real," Anne said. "The cat must have brought it in."

Julian was on his knees examining the toad. Sweat broke out on his forehead, and he could feel the pulse in his throat accelerate. His whole body went clammy.

"I'd better throw it out," he said, standing.

Anne turned to look at him, surprised by the new tone in his voice.

"I'll throw it out, if you want."

"No. No, I'll do it."

Julian looked around for something he could use to pick up the toad. He found a pirate mask, and next to it a green plastic dagger. He flipped the dried-out body of the toad onto a piece of cardboard. His hands shook so badly that the toad fell off, and he had to scoop it up once more. He threw it into the bushes outside the sunroom.

"God, I hate dead things," he said. "Look, I've got goose bumps all over my arm."

"Don't think about it," Anne said. "You should just do what you have to and don't think about it." She reached for his hand and shook it back and forth. "Eat your breakfast, silly."

But Julian had lost his appetite. All that day he was quiet and moody. When he spoke, it was to ask Anne how she thought the cat had brought the toad inside, or why, or why not until now. That evening they went to *The School for Scandal*, an awful production, Julian said, in which Lady Sneerwell was made up to look exactly like a frog. He sat up late drinking and slept only fitfully.

At sunrise he was wide awake again, his pulse racing, his legs straining to kick or run. He got up and went slowly downstairs to the kitchen. He looked around, prepared to find another dead toad, but there was nothing. He glanced into the sunroom and that too looked safe. In the garden Benjamin was curled up on the potting bench taking the sun. Julian sighed heavily and then smiled to himself. No toads. He felt as if a heavy rock had just been lifted from his chest. He went about making coffee.

"I'm on the brink, Benjy," he said, spooning out the cat food. "My celebrated mind is hanging by a thread. It's full of snakes and hoppytoads and death, death, death." He stroked the cat, who only continued to eat, and then he took his coffee into the sunroom and sat on a bench facing the glass doors. Immediately he saw the toad next to the wicker chair.

"Oh God, Benjy, not another one."

Benjamin came from the kitchen and went straight to the toad. He crouched, crept up, and then nudged it tentatively with one paw.

"Get away, Benj." Julian pulled the cat away, but Benjamin returned immediately, sniffing at the toad. Julian could see blood on the carpet, and there was blood on the toad too. "Come on, Benjamin, get away!" and he struck the cat lightly on the nose. He began to feel sick to his stomach. Saliva was running in his mouth. He wanted to spit. He got the plastic dagger and prodded the toad onto a magazine; as he did so the toad kicked out one leg in a kind of dying reflex, and a large, glassy eye moved in its head. Julian dropped the dagger and the magazine and ran to the kitchen, where he threw up in the sink. He let the water run while he stood leaning against the counter, staring out the window. After a while he washed out his mouth and, resolute, went back to the sunroom where quickly, almost cruelly, he pushed the toad onto the magazine and threw it into the bushes behind the potting bench. He was covered with sweat when he finished. It was hideous, this half death. He saw again the eye move in the head, the leg kick out.

He sat at the table with a fresh cup of coffee. He had to get hold of himself. This was ridiculous. He wasn't afraid of toads. It was just that he had had no sleep in too long a time. It was just that he wanted to make love to Anne and, somehow, couldn't. It was just that... Benjamin appeared outside the doors, crouched on the potting bench, then sprang into the bushes, cried, thrashed about, and in a moment reappeared with a toad dangling from his mouth. Julian began to feel nauseous again. Slowly he twisted the key to open the glass doors and clapped his hands at the cat, who turned and looked at him and then turned away. "Drop that, Benjamin! Drop it." He picked up a newspaper and slapped it against his thigh. Benjamin got a firmer grip on the toad and disappeared into the bushes. Julian closed the doors and leaned against them. "I'll kill that damned cat," he said.

He wandered from the sunroom to the living room and then out to the entrance hall, where there were some paperback books on a little table. He took one, Sitwell's *English Eccentrics*, and went into the kitchen and then into the sunroom, completing the circle. But from the sunroom he could see the garden, and suddenly he could not endure the sight of it. He took his book to the living room and sat on one of the Victorian nursing chairs that were so uncomfortable. He sat staring at the book, not reading it. Finally he heard Anne coming down the stairs, and as he looked up from the book, he looked straight at another toad. This one was much lighter in color, much larger in size, and it lay right at the foot of the stairs.

Anne put her arms around him from behind. "My poor husband never sleeps," she said, kissing his neck. "He's going to turn into a little raccoon." She traced the dark circles beneath his eyes.

"Look," he said, pointing.

"Not another toad. Where on earth are they coming from?"

"That damned cat is where. He's out there now, in the garden, with another one hanging from his jaws. I saw him with it."

"Oh, Julian." Her voice was halfway between sympathy and exasperation.

"Well, I'd better get on with it," he said.

She went to prepare breakfast while Julian once again got the plastic dagger and a magazine to scoop up a dead toad. But the toad was very much alive, and as Julian prodded and pushed, it suddenly leaped high in the air, thudding against the wall and then leaping off toward the center of the floor.

Anne rushed to the room when she heard Julian shout. He was standing with his back to the wall, his eyes horribly dilated, his face bloodless.

"I can't stand it," he said. "I've got to get out of here. I've got to get out of this house. The place is alive with frogs. I can feel them all over me and that cat, that vicious cat, keeps bringing them in. More of them."

She looked at him, a complete stranger to her. "Get out," she said. "Go into the kitchen. Julian, do you hear me? Go into the kitchen and close both doors. I'll get rid of it."

"I've got to," he said. "I've got to do it. I'm the man."

"Do what I say."

Trembling, white, Julian went into the kitchen. He looked out the back door and, as he expected, there was a dead toad on the step. Outside the sunroom he could see Benjamin hunting among the hollyhocks. There was another dead toad on the potting bench.

He sat at the table and covered his face with his hands.

Afterward Anne convinced him they could not move to a hotel since the Hills would not be returning for another two days. She insisted she could manage the cat. She would block off the cat port, keeping Benjamin outside the house during the day and inside at night. That way there would never be a time when he came in unobserved. Nearly desperate, Julian agreed to this.

That night, near midnight, they were lying in bed reading when they heard a racket downstairs in the kitchen.

"Somebody at the door," Anne said.

"No. It's that damned cat trying to get out." Anne had propped a carving board against the cat port but Julian, not taking any chances, had further fortified the board by placing a heavy chair against it.

In a few minutes they heard Benjamin scrambling up the stairs. He stood outside their open door and meowed. It was not the sound he made for food or for attention; it was a different sound altogether.

"Poor cat. She's lonely," Anne said.

"Poor cat, my ass. That damned thing is evil."

Benjamin moved across the carpet and then bounded onto the foot of the huge bed.

"Look. He's coming to get you."

"Poor sweet Benjy," Anne said.

Benjamin made no move to curl up. Instead, slinking, he moved slowly toward the head of the bed, his claws kneading the woolen blanket in what looked like rough play. He crouched for a moment and then moved up to her breast.

"See," Julian said, "he is after you," and as he said it, half-serious, the cat suddenly ducked its head and hissed, long and loud. With one swift movement Julian got his hands under the cat's front feet and lifted him high above the bed and then onto the floor. Benjamin sprang for the door and hid somewhere on the darkened stairs.

"My God, did you know he was going to attack?" Anne said.

"No, I was fooling. What do you make of that?"

"Maybe she was playing. It didn't look like playing."

"I think she's crazy. He's crazy. I think he turns into a predator at night."

"No. Not really."

"No wonder they associate cats with witches. With the devil."

"Poor Benj. You know, she scared me half to death? Could I have a drink, Ju? I mean, would you mind going down and getting it?"

"Sure. Man versus cat. Man versus forces of evil. Have no fear, m'dear, Julian is here." He laughed, trembling.

He threw on the lights for the stairs and started down. Benjamin appeared from behind him and raced ahead into the kitchen, where he began clawing at the chair blocking the cat port. Julian went to the refrigerator, but for once the cat didn't want food. He wanted only to get out. Julian made the drinks, glancing now and then at the cat. Benjamin was different, no doubt. He was possessed. For a long minute Julian stared at him and the cat stared back. It was as if they both knew something and neither dared admit it.

"Okay, cat, time's up," he said, and lifted him out of the kitchen into the hall. At once the cat wriggled free and returned to scratching at the chair that blocked the door. Frightened, furious, Julian pounced on him. "I said no." Holding the cat in his outstretched hands, he walked down the hall and threw him, with more force than he had intended, into the living room. The cat set up a furious screeching and began to tear at the carpet. Julian closed the kitchen doors both to the sunroom and to the hall and took the drinks and went upstairs. On the upper landing he turned and looked down at a sharp angle into the living room. He could see two gray eyes burning in the darkness. He shivered, knowing what he had to do.

The next night before bed, Anne packed their bags and tidied the house. She wanted things to look neat for the cleaning woman.

"It's been a strange vacation, hasn't it," she said. "First the sickness, then the Walpurgisnacht kids, and then the cat with all those frogs."

"I hate that cat."

"Poor Benjy. You know, I wonder if we'll ever come back here again."

"I have no desire to. You?"

"Not really. Something's different now. Spoiled." She was tucking makeup things into a silk traveling purse. "Julian? Can we, you know, make love? Soon? When we get home?"

"Maybe before we get home." .

"Well, no. Home is all right. But we need it, both of us."

"I know."

When it was time for bed, he said to her, "You sleep. I'm going to read downstairs for a while. In fact, I'll let the cat out and block the door."

"Will she be all right outside? What if it rains?"

"It's not going to rain. And then we won't have to worry about him going crazy in the house again."

"Okay." He kissed her. "And then maybe in the morning we'll get them old colored lights going. A little farewell gesture to Merrie England."

"I just want you your old self."

"I am, nearly. I've decided I'm going to invest in life. I'm going to join the human race."

Downstairs he poured himself a drink and waited. Benjamin ignored him at first, stalking from room to room, his head stretched forward, his tail erect and swaying. And then after a while he began to claw at the door. Julian thrust him roughly aside and the cat hissed. Deliberately taking his time, he poured himself another drink, sipped it, and only then moved the chair and the carving board away from the door. At once the cat sprang through the little opening. Julian opened the door wide and stepped outside. There was a quarter moon and clouds drifting across it. He inhaled deeply; a beautiful night; a perfect night. He heard the cat hunting in the bushes.

He found the red clay flowerpot he was looking for and brought it into the house. It was so heavy he had trouble carrying it; the earth inside had hardened almost to cement. He set it down in the sunroom next to the glass doors. He unlocked the doors and stood looking into the garden for several minutes.

Julian was sitting at the table composing a long note to the Hills when he looked up and saw Benjamin slink from the steps to the stone slab that served as a potting bench. He put down the pen.

He had just explained to the Hills that there had been trouble with the gang of boys next door, that they had stolen pears and broken branches and trampled flowers. He explained how they had repeatedly tormented the cat, how they had tried to beat him with sticks and pelt him with stones. He hoped the Hills would do something to ensure poor Benjamin's safety.

It was then that he put down his pen, seeing Benjamin outside the doors. He waited for a moment and, as he expected, Benjamin disappeared into the bushes and reappeared after a while, a toad hanging from his mouth, kicking but firmly hooked in those thin, pointed fangs. Julian moved to the doors, opened them, and stood watching Benjamin release the toad, poke it until it tried to hop away, and then swipe it with a swift paw, sinking his fangs into it once more. Julian watched this until at last the toad could make no more movements at all. Benjamin gave it a few more pokes, but when the toad failed to respond, he turned from it and assumed a totally different posture. His body seemed to inflate, and he arched his back while his fur stood stiff from his neck to his tail. And then he crouched, his belly flattened against the stone slab, his whole attention directed to something moving in the bushes. He inched forward, his claws still tucked in but his head already arched in its hunting position, his fangs bared.

Julian lifted the heavy flowerpot high in the air and brought it heavily, with both hands, down on the cat's head. The body convulsed and lay still. There was no sound. When he tipped the pot away with his foot, Julian discovered the head mashed flat. He stared at the bloody pulp and was relieved to feel nothing. Calmly, methodically, he picked up the cat by a hind foot and carried it across the garden to the compost heap. He kicked a small pile of weeds over the body. He returned to the potting bench, where he picked the dead frog up in his hand and threw it into the bushes. Then he tipped the hardened earth out of the pot onto the bloodied places where bits of the cat's fur still clung. He left the empty clay pot next to the potting bench.

Inside, he washed his hands and poured himself another drink.

He was perfectly calm, perfectly in control. He sat down and finished the note to the Hills, hoping they had had a pleasant holiday and promising to return next year with Anne so that they might again enjoy the delights of London, but especially so they might visit the beloved Benjamin.

Julian signed the note, placed the carving board and the chair against the cat port, and then went slowly, happily up the stairs. In the bedroom he would wake Anne. It had been a long night, a long vacation, and he was ready now, eager for mad, desperate love.

A FAMILY AFFAIR

1. In that country there was never a wind. Sun beat down from April to October, and the fields that surrounded the town grew pale yellow and then dark yellow and then brown. There was no green anywhere.

Dust hung in the air, flung by the wheels of jeeps as the soldiers tore down Finial Street to the Blue Spider Café. Cozy Oaks was also located on Finial Street; in fact, it was separated from the Blue Spider only by Adam's Bakery and Johnson's Wood and Hardware, but the soldiers never went to Cozy Oaks. The men from the farms went there, and the men from the foundry, but the soldiers went to the Blue Spider.

All during February and March they sang around the jukebox, and the sound drifted slowly past Adam's and Johnson's until the regulars at Cozy Oaks would shake their heads and shrug their shoulders, but nobody ever complained because, one way or another, everyone was a little better off since the soldiers had come. In April, with all the windows open, the singing and the short high whoops that meant they were having a good time could be heard far out in the fields and sometimes even beyond that, in the pocked desert where the base was located and where the lucky soldiers with cars brought the girls from the Spider who would go all the way.

It had been like this every spring of the past four years, even when the base was new and nobody had yet sorted out how they really felt about the soldiers. Beryl Gerriter gave birth that first spring to her son, Jason, her deep moans and howls punctuated with the drunken singing from the Blue Spider. Luke Gerriter had waited in the living room with his daughter, Elissa. They said nothing, though from time to time he would send her to the kitchen to get him another beer.

"Why can't I go in?" she asked him.

"Shut your mouth. You're not old enough."

"Twelve is old enough."

He held his beer can to his mouth for a long slug and then he looked at her. Nothing. A face like an ax, everything pulled out to a point, with her mouth pinched already like Beryl's, a worried face. And skinny. How in hell would he ever marry her off?

"Twelve isn't old enough for much," he said.

She knew his voice when he spoke like that, she was afraid of it, she didn't know why. She leaned over Pal and hugged him, rubbing the fur along his back.

"We should get rid of that mutt. It stinks. That's what the hell's the matter around here. That mutt. One of these days I'm going to take him out and shoot him."

She said nothing. He was just drinking; his threats didn't mean anything.

Voices drifted in from the Blue Spider. They were singing "Poor Lil." In the other room Beryl smiled sourly at the idea of poor Lil. Poor Berla, she thought, and she pushed again. By Christ, she'd never have another baby. She could feel her skin tear, she was being ripped apart. Someone mopped her forehead, someone pressed at her thighs. And that bastard in the other room, getting drunk, it was his fault. Oh God! She pushed again. There was a huge surge between her legs, and for a moment she went unconscious. She woke screaming.

Outside the room Luke waited out the scream and then slammed his beer can to the floor in fury. "If she don't hurry up in there! Hurry up, you!" he shouted at the bedroom door. "I said, hurry up!"

The bedroom door opened and Dr. Pharon stuck his head out. "We've got problems," he said, "serious ones. It's gonna be a while, and I can't promise anything. But I suggest, if you got a brain left in that addled head of yours, that you stop drinking and start praying and, whatever else you do, you shut up." He closed the door.

"I'll be at the Oaks," Luke said to his daughter. "You can come and get me when the mule is born."

Elissa nodded, her eyes glazed with fear, and she hugged Pal again. "It's going to be all right, Pal," she said, rocking back and forth, the dog's muzzle in her lap. "Everything's going to be all right. Everything."

She was awakened later by Dr. Pharon, who told her to go find her father; he had something important to tell him.

Outside she paused for a minute to think what she was doing. She did so many things automatically that sometimes she had to stop and tell herself what came next. She had trouble catching her breath; the sun had gone down, but there was no breeze. In the distance she could hear loud shouts and singing. She tried again to catch her breath, and in the still air she could taste the dust. She crossed the lawn to the evergreen tree and held a spiky branch to her face, breathing its sharp smell of oil and gum, a bitter smell, but special to her. The tree was yellow, almost green, and with her face buried in its branches she could forget the damp heat and the taste of dust.

Pal whimpered at her feet.

"It's all right," she said, and ran down the dirt road to where it met Finial Street. A small stone caught in the sole of her sneaker, and she stooped under the streetlight to poke it out. It had wedged between the rubber sole and the canvas lining, and the more she pried at the hole the deeper she pushed the stone.

A jeep roared by, throwing dust in her eyes and hair.

"Damn," she said, "damn it."

And then the jeep screeched to a halt and backed up, crookedly, weaving from side to side.

"Hi there, sweetheart."

"She's too young, Ron."

"They're never too young."

Elissa stared at them, not frightened. They were soldiers from the base. Nobody minded the soldiers. The men had jobs now that the soldiers had come. Even her father had a job.

"What do you say, sweetheart? You want a ride?"

He was blond, with a wide funny smile. He was the most beautiful man she had ever seen.

"I've got to go to the Oaks to get my father."

"Well, you jump right in here between me and my friend and we'll take you straight to the Oaks." He leaped out and held the low door open. She hesitated.

"Come on. You'll be all right."

"For Chrissake, Ron," the driver said.

"What about my dog?"

"Bring your dog too. Come on."

She climbed into the jeep and held out her arms for Pal, who wriggled from the soldier's hands into her lap. Ron climbed in beside her, slamming the small door. "And away we go!" he shouted as the jeep took off. His arm, thrown over the seat at her back, drifted gradually to her shoulder. She could feel his hand lightly touching her bare arm.

"What's your name, sweetheart?"

"Elissa," she said, throwing her head back to feel the air blowing in her face.

"Elissa. Well, that's some name. I never heard of a name like Elissa. I think I'd call you Cookie, 'cause you're so sweet." He put his hand on her knee and ran it slowly up her thigh.

"Ron, if you want to get your ass in jail, you're going in just the right direction," the driver said.

"What's the matter, for Chrissake? I'm only petting the dog." The two men in back laughed. Ron rubbed Pal's ears and his back. "Isn't that right, Cookie? No harm in petting the nice little doggy."

Elissa thought she had never been so happy. "My mother just had a baby," she said. "I've got to tell my father."

"That right?" Ron said, his hand going back to her thigh. "You gonna have a baby? Hmm? Would you like a baby?"

His hand was hot on her thin dress and she could feel sweat break out on her thigh and up higher. She wished he would move his hand there. She wanted him to touch her all over. But most of all she wanted to put her two arms around his neck and lay her head on his chest and just stay like that for a long, long time.

"Cozy Oaks," the driver said, slamming on the brakes.

And then she was out of the jeep and it was roaring off, the men in back laughing and Ron shouting, "See you around, Cookie!" She stood for a long while watching the trail of dust the jeep had left behind. She could still feel each of his fingers on her thigh and his thumb moving back and forth.

All the way home she repeated their conversation in her mind. I think I'd call you Cookie, 'cause you're so sweet, he had said. And he had asked if she would like a baby. She put her hand on her thigh where he had put his. For once she did not care that her father was stumbling along in the dark, cursing every goddamn stone in his path, the goddamn wife who called him away from his buddies, the goddamn baby that would put them all in the poorhouse. She had not even minded going into Cozy Oaks to get him. She had only half-heard the sarcastic comments of the men at the bar, the double-meaning jokes, the laughter. While he bought a round of beer for everyone, she had stood at the screen door looking down toward the Blue Spider, where Ron was probably dancing or drinking with some pretty girl he was calling Cookie because she was so sweet, but it didn't matter. He had been nice, and whether he meant it or not, he had said it.

"You said it's a boy."

"What?" She stopped and tried to wiggle the stone into another part of her shoe.

"The baby. You said it's a boy."

"Yes."

"Did you see it?"

"No. Dr. Pharon said to go right away."

"Then how do you know it's a boy?" His voice was angry.

"I don't know. I just think it is. I don't know."

She put her arm up to ward off the blow, but he had only meant to caress her. They stood looking at one another.

"I thought you were going to hit me."

"You're like your mother, you try to put me in the wrong, you try to make me look bad."

"No. I don't. I…" She lowered her eyes.

He put his arm around her shoulder now, stiffly, feeling the small tense muscles beneath his fingers. They walked this way, father and daughter in a book of photographs, until they reached the little house where all the lights were on.

Dr. Pharon explained patiently that Beryl had had a breech birth and, though there was not necessarily a connection, the child was mongoloid and would probably not live long. The mother had required many stitches, she was seriously ill. She should be in a hospital, but there was no hospital, and so Luke would have to pay Mrs. Botts to stay with her.

Luke Gerriter listened with his head in his hands, and when the doctor left, he saw him to the door. Then he went into the bedroom, where he looked in the crib for a long moment, for the last time. He stared at the gray figure in the bed.

"So you had to do this to me, too," he said. "One lay in three years, and you had to produce this. You bitch." He turned at the door to look at her again. "You miserable bitch," he said, and lumbered up the stairs to Elissa's attic room. Elissa would have to sleep downstairs in the living room.

Elissa stretched out on the battered couch and she stroked Pal, whispering over and over, "It's all right; it's going to be all right."

2.   The next morning Luke bought a bed frame that folded in half and a mattress to go with it, and he set them up in their tiny bedroom. He said nothing to Beryl—everything between them seemed to have been said already—and she remained with her face turned to the wall. She had not asked to see the baby.

With the double bed taking up most of the room and then with the dresser and the baby's crib, Mrs. Botts found she had no place for the chair she had brought in from the kitchen. So she perched on the edge of Luke's folding bed, knitting, talking to herself, and at regular intervals feeding the baby. This sort of thing had happened before; the answer was to wait. The little thing would die eventually or, if he lived and grew up, they'd adjust. People always did. She moved closer to the window, hoping to catch a breath of air, though she knew there was never a breeze here. Elissa would be along soon to relieve her.

Almost at once they had settled into a regular routine. At three o'clock Elissa returned from school and Mrs. Botts went home. Elissa prepared her father's dinner and then he disappeared until midnight or later, when he came stumbling home from the Oaks. Meanwhile Elissa sat with her mother, saying nothing. No one in the house said anything.

Elissa had instructions from Mrs. Botts about caring for the baby, and she went about the work methodically, automatically; it was the way she made dinner, the way she did schoolwork; it was as if there were some more important part of her that simply stepped out and walked away, leaving the methodical, automatic Elissa behind to do the work.

School was the worst part of the day. The others teased her about her idiot brother, and once one of the teachers had called her aside in the schoolyard and asked about her mother and her father and finally about her brother. She wanted to know if he had a big head and if his eyes were pink; she asked her to describe him. Elissa said she didn't know how and tried to pull away, but the teacher had hold of her arm.

"You tell me, you hear. I've got to know these things. I'm only doing my duty." She tightened her grasp on the girl's arm.

Elissa tried to run but could not get away. And then something inside her took over, and it was as if she were talking with her father when he was drunk and impossible. She said in her dreamy way, "He's just a baby, just a little ordinary baby. His eyes are blue, a pretty light blue they are, and his head is only as big as a baby's head. He cries when he's hungry and then my mother feeds him, but most of the time he just laughs and plays with his toys and sleeps. Just like any baby."

"Are you telling me the truth?"

"Yes, ma'am."

"That isn't what everybody says. What do you say to that?"

"Maybe they haven't seen him," Elissa said. "He's a real nice baby."

More and more she found herself alone; she played with the dog and sat with the baby in her mother's room, waiting.

Luke found himself in the center of things. Somebody was always standing him a beer at the Oaks, and the men went out of their way not to mention births or babies. Work was going well, too, with a good raise following the birth of the child and the foreman keeping out of his way at the foundry. It was only at home that life was impossible. He had to be very drunk before he could get courage to come back to that small bedroom smelling of sour sheets and milk and lie there knowing Beryl was not asleep and that thing lay in the darkness between them.

He thought sometimes he would get up and place a pillow over the baby's face and put it out of its misery. He thought of shooting it. Some nights as he turned off Finial Street onto the dirt road that led to his house, he saw himself approach the door and walk through the house and down the cellar stairs and get a gun—the small pistol maybe, with its shiny blue barrel, or one of the rifles—and go back up the stairs, through the sitting room and into the bedroom, and there...

He could not imagine the rest in detail, but there was one small shot into the crib and then a scream from Beryl, followed by two shots and then a silence. He held the gun at his own head. On those dark nights staggering home from Finial Street, he would weep at how rotten life was, how wrong everything had turned out. He would go home and fall into bed, and it did not matter anymore that Beryl was lying there awake, staring straight ahead.

Beryl seemed to be awake all the time. She lay in bed motionless, turning from side to side only when she had to be washed or when Mrs. Botts changed the sheets. She ate whatever they brought her, and when they asked if she wanted more, she shook her head no.

After the first day Mrs. Botts gave up trying to talk to Beryl but she could never be sure whether Beryl was asleep or awake. Sometimes it was as if she were staring even when her eyes were shut. She'd be plumb glad, she told herself, when this whole thing was over.

Only Elissa was indifferent to Beryl's silent stare. Often, coming home from school, she would stand at the bedroom door and look at her mother, thinking, She'll never come back, she's gotten away to someplace where there are trees and air and no more shouting and she'll never come back. She envied her.

And Beryl lay there, with her gray face on the pillow, staring. It was almost a month before she asked to see the baby. There had been no warning, no signs of a return to life; suddenly one afternoon she simply turned in the bed, lifted herself on one elbow, and spoke to Mrs. Botts. Her voice was clear and strong.

"Let me see it," she said.

Mrs. Botts looked up from her knitting. "How's that?"

"Let me see it. The baby."

"Well, now, Berla. Are you real sure you want to do that? Might be as how well enough should be let alone till you're feeling better."

"I'm real sure."

Mrs. Botts picked up the baby and laid him in the bed next to Beryl, who twisted beneath the sheet so that she could get a better look at him. She took a long deep breath, and her chest heaved twice, as if she were going to sob. And then she whispered "No," a breathy sound that turned into a deep moan. She picked up the baby and crushed it to her breast, bending from the waist and swaying her body from side to side as she clutched the white, unresisting thing.

Mrs. Botts stroked Beryl's hair and said over and over, "That's all right, Berla, you go ahead and cry. That's all right, Berla," and she went on stroking, waiting for the release of tears. But the tears did not come. Beryl stopped moaning and released the baby. She placed it on her lap and forced herself into a sitting position.

After a long while she said, "Look at it. Just look at it."

The baby had smooth, almost puffy skin, moist in the airless room. His ears were small and round, and his nose only a blob of flesh, not like nose at all. His lips were thick, the color of raw meat. Beryl bent closer and looked at his tongue. It had two deep grooves and protruded from his tiny mouth. But it was his head that astonished her most. It was small and hard and completely round. She had expected something huge, a monstrosity, an enormous watermelon head. Looking at him at first, she had been relieved, she had almost begun to hope. And then she recalled the doctor's warning. "He's mongoloid, he will never be normal, he will probably not live very many years," and she saw the huge lips and the tiny slits for eyes. With her thumb she gently pushed up one eyelid. The eye was milky blue and empty.

She had not wanted him, she had not wanted sex in the first place, and now this had happened. She crooked her finger under his tiny palm and looked at his hand. Even his hands were wrong. There was a space between his first finger and the rest. His feet had that same strange cleft, as if they were paws, as if he were Pal.

"Put him back," she said, and then a long while later, "I'm going to call him Jason." Her mouth bent in a thin, bitter smile.

She was herself again for a few months, and then in the fall she had a hysterectomy, and after that she left the baby's care entirely to Elissa. She never wanted to see him again, she said.

Jason died just before his second birthday.

3.   Elissa missed him. He was not mongoloid to her, some strange monster her father would not look at, or a mockery her mother hated. He was that ordinary little baby she had told her teacher about, a baby who cried when he was hungry, but who most of the time played with his toys and slept. She was able to feed him, change him, and never see anything but that ordinary baby. Ron's baby, she liked to think, or the baby of somebody, anybody, who loved her. She would have a baby of her own someday, in a place different from this one; and she would be loved someday too.

Elissa was fourteen now and plain. Her hair was long and thin, falling straight on either side of her wedge-shaped face. She looked nearsighted, though she was not. The glassy look in her eyes came from daydreaming, her teachers said, but Elissa knew it was something different from daydreaming. She was escaping, she was going away.

With Jason dead, no one teased her at school anymore. Among the other girls there was even some grudging admiration of her breasts, which were rounder and fuller than their own. They could tell she didn't use cotton either, as most of them did. But she was plain, she was no threat to them. They merely laughed indifferently when she was called on in class and admitted she hadn't heard the question. The boys ignored her altogether, except to joke about her breasts as they passed in the corridor. "Maybe with a bag over her head," they would say, cupping their hands in front of their chests. Elissa was oblivious. School would be over if you waited long enough.

Soon after Jason died, she had begun taking Pal for walks each evening. After supper, when her father left for the Oaks and her mother settled into her chair by the radio, Elissa took the dog and walked slowly down the dirt road to Finial Street. She pulled a stick of straw grass from a clump by the road and chewed on it, kicking stones ahead for Pal to chase. She walked slower as she came into sight of Finial Street, and under the streetlight she stopped and waited. When she heard one of the jeeps approach she bent over as if she were taking a stone from her shoe. She liked the feeling of the blood racing to her temple, the hammering in her chest. This was how she had met Ron. It could happen again.

And then one night a jeep did stop and come roaring back.

"Hi," a girl said, giggling. She was in the front seat beside a soldier, and there were two other soldiers in the back. Her dark red hair tumbled around her shoulders in big curls and her mouth glistened with lipstick. It took Elissa a full minute to recognize her as Florence Kath. Florence was also a freshman at the high school.

"Hi," Elissa said, her eyes darting from face to face. Ron was not there. "Oh, it's you. I didn't recognize you, you're so…"

"We're going to the Spider," Florence said. "Want to come?"

"Yeah, why don't you come?" a soldier in back said. "Here, you can sit right between us. We'll take care of you." The other just grinned.

"I'd like to," she said. "I really would, but my dog… I've got to get back home." She could not take her eyes off the soldier in front who had his arm around Florence and was pushing the shoulder of her peasant blouse lower and lower.

"Fresh bastard," Florence said, pleased, and she pushed his hand away. "Come on, Lissa, you'll really love it."

"I can't," she said, "I just can't. My father..." She stood there speechless as the jeep took off, scattering dust everywhere.

Elissa and Florence became friends. Each morning during third period they met in the girls' room and smoked a cigarette. And they ate lunch together. Though they ate in the cafeteria with everyone else, there were always empty chairs at their table. Florence was cheap, everyone said; Florence did it with the soldiers.

"You ought to come to the Spider, Lissa, it's really terrific. I go only on Saturdays now, but next year I'm gonna go on Fridays and Saturdays too, once I convince my old lady. You ought to come."

"My mother would never let me."

"Well, you ought to come anyway. Last Saturday there was this guy. Oh my God, he was so cute. He bought me a beer by buying it for himself, you know, and letting me drink it. He had real curly hair, black, and we necked like crazy right in the booth. I didn't care. And when he took me home, woo, woo."

"What happened when he took you home?"

Florence sang, "But I ain't gonna tell you what he did to me." She sang loudly so the kids at the next table would hear her. "I don't care about them bastards," she said. "I don't care about any of them. They all ought to go get laid."

"What happened when he took you home? Tell me."

"Nosy bitch, aren't you. I'll tell you on Saturday when we put up our hair."

Every Saturday morning they put up their hair in huge pink rollers, whispering and giggling at the kitchen sink, splashing water everywhere. Then they sat outside on the back steps letting the sun dry their hair.

Beryl would sometimes come out, not actually joining them, just leaning against the doorframe smoking a cigarette. She had put on weight since her operation, and the faded housecoat she always wore bulged now with two small rolls around her waist. She kept her hair tied back with a blue-and-white bandanna.

"Boy crazy," she would say, and the girls would giggle. "I know," she said, nodding in agreement with herself, "don't think for a minute I don't know."

Sometimes she would study the two girls. Elissa was developing a good bust. Funny about that, because she was so skinny, especially in the face. She'd get a man someday, all right. Beryl smiled bitterly to herself. Florence was pasty white, with a plump face and a red mouth that was always pouting. She's looking for trouble, Beryl thought, and she'll find it.

"You keep going to that Spider," she would say, "and you'll get what you're looking for."

And once she said, "You kids, you think you know. I was like that once. Everything looks rosy. You think getting married is going to be the greatest thing in the world. Ha!" She lit another cigarette, her face pinched in concentration. "I remember when I was a kid, about your age, maybe younger, I thought getting married was the best thing that could happen to anybody, just getting away, not having to answer to nobody for nothing. I thought men were…" She was looking out over their heads, squinting against the sun, and then suddenly she threw down her cigarette and ground it out. "Men," she said. "They only want one thing." She went inside and slammed the door.

Florence waited a minute until she was sure Beryl was gone and then she said, "Jesus, your mother, is she ever some kind of nut! She's worse than mine. My old lady just keeps nagging and nagging, but at least she's not crazy." She touched the rollers on top of her head. "You know something? I think she's really crazy. I really do."

"It's since the baby died," Elissa said. "And then her operation."

"Maybe it's the change. They get crazy during the change, that's what Tussie told me. Tussie's my aunt, and is she ever gorgeous. She's the one that showed me how to put on makeup and everything. She told me all about sex and everything. Woo, woo. As if I didn't know already." She shrieked with laughter, and Elissa laughed with her.

Florence rummaged through the large embroidered bag she carried everywhere with her. She pulled out her makeup box, flat plastic containers of base and powder and rouge, and she gazed into a small round mirror as she drew the crimson lipstick across her mouth. She was making it larger, she explained. Men liked lips that way, it was sexy. She held the lipstick lovingly, caressing her lips with it, gently expanding her lip line above and below its natural ridges. Her lips looked wet. She pursed them at the mirror, lazily stuck her tongue out and curled it to one side of her mouth, tossed her head back, and gazed into the mirror with half-closed eyes. She was thinking of tonight, of what might happen.

Elissa looked at her and ached. The pancake makeup, the hair in rollers, the glistening red mouth. Someday she would go to the Blue Spider. Someday all that excitement would be hers.

4. On the night before her fifteenth birthday, Elissa woke to angry shouting. It was a sweltering night and she had kicked the sheet off, but now she pulled it over her and pressed the pillow against her ears. Sweat was running from her forehead into her eyes. Her head ached. She took the pillow away from her ears. They were still shouting.

She could hear her mother's voice screaming "bastard" over and over against her father's drunken laughter, a choked, hollow laugh with no joy in it. Pal was whimpering at the foot of the bed. Her mother's voice grew louder and she heard her father's voice too, thick and angry, though she could not make out what he was saying. And then there was a crash. A table must have been tipped over or something heavy thrown. The voices stopped. The house was completely silent. A floorboard creaked and Pal whimpered once again, but the house remained silent the rest of the night.

The next day Beryl and Luke did not speak to one another and she wouldn't sit with him while he ate. When Luke returned from work the table was set for him and Elissa, and the dinner was ready on the counter next to the stove. Beryl sat in the bedroom looking out the window. Elissa and her father ate in silence, Elissa only toying with her food. She was not hungry.

On the third day Luke said to her, "Where's your mother?"

"In the bedroom."

"Doesn't she eat at all? When does she eat?"

"She eats before you come home." Elissa pushed the beans around on her plate with her fork. "Can't this stop?" she said. "Can't this all stop?"

She held her breath, fearing what he might say or do. But he only went on eating, mopping his plate finally with a piece of bread. He leaned over the table, his head in his hands. Elissa listened to the kitchen clock ticking, saw her father shake his head from side to side. It will always be like this, she thought, nothing will ever change. She will sit in the other room looking out the window and he will sit here with his head in his hands and I will be between them listening to the clock tick and tick and tick. She wanted to run, she wanted to scream, it was better to be dead.

Luke stopped shaking his head from side to side. He looked up from his plate, his eyes strange and wild, his face bruised-looking. He was not drunk now; she had never seen him look like this.

"Oh, Christ," he said, his face contracting, growing hard. "What's the use? What's the goddamn use?"

The next day he went back to his guns. He had three of them; two were heavy-gauge shotguns and the other was a .22 pistol, revolver size, with a snub barrel. He had not touched them since the soldiers came and he had gotten a regular job. But before that, in that endless time when there had been no work and he had a wife and daughter to support, he had spent the days hacking at the sand and stone that stretched for miles behind the tiny house, trying to coax the sterile land into producing vegetables. And at the end of the day, when they had eaten dinner, he would get out the guns. With Beryl and Elissa by his side he trudged to the end of the garden, where he placed tin cans on a large rock to use for target practice. He was quiet and methodical, setting up the cans and walking back to the shooting box drawn in the sand, lifting the gun to his shoulder, clicking back the safety catch, firing. Elissa watched as his face tightened in concentration, his jaw went hard as he focused on the target, and his chest expanded in a sort of sigh as the bullet struck the can and sent it spinning into the air. He did this over and over until it grew dusky, and then they went into the house. None of them enjoyed the shooting; it seemed, somehow, a necessity. He had taught Beryl to shoot the .22 and insisted that Elissa learn also. But all this had stopped once the soldiers came and there were jobs and money. He had not bothered since then to oil and polish the guns; weeds grew here and there in the patch that had once been the garden. They should have been happy, Elissa thought, but it had not worked out that way. And now he was back with his guns.

"What's he do that for, anyhow? What's he want to shoot tin cans for?" Florence narrowed her eyes and stared into the distance where Elissa's father was shooting. It was Saturday and they were doing their hair. "That makes me really jumpy, boy, that gunshot."

"It's just a hobby. He just does target practice."

"Jeez, your family. I'd be afraid to live here. Honest to God. With your mother in the change and everything and your old man shooting out back, I'd be afraid he'd go off his nut and shoot me. How do you know he's not gonna miss someday and hit somebody by accident? Or your dog, maybe. Where is he, anyhow? Maybe your old man shot him. Maybe he's using him for target practice."

"No, he's up in my room. He's afraid of guns. He's always been afraid of guns. The noise."

"He smells, that dog. He really does. If there's one thing I can't stand in a house, it's a smelly dog. I like everything really clean. That's why I wash all my own stuff. I like it really clean."

"Wait a minute. Shh." Elissa stared out across the ruined garden at her father. "I think he called me," she said. He was waving his arm at her. "He must have," she said, and began walking toward him.

"Watch out he don't use you for target practice," Florence said, adding softly, "what a bunch of nuts."

Luke was standing in a litter of tin cans holding a small bunch of purple flowers. They were weeds that had somehow grown through the barren soil and bloomed now in the shade of the rock Luke set the tin cans on. The stems were thick with brownish green leaves, and the blossoms were small but pretty. "Here," he said, handing the flowers to Elissa. "Wait a minute," and he stooped to pick two more and then a third stalk. "Here, take these."

"What should I do with them?"

"Take them in to her."

"What should I say?"

Luke had turned from her and was bent over, picking up cans.

"Don't say anything. Just give them to her."

"Should I say they're from you?"

"I don't care what you say. Say whatever you want. Just give them to her. Say, yes, you can say they're from me." He was lining up cans on the rock. He was sweating.

"I'll tell her," Elissa said.

"Oh, and kid, Elissa." He scratched his head and stared at the ground. He spoke so softly she could hardly hear him. "Tell me, uh, tell me what she says."

Elissa ran to the house, her heart pounding. It would end now, the fights and the anger and the silence. She showed Florence the flowers and then ran up the porch stairs.

"Flowers," Florence said. "Big deal. Big fat hairy deal," and she giggled to herself. Elissa had already disappeared into the house.

Suddenly she was shy. She did not know how to give her mother the flowers, how to say they were from her father. She went slowly into the bedroom and stood there. Beryl was sitting with her face to the window. Her blue-and-white bandanna had come loose and the hair at the back of her head stuck out in little clumps; it was matted and damp at the temples. She turned and blew a stream of smoke from the corner of her mouth. Her eyes were swollen and there were dark smudges beneath them. She looked at Elissa questioningly and then she saw the flowers.

"What are those? What the hell have you got there?"

"Look." Elissa held out the bouquet to her.

Beryl began to tremble, her mouth working furiously and her eyes darting from Elissa to the door behind her and then back to the flowers.

"Where did you get those?" she said, breathless. "Are they from him? Did he tell you to bring me those?" Her voice rose; she was almost screaming. "Get those out of this house! Get them out of here! Out! Get out!" She stood up, one hand at her hair.

Elissa backed to the door. "They're only flowers. He just wanted to give you some flowers."

"Look at them. They're death flowers. You put those on coffins. Don't you see? Don't you see what he wants? He wants to get rid of me. He wants me dead." She dropped her voice to a whisper. She was clutching Elissa's arm, her thumb and fingernails deep in the soft flesh. "He can get rid of me, you know. He has grounds. You can get rid of a woman like me. Once you can't have children anymore, once you're like a chicken with its guts ripped out, they can get rid of you. He'd like to, too, that's what he wants."

"He just wanted to make up. He just wanted to give you the flowers." Elissa pulled away from her but Beryl continued on, talking rapidly, in a whisper, her words piling furiously on one another.

"You're with him too. You're like him. The both of you, you want to drive me crazy. You want me to go crazy and then you can get rid of me. Bringing me those flowers. Death flowers." She began to scream again. "Get them out of here! Get out!"

Elissa ran out of the house and stood on the porch, white and gasping for breath. Inside she could hear her mother sobbing wildly. Florence was staring at her, motionless, one hand gently touching the pink rollers on her head, the other suspended halfway to her mouth. Somewhere in the distance Elissa's father was waiting. And all she could feel was the sun, beating heavily on her head and shoulders, numbing her entire body. There was a terrible crashing sound in her head, rhythmic and loud, like a gunshot; but it was not a gunshot, it was something inside her head and it would not stop. Florence was saying something, but she could not hear it.

"Wait. Wait," she said, "it'll stop."

Florence watched her come stiffly down the stairs, walking as if she were in a trance. Her arms hung limply by her sides and the flowers in her left hand trailed along the ground as she approached her father. He was standing with one foot on the rock, staring off into the space that stretched out forever behind the house. As she approached him, he turned and saw the flowers. He made a sound that was half laughter and half groan.

"She didn't want them?"

"No."

"What did she say? Did you say they were from me?"

"She said to get them out of the house."

"But did she say why?"

"She said they were death flowers. She said you wanted her dead, because... She said you wanted to drive her crazy, that we both did."

Luke's face went gray and he put the gun down carefully against the rock. He began walking toward the house. Elissa ran after him.

"No, oh please no," she said. "Don't say anything to her. Don't do anything. Please. Please no."

She was snatching at his sleeve but he pushed her away and kept on, a furious, determined walk. She turned and went back to the rock where he had left the rifle. She picked it up and held it in position, the butt against her shoulder, her eye at the sight. She turned the barrel toward the house, toward Florence, but Florence had gone home. Without thinking, she sighted the kitchen window and waited and waited, and then pressed the trigger. Nothing happened. She had forgotten to release the safety catch.

Voices came to her now, she could hear them shouting. The word "crazy" drifted toward her on the windless air and then "bastard." She shook her head; she would not listen.

And then—she did not know why—she turned the rifle so that the barrel pointed to her chest. She reached for the trigger, but her arms were not long enough. She crouched. She placed the gunstock on the ground. Nothing worked.

Yes, she thought, you'd have to use your toe. You put the stock on the ground, the barrel at your chest, and you push the trigger back, away from you, with a toe. It would work perfectly.

She smiled at the thought and then looked around, suddenly self-conscious. She put the rifle back, leaning it against the rock just as it had been, and she walked slowly to the house.

5.   "Look, kid, you can go if you want to, but if your father finds out, don't come crying to me."

Beryl had said this to her late at night on that same Saturday Elissa had brought her the death flowers, and now it was Saturday again, and she had been going to the Blue Spider for almost a year.

Elissa stood in front of the bathroom mirror touching her hair. She wore it in immense curls that tumbled about her head, some of them only half combed out, still springy from the rollers. Florence wore her hair this way; it was the fashion, she said. Florence helped her with everything. She had taught Elissa how to spread the thick layer of pancake makeup evenly over her face and how to blend in the little dot of rouge so that her cheekbones stood out flushed against all that pink. She had helped her pick the peasant blouse, elasticized at the shoulders, and the plaid skirt, yards of material that swirled around her when she danced and that concealed her thin legs and hips. And she had taught her how to act at the Blue Spider. She called Elissa Cookie, and Elissa called her Candy. The soldiers liked their names.

She smiled at her reflection, tipping her head from one side to the other to catch a glimpse of herself in profile. She pursed her lips the way Florence did. Minutes went by and Elissa continued to pose before the mirror, distracted from her own image by the thought of Len.

She had met him on her first Saturday at the Blue Spider. They danced once or twice that night, but she did not remember him a week later; she had been too excited, too confused. Everyone seemed to like her. They laughed and drank and danced. How could she have remembered one soldier out of so many? But when he reminded her that they had danced together only a week earlier, she was embarrassed and grateful. She fell in love with him at once, despite the scar on his lip. And now, every Saturday night, they drifted together early in the evening, kissing and touching in the booths and on the way home.

"He loves me," she said aloud to the mirror. She touched her hair one last time and then put on the soft pink lipstick her mother liked; she would put on the deep red just before she reached Finial Street.

"Don't get in trouble, you," her mother said.

"Oh, Ma."

"And you better get home before he does. If he finds out, he'll kill you."

"I'm always home before he is. Don't worry."

Elissa let the screen door slam behind her, but Pal had wriggled out before it closed and was wagging his stubby tail excitedly. "No, Pal. Go back," she said. "Go back!" She stamped her foot and pointed toward the door. The dog only lowered his head and put back his ears. "Goddamn," she said. Pal began to whimper. "Ma," she shouted, "call the dog, will you? He's gonna follow me." The dog slunk into the house.

Beryl watched her daughter walk down the dirt road, her hips swaying, her curls tossing with the movements of her head. "You look nice, Elissa," she said to herself, and then turned away, back to her empty house. Pal was in her way, sniffing at the screen door. "Get out of here, damn you," she said. "Damn dog." She kicked him lightly and he yelped and ran. Suddenly she found she was angry. "Damn you!" she shouted at the dog, and then she turned and leaned against the door, watching her daughter disappear down the road to Finial Street.

At Finial Street they were waiting for her in the jeep, but Len was not with them. The two soldiers in back made room for her, and even before she sat down the jeep roared away. One soldier had his arm around her shoulders, the other put his hand on her knee; she settled in comfortably between them.

"Isn't Len coming tonight?" She tried to sound casual. "Hey, is Len coming tonight?" The soldier repeated her question, laughter in his voice. He tightened his grip on her shoulder. "I don't know. Is Len coming tonight?" The other picked up the question, nudging her leg with his.

"What's the joke?" she said. "What the hell's so funny?" She leaned forward. "Hey, Candy, what the hell's so funny?"

"Wouldn't you like to know?" Florence said, rolling her eyes.

"Come on, tell me."

Florence leaned back and whispered in her ear. "Len's gonna get a car. And you know what that means." She laughed wildly, rocking from side to side, wriggling against the driver. "Woo, woo."

"Woo, woo," Elissa said, laughing, but her heart lurched and she could feel the blood rushing in her arms and legs.

She loved Len. She loved the feel of him as he pressed up against her in the booths or when they kissed in the jeep on the way home. She would twist around in the seat so that her whole body was touching his, and then she would move gently back and forth so that she could feel him thrusting against her. She wanted to be naked under him.

She looked down at her lap and then at the lap of the soldier next to her. She could see that soft bulge. She could reach over and put her hand right on it. What would he do? She didn't even know his name, and yet she could reach out and do something like that. She would, too, someday. She would tonight, maybe, with Len.

"See anything you like?" the soldier said, shifting a little on the seat. "If you were a squirrel I'd be worried."

"Bastard," she said, and hit him in the ribs with her elbow. She tossed back her head and began to sing the "Petaluma Polka." It was going to be a perfect night. Nothing could spoil it. She was still singing when they reached the Blue Spider and went in.

Elissa was thrilled by the air of excitement in the place. Everyone was in motion, talking and laughing. There were some girls in the booths already, but most of them were dancing, and there were soldiers lounging against the jukebox waiting for their turn. Someone called to her from one of the back booths. She waved to him and laughed. She was dancing, gliding backward to the heavy beat of the music, humming. She could feel the soldier's hands moving on her shoulder and at the small of her back. She didn't care. Let him. She was dancing with someone else now, she could feel his thighs against hers. She was floating, and always there was the music blaring and bodies touching hers. She was safe here. She was alive. Someone handed her a can of beer and she was surprised at the sharp bitter taste. She took a long slug from the can and everyone applauded.

"Jesus, are you ever the one!" Florence said to her, and then she whispered something to one of the soldiers. They laughed together and then he whispered to her. "You pig," she said, and pushed against his chest with her fist, laughing. They sat down in a booth.

Len had come in and was standing by the jukebox waiting for the music to stop. They were dancing to the "Chicken Bop," and every few steps the girl would pull away from the boy and do a little hop. It was a popular dance because it gave the girls a chance to show what they were made of, Len had once told her. Elissa moved away from her partner, hopped, and returned. He grinned and said, "What've you got down there?" He pulled at the elastic on her blouse.

"Pig," she said. She was flirting more than she would have if she had seen Len come in.

She swung out from her partner once again, did her little hop, and returned, and this time he said, "You've really got something. Let's take a look." And he pulled again at the elastic. The blouse slipped from her left shoulder, and she pushed it back easily with a flick of her thumb. But she was annoyed.

"Come on," she said. "Cut it."

The dance was about to end. "I'll be good," he said. He held her tight against him, but when she swung out and returned for the last time, like a small boy he said, "Just one little peek," and he pulled at the elastic.

She stopped dancing and stood there. "Now look what you done," she said. The elastic had broken and her blouse drooped low on the left shoulder.

"Let's see, let's see," he said, being funny. The music had stopped and everyone was beginning to stare.

"Come on, let's get out of here," Len said. He came between her and her partner.

"Hey, hold on there, soldier," he said. "You stealing my little girlfriend here?" And he pushed Len to the side.

"Look at this. Look what he done," Elissa was saying. "How can I go home with my blouse like this?"

"Quit shoving," Len said to the soldier, and took Elissa by the arm.

The soldier spun him around. "You didn't answer my question, friend. You stealing my little girlfriend here?" He waited for an answer. "Huh?" He pushed Len in the chest with the flat of his hand. "Huh?" Another push. "What do you say, soldier boy?"

The crowd around them had fallen silent, the faces hungry for a fight. Len glanced at them and knew what was expected of him. But he didn't want a fight. Not now.

"Don't try that again," he said, and spat on the floor.

"Try what? Try this?" He pushed Len harder. "This is easy, no trying involved." He pushed him harder still. "How'd you get that lip, soldier, blowing beer cans?"

And then before anyone knew what had happened, before anyone could holler "fight," Len lashed out with his right fist and caught the soldier on the side of the head. He lurched back, but as he fell, he struck the other side of his head on one of the upright beams. It made only a dull thudding sound. He slid down the beam to a sitting position, a look of surprise on his face, blood beginning to drip from the side of his head. Len took Elissa's arm and pushed her to the door.

"Hey, no rough stuff!" the bartender was shouting. Everyone was talking loudly. "Who got hit?" "Who did it?"

They stood for a moment outside the door, Elissa holding the blouse together with her hand. They were breathless, flushed with excitement.

"I got a car," Len said.

"I know it."

He paused, and she stood there fiddling with the material of her blouse.

"Do you want to?"

"Yes. Do you?"

"It's my first time," he said.

Laughing, they ran to the car.

"Yellow bastard!" they heard the soldier shout as they drove off. "Come on back and fight, you bastard."

They drove out of town, out beyond the houses and the fields and the base, deep into the pocked and sweltering desert. They were silent the whole way, an odd formality between them. Finally Len stopped the car and they got out. It occurred to Elissa that it would take forever to get home.

"This looks all right," he said. "What do you think?"

"Yes, this is fine," she said. What had happened? Len was a stranger, she realized, he was just someone else she did not know. But I love him and he loves me. We're going to make love, she told herself, trying to recapture the excitement of the Blue Spider. He was naked now, standing on the blanket he had spread over the sand. He was caressing his stomach.

"Come on," he said. "Get those clothes off. We haven't got all night."

They made love and afterward she said, "Is that all?" It had happened so quickly, just a brief hard pain that spread upward into her chest, taking her breath away, and then nothing more.

"What do you mean, is that all?"

"I mean, should we go home now?"

"Oh, yeah," he said. And as he picked up the blanket and walked to the car, he added, "You'll get better at this, don't worry."

"That's all right," she said. They were silent as he drove her home.

Luke had been home for more than an hour. He had gone upstairs and sat, waiting, on Elissa's bed and then he had come down.

"Where is she?" he asked Beryl.

"She's out for a walk. She was too hot up there."

"Yeah, I hear she's hot up there. I hear she's hot down at the Blue Spider too."

"Who says?" He was drunk, she knew, but canny drunk. It was best not to antagonize him. "Men gossip," she said. "They make things up."

"My own daughter, a friggin' whore. I have to hear about it at the Oaks. My wife don't tell me. Oh no, she's helping her do it."

"Who said..."

"It's been going on for a year, they tell me. 'Hey, Gerriter,' he says to me, 'I hear your daughter's getting it plenty.' I call him a dirty liar and he says, 'No, it's true.' So I'm gonna punch him in the face and they tell me, 'No, Gerriter, it's true. She's down there every Saturday.' And there I was listening to them laugh about my own daughter. I'll teach her. I'll beat her up to an inch of her life."

"I let her go. I'm the one. I said she could go as long as she got home before you did. So if you're gonna blame anybody, it's me."

"Yeah, I should beat you too. I should have years ago."

"You're not going to beat anybody, Luke Gerriter. Get that straight."

"I'm not gonna be made a fool of by my own daughter. I'm gonna teach her a lesson." He stormed into the kitchen and took a beer from the refrigerator. Beryl followed him. "'She's getting it plenty,' he says to me."

"Don't you touch that girl."

"I'll touch anybody I goddamn please."

They stared at each other in silence for a moment, and then Luke took a long slug from the beer can.

Beryl spoke very slowly. "If you put a hand on her, I warn you, I'll kill you." She continued to stare at him for a moment, and then she went to the bedroom.

She sat by the window, trembling. They had not fought for almost a year now, not since the day he had sent Elissa to her with the flowers. She had changed since then, she knew it. Something strange had happened inside her and she found herself, despite the stored anger between them, wanting him, wanting him with her in bed. She could not tell him this, but there were times when she ached, when she lay in bed listening to him snore and had to keep herself from going to his cot and saying, "Come to bed with me, I want you." And now it was all going to change again, within an hour, as soon as Elissa got home. She could see it already, the accusations, the hands curled into fists, the screaming. She shook her head to clear it.

In the kitchen Luke had finished his beer and took down from the pantry shelf the bottle of whiskey he kept there. He sat at the kitchen table and watched the whiskey rise in the tumbler; he filled it only half-full. He put his head on the table to rest, to wait for her. As the time passed and the whiskey sank in the bottle, he wept for himself as a betrayed father, for his daughter being used by filthy soldiers, for everything. He would grow angry and violent, pace around the kitchen, cursing and threatening to beat her half to death. And after a while he would sit down again. He dozed fitfully. By the time the small gray car turned off Finial Street onto the dirt road, Luke had finished most of the bottle and was thoroughly, violently drunk.

The car stopped in front of the house and Len and Elissa sat there in silence. It was very late. They had not spoken once since leaving the desert. Finally Len cleared his throat.

"Urn, there's something I should tell you. I'm being shipped out soon."

"Oh." As if she had expected it.

"Yeah, this week. They're sending me overseas."

"Oh."

"Yeah. Maybe I should have told you before. Maybe you wouldn't have wanted to do it."

"No, that's all right," she said.

"Well, anyway, it was, um, great."

"Yes," she said. She got out of the car and closed the door softly.

"See you around," he said and drove off, fast.

"That's all right," she said, and drifted toward the door, her hand at the shoulder of her torn blouse. Vaguely she noticed that the light was on behind the screen door. She couldn't breathe very well. She stopped by the evergreen tree, bending into its spiky branches to inhale the bitter smell. The screen door creaked, but she did not turn around.

Her head jerked sharply back and there was a tearing pain in her shoulder as Luke grabbed her arm from behind and pulled her into the light.

"Look at you, you whore, you pig," he said softly, staring at the curls and the makeup and the crimson slash at her mouth. He slapped her hard on the face. In the silence, the crack of his hand against her skin was like a gunshot, and involuntarily he drew away from her, hesitating for a moment. And then he saw the blouse. "Look, look!" he said. "Is that what happens in the cars, huh, they can't wait to get at you so they have to rip your clothes off."

Elissa backed away from him. He was crazy drunk. He might do anything.

"Or do you like it that way? Damned whore," he said, "some like it that way. Do you? Do you like it?" And with one hand he reached out and tore her blouse down the front. His anger grew as he looked at her. "Look at you!" he screamed. "Look at you." He tore at her brassiere and as she struggled it came loose in his hand. She stood stripped to the waist in the light shining through the screen door. "Whore," he said, "pig," and slapped at her breasts, pulling her closer and closer to him as they struggled. She was screaming, pushing him away, and he was calling her whore, while his neck and chest heaved with the violence of what he was doing. He felt fists on his back and he heard someone calling his name and then something struck his head.

"Luke, Luke," Beryl was saying. "Luke."

He took his hands from Elissa and turned, with the face of a stranger, to Beryl. He looked at her, confused.

"Get in the house," she said, her voice firm and low.

"She..." Luke said, pointing to his daughter.

"Get in the house."

Luke went up the stairs slowly, bent like an old man. He had not noticed the pistol in Beryl's hand.

Elissa and Beryl looked at one another, uncertain, questioning.

"Nothing happened, did it," Beryl said. Elissa continued to look at her. "Nothing happened," she insisted.

"No. Nothing happened."

"I know," Beryl said, "I know," and suddenly she threw her arms around the girl, sobbing uncontrollably. "Nothing happened. Nothing. Nothing happened."

6.   It was almost October and still the heat was unbearable. Luke wiped the
      sweat from his forehead with the back of his hand and then mopped his
      plate with a piece of bread, swooping down on it to catch the drippings.

      "How come she's sick again?" he asked. "What's the matter with
her?"

      Beryl pushed back her plate. "You want another beer?" She rose
to get it.

      "What's the matter with the kid?"

      She placed the beer can at his side and sat down at the table facing
him. "She's pregnant."

      "Oh no," he said, and groaned.

      "She told me this afternoon. She's over three months."

      Luke sat staring at his empty plate, his hands at his head. After a
minute Beryl saw his shoulders shake. He was crying.

      "How do you think I felt?" she said. "I told her she's gonna be
punished and good. I feel like she tore something right out of me,
like she killed something I had, the only thing I had."

      His shoulders shook again. He said nothing.

      The clock ticked above the table. They could hear Pal upstairs as
his nails clicked against the wooden floor. Beryl glanced at the ceiling
and waited for Luke to say something. Finally she couldn't stand the
silence any longer.

      "It's not yours," she said.

      He looked up at her, shocked.

      "It's not your baby. I asked her."

      He shook his head and looked back down at his plate. In the three
months that had passed since he had beaten Elissa, none of them
mentioned what had happened.

      "Well, I had to know, didn't I? After that…"

      "Yes," he said. She could barely hear it.

      "Do you want to know something? Do you?" There was fright
in her voice, and he looked up at her finally.

      "What?"

      "Do you know what I felt first of all? I was jealous."

He stared at her.

"You don't know what it's been like," she said. "Oh Jesus, sometimes I want to just die."

"It's not mine," he said. "I was drunk that time. I didn't know what I was doing."

"I know," she said. "Nothing happened anyway. Nothing happened."

There was a long silence between them and she moved her arm forward on the table until her fingers touched his. He did not move away.

"Can I tell you something?" she said.

He moved one of his fingers against hers.

"Sometimes I want it now. With you."

After a long moment he took her hand in his. "Oh Christ," he said, "what a mess." And for the first time in years, they went to the bedroom to make love.

Upstairs Elissa lay in her bed, one arm across her stomach. She studied the boards in the slanted roof above her head, and whenever Pal put his muzzle against her, she scratched behind his ears. But she noticed nothing, was aware of nothing.

At first, after that night with Len, she had tried to understand what had happened. He didn't love her, she knew that, but that hadn't mattered. Not that he was going away either. It was something different. Everything seemed to have come to an end—the excitement of going to the Spider, men brushing against her, touching her, knowing that something was going to happen, that it was all going to be different. But nothing was going to be different now. By the time she discovered she was pregnant, not even that mattered very much. That seemed only to prove what she already knew. She was trapped forever in the sweltering heat, fighting for a breath of air.

Around midnight they awoke and made love again. Luke collapsed against her, breathing hard, and then rolled away, half-asleep already.

"She's got to be punished," Beryl said. "She's got to be taught a lesson."

"I'll shoot her dog," Luke said. "She loves the dog."

"No. No, that's not enough."

There was a moment of silence.

"I'll make her shoot it," he said.

"Tomorrow."

Before dawn Luke walked to town and borrowed the Garners' car. He was back before the sun was fully up. Beryl had prepared a large breakfast for them and they ate it, as they always did, in silence.

Afterward Beryl said, "I told your father."

"You got to be punished," he said. "You know that."

Elissa pushed her hair back from her face but said nothing.

"We're gonna shoot that dog of yours. You're gonna shoot it, that is." Elissa nodded. "Now you're gonna take us out to where he did it and you're gonna show us the exact spot, and then you're gonna shoot that dog."

"You killed something I had," Beryl said, "and now you're gonna do the same."

Elissa nodded. It was all crazy. Nothing mattered.

The sun was high when they passed the last of the farms and took the road to the air base.

"Left here," Elissa said, numb. She stroked the dog and looked out the window. Miles and miles of sand, with the sun beating down. Nothing could live here.

"Where is it?" Luke said. "It must be around here somewhere."

How could you tell, she thought, everything was the same. After a while she said, "Here. Here's the place."

They got out of the car and stood by it awkwardly, looking around them. No one would ever hear a gunshot out here. They walked a long distance from the car until Luke said, "Where are you going? I thought you said it was here."

"Yes, it is here. It's right here."

Luke drove a stake deep into the sand and tied the dog's leash to it. He walked five paces distant, readying the gun. He cocked it, examined the shells, snapped it shut. It was only a .22 pistol, but at such close range it was enough to kill a dog. He released the safety catch and handed Elissa the pistol.

"Do it," he said. "Do it or we just drive off and leave you. It's your punishment."

Luke and Beryl moved off and stood at a distance, watching.

Elissa looked at the pistol, turned it over in her hand, and then looked at Pal, who wagged his tail and tried to come to her. She looked up at the sky, into the blinding sun, and thought she saw a cloud coming, perhaps it meant rain, but it was just the sun against her eyes, and when she looked back at Pal she saw only a blazing dog shape against the sand. Slowly, evenly, she raised the small gun, placing the barrel firmly beneath her right ear.

The only sound in the desert was Pal whimpering in the terrible heat.

NIGHTFALL

That summer during the late evenings and the cold endless nights that followed, young girls all over West Hadley lay awake hoping to hear the sounds of Rory O'Toole. The screech of his tires, the thunder of his terrible motor, and those girls turned luxuriously in their beds, knowing that at last Rory was laying rubber on their street.

Rory was an artist of the motorcycle and he was a female disturbance also, and Rebecca's mother said he was a disease. A pestilence. He was eighteen or maybe twenty-eight or thirty, with a heavy blond beard and low jeans. Rory was from Australia, however, and so at first the police and then later just about everybody realized it wasn't his fault, this female hysteria he excited. Nonetheless, he did excite it. Nonetheless, all those young girls were lying awake in hope and expectation. Nonetheless, he was to blame.

Rory's motorcycle was a Honda 750, with no extra chrome and no options, but he rode it as if it had once been wild, and he had roped and tamed it himself, and now it idled or roared or reared between his legs like some savage thing that he had made his own. His, only.

Rory was an incident. He was an occasion. Rory, Rebecca's mother kept saying, was a disease. Rebecca and her mother—each in her own way—were victims of this disease.

Rebecca's mother had been modern for a long time. She realized that they were living in the 1990s and so there was no chance of her

Rebecca's being ruined. Ruin had stopped in the 1960s, thanks to this new pill. Now all the girls—even the ones in West Hadley—had large breasts by the age of twelve, and they had experience too. They were sophisticated about safe sex and motorcycles and diseases. Rebecca's mother knew all this and did not really worry about Rebecca's possible ruin, but still she wanted something done about Rory, and she decided to get it done through the town selectmen. Her husband was a selectman, and even though he was personally useless to her, at least he was a contact. She could get what she wanted.

The selectmen of West Hadley also wanted something done about Rory, even if he was an Australian and couldn't help it. The selectmen were not concerned about ruin any more than Rebecca's mother was; they were concerned about water pollution, about sleeping nights, about getting that goddamn motorcycle off the side roads and onto the highway straight out of town. Who cares who screws who? Or what? Or why? Let's get some sleep, for Chrissake have some relaxation, could we only just watch *The Tonight Show* in peace?

Rebecca's mother sat alone with her pitcher of late-night martinis and said to the test pattern on the television: "Enough is enough. Rory O'Toole goes, or I go. And I'm not going." Too many nights now Rory's laid rubber and the peeling out of that infernal machine had awakened her to Johnny talking away, or David Letterman, or—worst of all—to a flickering test pattern, her martini clutched upright and in perfect balance, her mind fixed on Rory O'Toole. It was not that motorcycle thing he drove—the blatancy of it, the cheap sex of it—that wasn't what sickened her. It was… well, what was it? She put down her glass and headed for the stairs.

Let's face it. This is home. This is normal. This is a small New England town where there are no suicides and practically no murders. And who in hell is this Rory O'Toole that he can get away with terrorizing our children, destroying family life, etcetera, etcetera? There has to be a moral perspective on all this.

Thus she made it up the stairs and could go to bed. But first she looked in on Rebecca, who was twelve, going on thirteen, and who had fine large breasts, larger than her own. Rebecca was smiling toward the window, toward the last explosions of Rory's Honda 750. She ignored her mother, that drunk at the door.

"Rebecca," the mother said. "Forget him, this Rory. He's no good for you, sweetheart. He's my age. He's your mother's age."

"Go away," Rebecca said.

"Rebecca, my baby."

"Bug off," Rebecca said, still turned to the window.

There was silence for a moment.

"Let me tell you, kid," Rebecca's mother said, shifting gears. "In the showdown, either he goes or I go. And I'm not going."

"Look," Rebecca said, and she placed her pudgy hands firmly beneath her splendid breasts. "See?"

The mother looked as if she did not quite understand.

"In the showdown," Rebecca said, "you'll go."

Rory was coming for dinner and they were all going to get a chance to see him up close. At first Rebecca's mother didn't want him for dinner tonight because she had already invited three town selectmen and their wives. The cream of West Hadley, and Rory? No, it was impossible.

"Not in my home, Rebecca," she said. "Not for dinner. At least not tonight."

"He's coming. I asked him to come and he's coming."

"Rebecca, be reasonable. I'm your mother. You're only twelve."

"Going on thirteen."

"You're only twelve going on thirteen and he can't come here tonight. Not tonight, darling. Tonight is special. Look, I'm not even having a drink. For the company."

Rebecca looked at her with narrowed eyes.

"Let him come tomorrow night and he can have dinner, and if you want, he can stay over. You can sleep in the tent in the backyard. Okay? All right? Or you can have our room, the waterbed. But I don't want him in your room, darling. It's not right. I'm a mother."

"The things you say. If the selectmen only knew."

"It's the selectmen who want him out of town, Rebecca. He's an influence, Rebecca. He's disruptive. None of the girls are sleeping. It's his motorcycle, Rebecca. It's what it means."

"If West Hadley knew about you."

"Well, then, let him come. I'm through with arguing. I'm through with trying to be the sensible one. Let the selectmen see him up close, with his beard and that big thing. It's just a shame that it has to happen in my house."

And so Rory was coming for dinner.

The selectmen and their wives drank a lot before dinner, nervous at the prospect of finally meeting the legendary Rory. Rebecca passed chips and onion dip among the eight people, and everybody smiled at her and complimented her on her big breasts, but clearly their thoughts were elsewhere. Rebecca's mother said nothing and drank nothing. This was probably the best thing after all: Rory would condemn himself simply by being what he was. She could take satisfaction in having set everything in motion.

Rory arrived as they were about to sit down to dinner. There was a lot of talk about food and acid rain and air pollution and then they got down to business.

"So you're the famous Mr. O'Toole."

"Right."

"More of the roast, Mr. O'Toole?" That was Rebecca's mother.

"No."

"Rebecca?"

"No."

"Well, well. Mr. O'Toole of the motorcycle and the midnight rides."

"Right."

"The Mr. O'Toole who has all our young girls awake nights and… how shall I say it… palpitating!"

"It's my Honda 750."

"More broccoli, Mr. O'Toole? Rebecca?" The mother again.

"No."

"No."

"Do you plan to be working here in West Hadley for long, Mr. O'Toole?"

"I don't work."

"Ah. Well, then, you'll probably be moving on before long. Is that right?"

"Maybe. Maybe not."

"We'd be interested to give you a hand, to help you move on, Mr. O'Toole. If, as selectmen, there is any way we could help?"

"More rolls?" Mother.

"Stuff those rolls."

"Any way we might help."

"Enough is enough. I want a martini." Rebecca's mother got up and went to the sideboard where she poured straight gin into a tumbler and then returned to the table. "I'm making up," she said. "Enough is enough."

For a long time nobody said anything and then Rory spoke in his thin, caressing voice. "I like to drive my bike," he said. "I like to drive late at night up and down the side roads where all those middle-class birds live, the hot ones, around twelve or thirteen years old, and I rev my engine—get it?—and I sit way back, way back, and I bust through all that air that's out in front of me, blocking my way, and then I'm free, man, free."

"If as selectmen we could help?"

"You're old," Rory said caressingly. "You're dead men and you don't know it." He looked significantly at Rebecca and Rebecca's mother and the wives of the three selectmen. They looked back at him, fatally. Then he said, "They know. They want what I've got."

Someone cleared his throat.

"And I'm going to give it to them. I'm going to ride my bike and I'm going to take your women with me. All of them. They know what I've got."

"Have you no moral sense at all, Mr. O'Toole?"

"I'm just the temptation." He was purring. "You better look somewhere else for a moral sense." He ran his smile over the women.

Slowly then, Rory O'Toole got up and took Rebecca's hand and led her to the front door. "You can't leave," Rebecca's mother said through her martini. "I forbid you to go."

"I'm not going," Rebecca said at the door. "And Rory's not going." She placed her hands beneath those infuriating breasts. "You're the one that's going."

A week passed. Every night Rebecca left the house at eleven and returned, exhausted, at three. Every night her midnight cries and the explosions of Rory's motorcycle echoed in the streets of West Hadley. Rebecca's mother could endure it no longer. She woke Rebecca at five one morning, her glittering eyes holding the child awake.

"What is it like, Rebecca? Tell me. Tell me what he's got."

Rebecca gazed at her mother emptily for a moment and then said, "Listen to old raisin tits," and she turned to face the wall.

Enough is enough, Rebecca's mother had said, and it was. The selectmen talked a lot to one another about Rory O'Toole and, in secret, about their wives, and then they talked to the police. There were laws to be observed, the selectmen pointed out, not least of all the laws of proportion, and the police would simply have to do something. Rebecca was out every night roaring around town with that maniac, and Rebecca's mother was all upset, and who could tell who would be next? Besides, that is what police were for. To do something. Still, there was some worry and a lot of talk around the station house after they finally did it.

"But you're sure you got rid of him?"

"We beat him up. We kicked the shit out of him."

"But will he bring charges?"

"How can he? We're the police."

"Well, I hope it all looks clean."

"Looks clean? It is clean. This is West Hadley, for Chrissake. This is a normal New England town. We're just protecting our kids."

"What about the girl with him, that Rebecca? Is she going to be all right?"

"Well, that's a problem. That's a real problem. She's what you call a casualty. Her head got in the way, is what, but she'll be all right where she is. She'll never know the difference. Not at that place. They're all the same there, veggies, except most of them got born that way."

"Some knockers on that kid, that Rebecca."

"Not really. Thirty-eights. That's normal. She's almost thirteen years old."

"So long as O'Toole is gone, that's what matters."

"We did it for our kids. We did it for our women."

"He brought out the worst in people, that O'Toole."

"Well, he's a goner now."

But Rory was not gone. His jaw was broken in three places and all his front teeth had been knocked out by the tire iron across his face. One eye was damaged. And seven ribs were cracked. But his groin, despite the heavy boots of the police, remained perfectly intact.

He mended. He got well. Rebecca's mother, who had wanted it all to happen, who had invited the selectmen to put pressure on the police, felt bad about it now and brought him flowers and homemade soup. She brought him martinis. She brought him photographs of herself as a girl—at the beach, playing tennis, graduating from college. She touched the poor sore jaw, and his hurt ribs, and she moved her hand down beneath the covers. She liked to visit hospitals; and God knows there was no point in visiting Rebecca.

Within a month Rory was out and on his Honda 750, with his beard and his low jeans and a stunning leather patch over one eye. The police had decided on a hands-off policy because of the Rebecca incident, and the town selectmen felt bad too.

And so that autumn during the evenings and into the late cold nights that followed, Rebecca's mother and Rory O'Toole shattered the frosty silence of West Hadley as they tore through the side roads and up the expansive hills, laying rubber. At the sound of their going, the wives of selectmen throughout the town turned luxuriously in their beds, smiling to themselves, certain that their fate was inevitable.

NO STRINGS

Warren and Ruth had disagreed that morning over what Megan should
be allowed to wear to school. Megan was fourteen now and she looked
lovely in a short skirt, Ruth said, but Warren insisted that no daughter
of his was going to school in a skirt that made her look like a tart.
Tart? Tart? This is not the nineteenth century, Ruth said. Nor is it a
nudist colony, Warren said. You're a prude, Ruth said, you've become
a prude. The quarrel escalated from there. Those comic novels are
corrupting your mind, Ruth said, and Warren replied that *Ulysses* was
the greatest novel of the twentieth century and—just so you know—a
comic novel as well. Ruth said softly and with contempt: Joyce and his
bathroom humor. To which Warren, quietly superior, said, Belittling
my work is unworthy of you, Ruth. I can't believe you'd stoop so low.
Ruth, whose own work was not going well at the moment, replied to
the effect that Joyce was the most overrated writer in the canon and
she was fed up with hearing about him. And Murdoch. And Waugh.
Eventually there was shouting, a broken coffee cup, a slammed door.
Silence. Since Warren and Ruth rarely quarreled, their children found
this breakfast performance thrilling. The twins, Virginia and Vanessa,
quietly applauded their mother. Megan went off to school in her new
short skirt. Warren's day was ruined.

Now, as he gazed across his desk at Nicola Mantis, Warren considered
how unappreciated he was at home and how faithful he'd always been

to Ruth and what thanks did he get for it? This girl in his office was sexy and interesting and very likely persuadable. And those legs! Nicola Mantis! Warren thought of the mantis insect with its fantastic legs and extraordinary mating habits. Could it be true that, after mating, the female bit off her lover's head? He considered the metaphorical possibilities here. They didn't matter in any case, he decided, since he was not an insect.

Nicola Mantis, a graduate student in his Comic Novel Seminar, had been talking about irony in Iris Murdoch, eager to know what Warren thought? Where did irony begin and end in Murdoch, she asked rhetorically, and through what lens should we view the story within the story in *The Black Prince*? She stopped.

"You're not listening, are you?"

"I think you're on to something there," he said.

Nicola sat back, lazily. "You find me distracting," she said. She uncrossed her legs and crossed them again. Her webbed stockings made her legs look spidery, in a good way. "Am I right?" she said.

"Distracting, yes," he said. So she was indeed persuadable. But he was hopelessly inexperienced. He'd put it off and see what happened. "We should meet again after you've done more thinking about Murdoch," he said. Maybe nothing would happen after all.

They met again and she said, "Is it the stockings? I can see you're still distracted."

"I like being distracted." Uh-oh.

A few more double-edged remarks and the matter was settled.

"Let's be clear, though," Nicola said. "No strings. We're just in it for the fun."

"Perfect," Warren said, nervous, but ready to lose his head.

The fun began in the usual way, but Warren's natural awkwardness and his embarrassment at not knowing what came next, caused him to break out in a sudden sweat and, all thumbs, he made a hopeless tangle of her clothes. Nicola was obliged to help him out.

"Sex is no big thing," she said, to calm him. "It's just nature's way of saying, 'Hey there! Lookin' good!'" She gave his buttocks a hard squeeze, which made him jump.

Warren fumbled with his belt, but he couldn't unbuckle it. He had already made a fool of himself by getting his shaking fingers caught in those damned webbed pantyhose and, now that it was his turn, his belt seemed permanently attached to his waist. He yanked it hard but it only tightened more.

"Not to worry," Nicola said, and, with her deft little fingers, she had his belt off and his pants down with one quick motion. "Voilà!"

"I'm clumsy," he said. "I'm used to… well… Ruth."

"Here, let me," and, with his pants at his ankles, she lowered his shorts, slowly, slowly, like a magician about to astound the audience. "Voilà," she said again, and took him firmly in hand. "See how easy."

It was not easy. Nicola was perched on the edge of his desk and Warren was standing between her legs exactly as he had seen it done countless times in movies and on television, but here in real life the desk was in the way, and his position was impossible to sustain with all these arms and legs moving about, and the next thing he knew he had ejaculated all over the front of her shirt. He stood there, dripping.

"It's all right," she said. "It doesn't mean a thing. You're just not a desk man." He protested and apologized, staring like an idiot, waiting with his pants at his ankles for something else to happen. "That's it," she said, "*fini*," and, finally exasperated, "for God's sake, just put it away."

He turned from her modestly, muttering, "Sorry, sorry."

"Next time it will be a lark," she said. "It's fun, you'll see."

"I don't know about this," he said.

She said, "And next time we should lock the door."

They hadn't locked the door? Warren suddenly felt faint.

On the next Friday Nicola arrived at Warren's office carrying a duvet rolled into a tight little bundle. It had its own carrying case. They spread out the duvet and, eager to get at it, lay down on the floor like any old couple on a picnic. Afterward Nicola said, "See? It's fun. No strings attached."

Immediately back to work, she said, "Murdoch is relentless in manipulating her characters. What they think of as contingency is really Iris's authorial hand. Pushing them."

"Very true," he said. "She wants, ultimately, to prove other people exist."

"Who thinks they don't? Do you?"

"I think you exist and that's very nice."

They continued their conferences every Friday.

Warren had met and married his clever wife Ruth in graduate school. They had gotten their PhDs at the same time and, despite the odds against it, they had each landed teaching jobs in the English department of the same university. Now at forty-four, they were both tenured and free to relax, to write their books and raise their girls. Life with no stress. Sex had become a biweekly habit, and romance a matter of asking how the new book was going. They had a good academic marriage.

These days Warren was much more cheerful with his family—he kissed Ruth at the breakfast table, he roughhoused with the twins, he teased Megan about her boyfriends—but at work, teaching, he was constantly distracted and given to apologizing whenever he disagreed with a student. He had begun to stutter. He sometimes paused in his lectures and muttered, But what do I know?

What he knew was this: he was falling in love with Nicola Mantis and feared it might be true love at last.

Warren told himself that he recognized the danger of becoming that cliché: the middle-aged professor laid low by a student half his age. But, he knew, this was different. This was the real thing. Nicola was a splendid young woman. Short black hair and green eyes and those legs, of course. Perhaps her chin was a trifle strong, but she made up for that with a sly sexiness and an extraordinary self-assurance. Warren was in love with Nicola.

Nicola was not in love. Moreover she had no intention of being in love.

Breakfast this morning was french toast and everybody was happy about that. The twins, however, were at odds. Virginia wanted to start wearing a bra and she was playing her father off against her mother. Vanessa didn't care about bras. She was doomed to be flat chested and accepted her fate. Besides, she wanted to be a writer when she grew up and you didn't need boobs for that.

"But I need a bra," Virginia said. "Look." She puffed out her chest.

"Must we?" Warren said. "At breakfast? You're too young for a bra. You should talk to your mother. Privately."

Ruth said, "I agree. It's time for a bra, Virginia. A bra is fun when you're young."

"You should enjoy your youth," Warren said, "without bras."

Megan joined them at table, late as usual. "I'm enjoying my youth with a bra." Only yesterday she had gotten two compliments on her new breasts. "Nice rack," Billy Dillon had said as he brushed against her at their lockers. And later, in the copy room, her English teacher— "Hands" Hawley—touched her on the shoulder, casually, and said he liked her sweater very much. He made an appreciative sound deep in his throat. In fact Mr. Hawley often mentioned how nice she looked. Now, at breakfast, Megan said, "A bra makes you feel your sexuality."

"Megan!" Warren said, and Ruth said, "That too, of course."

Vanessa poked Virginia. "See what you started?"

"I wasn't the one that said *sexuality*," Virginia said.

"Sex is going to be central to my life," Megan said.

Ruth said, "But not today, I hope. Not this morning."

And Megan said, "You'll all just have to deal with it."

"Good Christ," Warren said.

Megan was a little bit in love with Mr. Hawley but she knew that this was not news for the breakfast table.

Friday afternoon in Warren's office. Nicola gave Warren a quick kiss and set down the duvet. She had questions about Murdoch and her blatant manipulation of character but Warren wanted to talk about his family.

"'Sex is a central part of my life,' Megan said this morning at breakfast. She's fourteen! And the two little ones, the twins, want to start wearing bras. At age ten, can you believe it?"

"I believe it."

"Well, to be fair, they're going on eleven."

Nicola had heard enough of this kind of thing from previous lovers to recognize where it was going. The end of the road.

"And then there's Ruth," Warren said.

"Ruth, yes." Nicola locked the door. "Let's get down to it."

Together and separately they shed their clothes. She folded hers neatly on the desk. He threw his in a pile on the floor. Ready.

Afterward—and it had been barely satisfactory—Warren was the first to speak. "Ruth," he said. "She's a terrific mother and I have to admit she's a devoted wife but…"

All married men are the same, Nicola thought. This fling has to end.

Megan was a features reporter for the school newspaper and—lucky Megan—she got the job of interviewing Mr. Hawley for the winter edition. She asked the usual questions about where he was from, where he had gone to college, how he came to be a teacher of English, and what he liked most about his job. The interview went well and, when Megan ran out of questions, Mr. Hawley thanked her and stood up, brushing hard against her front. He apologized. She said she didn't mind. He stood there for a minute, and then he put his hands gently on her breasts and, making that hard sound low in his throat, he said, If only you were eighteen, Megan. She blushed and murmured, Thank you, Mr. Hawley. Then, reluctantly, he turned and left the room. Megan clutched her papers to her chest, glad, and only a little frightened.

Another Friday afternoon and they were lying side by side on the duvet, recovering.

Nicola said, "This little fling has got to end."

"We should get married," Warren said.

"We were only in this for the fun. You agreed."

"But this is better than fun. I'm in love with you...."

"You've gone serious. It's over."

"I can be serious and still be fun. Look how much fun I am." He held up his penis, at the ready again, but Nicola was not interested.

"I'll explain this for the last time, Warren. Without irony."

This was the problem. She knew all she wanted to know about family life. She had enjoyed many uncomplicated affairs with men and women that had led her to conclude that sex was fine, and so too was a good emotional relationship that did not include sex, but, listen please, please understand, affairs with married men, especially when they have families, simply never work out. Period. Postscript: this means you, Warren!

She blurted this out as they lay, naked, on the floor of his office.

Warren listened in silence, half-crazed, reckless.

There was, of course, a knock at the door.

"Come in," Warren said.

The doorknob jiggled. "It's locked."

"You'll have to come back later. I'm taking an important call."

"How much later?"

"How about never?"

Footsteps retreated down the hall.

"Well, aren't you the cool one," Nicola said.

"But I was planning to marry you. I was planning to leave my wife. And my family."

"I'm getting dressed. I have a reputation to maintain."

"We could start a new life."

"Get dressed. Get off the duvet."

"Just the two of us."

"And an ex-wife with alimony and four children to educate."

"Three."

"You should get dressed. Now."

"I like being naked in my office. I like living dangerously. I think I've discovered the real me."

"I think you've lost your mind. Get off the duvet."

"It's part of the fun."

"Get up. The fun is over."

"Lie down with me and be my love and we shall all the pleasures prove."

"This is it," she said. With one great yank, she pulled the duvet from under him and he went sprawling, hard, against the bookcase. Several comic novels tumbled to the floor. She ignored the mess and rolled the duvet in a tight little bundle. "This is it," she said, again, *fini*. She scooped up her books and papers, slung the duvet over her right shoulder, and shrugged everything into place. She turned for a last look at him.

Warren was suddenly aware that he was naked and covered his privates with his hands. Then, feeling foolish, he uncovered them.

"Have a nice day," she said as she unlocked the door. "I had hoped we could end this in a dignified manner but I can see you have no sense of occasion."

"Murdoch is a closet Christian!" he shouted after her. He felt a complete fool.

A period of freakish weather had broken out. Days of perfect sunshine were spoiled by sudden bursts of rain. Warm days followed close upon cold ones, and at dusk there were winds that blew dust in everyone's eyes and turned a pleasant walk into a fight against nature. Everyone complained, but that's just how things were.

Ruth was deep into the final draft of her book, "Speechless: The Shock of the Transcendent in the Novels of Virginia Woolf," and so she hadn't noticed Warren's new indifference, nor did she mind that they had missed their customary lovemaking several times running. Life was good. Their marriage was good. The girls were doing fine— at least they seemed fine—and in any case they had to learn from their mistakes.

Ruth didn't worry about her girls, but now that she thought about it, she was worried about Warren. Sweet old Warren, her steady, loving husband. He was good, he was reliable. Then why was she worried? He was distracted these days. Was he developing a stutter? Out of nowhere it came to her that Warren might be having an affair. On Fridays. While she taught her Woolf seminar. She was ashamed for entertaining such a thought. Besides, she couldn't think of any of her friends he might have an affair with... or who might have an affair with him. However, Warren was still handsome at forty-four. She knew men got restless in their forties. And they carried age better than women. Men went gray and looked distinguished, whereas women... She went to the mirror and examined her hair. Mousy brown, but no gray yet. Still, it was time she did something with it. The french twist she'd worn for twenty years was easy to care for, but it made her weak chin appear weaker. Her blue eyes were fading to gray. She looked hard into the mirror. She was developing lines around her mouth that made her look severe.

"I am a severe woman," she said, with lots of *e*'s in *severe*.

She made a quick inventory:

Her frown lines were becoming permanent.

She often neglected to put on lipstick.

Her face was a catalog of failures.

She turned away from the mirror.

But this was just silly. She put the whole thing out of her mind. Nonetheless, she made an appointment with Hair by Helene for the next Thursday.

Warren and Nicola had never actually got around to a critique of her ideas on Iris Murdoch, but her seminar paper on *The Black Prince* appeared outside his office early on the date it was due, a Friday. A bitter Friday for Warren. Since their last, fatal encounter he had phoned her and left messages, all of them unanswered, and he had put notes in her department pigeonhole, and he had actually gone to her campus residence hall and stood outside hoping to run into her. By accident.

He stood there, gaping, until the faculty resident, Fats Colby, came by and asked if he needed help. "We all need help," Warren said in his new reckless way, adding, "How about yourself, Fats? You look to me like you could use some help." Professor Colby made a mental note that Warren, a likely stalker, deserved watching. Warren went home to give Nicola's seminar paper a good critical read. Not hostile exactly. But rigorous.

The paper, "Family Dynamics in *The Black Prince*," was full of compelling insights on family life in academe. The characters in Murdoch seemed to be alive and well on this very campus, "writing, teaching, fornicating," as Nicola wrote, "with little passion and wanton indifference." Her main point seemed to be that Murdoch manipulated her characters the way that God—she actually cited God—manipulated his characters. Murdoch, she concluded, was a closet Christian.

Warren reread the paper and wrote on the cover page, "Please see me in my office about your grade for the course." He would give her one more chance.

Ruth looked in the mirror at her new short hair and was giddy with pleasure. The mousy brown had been softened with blond highlights and cut at chin level so that her face was framed with this new silky bob that moved gently with the movement of her head, just like in television advertisements. Her chin looked stronger, the lines in her face had disappeared, she was almost beautiful. She told Megan and the twins not to say anything until their father had a chance to be surprised. It was thrilling to look young again.

Warren came home furious that he had been caught lurking outside Nicola's dormitory and so he compensated with hugs for Megan and the twins, a quick kiss for Ruth, and a brisk air of joy at being again with his family. They responded with silence.

"What?" he asked.

"Look at Mother," Virginia said.

Vanessa said, "What is the matter with you, Daddy?"

Megan said nothing, but her heart clenched like a fist.

"Your hair," Warren said. "What happened to your hair?"

Ruth had much experience in the close reading of a text. It was clear her husband was having an affair.

An ultimatum: "One more note, one more e-mail, one more phone message," Nicola said, "and I'll go to your wife and tell her everything."

That night Warren phoned her and Nicola said, "I warned you," and abruptly hung up. The next morning she made an appointment to see Ruth during her office hours. She arrived early, while Ruth was lecturing her class on the subversive heroines of nineteenth-century lesbians. Nicola sat in on the lecture, dazzled, indeed stricken, by this extraordinary woman.

"Your lecture was absolutely brilliant," Nicola said. "And you're so beautiful!" She remembered suddenly why she was here. "How could Warren be such a fool!"

Ruth said nothing.

"Forgive my gushing, Professor, but you're a revelation. You are! You're brilliant! And he never said how beautiful you are!"

Ruth was pleased, despite herself. And she was relieved to see that Nicola was no beauty. She was, in fact, plain. Ruth smiled and remained silent. Let the girl grovel.

"I came here to tell you about Warren and ask you to make him stop, but I see now he must be crazy... to leave a wife like you."

"Leave a wife like me," Ruth said, biting down on her words.

Nicola was stunned by Ruth's speaking voice, soft and rich, so different from the full-throated voice of her lectures.

"And your voice! It's like a musical instrument. Warren must be off his head. He said you were attractive, but I... Well, anyhow, it's over. It was meant to be just a harmless fling, with no strings attached."

"No strings. Only me and his three daughters. And his whole life."

"That's exactly what I told him. What a woman you are! You understand these things."

"I do understand," Ruth said, fury rising in her throat. "But do you understand I could destroy you?" She let this sink in. "Do you have any idea how easily I could end your career?" She let this sink in as well. "I could make sure you never get a job anywhere. Or even get your PhD. I'm not just Warren's wife, you see. I'm the next dean of Humanities." This was not true but Ruth knew it would be effective.

"It was meant to be just harmless fun," Nicola said again.

Ruth took a deep breath and let it out slowly. She piled her books and papers to indicate this meeting was over. "There will be plenty of time for me to decide your future," Ruth said.

Nicola did not take this as the threat it was. Instead, she said, "This is probably not the best time to ask, but would it be okay for me to sit in on your lectures?"

Ruth choked on her rage. Speechless.

"Lesbians are one of my interests," Nicola said.

"I'll see you dead first," Ruth said.

Warren continued to send Nicola e-mails and notes and leave her phone messages. He was crazy, he knew, but he was in love and his life was torture. He looked at his family and wondered, Who are they? Who am I? He was dying some terrible death, he felt, they were all dying. He blamed the constant rain. But he was wrong: the rain was not constant. There was no constancy left in nature.

Meanwhile Ruth brought to her lectures a new, vibrant energy. Word had got around about these hot new classes, and graduate students from Comp Lit and Classics and Sociology asked permission to audit. The presence of all these young excited students lent Ruth a new authority and she found she no longer cared about Warren's betrayal. She was more interested in what she was discovering about lesbian sexuality, and her own sexuality and, of course, about Nicola Mantis, who had interpreted Ruth's dismissal as permission to attend her lectures. She made Ruth her confidante in this business of getting Warren out of her life. They took long walks in the rain.

———

Nicola, desperate, went to the campus police and requested a restraining order against Warren. This very nice policeman, Officer Giroux, suggested that Nicola should first let him have a firm word with Warren and see what happened. His firm word with Warren was effective—the messages stopped—and, as a concerned policeman, Officer Giroux phoned Nicola to follow up on her case and inquire about how she was doing. His call was warm and caring and Nicola found him *très sympathique*. She phoned him back the next day to ask if he would join her for a coffee. Just to say thank you. Officer Giroux was a happily married man, with two young sons, one of whom was autistic and thus a constant source of pain and anxiety for him. He was glad for a short reprieve. "Sure!" he said, "what time?" They met that afternoon. They enjoyed their talk and they had a second coffee. Nicola found Officer Giroux witty and intelligent, even handsome in a refreshingly nonacademic way. They became good friends at once. Just friends.

A week passed and Warren remained crazy but quiet.

Nicola confided all this to Ruth since, after all, they were both victims of Warren's treachery. With her cold eye, Ruth contemplated her own relationship with Nicola Mantis and concluded the girl was dangerous but delightful, with a quality of innocence that was totally unexpected, given her past history with Warren and her present entanglement with Officer Giroux. Ruth would never trust her, though she could see how Warren had been stricken by her. And then the handsome policeman, stricken also. To be honest, Ruth was a little stricken as well.

Months passed. The unpredictable weather unfolded with complete disregard for the television experts, who grew visibly cranky, even on air. Life for Warren was uneventful, except for his new, enforced silence as he resigned himself to the loss of Nicola Mantis, and apparently to the loss of his wife. And perhaps his family as well. He was surly and uninterested and his teaching was very poor.

For Officer Giroux, however, these months were eventful indeed. He had told his wife he was leaving her and the two boys to start a new authentic life with Nicola Mantis, if only he could persuade her. His wife replied that she would sue him into poverty, and, like a member of one of those girl gangs, she'd take a razor to Nicola's face. And he knew her. She'd do it.

The time was eventful, too, for Ruth, who seemed younger every day, and now totally committed to her new field of lesbian studies, perhaps a consequence of her scandalous romance with Nicola Mantis. She made no effort to conceal it, though she was deeply embarrassed when Vanessa and Virginia came to her office to get lunch money and walked in on their mother and Nicola, engaged in what was clearly more than a conference. Vanessa made an entry on *l'amour fou* in her new *Writer's Notebook* that night. It rained again, she noted, and a sudden fog had descended on them. She had been carefully recording the weather.

These months were especially eventful for that same Nicola Mantis, who found herself now at the center of a sexual tornado, when all she had wanted was a little fling, just for fun, no strings attached. She was hopelessly in love with Warren's wife. And with Officer Giroux, of course. And who knew what would happen next?

Time speeded up, and it was impossible to respond to one disaster before another took its place. And always now, there was the weather.

Life and nature were out of joint.

Mr. Hawley—"Hands"—was arrested for sexual molestation one morning, immediately following his class on *A Midsummer Night's Dream*. The victims were two girls in his advanced placement class. Though they had not lodged a complaint against him, their parents had. Mr. Hawley appeared on the evening news, in handcuffs, but by the next day his devoted wife had bailed him out. School administrators were outraged. Counselors were made available for all the students.

No bacon and eggs this morning; breakfast was cold cereal. Ruth had lost interest in cooking and, besides, all of them—even the twins— were preoccupied with the sensational news about "Hands" Hawley.

"It's outrageous," Warren said. "A child molester in our school system. How was he ever appointed in the first place? Did you know him, Megan? Did you know about him?"

Megan mushed her Cheerios with her spoon.

"Wasn't he your English teacher last year?" Ruth asked. "Or was it this year?"

"Sweetie? Did he ever... you know... approach you?"

"Your father means did he ever touch you... unnecessarily?"

"Megan says he's cute," Virginia said.

"And sexy," Vanessa said. Vanessa loved learning the new terms for these things. "Megan says he's hot."

Megan pushed her fist against her cheek so as not to cry.

"Megan?"

"I love him," Megan said, tears falling into her Cheerios. "He would never hurt anyone. He's very gentle."

"What do you mean, he's gentle?"

"Good God!"

The twins fell silent. Warren and Ruth exchanged looks and, together in this, they sent the twins upstairs to get ready for school. Vanessa said, "We understand, you know," and Virginia said, "It's on the news, even," but they left the room as they were told. "We miss everything," Vanessa said, lingering.

Warren cleared his throat. The inquisition that followed revealed that—according to Megan—Mr. Hawley had only complimented her on her sweater and said he wished she were eighteen. He had never touched her. He was very gentle and polite. The parents pretended to believe her.

"You're a good girl, Megan, but you can't go falling in love with grown men. You'll only get hurt."

"And he's twice your age," Ruth said. "Listen to your father. He's an expert on these things."

Late morning and they were still fighting. Their concern for Megan had turned almost at once into blame and accusation until finally Ruth called Warren a hypocrite and a liar and Warren rose to the challenge and shouted, It's impossible to talk with you! Your blindness. Your arrogance. Your Woolfian superiority. No wonder I had a love affair. You drove me to it. He stopped to catch his breath. But he had unleashed the months of coddled rage Ruth had masked as indifference.

Now she denounced him, his hurts and betrayals, his months of deception. He was a liar and a traitor with his comic novels and James fucking Joyce, and how—*how*—could he have hurt her this way with a student half his age, for God's sake, and people knew, everybody knew.

Then suddenly she was done. She had resisted the impulse to cry, but Warren broke down and cried for both of them, begging forgiveness. The affair meant nothing, he said, it was just a fling, and he was sorry. She was right, he was a hypocrite and a liar. He was a selfish pig. But he wanted to start over. It was family that mattered. He was so sorry.

Ruth let him go on saying he was sorry, begging forgiveness, humiliating himself, and she said nothing. She felt no guilt for her own duplicity in this matter.

About this time, the sky began to darken and Ruth turned on a lamp. It threw an interesting shadow across her face, and Warren felt something important was about to be revealed to him.

"We have to pretend this never happened, Warren. For the children." Her voice was oracular. "But from now on you'll sleep on the couch in your study. And we'll never talk about this again."

In this way they achieved what looked like peace.

Weeks passed. Gloom. Depression. Ruth's silence was terrible and the tension grew daily more oppressive.

Megan was eating less and less. Ruth took notice but said nothing.

From time to time Warren would try to say he was sorry, but Ruth merely held up her hand, palm toward him, and said nothing.

The twins began to act up. Their homeroom teacher asked to see the parents and, after a futile half hour of talking at cross-purposes, she recommended that the girls see a therapist. The parents might want to see one at the same time.

Warren said, "This has to stop. Now!"

Ruth smiled at him, coldly. She was happy with Nicola.

Megan's student counselor phoned Ruth and asked her to come for a meeting. Megan was clearly anorexic and something should be done. Ruth said, Thank you, they would consult a doctor.

The doctor recommended a therapist.

The twins set fire to a bush next to the back porch and nearly burned down the house.

"You don't care about us anyway," Virginia said.

Vanessa said, "All you care about is Nicola Mantis."

Warren took a deep breath. So even the kids knew.

But Ruth clarified the situation for him: Vanessa was not referring to Warren's affair with Nicola. *Au contraire*. Ruth had taken up where Warren left off, and she was having a very satisfying affair with Nicola, at least for now. There were, on Ruth's part, no strings attached. Warren was speechless. He was living with a criminal.

More time passed, a time of ugliness and sorrow that was mirrored in the cruel weather.

For the twins' birthday Ruth made a special afternoon treat with peppermint tea and chocolate éclairs. They invited two friends but they were busy with other things.

"Was it a nice birthday?" Ruth asked.

"I liked it better when you and Dad were friends," Virginia said.

Vanessa said, "I liked it better when you didn't hate each other."

Megan lost more weight. She fainted in gym class. The parents were notified that Megan had a medical problem and perhaps a psychological one as well.

There were tears at every meal.

Nicola phoned Ruth to say that Warren insisted they meet at the college cafeteria, on the outside patio where they could have privacy. Nicola said she was bringing Officer Giroux for protection. Ruth protested that she was not going to be left out, since, after all, she was the major injured party here.

They gathered at the same time, not by accident, since the two couples—Warren and Ruth, Nicola and Officer Giroux—had been keeping watch so as not to be the first to arrive. They shook hands and Warren introduced himself to Officer Giroux, who said, "Call me Luke, please." It was all very civilized. They ordered coffees and for a long time sipped in silence.

Officer Giroux broke the silence with the information that his heart was broken.

Warren said, "Forget about hearts, my whole life is ruined."

Nicola put a hand on the hand of each and said, "Poor babies."

"Nicola and I, however, are having a good time, at least for now," Ruth said.

Nicola looked at her, shocked. "For now?"

"No strings attached," Ruth said.

That was how they began, quietly. The denunciations and recriminations, the tales of broken vows and lies, lies, lies, occupied them for the rest of the long afternoon. Nothing was salvaged, nothing was resolved.

The dusk had obscured their thinking and finally they fell silent again. A wind began to blow and suddenly there was a chill in the air. The other people on the patio went inside, but the four injured lovers seemed unable to move. They sat there, waiting for whatever would happen.

The wind intensified and Luke Giroux said, "This could be dangerous."

"Yes," Warren said, and the women nodded in agreement.

Still, nobody moved.

This was not tornado season, nor was it tornado country, but a small, unimpressive tornado descended on the patio nonetheless. Papers began to fly everywhere, there was a roaring sound, and an overturned trash bin spilled its smelly contents into the air. A huge green canvas awning came loose from its anchors and raced across the patio. Tables fell over and chairs began to lift off and fly dangerously close to the four lovers. They lay their heads on the table and shielded them with their arms. This surely was the end. Eventually the roaring noise wound down and the dusk cleared and the wind let up.

They raised their heads and, dazzled, looked around at where they were. The patio was no longer littered with papers and trash, and even the flying chairs had been spirited away. What remained were ashes, ashes as minute as dust, ashes large as chunks of bone, and they were everywhere, carpeting the patio floor. A breeze came up, gentle and warm in the wake of the troubling storm, and it moved the ashes from place to place, as if they might mean something.

Suddenly, a poster that had survived the storm detached itself from the cafeteria wall and skittered across the patio to the four people sitting, mute, at the table. The poster announced the annual Kiss a Stranger under the Full Moon Festival.

Excitement!

A chance to make new friends!

Maybe even a new romance!

Fun! And it's all free!

Janet Gray was our next-door neighbor, and my parents seemed to think she was peculiar, so I did too. I was thirteen, and a spy, and I wanted to know everything about her. At first she didn't look peculiar to me. She looked like anybody else, except she always wore the same pink housedress, like an apron with sleeves, and she smoked cigarettes outside in the yard, and she had a pale, frightened face. She was younger than my parents but she looked older. She would be attractive, my mother said, if she'd just fix her hair and put on some lipstick. Janet's husband, Lester, drove a delivery truck—Gray's Foods—and he periodically went on drunken binges. He was fat and balding, with a powerful beer belly that gave him a stumbly walk. They had a three-month-old baby, Marian, who never cried or screamed or carried on, so I wondered about her too. Very soon I learned that Janet was an abused wife. A new idea, "abused." I had read about such things in the newspaper and heard about them on the radio, but they didn't happen on Garby Road. So it was exciting, and awful, to imagine the Grays' mysterious lives.

I spied on them from my upstairs bedroom window and I lingered on their back porch when I delivered the evening newspaper. I was thirteen and I wanted to know and to know.

The Grays had moved here a couple years ago. Nothing dramatic ever happened on Garby Road, so a few days after the Atlas van pulled away, even before anybody had had a chance to welcome them, we were all astonished to wake up around midnight to the sound of a police siren. An ambulance, my father said, it must be old Al Burroughs, but my mother said only police use a siren in the middle of the night so it must be them. One or the other, my father said, let's get some sleep, and my mother said, I'll find out tomorrow.

The next afternoon my mother baked a cake and around dinnertime she went next door to welcome Janet Gray. The back porch was glassed in, a sort of room by itself, and my mother waited outside. The porch was a mess of moving boxes and golf equipment and empty beer cases, so my mother decided to make this a quick visit. It seemed a long time before Janet came to the door.

"Yes?" Janet said.

My mother introduced herself and said she figured Janet was still getting settled and must be short of time, so "I've brought you a cake I baked for you. To welcome you to the neighborhood."

Janet made no move to invite her in. "What's this about?" she said. "I'm kind of busy."

"It's a cake," my mother said. "It looks a little lopsided, I guess, but anyway it's homemade." She was staring at the red bruise on Janet's cheek.

Janet raised her hand to her face and said, "I bumped into the cabinet door. I'm clumsy."

"But you're all right? It's just a bruise?"

"I'm always bumping into things." Janet kicked at an Atlas Movers box. "It's getting late and the baby…"

"Of course, of course, the baby. I just dropped by to say I hope you'll enjoy it here, Janet. It's a nice neighborhood." She held out the lopsided cake. "And I hope you enjoy the… it's chocolate."

Janet took the cake without looking at it and said, "Lester will be home any minute. You shouldn't be here."

My mother was embarrassed, but she gave Janet a warm smile and said, "I'd better go."

As she was about to make her getaway, a truck came roaring up the driveway, slammed to a stop, and Lester—the husband—got out. He was carrying a case of Budweiser in one hand and in the other a ratty bouquet of flowers. He was not happy. "That fucking foreman," he said. "He wanted me to make a late delivery. I told him where he could shove it." He tossed the Budweiser on top of a case of empties and thrust the flowers at Janet. "Here," he said, "on account of last night. Sorry." He looked at my mother with suspicion. "Who are you supposed to be?"

My mother, still unnerved at hearing someone actually say the *F* word out loud, found herself speechless.

"And what's this?" Lester asked. "A cake?"

"I baked it to welcome you...."

"Are you one of those nosy neighbors? Yes? Are you the one that called the cops?" He leaned into her. "That's some kind of welcome. And then you show up with a cake? Well, we don't want your fucking cake." He took the plate from Janet and, in one quick movement, he tipped the cake into an empty Atlas box and handed the empty plate to my mother. "Thank you. It was delicious," he said, and to Janet, "Now, get inside, you."

My mother came home and we had dinner. My father asked my brother, Charlie, about football, and he asked me what I was reading these days, and when he got to my mother, she said, "I visited the Grays this afternoon. I'll tell you later."

"Oh?" my father said.

"Yes," she said. And that night after I was in bed she told my father everything, including the *F* word. "He actually brought her flowers," and then my mother lowered her voice. "An abused wife."

I kept my door open a crack, eavesdropping, and in the morning I wrote it all down. Whenever I got to a place I couldn't remember, I thought really hard and, if I still couldn't remember, I made it up.

This is a story about Janet Gray, and about me, and about how we came to misunderstand one another. My brother, Charlie, comes into it, and my parents of course, but they all have minor roles. Charlie was a senior in high school and he played quarterback on the football team. He was very popular. His whole life was spent getting ready for college and hanging out with guys his own age and dating girls. He had little interest in me and even less in Janet Gray. My parents were nice people who worked hard and mostly kept to themselves.

When I first met Janet, she talked all the time about boredom and loneliness, adult things. I didn't mind because I had already failed at being a normal teenager. My emotional life was a mess. I wanted to be first in everything and at the same time I didn't want anyone to notice me, never mind the contradiction. I was interested in books, not sports, and I had no neighborhood gang to hang around with. I lived mostly in my imagination. I hated being thirteen.

And I hated delivering newspapers. My paper route stretched from the cemetery at one end of Garby Road to the highway at the other. It was a long country road that meant a lot of walking and a lot of wasted time that I could have spent reading. Delivering papers was the worst. I was embarrassed at that *Sentinel* bag slung over my shoulder, afraid that someone from school might see me. I was embarrassed to make Wednesday night collections, stopping at each house with my hand out for the eighteen cents delivery money. I was embarrassed at taking the school bus. The problem was simply sociological, I told myself. The baby boom following the war had produced on Garby Road a pack of kids who were either in their late teens like Charlie or just babies like Marian next door. There was nobody my age. I was alone and I was skinny.

School was fun, except for math and science… and not fitting in. The other kids considered me smart because I had skipped a grade, but that only made me feel freaky. Nobody bullied me—there wasn't much bullying in those days—but they made it clear I didn't belong. I was one of those kids who was friendless and knew it. I pretended not to care.

So I read. The Thornton Burgess books, the Lone Ranger books, the Hardy Boys. Then I read the books in our living room bookcase: *David Copperfield, Robinson Crusoe, Wuthering Heights,* and others I couldn't half-understand. The more I read, the more I wanted to be a writer and tell stories. I knew that writing was supposed to be hard and you had to be willing to rewrite, but I discovered that I liked to rewrite. It surprised me that you could tell a story in different ways—you could even change the facts—and make it more interesting. I wrote every day in my journal, and the more I wrote, the more I found to say about Janet Gray.

Lester continued to keep us at a hostile distance but, while he was away at work, Janet made tentative gestures of friendship toward my mother. She would stand in her backyard and talk across the line of shrubs that separated our houses. At these times Janet was lethargic, sloppy even, smoking her cigarettes and complaining about the baby's colic and the boredom of married life and the simple fact that there was nothing to do here. Read a book, read *Gone with the Wind*, my mother would say, read *Forever Amber*, or take Marian for a walk. Well, no, Janet said. Or, Well, yes. Or, Well, what can anyone do about it? and she'd let out a short, barking laugh and shake her head in resignation. Poor soul, my mother would say at dinner. She's not very bright.

During one of these chats, while Janet stood there smoking and my mother knelt, weeding the flower beds, she realized she had not seen Janet's baby in some time.

"How is the baby doing?" she asked. "Is she over her colic?"

"What baby?"

"Your baby, of course. Marian."

"Oh, that baby's gone," Janet said, her voice flat.

My mother stood up and looked at her. "Gone where?"

"She died."

"You can't be serious, Janet."

"It was a crib death. One morning she was just dead."

"Janet! Janet, I'm so sorry." She did not know what to say and she could not understand Janet's indifference and so she babbled on. "You must be distraught. She was such a good baby. And sweet. This is terrible. When did it happen?"

"She didn't suffer much. It was a quick death."

"Oh, Janet!" my mother said, stricken.

"I don't want to talk about it."

My mother looked long at Janet. "I don't know what to say." She turned away, slowly, and went inside the house. She had a fever—this was too much to grasp—and she lay down for the rest of the afternoon.

That night, before bed, she told my father what had happened.

I wrote it all down without changing any of the facts.

A month passed before we saw Janet again. One evening when I delivered the paper, she met me on the glassed-in porch, cigarette in hand, ready for one of our talks. She leaned against the door as if nothing had changed and asked how my brother was doing as quarterback. And how I was doing at school. And if my parents ever talked about her. The old Janet was back.

As the year went on she began to ask about my girlfriends, she thought I must have lots of them, she said I'd better be careful. She gave that short barking laugh.

Eventually she got onto the subject of Lester, telling me how they married because she was expecting and how she lost the baby— an earlier crib death, it happened years ago, she didn't want to talk about it—and now she was afraid of him because he drank so much, and sometimes he got violent when he drank. And then he'd attack her. His fists against her face, her stomach, her breasts.

She put her hands on her breasts and said, Do you know what a good beating is like? Do you? No, you're too young. You think life is easy. Besides, you're too smart to get caught like this. Married. In a trap. She talked faster, she was excited. But now listen to me! Listen! You can't tell this to anybody, especially not your mother and father. Promise me you'll never tell.

I was thirteen. I promised not to tell. And Janet told me everything.

First of all, Lester was only the nephew of Gray's Foods, he didn't own the company. He was hardly family at all. He had started out in management with old Upton Gray, but after a while, when he didn't do so well, he was demoted to sales and eventually to deliveries. He stayed in charge of deliveries until they noticed his drinking and, after his second DUI, he was pushed to the end of the line where he worked now as a driver. The older Grays had kept him on the job because, though he was only a nephew, he was still a Gray. It was the Upton Gray who owned Lester's house and they were the ones who periodically bailed him out of drunk driving charges. Janet talked compulsively, piling these secrets on me as if she was trying to get rid of all the junk in her life. But there was always more.

"Promise me? You'll never tell?"

I promised not to tell, but one night I asked her why she didn't leave him. He would kill her, she said, he'd get crazy drunk and find her wherever she went and he'd beat her to death.

"But you could get a divorce. You could go live in New York."

"He'd kill me. He would."

"Maybe you should fight back."

The sound of a truck coming up the drive. Lester. I had to get out of there in a hurry. I turned to leave and saw her cigarette tremble and fall from her hand; her face went white; she began to shake. She plucked at her housedress as if it were on fire.

"Go!" she said, "Now!" and I went.

Halfway down the front walk I heard Lester shout, "I told you, I don't want you talking to that little creep!"

He's right, I thought, heavy with secrets. I am a creep.

That night I wrote down our conversation in my journal and concluded, "Janet Gray is an abused wife, and a very disturbed woman, with problems both sexual and emotional. She should divorce her husband or maybe kill him. The two of them suffer from some kind of sexual dysfunction."

Dysfunction had been on yesterday's list in *Word Wealth*.

A year passed and Charlie went off to college and I started high school. The Proctor High kids came from three different grammar schools so they all felt uneasy and it didn't matter to anybody that I had skipped a grade. Nobody really knew me and in the confusion of the first weeks I was elected freshman class president, which meant that I was in charge of planning the Halloween hop and had to meet once a month with Student Council. To use up my free periods, I joined the school paper as a reporter. I still had no friends, but at least I was growing taller. I had shot up three inches during the past year and my pants were always too short, so I pretended I liked them that way. Back on Garby Road I was still delivering newspapers and was more embarrassed than ever.

"You're getting so tall," Janet said. "You're going to be as big as your brother."

"I hope so," I said. "I just turned fourteen."

"But you're thin, like your mother. Your brother is a hunk."

I turned red and shifted the newspaper bag to my other shoulder.

"Don't blush," she said. "It's good to be a hunk. It's sexy. You wouldn't believe it now, but Lester was a hunk when we married. We were in love then, I can tell you. We made love all the time."

"I've got to go," I said, annoyed, and glad for a moment that she was stuck with Lester, the former hunk.

Sometimes Janet would fiddle with stuff that had just come out of the dryer—the porch had been cleaned up and served as a makeshift laundry room—and she'd ask me to help fold things before Lester got home. Don't be embarrassed, she'd say, and she'd hold up her nightgown and I would flush red and say nothing. I thought, though, that if I were a little older and she a little younger—maybe ten years younger—this could look like a seduction.

I thought a lot about seduction. I secretly read Charlie's stash of *Playboys* now that he was in college pursuing the great unknown: a sex life. I myself was not ready for a sex life, despite being desperately in love with Amanda Fuller. Amanda was beautiful and very smart— she knew all about Italian opera and French film directors—and she was an atheist. Atheism was simply a reasonable choice, she said, once you've thought it through. Look: even if you accept the Adam and Eve story as a myth or a metaphor, you're still left with the notion of original sin, which is intellectually insulting. She found religion boring. And me, as well. I was a Catholic, so marrying Amanda would be a problem, but there was still the possibility—the necessity—of a sex life. Eventually. When I was ready. In fact, the whole sex enterprise, as I understood it, terrified me: getting naked in front of a girl, not knowing where to look, making the first move, whatever that should be. It was all horribly complicated and I was sure I'd make a fool of myself. Meanwhile I was regularly embarrassed by erections at the most awkward times: when I talked to girls or when I got called on in class or in the morning when my mother insisted I get out of bed, *now*, and there I was at full attention. Daily life was difficult, but it was made more so by this unmanageable thing attached to me.

Love and desire and Amanda Fuller. Time seemed at a standstill while I studied Latin and French and English. I wrote boring news stories for the school paper. I took art to fill up my second study period and I skipped phys ed whenever I could get away with it. Nothing happened.

Then one day in spring I ate lunch with Charlotte Smith and, with no preliminaries at all, Charlotte offered to teach me to dance. Charlotte was not as pretty as Amanda, but I was flattered, and learning to dance sounded promising. We walked together to her house and, when we got there, she explained that her mother was a nurse who worked afternoons so we would have the place to ourselves. Oh good, I said to her, learning to dance is not a public thing, and to myself I said, So, is this it? Is this the first step toward the great unknown? I felt ready. We danced for a while; or rather, Charlotte danced and I tried to avoid stepping on her feet, and then, because it seemed right, we kissed, and kissed again, and then we lurched to the couch and made out in a clumsy but satisfying way. We pretended, as if by agreement, that the erection solidly between us did not exist. At five, Charlotte's mother returned from work and, while Charlotte memorized the third conjugation, her mother drove me home to Garby Road. After that Charlotte and I frequently did our homework together, Latin and French, with periodic study breaks for "dancing," as we called it.

We were both Catholics and we knew that this was probably sin, but it didn't feel like sin, so we just enjoyed ourselves.

I was going on fifteen and I had a serious girlfriend.

Reading my notebook you'd think Janet Gray had withdrawn into the background of this story. And she had, in a way, although I saw her every evening when I delivered newspapers. She still told me things about Lester's drinking, how he threatened to kill her, and how she would fight back. The way you wanted me to, she said. In fact, I only wanted not to be involved. Worse than this, she would interrogate me about my girlfriends. I told her nothing, but she persisted; how many did I have, and who was the prettiest, and then she would joke about how sexy my brother was. What a hunk, she said. One evening she astonished me by saying, Lester loves me, you know, and I love him. He's a different kind of man. You should be more understanding, at your age. And another evening she said, Good lovemaking goes a long way in marriage. Remember that. I knew it was not just harmless talk. It was sexual provocation, and in a way I was intrigued by her. But I told myself to get real: she was just a lost and lonely—and abused—woman who enjoyed harmless flirting. And I had no temptation to tell anybody, far less my parents.

Then came the night Lester attacked Janet and she ran to our house for protection. It was 1953, on the day the New York Yankees won the World Series against the Brooklyn Dodgers.

Lester had asked the whole Gray clan to a baseball barbecue, and he had laid in many cases of beer and an array of steaks and sausages and chops. There were lounge chairs and two big beach umbrellas. He ran an extension cord from the house to the backyard and turned the radio up to full volume. He made sure everybody had a drink.

At our house everything was quiet. My father was reading *The Power of Positive Thinking* from the Book of the Month Club and my mother was listening to the radio. I was in the middle of *Great Expectations* and thoroughly bored.

A shout from next door. Billy Martin!

"Billy Martin," I said. "Even I know him."

Neither of my parents cared about Billy Martin.

"They're having a family reunion," my mother said. "I'd love to get a gander at that."

"Spare me," my father said.

"But it's probably nice for Janet that they're all together."

My father gave her a hard look. "With enough booze to float a ship," he said.

"Janet's alone all the time."

A loud burst of laughter from next door and my father said, "I'm afraid this won't end well for Janet."

"Don't say things like that," my mother said, "saying it makes it happen."

I put aside *Great Expectations*. My mother had said, I'd love to get a gander at that, and without telling her—frankly, I was ashamed—I went upstairs and stationed myself at my bedroom window for a few minutes of spying. It crossed my mind that I'd never tell Charlotte about this—my life was a clutter of secrets and lies—but then I settled down to enjoy a perfect view of the Grays' barbecue. Janet was dressed up in black slacks and a white blouse and I could see she was wearing lipstick. She looked young and pretty. There were a lot of people, maybe twelve or more, and some of the real old ones were stretched out on lawn chairs, but the ones who were my parents' age stood around talking and drinking. Every so often I could hear our name shouted and then Lester's roar of laughter and someone saying, "Not so loud! They'll hear you." My legs got stiff from crouching by the bed and I was glad when the game ended, Yankees, four, Dodgers, two.

My few minutes of spying had stretched out to an hour and then two hours. Next door they turned off the radio and the voices grew louder, but the sounds were just party sounds until suddenly I was surprised to hear my own name. It was Lester and he was saying, "The boy genius next door... the newspaper boy. He's president of his class and he's too intellectual for the rest of us and—are you ready for this?—Janet is his girlfriend." A lot of laughter, and then Janet said something I couldn't hear. I felt hollow inside, and sick. How did he know about me? "You oughta hear him... he's got this voice..." And he did an exact imitation of me, with that voice I hated. High and nasal, with precise enunciation. Lester roared, "He sounds like a girl, if you ask me!" I turned away from the window, ashamed, sick to my stomach. It's true that Miss Brown had tape-recorded me for speech class, and in her critique she said that if I worked on my voice exercises I would develop a lovely baritone but right now, despite my excellent enunciation, I sounded "raspy and unpleasantly nasal." I wanted to tell Miss Brown to go to hell, but I knew she was right, and I knew Lester's imitation was perfect. I lay down on my bed and covered my face with my hands, wishing I were dead.

At dinner we talked about *Great Expectations* and then I left to deliver my papers.

The Grays' cookout had broken up by now and the older ones had gone home. Lester and a couple men his age slouched in lounge chairs drinking beer straight from the bottle while Janet and one of the wives cleared away plates and cutlery. As I came up the drive Lester shouted, "Here he is, your boyfriend, the genius himself!" His friends laughed uncertainly, but Lester went on. "Tell us about your father, genius, tell us about his days on welfare. When me and my friends had to support him because he didn't have a job. The American taxpayers. That was before they got so high and mighty." He turned to his buddies. "They've got money now and they think they're better than everybody else." He floundered about for something else to say. "Some genius! His father never even went to college."

"Neither did you," Janet said in a brittle voice, and his two friends laughed.

There was a sudden silence.

"I went," Lester said. "I just didn't feel like staying."

"You were thrown out."

I stood, speechless, stupid, afraid for Janet, afraid he would attack her right here. Finally, in my deepest voice, I said, "Here's your paper, Mrs. Gray," and turned down the drive.

Lester went silent, but then I heard him say to Janet, "You can be brave now, you, but we'll see how brave you are when we're alone."

He was like a malicious child. He saw that she was broken and now he wanted her crushed.

It took me a long time to deliver my papers, and by the time I got home, it was quiet next door. The woman I'd seen helping Janet had left and now there was only Lester and one of his drinking buddies. I settled in to read Dickens, but all I could think of was Janet and Lester, alone. I went to bed.

I woke sometime later to Janet Gray's shrill voice downstairs in our living room. "He wanted to kill me," she was saying, "he tried to kill me," and my father kept saying, "It's over now, Janet. Shh. Calm. Everything will be all right." My mother made consoling sounds.

I knew instinctively that this was a time when I should stay out of sight. I crept down the stairs and huddled at the door to listen.

Janet continued to wail, only more softly now—my hand is broken, look at my fingers, he tried to kill me—but gradually my father calmed her down and she told him what had happened.

She had gone to bed expecting the worst, so she was terrified but not surprised when Lester came up the stairs shouting her name. As he stumbled into the bedroom, she slipped out of bed and into the closet, watching while he tore at the empty sheets. Where was she? He flicked on the light and looked around. Janet bolted for the door, but he grabbed at her as she tried to get by him, and he twisted her hand so that her fingers—look at them!—were bent back to her wrist. She tore away from him and he lunged at her but he lost his footing and crashed headfirst into the wall at the head of the staircase. He just lay there, barely moving. She ran down the stairs and out. But look at my fingers!

Quietly, I opened the door to see for myself what was going on. My parents were sitting forward on the couch, listening to Janet as she stood in the middle of the living room, barefoot and wearing only a nightgown. She was waving her arms about, and I could see that two fingers of her right hand—the index and the middle—were pointing backward toward her wrist. It was hideous. I got a pain behind my knees just looking at it.

"Mrs. Gray," I said, but my father put up his hand, the palm toward me—not now!—and I went back upstairs.

"You've got to see a doctor for that hand," my father said, "and you've got to call the police."

Janet insisted, mumbling, that Lester would kill her.

"In fact," my father said, "you've got to call the police, now, and they'll take you to a doctor."

"Not the police. I can't."

"Janet," my mother said. "He's gone too far. He *will* kill you."

"You've got to call," my father said, and my mother said, "You've got to."

Finally Janet was persuaded. She was barely coherent, but the police recognized her address and in a short time they arrived in two cars, one to take Janet to the hospital and one to take Lester to jail.

My father poured a glass of wine for my mother and a shot of brandy for himself. I had a Coke, and for the next hour we talked about the Grays' problems, openly, as if I were old enough to hear about an abusive marriage and responsible enough not to write it all down.

Three days passed. Lester and Janet were home, we knew, but nobody saw them. I dropped the paper at the door each night and got out of there quickly. I wasn't sure which one I most dreaded seeing, and I was doubly glad I had told the *Sentinel* I was quitting my paper route at the end of the month. I wanted to spend more time studying but mostly I wanted to be free of Janet Gray.

On the third night, when I dropped the newspaper at their door, I heard Lester and Janet fighting. Lester was drunk, I could tell, and Janet's voice was different. It was loud, for one thing, and it was defiant. I thought of my father saying, I'm afraid this won't end well for Janet. But tonight Janet seemed to be holding her own.

Nothing happened that evening. I practiced my French conversation, we listened to the radio, we went to bed. Toward morning, we were awakened by an ambulance and a police car pulling in next door. And not long after, while we were having breakfast, we were visited by an exuberant Janet Gray. Her right hand was in a plaster cast and she cradled it in her left.

"I'm sorry to break in on you, but I have to tell you." She was ecstatic. "Lester is dead and I'm just about the happiest woman in the world. Thank God, oh, thank you, God!"

My mother and father exchanged a look but neither said anything.

"Dead?" I wanted to be sure.

"Sit down, Janet," my mother said, "and let me get you some tea. Chamomile. It will settle you a bit and then you can tell us about this."

My father pulled out a chair for her but Janet ignored it and said again that she was happy that Lester was dead.

"How?" I asked. They all turned to look at me. "Well, how did he die? I want to know."

Janet told a story very much like the one from three days before. Lester was blind drunk and he had attacked her in bed but she had fought free of him. She ran from the room and he ran after her, and though he was drunk and fat and unstable, he cornered her at the head of the stairs. He slapped her face with his open hand, and when he pulled back to do it again, he struck the cast she held up to protect herself and he lost his balance and pitched headfirst down the stairs. It was all so quick. I barely touched him. And then he was dead.

We all listened, and when she finished talking, I looked at her and she looked back and for a moment we were all silent.

"You pushed him," I said.

"No," she said, "I just put my hand up to protect myself."

"Yes," my mother said, "of course," and my father said, "It was a terrible accident."

"I'm so happy he's dead," Janet said. "Thank God. Oh, thank God."

I decided to think it was an accident. Like those two crib deaths.

Eventually it was time for me to catch the bus and, reluctant, guilty, I left for school.

Janet remained happy and distraught until nearly noon when my mother was able to quiet her down and take her home and put her to bed with two sleeping pills. My mother checked on her throughout the day, and by late afternoon Janet was able to get up and take a hot bath and face her new life without Lester. As it happened, I was the first one she faced in her new life.

I opened the porch door and tossed the paper inside. Then, for no good reason, I waited to see if Janet would come pick it up. A moment later she opened the door a crack, looked at me, and opened it further. She was wearing only a nightgown.

"It's you," she said, and stepped out on the porch.

I didn't say anything. I only looked at her.

"What?" she asked and took a step forward. "Why are you looking at me like that?"

I was fifteen now, I had a girlfriend, and I knew what was right and wrong. I knew Janet was wrong. I did not know that I was still very young.

"I know," I said. "You pushed him."

"I don't want to talk about it."

"You pushed him down the stairs. I know."

"You know! You know! You think you're so smart. You think you know things, but you don't know anything." She grabbed me by the shoulders and shook me. "You told me to do it and now you'll ruin everything!"

She put her arms around me and pulled me close. I dropped my *Sentinel* bag. "Please," she said. She pressed herself against me, hard, and felt the erection I had hoped to hide.

"Oh," she said. "I get it now. I know you." She reached down and pressed her hand against my crotch. My whole body ached.

I was suddenly clearheaded. This was not like love with Charlotte. This was an unholy bargain. It was wrong, it was savage, and I wanted to do it. I was going to do it. I unbuckled my pants and Janet pushed them to my feet and, as if we were experts at this, we coupled there on the glass porch of her house, visible to the whole world and, should they have looked out the window, to my mother and father as well.

In a few short minutes it was over. "Now you'll never tell," Janet said and gave me a knowing smile. "That's the end of it."

"That's the end of it," I said, empty and numb.

But that was not the end of it. Many, many years went by before I could write down this last encounter with Janet Gray, and by then my tired brain was less sure about right and wrong, my memory had grown hazy on details, but one thing remained certain beyond all doubt: my unholy bargain with Janet Gray had left on my imagination—and perhaps on my soul—something more than the stain of a little original sin.

THE PRIEST'S WIFE:
THIRTEEN WAYS OF LOOKING AT A BLACKBIRD

1.   The priest and his wife were seen skiing together before they were married; or, rather, she was seen skiing and he was around, somewhere.

She took the lift to the slope reserved for advanced skiers. She was wearing a black parka and formfitting ski pants, also black. Her blond hair hung loose and straight.

Those who watched with binoculars from the deck of the lodge said it was an exercise in discipline. She allowed herself none of the indulgences of the advanced skiers. She plunged straight down vertical slopes, shooting off at an angle over horizontal ones, slaloming between invisible poles even when her momentum would have seemed to indicate certain disaster. She never shifted weight suddenly from one leg to the other. She never skidded, never fell. She crouched, swerved, straightened, her body always completely in control.

An exercise in grace, someone said. No one could take their eyes off of her and so no one was sure who said it. It may have been the priest.

Snow had begun to fall, so they all went indoors for hot buttered rum and a little fooling around by the fireplace. Every now and then somebody would look out the window and see her mounting once more that precipitous slope, and then the lightning descent, the perfect turn around the invisible poles.

Among twenty snowy mountains she was the only moving thing.

2.   After he met her the priest was of three minds regarding what he ought to do. After he watched her skiing on the slopes he was of one mind. He wanted to be a poet and write perfect love songs. For God, naturally. And then eventually perhaps for publication. And finally just to create a good thing. To make something. He was of one mind about that.

With such an attitude, it was inevitable that in time he left behind him the order, the priesthood, and—he sometimes thought—common sense. Burdened with an artist's drive and a priest's training, he did what anyone would do. He married her and became a teacher of high school English.

3.   She had a face like a woman in a novel. Her grandfather said that to her once when she was nine or ten, and it pleased her. It gave her an existence out there, in the real world, in a book.

She was Katharine Stone, age nine or perhaps ten, and she was called Kate. Her father was a psychiatrist and her mother was a psychiatric nurse; they employed a cleaning woman, a part-time gardener, and a part-time cook. These people, and her German shepherd, Heidi, were her serious world. Her play world was at school where nothing was serious, really, not for a girl who had a face like a woman in a novel.

When Kate grew up she scrutinized novels, old ones particularly, in an effort to discover what her grandfather had meant. When she grew up some more, she turned to psychology in an effort to discover which woman in which novel she might be. In time she came to know certain women well, in and out of novels.

Even though she knew she was not beautiful, she worried that she might be Anna Karenina, a woman she knew by instinct, a woman she feared. Anna, with her red leather bag, getting on the train at the beginning; Anna, with that same red leather bag, plunging beneath the train's wheels at the end. Why the red leather bag? Why the train? Surely Anna's fate was in some way connected to the fact of her face. Surely one day she would unravel what that mysterious connection might be.

Perhaps she should write a novel of her own, as Cora had told her. Perhaps she would someday. In the meantime she entered the convent. It was autumn, and as the sisters walked in twos from chapel to school, the wind caught their veils and whirled them about so that they flapped like the wings of blackbirds.

4. Cora Kelleher had been the cleaning lady for the Stones ever since Kate's birth. She had seen Kate Stone grow up plain and skinny, she had seen her enter the convent, and she had seen her come out ten years later, blond and beautiful. In jig time Kate had gotten herself a husband, a job with IBM, and had taken up skiing, would you believe. There was no sign Kate was pregnant or about to be. Cora herself had had seven.

"I don't see she's pregnant," Cora said to Eunice, the part-time cook.

"Who would that be, now?" Eunice said, moony as ever.

"Kate Stone, that was." She snorted. "The priest's wife."

"A lot of them today use the pill."

"A lot of them today use a lot of things."

"She's a beautiful girl, though." Eunice stopped peeling potatoes and gazed out the window dreamily. "And her a nun once."

"Her a nun and now that marriage. There's no luck on that marriage, let me tell you that."

"He teaches school," Eunice said, peeling again.

"Only high school. For all his priest education, he only teaches high school."

"She's a beautiful girl, though."

"Well, she was a plain stick of a thing when she was little. I remember once when she was no bigger than this, she says to me, giving herself airs, she says, 'Grandpa said I have the face of a woman in a novel.' 'And why is he telling you grand things like that?' I says. 'Because I asked him if he thought I was pretty,' she says. So I told her, I says to her, 'Well then, you'll have to write it yourself. There are no novels about skinny little things like yourself,' I says."

"Beautiful hair she has," Eunice said, peeling.

"She was always uppity. Another time, after her grandpa died, she said to me, all serious and with her eyes big, she says, 'I'm going to practice dying. Like Grandpa. I'm going to spend my whole life getting ready.' 'Are you, now!' I says to her. I says, 'Well, you're going to die anyway, ready or not, once it's your time.' Uppity she was and uppity she is."

"And her a nun once," Eunice said. "I could have been a nun once. Of course it's too late now." And she ran the water loudly, so Cora Kelleher had to shout.

"There'll be no luck on that marriage, you mark my words! A man and a woman are one thing. But a priest and a woman? It's like having a buzzard sitting right square on your tombstone."

5.   It had been one hell of a day for him at school. The kids had been maliciously thickheaded and they had talked all through his exposition of Yeats's "Second Coming." So what was the use? And in the two hours before Kate got home from her office, he had accomplished absolutely nothing. The poem simply wouldn't come right, he just didn't have it, he wasn't a poet.

"You are a poet," she said, "you're a wonderful poet. Why don't you let me take a poet to dinner? Anywhere you want. Or you take me. Either way I get to dine with a poet. Bewitching."

So they went out to dinner and afterward to a movie and by then he'd cheered up and they made love. Kate had office work to do but she kept quiet about it and, for his sake, pinched and poked him until he felt like doing it again. After the second time they lay, exhausted, staring at the ceiling.

"I'm going to take one more try at that poem," he said.

"Good for you," she said. "And I'm going to take a shower and fix you a nice drink—I won't disturb you—and then I'll go do a little work too."

He heard the water come on and the glass doors slide closed. She was being awfully good; she always was. And he knew what a bore he must be, what a pain in the ass about being a failed poet. And God knows, he didn't mean to rage; he just couldn't help it. He'd make it up to her and surprise her in the shower.

He opened the bathroom door softly, though there was no need for stealth since the water was running wildly. He was about to slide open the glass doors to the shower when he saw—as if in a film—the long line of her body, complete, perfect. She had her head back so that the water struck her full in the face. He traced the long neck to where it disappeared in the rise of her small breasts. And then the rib cage and her little belly and the long severe thighs. Perfection.

He sat down on the toilet seat, his head in his hands.

"Will I ever know her?" he whispered, and then again, "Will I ever know her?" He had folded that body so completely into his own so many times now during these past three years, and still he had never seen her... he could not find the words... her naked face. "I will never know her," he whispered, but already he was thinking something else. He was thinking, I will never be a poet. Never.

He left the bathroom, angry, and went to his little study off the kitchen. Kate had shopped everywhere to get him just the right desk and she had decorated the study according to his instructions, but still he never used it. His desk was heaped with books and papers, so there was no room to write. He wrote either at the dining table, which he also kept heaped with books, or sitting in his easy chair. "You don't need a study if you can't write anyhow," he had told her, though it was he who had insisted on the study in the first place.

He could hear her tiptoeing around the kitchen as she got his drink ready. How could he concentrate knowing she might interrupt him at any second? "I don't want to bother you but..." He sat there, daring her. She glided into the room in her soft slippers and placed the drink on a coaster near him, patting him twice on the shoulder.

"God dammit," he shouted, "I'm trying to write! Is there no place in this goddamned apartment I can work in peace?"

"I didn't say anything," she said, defensive, accustomed by now to these outbursts. "I just gave you your drink."

"You bumped me on the shoulder. You poked me twice. I was just getting it right and you interrupted and now it's gone." He looked at her with hatred and then took a good slug of his drink. "I'm sorry. I hate to sound like a bastard, but Jesus Christ!" He had been penitent for a second and now he was furious all over again. He slammed down the glass and the liquor sloshed onto his papers. "You always do this! You always ruin it! You always…" But she had gone. He followed her into the bedroom where she had her papers spread on the bed. She bent over the papers, not looking at him.

"Don't," she said. "Not again. I can't take it."

"Sometimes I detest you," he said. "Sometimes I curse the day I ever laid eyes on you."

She stared back at him in silence. And then she said, "Someday you'll say one thing too many. I give you warning. Now."

He backed out of the room. Several drinks later he woke her up. "Forgive me, sweet. Katie, forgive me, please," he said, and buried his head in her breasts.

"I know," she said. "It's all right. I love you."

"Friends?" he said.

"Friends," she said.

And so it was over, this time.

6.   They had been married five years now, and it was winter. Icicles filled the long window that looked out over the ruined garden. It was evening and shadows in the garden and shadows in the living room flickered as Kate moved back and forth in front of the light, watering the indoor plants. She wore a red gown, knotted at the neck and waist, and it created for her a mood in which she could feel withdrawn but not unpleasant. Her husband sat with his chin in his hands, watching her, watching the shadows she cast. He had just despaired, yet again, of ever being a poet. And besides, he had a terrible sore throat. And so they had their last fight.

It was about her habit of visiting her widower father, that bastard, every Saturday, and about her job at IBM. And it was about her way of being vague with him, as if what he said required only half her attention, as if he didn't really matter. And it was about his failure as a writer.

Five years of this and now, at last, she had had enough.

"I can't live your life for you," she said. "There are some things you've got to do for yourself. You've got to breathe, you've got to eat, you've got to crap, and God dammit, you've got to live. And if you hate your job, then do something about it. And if you resent mine, which you do, then why don't you..."

"Go ahead, say it! Say it! You've been wanting to."

But she didn't say it. She went to bed and he went to the kitchen for a drink. He had a second and a third and then he went in to wake her but she wasn't asleep yet anyhow. He apologized and she apologized and it was almost over.

Deliberately he looked at her hand. He had had a sort of vision once of who she was and how she loved him and it had split him down the middle. He had thought at the time that he had become two people, both of them crazy. And all because of her hand. She had placed it on his knee during a quarrel—afterward he could not remember what the quarrel was about—and he had watched it crumple and break like an autumn leaf, while his words continued angry and smooth and satisfying. In those days he had had all the words. And then, as the hand fell from his knee, he stopped and said to her, "I'm not a good person. I'm not like you." He cried then, and he had not cried in fifteen years. That was during the first week of their marriage.

Now, five years later, he sat on the edge of the bed looking at her hand, white and small with long, tapered fingers, trying to make it happen again, that vision.

But nothing happened.

"Friends?" he said.

"Friends," she said.

In bed, they both pretended to sleep. After a long while she got up and poured herself a drink and sat in the dark living room. She finished it and poured herself another. Then, not really knowing what she was going to do, she put on the light and got out a pencil and a legal pad and wrote, "I want out. I want a divorce." She stared at the words for a long time, and then she wrote them again. And then again. She found a peculiar satisfaction in forming the letters, in putting down on paper those words that finally said the unsayable. "I hate him. I hate what he turns me into. I hate the way he hates himself." She made a list of the things she could not say, and she said them. She wrote out their most violent quarrels, including in parentheses the words she had not said because they might kill him. ("You'll never be a poet." "You have a gift for words but no gift for poetry." "You're wrecking your life and you're trying to wreck mine, but I'm not going to let you." "Why didn't you stay in the priesthood and just drink yourself to death?") And it was astonishing. Words did not kill, at least not on paper. Rather, they gave her a wonderful feeling of release, of freedom. She got herself another drink and went on writing until, hours later, she had run out of things she was angry at. Without a pause she moved into a description of how she had first met him, her husband now, in the train station. The strap had broken on her red leather bag and he had offered to help her with it. But the bag was square, and with his hands occupied with skis and his own suitcase, he hadn't been able to get a good grip on it; he dropped it and it opened and spilled out keys and makeup and God knows what else. She had laughed at him then and he had laughed too.

She stopped writing—these notes, in time, would find their way into her first novel—and looked out at the garden where the sun was just touching the silver branches of the trees. A single blackbird lit on the end of a branch, making it bend, sending down a thin sifting of snow. Smiling to herself, she recited the Magnificat, as she had done every morning for the past twenty years.

And so the divorce was put off for eleven months.

7.   During those eleven months they often walked by the river together. And they often dined out. He appeared to be the more talkative but in public she did most of the talking. If the marriage was not a happy

one, they at least put a good face on it, and five years is a long time to put a good face on anything.

Acquaintances who had known them off and on for years said that marriage made them both merely conventional. His wild imagination and flights of whimsy disappeared altogether, replaced by a kind of watchfulness and a mildly sardonic humor. She talked politics a lot and, when the conversation turned to religion, she avoided discussion of how much she still believed, dismissing the topic with a remark about how bored she was with Sunday sermons.

Friends of hers who visited from the convent said the couple was supremely happy. She had taken to wearing high-fashion clothes, finding it necessary to be more feminine now that she had so many males directly responsible to her. She had a big job with big obligations. Friends of his who visited from the monastery said she had done wonders for him. He had put on weight and he was no longer so volatile. He had settled down to being a high school teacher; her big job with IBM obviously posed no ego problems for him.

They had private jokes and sometimes on the street they were caught laughing immoderately. They held hands at these times. They also held hands in restaurants, though not so frequently as on their walks. This was not natural in people married so long; it was probably a cover-up for something.

After eleven endless months they separated.

8. In the two years of their separation he had seven job promotions with his ad agency and she wrote two novels, both of them flops.

He had moved to New York, and by some fluke, or by talent, managed to put together a trendy portfolio. In no time he was making as much money as Kate, and by the end of the two years he was making a good deal more. He was happy and fulfilled, except of course that he missed her. He was a different man now. It was the writing that had made him so miserable. She'd see. Would she take him back? Would she agree to drop the divorce business and give the marriage another try? And, ahem, would IBM be willing to transfer her from her new job in Gaithersburg to a newer one in New York?

She smiled. She would think about it. But he'd better be clear on one thing: she was fiddling around with a novel and she didn't intend to give it up for anybody. Got that?

The first two novels had been mistakes, no doubt about it. She had begun with a description of their meeting in the train station, a nice, tightly written scene, but when read aloud it sounded so like a murder mystery that she decided to turn it into one. She killed herself off in the first chapter and then... well, it didn't work out. Her murders were clumsy and her murderers uninteresting; she was more preoccupied with psychoanalyzing the bereaved than with moving the damned plot along. Five publishers turned it down before she realized that it was a mistake, that she just didn't know anything about murders and she didn't care much either.

With the second novel she decided to stick to what she knew: life in a convent. She put in the mistress of novices and her more colorful teachers and her eager and ambitious nun friends, all of them meticulously drawn. She had gotten down every revealing gesture, every idiosyncrasy of speech and behavior, and yet somehow nobody came alive. The book was a jumble of real people rather than fictional characters, and it was rejected everywhere.

Her next novel, the one she wouldn't give up for anybody, would be different. She would write about what she knew as if she didn't really know it. And she would put herself in it. One thing was certain: whatever it was that she knew and was able to get down on paper, she herself was involved in it.

Meanwhile she would think about dropping the divorce suit. She might even think about requesting a transfer.

9. In Utica, New York, the priest's mother heard the following established facts at the Ladies' Guild:

    1. Katharine Stone had grown up in Utica and moved to Boston when she was five. She was an airline stewardess for seven

years and often flew back and forth between Boston and upper New York State. Now that she was separated she had gone back to United. She had been seen in her uniform only last week. In Utica. Many people in Utica knew her well.

2. Kate Stone was a staff editor of *Ms.* magazine and had formerly been a fashion model. She was six feet tall and beautiful. She dated married men.

3. Katharine Stone was a former nun who grew up in DC but who lived, at the time of her marriage, in Baltimore. She was from a distinguished family of doctors in which all the men went to Harvard and all the women to Radcliffe. She was, despite this, not the least bit snobbish and was quite content teaching high school English. Her family would never permit a divorce.

4. A friend of the guild's president's daughter had gone to Noroton with Kate Stone and there they had both known the Ford girls, Anne and Charlotte. They, the four, had not been close since she entered the convent. Kate Stone, of course. Anne Ford had not entered the convent and neither had Charlotte.

5. Kate Stone had been a dancer until she broke her foot. Since then she had worked for IBM and spent all her free time skiing. She was going to get a divorce and then marry her ski instructor.

The priest's mother went home and cried until ten, when *Kojak* came on.

10. In the spring of that year they both got transfers to Boston, where they bought a house and took up where they had left off, only a lot better. Kate was involved in writing her novel and her husband was all worked up over a new ad campaign, and so they were happy. They even put in their names to adopt a child.

That summer they drove to Baltimore to visit Kate's friends in the convent. Kate was all in white and very tanned though it was still only the end of June. He was wearing his white suit and his white shoes, too summery perhaps, just this side of affectation. They knew they looked good.

Kate's friends came to the visiting parlor in twos and threes. Visits were not so exciting as they had been years ago, before the cloister had moved into the world. These days a visit from outside meant little. Still, everybody was curious to see the couple now that they were reconciled. How long would it last? Kate looked wonderful, but he was putting on weight. He was polite, said very little. Whenever they asked about him, he answered briefly and directed the conversation back to Kate and her friends. There was no telling from the way he acted whether or not he'd take off again for New York. Poor Kate.

At noon some of the sisters went to chapel for midday meditation. Kate and her husband went for a walk around the grounds. Hand in hand they walked down the long slope of grass to the lake. A small dirt path ran around the lake and they followed it for a while, disappearing among the overhanging willows and high swamp grass. There were pine needles everywhere. He wanted to lie down on them but she said no, it was time to turn back. They lay down for a little while anyway.

As they came out from under the trees, they paused and looked across the lake. The sun turned the water green and cast a green reflection on their faces and clothes.

The sisters, coming out of chapel, paused on the cloister walk to gaze out over the lake. The sisters saw the man and woman, their hands joined together, their clothes of dazzling white drenched green in the reflection from the lake. Just those two white figures, joined, against the world of green.

Someone cried out in disbelief.

11.   And so she finished the damned book, as she said, and got a publisher, and sold sixteen hundred copies of it. The *New York Times* said it was a promising start and the *New Republic* said it was witty and disturbing. Nobody else said anything about it.

What she wrote was, in actuality, a pack of lies about her friends at IBM and about her husband and—in a peculiar way—about herself.

The characters numbered thirteen and they were as diverse in their morals and desires and preoccupations as even God or nature would have made them. There was a man who was so insecure he dared to communicate with his employees only when he had worked himself into a rage. There was a man whose sole love was for machines and who had cut himself off from human intercourse completely. There was a housewife whose loneliness and vulnerability drove her into affairs with any man who presented himself. And another who wanted to write poetry and instead was drinking herself to death. And a female executive who made passionate love to her husband each night, moaning and tearing at his flesh, and then went to the bathroom where she calmly and coldly masturbated before the full-length mirror. They were unscrupulous people and hateful people and pitiful people. And all of them, so her husband recognized, understanding at last, were Kate Stone. In some way, at some moment in the story, they all wore her face.

He was grateful for the book. She existed now, in reality, for him.

She was grateful too. The book was done, some kind of awful duty was discharged, and she felt no desire to write another. All she wanted to do now was to take up skiing once again and to conquer at last the dark fear of hers that plunging down that slope was somehow entering the valley of the shadow of death.

12. It was their anniversary and she gave him a card she had made herself. Inside it she had written, "This river that carries us with it, out of control, out of any control, at least carries us together."

He did not know what she meant, he never knew what she meant, but it no longer mattered because he had seen her naked face and loved her.

13. Time passed for them. There may have been children, a boy and a girl, adopted. There may have been a dog. There may have been... but the snow falls and everything recedes into uncertainty, except that we die and we do not wish to die.

"It's snowing," she said.

"And it's going to snow," he said.

The light on the snow had been pale purple all afternoon and, though it continued to snow, she insisted nonetheless on going skiing.

They were seen leaving the lodge where everyone was sitting around drinking hot buttered rum by the fireplace and they were seen again later taking the lift to the highest slope. Slowly at first, and then with lightning speed, they descended, two black figures against the white snow, darting across each other's path, plunging straight down and then veering off at an angle, dodging invisible poles. For a long while people from the lodge watched them, but then the sun dipped behind the trees. Nonetheless they went on ascending and descending that hill.

In the first dark an owl hooted and some winter bird shifted on his perch in the cedar limbs.

DOUBTS

THE RISE AND RISE OF ANNIE CLARK

A SIGN

Annie Clark is a modern woman. It's 1950, smack in the middle of the century, and she knows that the second Great War is over and women were the real winners. Everywhere women are taking charge of their lives. But Annie is Catholic, so she has to go slow.

Today, for instance, she is being extra patient with this young waitress—Patsy P.—who is stout and clumsy and may be new to the job. Annie is waiting for her dessert, apple pie with cheese, and she figures they must be baking the pie fresh because it's taking forever. Finally the girl brings the pie and shoves it in front of Annie and heads off without a word. Annie looks at the speck of cheese on her plate and immediately says, "Miss," but the girl keeps going, so Annie raises her napkin in the air and says loudly, "Miss!" Everybody turns to look at Annie except the waitress. She's gone. After several minutes she comes back from wherever she's been hiding.

"Miss," Annie says, the voice of endurance. "What is this, please?"

"It's what you ordered."

"No. I ordered apple pie with cheese."

"That's what you've got," the girl says, staring beyond Annie at a future without people like this.

Annie is about to say, "Bring me a slice of cheese big enough for me to see!" when suddenly she is struck by how much the girl resembles Annie herself at twenty. Patsy P. is unattractive, with bad skin, and she is running to fat already, so nobody notices her now and nobody ever will, except to take advantage of her. It was that way for Annie too. In her teens she used to joke that she was Cinderella, but without the fairy godmother. She's been taken advantage of always. Even in the convent. Faced now with Patsy P. in all her unloveliness, Annie is moved nearly to tears at her own life.

She manages, nonetheless, to ask for—and get—a larger piece of cheese.

Annie eats her dessert slowly, meditating.

Her kids. This morning she left for seven-thirty Mass while they were still quarreling over their Wheaties, so God only knows if they got to school on time. They hate school and they're rude to the nuns. Annie admits it must be hard for them. It's a Catholic school, Sacré Cœur, where all the classes are taught in French, but of course her kids don't know French. Catholicism comes first for Annie and she has great sympathy for nuns, except for the mean ones.

She herself wanted to be a nun. She applied to the Daughters of Saint Joseph and, after a lengthy interview, she was told to wait a year. Or two. In time she was accepted and, taking the name Sister Angelica, she was happy doing for God the very work she had so disliked at home.

But then she was assigned a month's kitchen trial under Sister Hildegard, a German sister who took the word *trial* literally. In her abrupt way, Sister Hildegard asked Annie—Sister Angelica now—to go down to the cellar and bring up a bag of sugar. The cellar stairs were steep and the treads were narrow. It was a descent into the great unknown.

Annie, obedient, made the descent. After a brief search she located the bags of sugar, chose one, and started back up the stairs. But she was holding the bag clumsily and, when her foot caught in the hem of her habit, the bag slipped from her arms and she went pitching forward on the stairs. The noise of her fall was terrific, and she lay there expecting someone to come and help her. She waited only a short time before realizing nobody cared. She recovered the bag of sugar and, clutching it in one hand and her habit in the other, she made her way up to the kitchen.

"Oh, no," Sister Hildegard said, "not a ten-pound bag. I need a twenty-pound bag."

"I just fell on the stairs. I could have been killed."

"Then you must be more careful," Sister Hildegard said.

Annie returned to the cellar and got a twenty-pound bag. She climbed the stairs and plopped the bag down in front of Sister Hildegard.

"There!" she said.

Sister smiled at her and pointed to the bag's fancy gold label, which read "Select Brown Sugar." "Not brown. I need white," she said, adding, "one more trip, please."

Annie stood looking at the old nun until, for the love of God and the vow of obedience, she took to the stairs once again. In the cellar she sat down on a case of Bon Ami to rest for a while and to examine the state of her vocation. Had she really heard a call from God? She knew life in the convent was meant to be a trial, but she had expected trials of a spiritual nature: tests of faith and things like that. Not Sister Hildegard and her twenty-pound bags of sugar. It was asking too much. She sat on the Bon Ami, despairing.

Then, hoisting the bag of white sugar high in her arms, she struggled once more up the stairs to the kitchen. She placed the bag of sugar before Sister Hildegard and waited for some new outrage. She did not have to wait long.

"I've changed my mind," Sister Hildegard said, but, before she could say anything more, Annie fairly shouted at her, "Whatever it is, you can go to hell and get it yourself!"

That evening, in conference with Mother Superior, it was decided that Annie could best serve God in some other vocation, and thus Sister Angelica was no more.

Now, as she finishes her pie and cheese, Annie recognizes that "You can go to hell and get it yourself" was the moment when she took charge of her life and stepped bravely into womanhood.

———

Annie lost weight in the convent, and her hair, chopped off to wear beneath a veil, grew out to a fashionable length. With her new, surprised expression, she looked young and attractive.

So she stumbled from the convent into the arms of Willy Hébert—remaining, in her Irish heart, Annie O'Flaherty Clark—and in the next seven years she popped out four sturdy children. They were easy births, but four was enough, too many in fact, so she told Willy the sex part of their marriage was over. From now on he would have to grind out his satisfactions elsewhere. She was secretly relieved when he chose drink for his pleasure, because she had not been looking forward to another woman in their life.

The kids are now in their early teens—David and Mary anyway—and they are constantly in trouble. Annie's feet hurt and her heart beats too fast. She thinks she may have a condition.

Her troubles are beyond number.

Only last week a cop came to the door with questions about David, who was accused of stealing candy bars from LeDuc's Grocery. She put the cop in his place, telling him a thing or two about false accusations and prejudice against the Irish, but it turned out that he, too, was Irish. Officer Murphy.

She gets that chest pain again.

She wonders now if she is pleasing to God. If so, she'd like some evidence of it; nothing big like the saints had, but just a little something to keep her going. It's not as if she were asking for something like Lourdes. She decides to go and see a priest at Saint Patrick's, the Irish parish, even though technically she belongs to Saint Joan of Arc, mostly French.

Annie dresses formally for her visit to the priest. She struggles into her girdle and her dark blue dress and then checks the mirror. She is in her forties but she looks sixty and she knows it. God does not care, and nobody else matters, so why should she fuss? She always uses face powder and sometimes she remembers to put on lipstick, but she doesn't go in for makeup. She wears her hair short, brushed straight back, and that's fine for her. She is ready to go.

She knows how rectories work. You don't just knock at the door and get to see someone, but she gives it a try anyway. She tells the housekeeper that she's got to see a priest; it's urgent; she'll wait until Father is free. Any father. No matter how long.

Annie is taking charge of her life and bringing her troubles to God, or at least to the local priest who stands in for him. She waits a long twenty minutes until finally Father O'Malley enters through a side door, like a sneak. He is a young priest, tall, with reddish hair and thick glasses. They're so thick that she wonders how he can see out of them.

He smiles, officially, and says "Sit down," even though she's already sitting. He goes to the desk and assumes a listening pose.

Annie plunges ahead. She is at the end of her rope, she says. It's her kids. They're into everything and there's no controlling them. The oldest steals things from LeDuc's. Imagine! She herself is a daily communicant and says the Rosary constantly for the pope's intentions, but nothing seems to help. Four children and they're all wild, they use terrible language, they pay no attention to the sisters at school. Sacré Cœur. They're French, the sisters. Annie takes out a handkerchief, Irish lace, that she has brought for the occasion. Her husband drinks. She has this pain, terrible, in her heart. It's all too much. Why has God sent her this cross to bear? She dabs at her eyes with her handkerchief and takes a deep breath. "I know. I know. His will be done," she murmurs.

Father O'Malley hears "His will be done" and dives right in. She is a good woman, he says, a responsible mother, and children can be a trial. But marriage and family are meant to be a trial. God intends that. He has ordained marriage for a reason, and he has blessed it with children. Hers don't sound any wilder than most kids that age. She should remember that God has a sense of humor. God likes to see us rejoice occasionally. Father squints to get Annie in focus. She is very conscientious, he says. Perhaps even overconscientious. Pray for patience. And pray for joy.

Annie interrupts to ask if he will have a private talk with David, the thief? David doesn't listen to her, but she knows he would listen to a priest. She could bring him in anytime.

Father O'Malley does not seem to hear her.

"Remember," he says, "that God never gives us a heavier cross than we can bear."

Pushing back from the desk, Father O'Malley says that he will pray for her, and meanwhile he manages to get her to the door. Annie turns to say one last thing about her troubles, but he's too quick for her, and she finds herself outside, saying goodbye.

"I hope our talk has been a help," Father O'Malley says and lifts his hand in a sort of blessing before he closes the door.

Annie stands for a moment on the front steps of the rectory. What just happened? Was she given the bum's rush? Is O'Malley one of those priests who doesn't understand real life? And what is this about God having a sense of humor? If she believed that, she'd give up on religion tomorrow.

She goes next door to the church to pay a visit and say the Rosary, even though she's not in the mood. The church is empty at this time of day, the way Annie likes it, because it shows she's doing something extra. She sits back a little so her behind is braced against the pew. Father O'Malley said she is a good mother, but maybe too conscientious. He could have gone into more detail on that. She would like some kind of sign. She has always wondered about divine signs and how they come to you. The stigmata, for instance. Or levitation. If you levitate, are you aware of being in the air? How high, exactly? Does it hurt when you land? She's had trouble with her knees ever since the convent. Saint Teresa of Avila levitated all the time, but that was in the olden days and, let's face it, nobody gets signs like that anymore. She sits farther back and tries for a comfortable position, but the pew is hard as stone and her girdle is killing her.

It would be nice right now to go to a movie, one with those new plush seats, but she continues to sit in the pew until she finishes her Rosary.

Jezebel is playing at the Orpheum, and the theater is crowded.

Annie doesn't approve of Jezebel—not the one in scriptures, and not Bette Davis, either—but the movie should take her mind off Father O'Malley. At least he said she was a good mother. A very responsible woman, his exact words. She imagines that his own life is not easy. On the whole, she thinks, Father O'Malley tried to do his best. She replays their conversation, still dissatisfied. And then suddenly, with a great swell of music, the movie is over. Annie smiles. It's wonderful to see a bitchy woman like Bette Davis get her comeuppance. But she is late now, so she leaves the theater while the credits are still rolling, and she finds herself outside in a heavy rain. She will be soaked through by the time she gets home.

Annie puts spaghetti in a pot of water and sets it on the gas at the lowest heat. Usually Willy does the cooking, but today is payday so he'll stay late at the bar drinking their money away. Willy is the cook at Granger's Bar and Grill, where he shovels out hamburgers and hot dogs and shepherd's pie to a bunch of millworkers who also drink up their payday money. Annie doesn't complain. She knows Willy has to drink, so once a week she struggles to make dinner.

She is upstairs changing into dry clothes when the kids come home, all of them piling in at the same time. Annie's heart races.

"Ma-a-a-aah!" Mary calls out in that razor voice of hers.

"Oh shit," David says, looking at the stove. "Ma's cooking tonight! Cut lay donk."

"What does that mean?" Virginia asks. "Is it dirty?"

David points to the pot of spaghetti, now on the boil. "Cut lay donk! It means 'Look at that!'" David shouts, "Hey, Ma, are you home? Ma! Hey, Maaaaa!" and the others shout too until Annie can't bear it any longer and comes downstairs.

She greets them with a nasty look and goes to the stove. The spaghetti is overcooked, but what can she do? She opens a can of stewed tomatoes for the sauce. "Somebody set the table," she says. She is busy cutting the tomatoes into small pieces that she dumps into a saucepan and puts on the heat. To her surprise, the kids set the table without complaint. If only they could be nice all the time.

The youngest, Eddie, says to Annie, "What they're trying to say is *Regardez-les, donc*. It means 'Look at that!'"

Annie bends over and kisses Eddie's head. "I knew you'd catch on. French should be easy for you. Your father is French."

"I know *merde* and *putain*."

"Don't say *merde*. It's a bad word."

"It means shit. What about *putain*?"

"I'm busy now," Annie says, and upends the spaghetti into a strainer, and from the strainer she dumps it into a bowl. She can see it's a disaster, but she pours tomatoes on top and hopes for the best.

"What about *putain*?" Eddie asks again.

Everybody sits down at the kitchen table and Annie tries to say grace, but before she can get beyond "Bless us, O Lord," they have discovered that the spaghetti is stuck together in a solid mass.

"We can't eat this, Ma!" David holds the bowl out to Mary, who digs into the spaghetti and says, "This is a bowl of caca, Ma! It's not spaghetti, it's shit!"

"Watch your language, young lady!"

"It's *merde*," Eddie says, delighted. "We're having *merde* for dinner."

"Eat the sauce," Annie says. "Tomatoes are good for you and I'll open another can."

"*Je m'en fiche!*" Eddie says. "*M'en fou*."

They sit and take turns poking at the glutinous mass while Annie opens a large can of tomatoes. "Mary," she says, "give me a hand and get out the soup bowls. We'll have a tomato salad, sort of." She chokes on a sob. "I'm not a cook like your father."

"You can say that again."

Mary gets the soup bowls and passes them around.

"I'm sorry," Annie says. "God help me, I'm doing the best I can." She wishes she had not gone to the movie. She could have cooked something delicious. "You poor kids," she says.

"Tomatoes aren't even a meal. They're a vegetable."

THE RISE AND RISE OF ANNIE CLARK

"They're *merde*."

"Willy would never serve us a meal like this."

"Yay for Willy! Willy don't serve us *merde*."

Annie is about to break down and cry when she is saved by the unexpected arrival of Willy himself.

The front door opens and he staggers in, drunker than usual on paydays and relieved that he has made it home to his family.

"Willy!" they all shout, "Willy's home!"

"She's trying to give us tomatoes for dinner," Mary shouts, and the others add shouts of their own.

Willy holds out a large brown bag he's been cradling in his arms and tries to say, "Spaghetti," but he can't find the word. The kids take the bag to the table and have at it.

So he has saved Annie, who is grateful and resentful at the same time. She tries so hard, but she can see God never meant her to be a mother. She puts her shameful bowl of spaghetti on the kitchen counter behind the Wheaties box where nobody can see it.

Willy's restaurant spaghetti is delicious and the kids devour it as if they've been starving. Annie, sick with a sense of failure, leans against the counter while Willy dozes quietly in the rocker. Anyone looking in would think that this was an ordinary family having dinner. Then suddenly a quarrel breaks out.

Annie has no idea how it started or what it's about, but suddenly David has found her sodden bowl of spaghetti hidden behind the Wheaties and set it down in the middle of the table, saying, "Okay, I dare you." Virginia, the quiet one, reaches into the bowl and makes a spaghetti snowball and throws it, hard, at David. He is covered in the mucky stuff. Startled, he grabs a handful of mush from the bowl and throws it back at her. She dodges, and it hits Eddie instead. "*Putain!*" Eddie hollers. "*Merde* on you!" and suddenly they're all fighting for the bowl, shouting and laughing, and they get louder and wilder, until finally Willy wakes up.

He is cross now, and his speech has returned, so he shouts, "Cut it out! Show some respect for your mother!" though he has no idea what is going on.

Annie bites her knuckles, fighting the urge to scream.

They all quiet down and wait to see what's going to happen.

Willy begins to understand the situation. He is the father here. He should take charge. "Your mother works all day to make you a beautiful dinner and you don't appreciate it," he says. "You should be ashamed. She's a weak woman, in her condition." He wanders off course. "Responsibility begins at home, you kids should know that, and some day I'm gonna put down my foot... down." He leans back in his rocker and closes his eyes.

The kids laugh, but they recognize that the fun has ended.

"*Merde*," Eddie says, "*putain*."

Annie has had enough. She was not raised this way. She has been a nun in a convent. She is an independent woman.

She goes to the front room to phone her sister, Millie, and ask if she can stay with her for the night. Millie says yes, though Annie can tell she is hesitant. Well, too bad about Millie, who has everything and who does nothing.

With a prayer of thanks to Jesus, Annie seizes on her power as a modern woman. She will take her life into her own hands and let someone else do all the work for a change. She may never come back.

A REFUGE

Annie is sitting in Millie's breakfast nook where the sun pours in through the huge window, a bright beginning to a new day. Millie has been busy making french toast, getting the boys off to school and Charlie off on a trip to New York, even though she is supposed to be resting.

Millie has had two miscarriages since the boys were born and, after months of trying, she is finally pregnant again. And she is hurt that Annie has not asked even once about the baby. This baby is the center of her life, and Millie is terrified that something may go wrong with her pregnancy. So she is annoyed today by Annie's doom and gloom, and she is unable, in particular, to cope with her religious obsessions.

Still, Annie is her sister and she loves her.

Now Millie has tidied up the kitchen and poured them fresh coffee, and they get comfortable in the living room.

"Well," Millie says, warm, determined, "tell me all about it."

Annie starts with her visit to Father O'Malley. "We had a very good talk. I think he's nearly blind, Father O'Malley. And he's got red hair." Annie pauses, and repeats, "He's got red hair."

"Red hair," Millie says. "I heard you."

But Millie is not listening, Annie can tell. Millie has an easy life, with a devoted husband who doesn't drink and two boys who are smart and well behaved. No trouble with the cops for them. Millie was always the lucky one.

Annie begins to cry.

The baby, five months in the womb, shifts a little and Millie says, "What's wrong, Annie? But don't tell me if it upsets you." As if anything could stop her.

"It's a cross, my whole life. The kids are impossible. They make fun of the nuns, right to their faces. They say things in English but with a kind of French accent, as if they're talking French, but the only French words they know are filth. I hate to judge, but sometimes I wonder about those French nuns."

Millie is listening now, mystified. French nuns?

"And the two youngest, who used to be so good, hollered at that beautiful girl, the one that's the airline stewardess, 'Hey, lady, you want an enema?'" Annie laughs quietly. "Can you imagine it?"

Millie goes red with embarrassment. She does not want to imagine it.

"It's partly my fault," Annie says. "Whenever they acted up around the house I used to threaten them with an enema. The doctor said that constipation can make them, you know, act up. And to tell the truth, they were just saying, 'Hi, pretty lady. Hi, pretty lady,' and they were being nice. That stewardess dresses like a fashion plate. They were saying, 'Hi, pretty lady,' and when she didn't answer, their feelings were hurt, and they started hollering, 'Hey lady, you want an enema?' and they followed her halfway down the street. God forgive me, I shouldn't laugh," Annie says. "But they're only kids, after all, having fun."

Millie says, "I've got to lie down, Annie. The baby."

Annie can see she's exhausted. Millie has everything but she hasn't really taken charge of her life.

Annie will say a Rosary for her. On the bus to Florida.

Annie is listening to *Stella Dallas* on the radio when Millie's kids get home from school. They are full of energy but keep their voices low because their mother is resting. They give Annie a quick kiss and then disappear into the kitchen for a snack before they go upstairs to do homework.

Annie, grim, thinks of her own kids coming home from school. It's like a gang raid. They attack the kitchen, complaining loudly that there's nothing to eat, they push and laugh and fight for leftovers, and when they're done, they flee the scene, leaving Annie to deal with the open jars of peanut butter and the smears of jelly and David's candy bar wrappers from LeDuc's.

Curious, Annie looks in on Millie's kitchen once the boys are upstairs. The counter—one of those new tile ones, very pricey—is immaculate and the whole kitchen gleams. It's true; Millie does have everything.

But now *Stella Dallas* is over and Annie has missed the whole damned thing.

Annie wakes Millie from her nap in case she'd like a cup of tea and a chat. Millie sits up in bed, groggy after those new pills. She feels cranky and wishes Annie weren't there. But Annie is her sister.

"Should I make you some tea?" Annie asks.

"No, I'll make *you* the tea," Millie says, determined to be nice, "and we can have a good long talk before dinner."

Millie makes tea and Annie talks. "Have you ever thought about the stigmata? I've often wondered if the blood just leaks out or if it gushes. I imagine it must hurt. I wonder what it's like the first time it happens to you. Do you ever think of that?"

"No, I never think of that."

"There's this Padre Pio. He's a monk in Italy, and they say he has the stigmata. I wish they'd advertise it more. A miracle in our own times." She pauses before she risks saying, "Sometimes, I wonder what I'd do if I received a sign like that."

"For God's sake, Annie, talk about something real."

Annie bites her lower lip and Millie finishes making the tea. There is a short, stressful silence. But then Millie comes up with some very good spice cookies, and Annie, encouraged by the appearance of this new treat, forgets about signs and wonders, and catches Millie up on the movies.

She tells Millie about Bette Davis in *Jezebel* and then, with more enthusiasm, about the real Jezebel, the one in the Bible. Annie is pleased to show off her ease with scripture. "It's a wonderful story," she says. "The books of Kings. Kings one or two, I'm not sure. Don't you love that story?"

"Tell me more," Millie says, eager to put off until later the endless saga of Annie's troubles.

The boys have gone to bed. Millie and Annie sit on the couch, sisters and friends. Millie is waiting to hear the new personal tragedy Annie will reveal and Annie is waiting for the right moment to tell Millie that she has walked out on her family—for good, this time. She can't live like this any longer. She was once a nun. She has resolved to get on with her life.

"What is it, Annie?" Millie gives in first.

Annie settles into confessional mode. Her voice drops to a lower register as she begins to feel the drama, and already she is fighting tears. It all seems to have happened a year ago, but now, as Annie tells Millie the story, the horror is immediate, and she wonders why God allows such things. But Annie is resolute and fights through to the end of her story.

"They say filthy words in French. They make fun of Willy, their own father. And they throw food. Food was scattered all over the kitchen. God's good food, while people in China are starving to death." She chokes up.

Annie is overwhelmed with sorrow at the waste of her life when suddenly she realizes that Millie, her foolish, foolish sister, is bent over with laughter. Millie thinks the solid bowl of spaghetti is funny. And Annie's indignation makes her laugh until tears run down her face. Incredible as this is, she finds Annie's tragic life comic.

Millie laughs and says, "Oh, Annie."

"Sometimes I just don't get you," Annie says, "but I can assure you, my life is not a joke."

At once Millie stops laughing. She finds she has run out of patience, completely out, and her long day of listening is now over.

"Oh, for God's sake, Annie. You tell a funny story, you've got to expect people to laugh." She is exasperated and wants to say more, but she holds back.

Tentatively, Annie says, "I think I wasn't meant for marriage." Millie just has to understand. "I was meant to be a nun."

"I believe you tried that once before," Millie says, bitchy, like Bette Davis.

"Well, I've made up my mind and I'm leaving them. It's my heart. I've got a condition and I'm going to Florida for a rest."

Millie asks what she will do in Florida.

"What I do here: work my fingers to the bone for ingrates!" Annie has decided that two can play at being Bette Davis.

"Poor Annie. The eternal martyr."

"I'll pray for you, Millie. You'll need my prayers."

"Did you get a sign from God? Finally? Is that it?"

Millie has invaded Annie's spiritual life, and she is outraged. Betrayed.

"Was it a sign pointing to Florida? A sort of divine traffic sign?" Millie laughs, pleased with herself.

It takes effort but Annie rises from the couch and stands as tall as her short figure will allow. "I will not stay in a place where God is mocked. God will not be mocked!" she says and thunders off to bed.

She will never forgive Millie. This is the end.

In the morning Annie leaves by the front door, quietly, while Millie is in the kitchen making pancakes for the boys. She does not say goodbye.

Outside in the chill air, misery descends on her like rain. In fact, a hard, cold rain begins to fall, and she is overwhelmed with sadness as she waits for the bus that will start her on her new life.

She wonders, frightened, if this rain has been given to her as a sign. That she is a selfish person. That she failed as a nun and now she is failing as a mother. What does God think? And what is the matter with him, anyway? Why does he stay so remote when she prays constantly?

She gets off the bus and stands there, seeing herself: a woman, alone, in the rain.

For a second she senses the answer to her prayers. There is no flapping of wings, no angelic greeting, only silence. And then a greater silence. She makes no defense against this wordless revelation: if she could stand naked before God, silent just like this, and stop all the noise about who she is and how God feels about her, she might rise above it and become Saint Annie. For that second, she understands, almost.

But she loves her noise too much—it is her—and this cannot be the sign she has prayed for, so she snaps out of it.

It is sinful to ask for signs. Annie knows that.

The rain is only rain and not a sign of anything.

Annie packs a small suitcase with basic necessities and then writes two notes, one to the family and one to Father O'Malley. The family note is brief—"Bad heart. Gone to Florida"—and she tucks it beneath the clock, where they'll be sure to see it. Her note to Father O'Malley is more detailed, wishing him good health and explaining her need for rest and quiet. She asks him to stop by her place now and then, if it isn't too much trouble, to check on the family now that her husband, Willy, is in charge. She smiles as she finishes the notes. Let them all find out how easy it is to run a family.

Au revoir, the whole crowd of you, au revoir!

A KIND OF MIRACLE

Annie has been in Florida for nearly two months when Mr. Savage, the manager of the Hotel Howard, calls her in because of an ugly problem with theft. He mentions the police and arrests, but after talking with her for a while he is convinced that Annie is not a thief but just another cleaning lady in flight from a difficult life and now the innocent victim of a scam. He finds Annie refined but naive, and probably a little stupid; she is a perfect scapegoat for a hotel thief. It is an old trick: you take your valuable gold necklace from the hotel safe, being careful to sign out for it, you leave it on your dressing table, and after the woman from housekeeping has cleaned the room, you discover that it has gone missing. The cleaner is the only one who has been in the room. And chances are she has been accused of something at least once before. Annie admits trying out the woman's perfume, just a couple sprays of Chanel No. 5, but everyone knows that the step from perfume to necklace is an easy one. The guest wants compensation for her loss.

Annie sits in Mr. Savage's office and waits for him to decide her fate. Meanwhile, she says the Rosary and tries to stay calm.

But Mr. Savage is on her side. But the Howard is an expensive international hotel that cannot afford the bad publicity of a lawsuit, so he resolves the matter discreetly with a small financial settlement for the guest. In his subtle way, however, he lets this amateur know that he's not fooled for a minute, even while assuring her that Annie Clark will go. And so Annie is fired, with a week's wages for consolation. She sobs quietly and Mr. Savage, a softy at heart, slides three extra twenties across the desk to her.

Suddenly, out of nowhere, he rises from his chair and, in a way that she finds shocking, he takes her two hands in his. He looks at her and says, as if he cares deeply, "This isn't good, Miss Clark. This is no good for you. Go home to your family." He continues to look at her in a way that says he knows every single bad thing about her, and it's all forgiven.

She bursts into tears again, and the Florida experiment is over.

———

The bus trip from Florida seems to take forever, but eventually Annie sees familiar churches and Sacré Cœur and knows she is home.

She is not sure what to do next. She should call Millie and get that over with, and then she can face the family. When she first got to Florida she wrote the kids a postcard, saying, "In Florida for my health. Love to all." And to Millie, conscious of past favors and possible future needs, she sent a card wishing her good luck with her pregnancy.

The card arrived, however, the week that Millie lost her baby. The miscarriage proved nearly fatal because Millie bled uncontrollably and, to save her life, they had to perform a hysterectomy.

Annie knows none of this when she phones Millie to ask if she can stay the night with her. Millie is cold at first, but when Annie tells her about the necklace and the false charges of theft and how she almost went to jail, Millie softens and says, "Yes, come ahead, Annie. But I'm not well, so it's just for one night."

Charlie hears that Annie is on her way and says, "Are you up to this? Really? I'll stay if you need me, or want me, but otherwise I'm not up to this." And, full of guilt but with Millie's blessing, he leaves to spend the night at his sister's house.

Annie arrives after dinner and makes herself at home. She is at her best with genuine loss, even when it is not her own, and she folds Millie in her arms and they cry together. They say little. No words of consolation can change the hard facts: Millie has lost her baby and there will not be another one.

The boys are welcoming but subdued, and they seem glad to spend the evening upstairs with their books and their radio.

Annie and Millie sit together on the living room couch.

Annie starts off dangerously. "God's ways are a mystery, aren't they? You can never tell why things happen to you. I mean, who would think this would happen to you, a good Catholic from a good family."

"I don't want to talk about it, Annie."

"I sometimes think God gives us a sign we can't understand." She suddenly recalls Millie's terrible words—like Bette Davis—asking if the traffic sign pointed to Florida.

"I sometimes envy the life of a nun. They're so close to God."

"I suppose."

"God works in mysterious ways. Don't you think so?"

"Yes."

"And his ways are not our ways."

"Annie, for God's sake, stop! You sound like a fortune-teller."

"Oh, Millie."

"It's time for me to take my pills and then let's have a snack."

Millie's pills are called "nerve pills" and they're something new for when she's depressed. Her doctor has said to take one or two when she feels anxious or sad, and she finds they actually work. She takes two now, even though she took two before Annie arrived.

Over the past months, Millie has tried to see Annie with a loving eye. And she does, but she sees her coldly. Annie is lazy, judgmental, and self-indulgent. She neglects her family shamefully. She is impossibly selfish. She hounds priests. She nags God for a private miracle— something cozy just between the two of them—and she must bore him to death with her constant praying.

Meanwhile Annie prays for Millie. Millie is her beloved sister, but she is not accepting her miscarriage as God's holy will. "God's will be done," Annie prays, and while she has his attention she adds a prayer that he will be merciful tomorrow when she returns to Willy and the kids. She will not ask for a sign of his approval, but… and then here is Millie, changed into a dressing gown and looking beautiful, as if she had never had a miscarriage at all.

Millie makes hot cocoa and, when Annie says, "I'd love one of those spice cookies with this, or even some Ritz crackers," she opens the bread drawer and there are no cookies but she finds the bag of dinner rolls left over from Sunday. They're hopelessly stale and will have to be thrown out.

Millie feels funny. The pills have begun to work.

"Sorry, Annie," she says. "We're clean out of cookies."

A mad thought comes to her suddenly and she bends over the drawer laughing. She can't stop, because it's all too funny. She tries to say, "It's God's holy will, Annie," but she can't speak for laughing.

"What is it?" Annie asks. "What's the matter with you?"

Millie stops laughing, and with a perfectly straight face, she says, "I'm sorry, Annie, but I've got to hit you with one of these rolls." She chooses a roll with care and pitches it at Annie.

The roll strikes Annie's breast and she yells in surprise. She looks at Millie, indignant, and reaches for her cocoa. "Foolish!" she says. "You're just being foolish." And she turns away in disgust.

Millie throws another roll and Annie bats it away. "I'm sorry, Annie, but I've got to do this. It's God's holy will." She throws another and Annie screams in genuine fright and runs from the kitchen. "You're crazy," she shouts, "you've lost your mind!" She hides behind the dining room door.

The boys come running downstairs and applaud their mother. "Go, Mom," they holler, "go for it!" And Millie does.

She chases Annie from the dining room through the living room and down the hallway, pelting her with the last of the rolls until, with one final scream, Annie locks herself in the bathroom and the excitement is over.

The boys are proud of their mother—it's like old times—and reluctantly they go upstairs to bed. Millie subsides on the living room couch, exhausted but happy. Those nerve pills, she thinks, will make me crazy in the end, but oh what a relief from Annie's piety!

Annie sleeps that night, but it is a restless sleep, disturbed by anxious dreams.

Millie sobs for hours before she falls asleep, but she rises early the next morning to say goodbye to Annie. Millie's voice is kind and loving, but to Annie it is the terrible voice of the pagan Sibyls. "Stop pestering God, Annie. Just leave him alone."

Annie kneels, determined, before the statue of the Blessed Virgin and tries to pray. Everything in her life is terrible. She herself is terrible, a woman overwhelmed by troubles that keep her from being a good person. She finds she cannot pray; she cannot even think. Her mind is a beehive of doubts and accusations.

Less than an hour ago she knocked on the rectory door and Father O'Malley himself answered. He was abrupt, even hostile, and he seemed to think she was wrong for having gone to Florida for a rest. Regarding the dictates of her note, he said, he had checked her house from time to time and found everything in good order. Willy had transferred the children to public school where they were doing well. David seemed to have taken over the cooking. The girls made the beds and cleaned the house. And Eddie was learning French with the help of a nun from Sacré Cœur. Father O'Malley hoped Annie had had a good rest—in Florida, he added, his tone sarcastic.

So everyone has turned on her. She is lost and she knows it. If only she could reclaim that moment of silence when she almost saw where it was that she stood in the eyes of God. Did she almost see that? Or had she deceived herself?

She closes her eyes and immediately she hears herself thinking—and surely she is now her own miracle—I don't care anymore. I don't care about how much I matter. Or how much You matter. I don't need to know anything. I just give up. I give in. I want nothing. I surrender.

And with that she falls asleep. Kneeling upright at the altar rail before the statue of the Virgin Mary, Annie sleeps a good, unfeeling sleep. She knows nothing. She wants nothing.

Now slowly, gently, she rises in the air, kneeling upright as she ascends to a height of exactly three feet and two inches, still sleeping soundly, aware only that she has surrendered, whatever that means. She knows nothing of what is happening to her.

Father O'Malley comes from the sacristy, genuflects before the altar, and stops to stare with his single eye, blurry as it is, at what looks to be a woman levitating. He stares harder and sees that she is that tiresome Annie Clark, and without a doubt she is kneeling on the empty air. He blesses himself, genuflects again before the altar, and goes back into the sacristy.

Annie eventually descends from the air, sleeping still, and when she wakes, she has no knowledge of what has happened. She is embarrassed at having fallen asleep in church, and her knees hurt from kneeling so long in the air, but she is strangely rested and refreshed.

In the sacristy, Father O'Malley ponders. To what end would God suspend his law of gravity this way? For whose benefit? And why? Annie Clark seems an unlikely candidate for special attention. As is he himself, half-blind and half-useless. Still, he is pleased to have been chosen as witness to the levitation of this annoying woman.

Perhaps the age of miracles has returned? Or, more likely, God is simply in one of his antic moods.

It is not useful to examine this kind of thing too closely, he knows. Still, you have to wonder.

COMMUNION

Snow had fallen all through the night and it continued to fall through the short bleak morning of the day before Christmas. Though the sky remained overcast, the snow stopped falling about noon, so the plowing crews were able to clear the main highways and some of the side roads. Conor was glad about this because it meant he would be able to get through to his weekend call.

Conor had been ordained a priest the previous June and this would be his first Christmas Mass. He was still studying at Shadowbrook, completing the fourth and final year of theological studies required by the Jesuits, and though he offered Mass privately each morning, he was eager to be out in a parish, hearing confessions and saying Mass for real people facing real problems in the real world. It would mean missing the mulled wine after midnight services at Shadowbrook, but they'd probably give him a drink at the parish anyhow. And it was good to get away. Life at Shadowbrook was fine; it was all that a young priest could hope for; but with nobody but Jesuits living there, it was a hothouse of spirituality, and Conor saw little point in preaching the Gospel to other preachers of the Gospel.

And so on the morning of Christmas Eve Conor packed his overnight case and went out to the back step of the theologate to wait for the car that would pick him up, along with five other newly ordained Jesuit priests who would all be dropped off at parishes around the city. They were a somewhat suspect group in the parishes, filled as they were with radical new ideas about scripture and the sacraments, but at Christmas all the local pastors were shorthanded and so these young Jesuits were welcomed for the work they could do... even though three of them sported beards.

Conor felt happy, he felt fortunate, as he charged out into the snow to do good, to bring a little peace into this world, to make people feel loved and valued and saved. How lucky I am, he thought.

He arrived at Our Lady of Victories parish with an hour to spare before afternoon confessions. The parking lot at the side of the church was still not plowed and no path had been cleared to the front door of the rectory and so Conor, with only rubbers on his feet, plunged into the snow and waded, knee-deep, up the nonexistent path to the stoop. He shivered as the snow seeped down inside his shoes; he would get a cold out of this, for sure.

A snow shovel was propped against the wall next to the door. Conor was just about to ring the bell when he thought, Oh hell, it's Christmas, and he put down his overnight bag and began to shovel the stoop. When he finished, he cleared the stairs. He had made a good start on the cement walk when suddenly the front door opened and somebody yelled at him.

"What the hell do you think you're doing?"

Conor turned around and saw, standing in the doorway, an elderly priest with a red face and glasses. He was wearing a white T-shirt and black trousers, and his belly hung over his belt. His right hand curled around a coffee mug as if it were a grenade.

"You deaf?"

"Oh, sorry, Father," Conor said, all innocence and charm. "I saw that the walk hadn't been shoveled, and I thought I'd just give you a hand."

"Get in here; it's freezing out there."

"Why don't I just finish this walk?" Conor said. "It'll only take me a few minutes and I'm almost..." but the door slammed before he could complete the sentence. Conor stared at the closed door for a moment, blushed, and said, feeling like a fool, "Done."

Snow had begun to fall again in heavy wet flakes and Conor pulled his scarf tighter around his neck. Yes, he'd get a cold from this; with any luck, he'd get pneumonia. God damn.

He finished shoveling the walk and then stamped his feet several times to shake off the snow. He stood on the stoop and examined his overnight case. He blew his nose. He took off his rubbers and placed them next to the door. Then he picked them up; they should go inside the door or they'd freeze. This was awful. Should he ring the bell? Should he just walk in as if nothing had happened? He waited there, in dread. Finally he pushed the door open and went inside.

"Out here," someone called, and Conor put down his rubbers and followed the voice into the kitchen where the priest sat at a table hunched over the sports page of the newspaper while the cook stirred something on the stove.

"Happy Christmas!" Conor said.

The cook turned and looked at him for a moment and then went back to her stirring. The priest said, "Have some coffee," and kept on reading his newspaper.

Conor took off his coat. "Good afternoon, Father. I'm from Shadowbrook? I'm here to help with confessions and Mass. Gosh, that's some snow. I was afraid I wouldn't be able to get through." He looked around for someplace to hang up his coat. "You're Father... ?"

"Just toss it anywhere," the priest said, folding his paper and scooting back his chair, all action suddenly. "Have some coffee. What's the matter with you anyway, shoveling the walk. You're a Jesuit, right? Beard and all. What are you, *New Breed* or something?"

"I don't know what you mean, Father. New Breed."

Conor knew exactly what he meant. Any priest this old and this fat used the term *New Breed* to mean all those things that menaced his existence: antiwar activists like the Berrigans; folk masses with guitars; the usual threats—the threat of English in the liturgy, the threat of birth control, the threat of every single thing they were now talking about at Vatican II, a council already in its second year and bound to turn out liberal and disastrous. That's what he meant.

The priest merely stared at Conor and Conor stared back.

"Have some coffee," the priest said, and this time he pointed to a little side table with a coffeepot and some cups. "How long have you been ordained, Father?"

"Six months; almost six months to the day."

"Six months. That's not long, even for a Jesuit. You burn draft cards and that sort of thing? You want to stop the war?" He waited for an answer, but there was none. "What kind of last name is that you've got, anyway? French? You French?"

"I'm half-French. Half-Irish. Hence Conor for a first name."

"Hence," the priest said, with a laugh. And in a prissy voice, "Hence."

Conor stared into his coffee cup. "And your name, Father?"

"Pure Irish. Mahoney. And this is Mrs. Carberry; she's Irish too."

Mrs. Carberry turned and frowned at them both just as another priest entered the kitchen, this one also in a T-shirt and black trousers. He was thin, scrawny even, with a pointy face and the smell of alcohol on him. He could have been any age between forty and sixty. "And Father Riley is my assistant. He's Irish too. This is the Jesuit, Riley. Father here is a French Jesuit. With a beard. Shovels walks, he does."

Father Riley rubbed his eyes and yawned. "Can't wake up," he said. He walked to the refrigerator and stuck his head inside. "Nothing here but a load of cast-iron crap," he said.

"Now, listen up, sonny," Father Mahoney said to Conor. "Everything around here is done by the rules. In liturgy, we follow the rules of the church. And around the house, we follow my rules. Got it?"

Conor smiled. "But of course."

"But of course," Father Mahoney said, in that voice again. "But of course. So, here are some rules. Confessions this afternoon from three thirty to five thirty. Dinner at six. Not six fifteen. Six. Confessions again from seven thirty to nine. Midnight Mass at midnight. Get there at a quarter to. It'll be a High Mass, but don't panic; I do most of the singing. One thing Jesuits can never do is sing. I'll be celebrant, Riley here will be deacon, you'll be subdeacon. There's a rubrics chart in the sacristy, so study it sometime before Mass tonight. One thing Jesuits never know is rubrics. Got it?"

"Got it. And I do happen to know the rubrics."

"You happen to. Good. Now do you happen to know why I don't want you doing any more shoveling?"

"Father, it's Christmas," Conor said, the peacemaker.

"I don't want you shoveling because we pay a man, pay him very well, to do exactly that. But he's out today... on a bender. And when he comes in tomorrow or the next day or whenever he finally makes it, I want him to see just how much trouble he's caused us. See?"

"See," Conor said. Father Mahoney took one last sip from his coffee cup and left the kitchen. Conor turned from him to Mrs. Carberry, who was now busying herself at the sink. He turned to Father Riley, who still stood with his head in the refrigerator.

"I wonder if someone could tell me where my room is?" Conor asked. Without a word Mrs. Carberry pointed to a door at the far end of the kitchen.

"Happy Christmas," Conor said.

"It's *merry* Christmas," Mrs. Carberry said.

Above the door to the confessional was a slot for the visiting priest's name. Conor was just inserting a strip of white cardboard printed with his name, followed by the SJ, when Father Mahoney came up behind him and said, "I see you're advertising the SJ. That should bring the customers in."

Conor could tell some answer was expected, but he refused, and offered the old priest only a hard smile.

Father Mahoney took a step backward and said, almost apologetically, "It was only a joke," and when Conor continued the hard smile, Father Mahoney turned and made his way slowly down the aisle and across the church to his own confessional.

Conor sat in the darkness and thought of his wet feet. He caught cold every year, and once he'd caught it, it would stay around till spring.

He'd dried his hair and changed his socks before coming out to hear confessions, but he had only the one pair of shoes and of course they were wet all through. It's that damn Mahoney, he thought, and then asked God's forgiveness because Mahoney was probably a good priest according to his own lights, dim though they were, and who could guess what private suffering Mahoney had to endure, etcetera, etcetera.

There was no room for emotion, hot or cold, in Jesuit piety, Conor liked to say. No room for hate or even resentment, and certainly no room for sentimentality. And so, who was he to judge the Mahoneys of this world? The long course of Jesuit training—fifteen endless years— was intended to produce men with a naked and ruthless knowledge of self. It went without saying that self-knowledge presupposed the desire and commitment to reform the self in the likeness of Jesus Christ. And he himself was as far from that likeness as you could get, Conor knew. So leave poor Mahoney alone. And at once he found himself thinking, Yes, leave the dead to bury the dead. But at just that moment someone entered the confessional on his right, and Conor immediately forgot his failure of charity, his head cold, the unspeakable Father Mahoney.

"Bless me, Father, for I have sinned. It is two weeks since my last confession, and these are my sins."

"Mm-hmm," Conor murmured, an encouraging sound.

"What?"

"Nothing. That's fine. Go right ahead."

"Oh, okay. Bless me, Father, for I have sinned. It is two weeks since my last confession, and these are my sins." Pause. "I was mean to my little brother twice; I told a lie once; I sassed my mother seven times; I masturbated six times; I forgot my evening prayers twice; and I took the Lord's name in vain nineteen times."

Ah, Conor thought, the sin sandwich. They all did this, dropped the big sin in the middle of all the little ones, hoping it wouldn't get too much notice. "I see," Conor said. "Well that's fine. It sounds as if you're trying hard to be a good guy. How old are you anyway?" There was silence. None of them were used to being spoken to as if they were people. After a while, the boy said, "How old?" And then, "Fourteen."

"Fourteen!" Conor said, as if he were astounded that anybody could be fourteen. "Well, that's a really rough age. I had a terrible time when I was fourteen. Let me ask you something about your confession, okay? You said you were mean to your little brother; how old is he?"

"Six, Father."

"Oh, six. Well, they can be an awful pain in the neck at six, right? But of course, you're so much older—you're practically a man now—you can be patient with him. I mean, you want to be, don't you."

"Yes, Father."

"Sure, of course you do. I know you do. Now, the other thing. Taking the Lord's name in vain. What do you think about that anyhow?"

"It's a sin, Father."

"Well, I don't know how much of a sin it is, but it *sounds* lousy. Don't you think? I think so. Oh sure, all the other guys say it and we figure we sound like one of the guys, you know, we really fit in if we say it too. But it sounds like hell. It's a bad habit."

"Yes, Father."

"Now I guess that's all. Oh, wait, you mentioned something else; masturbation, was it? Well, a lot of fuss is made about that. I don't know. Just do your best and try to help around the house. And be nice to your little brother, especially tomorrow, because it's Christmas and he's gonna be very excited and will probably drive you crazy. But just try to make it a nice day for him and for your folks, your mom and dad, all right?"

"Yes, Father." Relief in the voice.

"You're a good kid, don't forget that. Now, for your penance say one Our Father and thank God you've got such a good family."

Conor gave the boy absolution, sketched a large sign of the cross in the air, and slid the little window closed. He sighed once, happy, and tilting his head to the other side, slid open the little window on his left.

Let me help, he prayed silently, let me just help.

"Bless me, Father..." It was a woman's voice—birth control, of course—and Conor's long afternoon of confessions began in earnest.

The same old sins. There were no new ones. Fornication, adultery, masturbation. Birth control. Drunkenness. Theft. Wife-beating. And then the nice category nobody minded confessing: sins against charity. Uncharitable thoughts, uncharitable conversations, uncharitable actions. No murderers and no rapists; apparently murderers and rapists made their confessions only after they'd landed on death row. And so Conor sat there for two hours and heard the endless catalog of small failures. Of good people. Because only good people came to confession in the first place.

"God bless you, you're a fine woman," Conor said, and gave her as a penance that she do some nice thing for herself; nothing big, necessarily; just buy herself a magazine she wanted, or take a morning off and watch television, or something; just to thank God that life is good. He gave her absolution then, and as he slid the window shut, he prayed—a little self-conscious about the words—oh you whom I love, please let me help.

During the final hour he had begun to sneeze and his handkerchief was already soaked through, but he didn't mind. This was wonderful. This was the priesthood at its most intimate and effective. He could sit here frozen and sneezing forever.

Conor, busy in the confessional, was very late for dinner. Father Mahoney gave him a long look as if he suspected him of criminal activity, and then he explained that they had to serve themselves tonight because Mrs. Carberry had the evening off, that Conor had already missed the soup course that was Mrs. Carberry's masterpiece, that out of respect for Mrs. Carberry's troubles—she had buried her husband earlier this month—they would eat their small meal in silence.

Conor was surprised that the laconic Mrs. Carberry—it's *merry* Christmas—featured so largely in the life of the rectory, but he was grateful for the silence because he had come to dinner fearing another inquisition. Beard, birth control, New Breed. He shot a quick glance at Father Riley who, very clearly, was drunk. Conor gave his complete attention to chewing the stringy meat. Veal?

When Father Mahoney got up to clear the table, Conor started to get up too, but Father Mahoney gestured him back to his chair.

"But I'd like to help," Conor said.

Father Mahoney repeated the gesture and then gathered the plates and took them to the kitchen.

"Well, that was delicious," Conor said, half to Father Riley and half to his plate. He looked up and saw Father Riley staring at him, curious.

"What was it?" Father Riley said.

"The dinner," Conor said. "It was delicious."

"But what was it?" Father Riley repeated.

Conor looked at him blankly.

"I'll tell you what it was," Father Riley said. "It was a goddamn rubber boot, that's what it was."

Conor laughed at what he presumed was a joke, but Father Riley merely continued to stare at him with that same curious look.

Father Mahoney returned with a pot of coffee and two wedges of chocolate cake. "Devil's food," he said, smiling, and told them to leave their plates on the table; he would get them later. "Fathers," he said, bemused, and left the dining room.

They were silent for a moment and then Father Riley lifted the coffeepot and said, "Some?" He filled Conor's cup but poured only a splash or two into his own. From deep inside his cassock pocket he pulled out a half pint of scotch and poured at least half of it into his coffee. Conor stared at him, astonished, and Father Riley said, "I'm not hearing confessions tonight." And then, when Conor continued to stare, he added, "It's all right. It helps me relax."

Desperate, Conor asked, "Does Father Mahoney always serve at table? That's very impressive."

"Once a month. It's a thing with him." For a moment he assumed Father Mahoney's mocking voice: "*So he'll never forget that he's a servant of God, and therefore a servant of man.* Or so he says. I think he just likes to do it."

"Well, it's very impressive."

"There's something I want to ask you." Father Riley stared at Conor with his curious stare, and then took a long swallow of his drink.

"Yes?"

"'Yes?' 'Very impressive!' 'Quite delicious!' You are the proper little priest, aren't you." He raised the cup to his mouth. "Well, you're young."

"I think I'll go take a look at the rubrics for tonight's Mass," Conor said, and started to get up.

"No, please. I'm sorry. I do want to ask you something and I am sincere about it. Okay? Okay. So keep your seat. What I want to know is how you Jesuits get away with preaching birth control. And why do you want to? I mean, the pope has said we can't. Period. And that's that."

"Well, I'm afraid I see it as a little bit more complicated than that, Father. Maybe sometime we could talk about it. Right now... well."

"Right now I'm too drunk to understand, you mean. Right? Try me. Go ahead, explain."

As soon as he saw he had Conor hooked, Father Riley pulled the bottle from his pocket and refilled his cup. "It helps me concentrate," he said.

And so, doubting he should do this but unable to stop himself, Conor explained the complicated process of reasoning by which he— and indeed most of the other young Jesuits from Shadowbrook— concluded that he was not preaching birth control but only helping concerned Catholics to form their own consciences in an intelligent and responsible way. "Do you see the difference?" he said.

"But how do you actually do it?" Father Riley asked him. "What do you actually say?"

"You just help them see where they feel their duty lies. It's their conscience, after all."

"But how do you get them to see? What do you tell them?"

Conor gave Father Riley a long hard look. How drunk was he? And was he sincere? Or was Riley just getting the goods on him so that he could stagger off to old Mahoney, or even to the bishop, and cause all kinds of trouble?

"You could help me," Father Riley said. "Sincerely."

Conor blew his nose and thought about it. This could be very dumb. Everybody knew that parishes were the last outposts of the scalping conservatives and here he was about to tell a drunk how he advised penitents in confession. There would be trouble with the pastor. There would be trouble with the bishop. There would be trouble back at Shadowbrook. And eventually Conor himself would have his ass handed to him. No, he should simply refuse.

"I'm coming down with a terrible cold," Conor said.

"Help me," Father Riley said.

Oh God, Conor said to himself, help me. And to Father Riley he said, "Well, I do this. First off, I talk to them about the other things they've mentioned—you know, the usual stuff, impatience with their kids, missing Mass, sins against charity; stuff like that. And after I've talked for a while, I say something like—let's see—'I think you mentioned that you've been practicing birth control? Is that right?' And they'll say they use the pill, or they've been trying to stop, or they know it's a sin. But the thing is to ask them, right away, why they think it's a sin, and invariably they'll say: 'Because the church says it is.'"

Conor paused to see how Father Riley was taking this. He was hunched over his coffee cup but not drinking.

"And then?"

"And then I try to explain that it isn't just a question of what the church says; the birth control issue is far more complicated than that."

"But what do you *say?*"

"I say that, yes, the church sets down as a general rule—and I underline those words for them: as a general rule—that Catholics shouldn't use birth control. But the issue, I tell them, is essentially a personal one, involving private rather than general norms of morality, and so it's the responsibility of each of us to *in*form our minds on the matter so that we can properly *form* our own *consciences*. You see, I've got it down to a rote speech, practically."

"And then you help them inform their minds."

"An informed conscience is absolutely essential."

"Got it."

"I tell them they should ask themselves three questions. Like this. I say: 'First, you should ask yourself if you are shirking your Christian responsibilities; that is to say, do I just want the pleasure of sex without the responsibility of children? Now, you've already got three children, you said, so obviously you're not out just for pleasure.' Or, if they don't have any children, I say that 'probably you'll want to have children later, someday.' Anyway, I take away their worry about the sex part. 'Second, you ask yourself if there is some real need for you to use birth control. But you've already indicated financial reasons... or psychological, or physical, or whatever. I just fit the answer to the case, you see. 'Third, you should ask yourself if this is going to help you and your spouse lead a fuller, happier, more responsible Christian life. Now only you and your spouse together can answer that, so you should have a discussion with him or her, and then once you've made up your mind to use or not to use birth control, then just go ahead and live comfortably with your decision. And whatever you do, don't mention it in confession again, because eventually you're sure to run into some crazy priest who'll scream and yell and say you're committing mortal sin.'"

"Fantastic."

"Wait. I'm not done. Then—because by now they're usually so excited they're liable to forget—I give them a quick run-through once again. I say, 'Now I'll repeat those questions just to make sure you've got them right.' And then I send them on their way. Rejoicing."

"Fantastic."

"Well, it's sound morality, I think. And it helps people to assume responsibility for their own lives." Conor paused a moment and then added, "I try to get them past fear, past blind obedience." He paused once more. "I try to help them see it's only love that matters."

Father Riley, saying nothing, looked past Conor into empty space. At once Conor felt trapped; he turned to see what Father Riley was looking at, expecting to see Father Mahoney, expecting to be denounced for hypocrisy, for New Breedism, for God knows what. But no one was there; Father Riley was merely looking into a new world of possibilities.

Conor let out a long breath and turned back to Father Riley.

"Well, I hope that helps," he said, but he was thinking, I've done it now; I'm gonna pay for this.

"I always wanted to be a priest," Father Riley said, and a boozy tear slid crookedly down his cheek.

Conor excused himself to go get ready for evening confessions.

A number of people were lined up at his confessional when Conor arrived, but now he had heard them all and was free to think about himself for a moment. On the walk over to the church he had helped push a stalled car, and when the wheels suddenly caught traction, they sprayed snow and slush all over him. His feet were wet again and his cassock was soaking from the knees down. He blew his nose, too hard, and got a terrible pain in the ear. And he was sweating. Pneumonia, just watch.

He wanted a drink. Maybe Father Riley would still be in the kitchen after confessions, maybe with a new bottle, and Conor could have a good belt and then lie down until midnight. But of course he couldn't lie down; he'd have to study rubrics for the midnight Mass. Because of course that damned Mahoney was right; Jesuits never knew what to do or where to go during a High Mass. Still, as subdeacon, he'd have very little to do; it would take only a few minutes to go over the rubrics.

Conor thought of Father Riley. He was supposed to be the deacon. Could he do it? With all that booze in him? Worse yet, with all that booze in him, would he blab to Mahoney about the birth control stuff? And, oh God, this filthy cold coming on.

I've got to learn prudence, Conor told himself. Prudence in speech. Prudence in action. What a boring virtue. "Prudence, the ugly stepsister of incapacity." Blake? Yeats?

There was a rattle and a clunk in the confessional on his left, so Conor closed one window and opened the other. He would have to think of prudence later. After a moment of waiting for the penitent to start, Conor said, "Fine. You can begin anytime."

"I can't see you." A woman's voice.

"That's okay. So long as we can hear."

A long pause.

"Can you hear me?" he asked.

"Do you have a beard?'

"Um, well, yes. But what is the point?" Conor began to feel very uneasy. This is not how confessions were supposed to go. There was no room for the personal here, no room for chats. If there were any chatting to be done, the priest would do it. "What is the point of asking if I have a beard?"

"A friend who came to confession this afternoon told me about some priest. She said to be sure to go to the one with the beard, but I can't see through this screen."

"Well, perhaps we can begin," Conor said, a little icy, and the woman, picking up his tone, began at once. Birth control again.

It was like that for the next hour: a succession of women and men who had not been to confession in months, a year, in several years. Conor was moved and sympathetic, but he had been rattled by that first woman, chummy and chatty, and so he was careful to remain a little distant, a little formal, a little... he searched for the word... a little priestly.

His head ached and his throat felt raw. Between the penitents he checked his watch; it was eight thirty. Good. He wanted to lie down.

And then, just as he was about to slide the screen open, he heard the voice of Father Mahoney booming from the other side of the church. "You people kneeling over there. Yes, you. Come over to this side and I'll hear your confessions."

My God, Conor thought, talk about bringing in customers! What a scandal Mahoney was. What a woebegone wreck of the priesthood. What a commentary on how hopeless priests were. But what could you do about it?

Conor slid the window open and yet again it was birth control. And yet again he launched into his three-point speech. Love is what matters.

"You three over there." It was Mahoney's voice, booming. "Two of you come over here. It's nine o'clock and we're closing now. So you two come over here."

God, I hate that man, Conor thought.

He refused to be rushed with this last confession. He was saying the words of absolution and had just raised his hand to begin making the sign of the cross when someone knocked hard and long at the door to his confessional. Mahoney, of course. "Father? You! Father! We're locking up now, so finish up here and leave by the left rear door. The left. Rear. No more confessions after this."

Conor repeated the words of absolution, apologized to the penitent, and then sat silently for a moment, blushing, furious. That utter fool!

As Conor went out by the left rear door, he was startled to find Father Mahoney there, shouting at three young men who were standing at a little distance, up to their knees in snow.

"This isn't a supermarket, you know," Father Mahoney was saying. "If you want to go to confession, you get here on time. You can't just come in here any old time you want. This is not Safeway."

The three young men continued to stand there listening, uncertain what to do. Finally, one of them turned and started making his way out to the street. The others followed him.

Father Mahoney cleared his throat noisily and said to Conor, "I know that type. Confession once a year and then three hundred and sixty-four days of sin."

Conor had watched the scene in disbelief, his annoyance at Father Mahoney giving way to embarrassment and then to rage. Suddenly he came to himself. He jumped down from the steps and took off after the young men. "Wait!" he shouted as he plunged through the deep snow. "Please wait."

He caught up with them at the street, out of breath and soaking wet all over again. He apologized for Father Mahoney; he grimaced and shook his head conspiratorially so they would know he was on their side; and then he led them off one by one to hear their confessions. He stood on top of the church steps, his back turned, his head lowered. It was just as Father Mahoney had said; none of the three had been to confession in a year. All the more reason, Conor thought, for hearing them. It was like the Middle Ages, really: priest and penitent huddled at the church door, the once-a-year reconciliation on the feast of Christ's birth, the snow falling. It was romantic, beautiful. It was an act of love.

Conor absolved the last of the three, shook his hand, and waited as he went down the steps to rejoin his friends. They turned and waved to him. "Happy Christmas," Conor called after them. He watched as they made their way down the snowy street. One of them jumped in the air suddenly and let out a war whoop; the others laughed, and one of them scooped up a snowball and threw it at the one who had whooped.

"I have done a good thing," Conor said to the empty air, and then he descended the steps and walked slowly through the snow to the rectory and to the inevitable encounter with that fool Mahoney.

Conor paused inside the front door, listening. There were loud voices in the kitchen; Father Riley, thoroughly drunk by now, was trying to explain something to Father Mahoney, and Father Mahoney was trying to convince him to go to bed. Conor was shucking off his rubbers when suddenly the voices grew louder and he heard Father Riley say, in his muzzy voice, "Listen to me. I'm serious. We just have to tell them to ask themselves three questions, and then it's all right and they can practice birth control." And he heard Father Mahoney say, "Go to bed, Father. Now." Father Riley protested further, and again Father Mahoney said, "Now," and then Father Riley broke off in the middle of a sentence, walked unsteadily into the living room and, without a word to Conor, went up the stairs to bed.

So, this is it, Conor said to himself, and squared his shoulders, ready for the fight. But when he entered the kitchen, expecting to find Father Mahoney red-faced and righteous, he was astonished to find him instead with his eyes shut and his hands knotted in prayer. Conor stood there waiting for Mahoney to open his eyes and get on with it, but the old priest continued to pray for what seemed like minutes.

Conor stood silent all this time, waiting.

"Ah, it's you," Father Mahoney said finally. "I didn't hear you come in."

"Little cat feet," Conor said, his voice cold, his wits ready for combat.

But Father Mahoney did not seem to hear him. He took a deep breath and Conor, watching him, realized suddenly that Father Mahoney was a very old and very tired man.

"My son," he began. He ignored Conor's smile, which might have been genuine or merely ironic, and continued in a tired voice, "You are a very, very young priest. What you say in confession is between you and God, and therefore between you and the bishop as well, but it's God finally that you're going to have to answer to. But since you're preaching birth control—in the confessional of all places—and here in my parish, I feel it is my duty to say this to you."

Conor's smile was certainly not genuine.

"I want you to ask yourself one question. Not three. Only one. You make a lot of people happy by what you say in confession. They wait outside your confessional. They stand on the church steps in the snow. And they think you're wonderful. Of course they do. Of course they do. But I want you to ask yourself this question. Whom are you serving? Who is your God?"

Conor had been ready for a direct attack, for bombast. By the time he was able to take in just what Father Mahoney had said, the old priest had turned and walked slowly from the kitchen. Conor stood there in silence, listening to the slow soft footfalls as Father Mahoney ascended the stairs.

I'm getting pneumonia, Conor thought; I'm going to die of this. There is a large wet cat asleep in my head.

His mind was racing back and forth through the day: his cold, confessions, Father Mahoney, poor old drunken Riley, the three guys whose confessions he had heard on the church steps. But always he came back to Father Mahoney asking him, "Whom are you serving? Who is your God?"

Conor was sitting with his hands folded in his lap, his eyes lowered, the model of religious propriety. Father Riley was sitting next to him, he too a model of religious propriety. Father Mahoney was—forgive the expression, Conor said to himself—preaching. They were halfway through midnight Mass and everything was going smoothly. Except for the cold. His throat was raw and his nose was stuffed and he wanted a drink. Surely old Mahoney would loosen up after Mass and give them all a Christmas belt of Irish whiskey.

Conor shot a glance at Father Riley. Amazing. He was sitting there, hands folded, eyes straight ahead, as if he had never had a drink in his life. How had he done this? Evidently his powers of recuperation were mammoth. Two hours earlier he had scarcely been able to walk and talk and now here he was, clean shaven and clear eyed, the perfect little Irish priesty-poo.

Priests. They made him sick. Always so right, so righteous, so complacent. Look at that old fool Mahoney up there, mouthing platitudes about the stable, the shepherds, the wise men. The *wise* men; my God!

Conor forced himself not to listen. He had spent the past two hours going over and over tomorrow's homily and now he mentally recited it one more time. He had written it a week earlier and had timed it with a stopwatch. Seven minutes exactly. Theologically sound. And to the point. "Love shows itself in deeds, not words. The word of God is love."

Father Mahoney stopped preaching, finally, and the dreadful choir began the Credo. Conor tried to give his attention to the Mass itself but his mind would not stop racing. Then the last notes of the Credo faded away and he came back to himself. At that instant he decided he would say tomorrow's Mass in English. He had made the translation himself and, though he had never yet used it publicly, he always carried it with him on weekend calls. Just in case. It was only a matter of time anyhow until Rome authorized the Mass in the vernacular, so no one would care. Except Mahoney. But he'd never find out.

In no time at all they were at the consecration, and then they were distributing Communion, and finally—Conor's mind was still on tomorrow's Mass in English—Father Mahoney was giving the last blessing and the choir was bleating out "Joy to the World" and it was all done.

They took off their vestments in silence. Conor kept hoping Mahoney would propose a nightcap or two, but perhaps this wasn't the right moment. Father Riley disappeared almost immediately, in pursuit of his own nightcap, no doubt, and then Father Mahoney got involved in a long conversation with the head usher, so Conor had no choice but to walk back to the rectory alone. Could it possibly be that Mahoney had no intention of offering drinks at all?

Snow was still falling, and it was very wet now, so the street was deep in slush. Cars were stuck in the snow and horns were honking, but everybody was calling out happily to everybody else as if—Conor found himself thinking—as if it were really Christmas. He was suddenly very depressed.

"Father? Have you got a second, Father?" A bald-headed man in a red-and-black mackinaw thrust a package—unmistakably booze—into Conor's hands. "It's for Father Mahoney, could you give it to him for me? It's a little Christmas cheer. And Father. No sampling, right?" He let out a loud laugh and punched Conor on the arm. "Get it? Just a joke. Merry Christmas, Father." And he was gone.

Conor sat in his bed, comfy, propped up against the pillows. "Fate and free will," he said, filling his glass with scotch. "Here's to Father Mahoney, who alone has made this possible."

Now that he had opened it, he would have to take the bottle back to Shadowbrook. The card too. Imagine becoming a thief for a bottle of booze.

"Here's to you, Father Riley."

Conor refilled his glass and put the light out. The last thing he wanted now was for Father Mahoney to stop by and invite him to have a drink.

"And to you, Mrs. Carberry."

He sat in the dark, drinking and toasting penitents everywhere. "Happy Christmas to all," he said. "God bless us, every one."

Conor woke at six, his eyes on fire, his throat raw. At first he could not remember where he was, but then he saw the half-empty bottle beside his bed and he remembered: Our Lady of Victories parish. And he had the seven o'clock Mass to say. And then the ten o'clock Mass.

He was sick. The cold had settled in all right, but the hangover was the worst part of it. He knew how it would be: dull pain for a few hours, and then nausea for a while, and then—after the entire day had been ruined—recovery. The important thing was to get through Mass before the nausea set in. Oh God, how did these things happen?

He blew his nose until it began to bleed and then he dragged himself to the shower. A shave, a clean shirt, a forced fleeting smile in the mirror; he began to feel a little better. But when he came through the passage into the kitchen, the smell of cooking made his stomach turn and he thought he was going to be sick. He put his hand to his mouth and concentrated on keeping a calm stomach.

"Good morning, Father, and a merry Christmas to you!" Father Mahoney was full of high spirits this morning. Conor mumbled a good morning and made his way to the little table with the coffee cups.

"I'm making french toast especially for you," Mrs. Carberry said. "So you'll have a French merry Christmas. Right after your seven o'clock holy Mass."

The thought of french toast made Conor's stomach turn once more.

"You're very kind," he said.

"Sure, it's only the start. There'll be ham and eggs and coffee cake and my own biscuits…"

Mrs. Carberry went on listing the things they would have for breakfast, but Conor interrupted her. "I never have more than coffee," he said. "But it's nice of you to go to all that trouble."

"Trouble! It's no trouble. It's all the pleasure I get in life, baking this and that, a little peach cobbler, a little…"

"Merry Christmas. Merry Christmas. A Christmas kiss for you, my dear," and Father Riley, fresh from his five-thirty mass, planted a kiss on Mrs. Carberry's cheek. "Merry Christmas, Father," he said to Father Mahoney. "And to you, Father."

They're all mad, Conor thought; they're all possessed. Yesterday nobody would speak a civil word and this morning nothing can shut them up. He took a long drink of coffee and immediately choked. "Excuse me," he said, and made for his bedroom.

Only twenty minutes until it was time for Mass and his head would not stop pounding. Just so that I don't get nauseous, he said to himself, anything but that.

He got out his English version of the canon—yes, that will make them a wonderful Christmas present—and folded it into his breast pocket. He glanced at the opening paragraph of his homily. Even hungover, he had that by heart. If he could just pull himself together a little more, everything would be perfect.

Walking over to the church he was dazzled by the sun. The snow had stopped and it was a beautiful winter morning, the air bright and clear. Conor slit his eyes against the light.

Mass started out well. The altar boys knew their Latin responses and the organist was on key and—proving the existence of a merciful God, Conor thought—the choir did not sing at the early morning masses. But everything began to go wrong at the Gloria. Conor went suddenly cold and his forehead broke out in sweat. He couldn't concentrate. Reading the Epistle and then the Gospel, he couldn't get any genuine feeling in his voice, in his heart. And now it was time for his homily.

"Love shows itself in deeds, not words. The word of God is love." But everything he said sounded flat, rehearsed. It was all words. Only words.

Desperately, Conor tried to feel something. Anything. And so, while the words fell from his lips in perfect order, the sentences balanced, the images sharp, Conor's mind raced through this weekend for something to draw meaning from: the confessions, the good advice given, the sincerity and warmth of the people he had counseled. He thought of these things, but he felt nothing.

And then after the homily, while he was pouring the wine into the chalice, the smell of it went straight to his head and from there straight to his stomach. His eyes burned and his head swam. He was going to be sick. But by an act of the will, he choked back the nausea and went on. The important thing now was just to get through this.

But then all at once, as he was about to say the words of consecration over the bread, he realized that he had completely forgotten to say the canon in English. He should be saying "This is my body," instead of "*Hoc est enim corpus meum.*" He forgot his nausea for a moment in the sheer annoyance of it all. He had brought the canon with him. His own translation. His own words leading up to the consecration of the bread and wine.

Illogically, Conor found himself thinking, It's all Mahoney's fault. And immediately, as if by thinking of him he had made the man come alive at the altar, he heard Father Mahoney's sad little question, "Whom are you serving? Who is your God?"

Conor bent low over the chalice for the consecration of the wine. He spoke the words simply, feelingly, in English. "For this is the chalice of my blood, of the new and everlasting covenant, the mystery of faith, which shall be shed for you and for many others unto the forgiveness of sins."

He could feel a stir in the church as the people, probably for the first time in their lives, heard the actual words of consecration in language they could understand. He felt proud, even brave, to be shattering the verbal constraints of this old religion.

Conor spoke the last of the words: "As often as you shall do these things, you shall do them in memory of me."

He paused then and gazed into the amber wine, this sacred drink that is the true blood of Christ, and saw mirrored there only his own hard eyes, swollen, scorched. And for a second that would last forever Conor knew who it was he served.

BROTHERS

Finn said an awkward goodbye to his parents and watched them drive off in the new Buick they had bought in case he changed his mind. They were pleased, of course, at Finn's decision to study for the priesthood, but they were wary. It was 1954 and priests were still thought to be holy, and Finn... well... Finn knew that he wasn't holy, but during a retreat in college, he had succumbed to a fit of piety and, dizzied by the idea of sacrifice, he had applied to join the Jesuits. They had put him through a series of interviews and let him know he seemed altogether too caught up in theater, but in the end they had accepted him. So now here he was, almost a Jesuit, and this annoying Brother Reilly kept calling him "Brother."

Brother Reilly had given him a short tour of the public areas—the chapel, the guest parlor, the dining hall—and then escorted him to the front veranda where the other new men were gathered to admire the grounds. A green lawn cascaded down the hill to a small wilderness of trees, with a lake beyond. Everyone agreed it was beautiful. They stood in little groups, sweating in their jackets and ties, while the novices—the real Jesuits—made awkward attempts at conversation. Finn introduced himself to the group around Brother Reilly and, after the expected hand-shaking, silence descended. Finn was not good with silence, so he cleared his throat and wondered aloud if they all felt as strange as he did in his jacket and tie. There was eager agreement and a little self-conscious laughter that encouraged him to wonder further when they would get to wear a cassock—"If it's okay to ask," he said.

"A habit, Brother Finn, not a cassock," Brother Reilly said quietly, a gentle rebuke.

"Sorry; a habit," Finn said, "but when?"

"In good time, Brother Finn."

Finn realized he should shut up, but he couldn't help himself and, attempting friendliness, he said, "Just call me Finn. *Brother* Finn creeps me out."

Brother Reilly, with a show of patience, explained that in the Jesuit order, all novices were called Brother—he pointed them out—Brother Quirk, Brother Matthews, Brother Lavelle, etcetera. And then, lapsing from charity, Brother Reilly added, "You are now *my* brother, Brother Finn, and I don't like it any more than you do." Nervous laughter, a fit of coughing from Brother Lavelle, and then silence.

Finn blushed and muttered to himself, "Ah have always depended on the kindness of strangers."

That night Brother Reilly made a note in his manuductor diary about Brother Finn's "singularity"—Jesuit speak for self-importance—and he added, "I wonder how long Brother Finn will be among us." Then, during examination of conscience, Brother Reilly went to confession and accused himself of disedifying conduct, sins against charity, and anger against one of his new brothers. Anger was a habitual failing, he admitted. He would try harder.

Brother Reilly had been appointed manuductor—"he who leads by the hand"—because even now, as a second-year novice, he was brusque and withdrawn, inclined to hang back from group activities. He had served as a marine in Korea and he had remained gaunt and hungry-looking, with an intensity that seemed to border on the dangerous. His superiors had judged that he was ill-suited to the role of manuductor, and therefore it would be a useful trial for him and an instructive one for the novices.

———

"Feelings," Father Superior explained, "are always to be distrusted. Jesuits are men of the will. The good Jesuit may feel excited or depressed, but—remember—he never shows it. He is never singular. He disappears into the long black line."

This was a talk Father enjoyed giving. It was essential that novices learn self-denial. And denial of feelings came first.

"*Agere contra*—to act against—here is your safeguard against the dangers of feeling. If you feel depressed, smile. If you feel elated, exercise self-restraint. If you dislike someone, pray for him, take note of his virtues, imagine he has virtues even if he has none. *Agere contra*. Be a man of the will."

Finn listened, eager and anxious, certain they would never have let him in if they knew what a shit he was.

But maybe this was a feeling he should just ignore. By an act of the will.

"Brother Reilly must be a holy man," Brother Quirk said to Finn.

"What makes you think that?"

"Well, they chose him as manuductor, and he never violates silence."

"Maybe he just has nothing to say." Finn thought for a moment and added, "That was uncharitable of me. I'm sorry."

Brother Lavelle cleared his throat and spat.

Brother Quirk and Brother Lavelle and Finn had been assigned weeding duty during recreation—weeding the tomatoes where there were in fact no weeds—and since they were outside the house, talking was allowed. Inside the house, talking was forbidden except in emergencies, and then you had to speak in Latin. If your Latin wasn't good, you were expected to learn it or shut up.

"Also, he was in Korea," Brother Quirk said.

"God help the Koreans." Then, to change the subject, Finn added, "These tomatoes are on their last legs. What do you think, Lavelle?"

Brother Lavelle never talked, but now he sat back on his heels and said, slowly, deliberately, "I think this whole fucking thing is a mistake." He stood up and looked around. "Christ," he said, and without asking anyone's permission, he walked back to the house.

Finn, for once, remained silent, but later he noticed that Brother Lavelle was absent from dinner and evening prayers.

"One down," Finn said as they left chapel that night. Brother Reilly heard him and gave him a hard, knowing look.

In conference, Father Superior explained the use of what were facetiously called "scroop beads." A tiny string of beads attached to a safety pin and worn inside the habit allowed you, unobtrusively, to pull down a single bead each time you broke silence or sinned against charity or had an unkind thought. The beads kept you scrupulously aware—hence *scroop*—of your failings and came in handy at the twice-daily examination of conscience. Wearing them was, of course, optional.

Finn waited for Father Superior to say "Just joking," but Father Superior was not given to jokes.

The new men, still wearing jackets and ties, finally began their eight-day retreat. Silence was absolute and time stretched out endlessly before them. Their whole world contracted to an intense focus on Father Superior's conferences, three a day, followed by an hour of private meditation in which they tried to engage each of their five senses in the day's topic: sin, heaven and hell, the life and teachings of Christ, the Gospel mysteries, the wonders of living the Christian life.

Finn thought of Brother Lavelle. Maybe this was all a fucking mistake. But as the eight days passed Finn found himself surrendering to the power of silence and meditation.

Most nights he lay awake while the others slept. On the last of the eight nights, his mind wandered from Christ's resurrection and the empty tomb to the summer theater in Vermont. Gillian Cantrell was his girlfriend that summer, a sophomore at Brown. She was a good actress, full of life and wit, and she was very sexy—too sexy for him. Gillian. Sexy Gillian. He thought of that last night with her. He found that he was getting aroused and forced himself to think of Mary Magdalene at the empty tomb.

The problem was that Finn had always wanted to be an actor. He had spent the summer after high school studying at the New Theatre Academy in New York, and after his first year of college he had acted in summer stock in Vermont. Acting was fun. Acting was thrilling. In his sophomore year he acted in every play the Drama Department put on. At the same time, he had this secret life in which he gave himself over to prayer. One night on his way back from the library he'd decided to make a quick stop at the college chapel. The place was black with only the red sanctuary light blinking next to the altar. It was sort of spooky and Finn was glad that nobody could see him. He knelt in the back pew and closed his eyes. After a while he felt foolish, as if he was faking some kind of piety, so he decided to leave. But when he opened his eyes he was startled to see the flickering red altar light move toward him. He blinked and it moved again. The dark, and the single red light moving toward him in that dark: it had to be just an optical illusion. But for a moment his heart stumbled and, looking back, he knew that that was when he'd seen it clearly: acting was not enough. The best thing he could do with his life was sacrifice it, and what better way to sacrifice it than as a Jesuit.

Suddenly from the bed nearest the door, there came a terrible shout. It was more than a shout; it was a wail of pure terror and it seemed to go on and on before trailing away into silence.

Someone turned on the light. Someone else said, "It's Brother Reilly. It's the manuductor."

Brother Reilly, the manuductor, still fighting his way out of his dream, pulled himself together and said in a shaking voice, "Everything's fine. There's nothing the matter." He turned off the light, saying, "Sleep, everybody," and he left the room. Incredibly, they all slept, even Finn.

The next morning, their trial period behind them, the new novices were accepted into the common life of the Jesuit community. It was a free day, with a sung mass in the morning and a special feast in the evening and Benediction before bed.

Finn was at last a member of the long black line.

ONCE IN A DARK WOOD

Brother Reilly had had a fit. The word went around during *laborandum*, the afternoon work period.

"It happened once before," Brother Quirk said, "when he was in his first year."

"It was worse," Brother Matthews said. "He woke us all up howling. He dreams he's back in Korea."

"My brother was in Korea and my father was in the last war—in Germany—but they never wake up howling."

"I wonder why he does it. Why it happens, I mean."

"It's a cross to bear." Brother Quirk paused, then added, grimly, "The real cross is that he may have to postpone vows. For a year."

"For howling?"

"It's canon law. His mental state... his fits may be an impediment to ordination. Like epilepsy or schizophrenia or even facial disfigurement."

"You mean if you're too ugly, you can't be ordained?" Finn doubted this. "That would mean a lot of priests got through by accident."

"Father Taylor, for instance."

"Or Father Hanson."

"You'll be a close call yourself, Quirk."

"Very funny, Brother Finn. We should pray for Brother Reilly and we shouldn't be talking about it anyway. It's not charitable."

Brother Reilly, meanwhile, was resting in the infirmary. It was called rest, but he knew that, in fact, he was under observation. Superiors wanted to know if his fits were incapacitating or if, as the neurologist had assured them, Brother Reilly was merely having a flashback to the war. They should just wait, the doctor said.

Brother Reilly knew all about waiting. When he first applied to the Jesuits, he interviewed with the psychiatrist whose job it was to vet all incoming novices, and it emerged that, as a marine lance corporal in Korea, Reilly had spent a good deal of his downtime with local prostitutes. The psychiatrist thought it wise for Reilly to see if he could get by without sex for a year, and so he recommended postponing entrance. Reilly endured his year of chastity and applied once again. This time, he was approved by the psychiatrist. He was a dutiful novice, if quiet and withdrawn, but then one night he woke up screaming. It was his first fit, which he passed off as a bad dream.

But now it had happened again.

Finn was tempted to make a smart-ass remark about Reilly, but for once he held his tongue. He was briefly proud of himself. Then ashamed of his pride. Mentally he pulled down a scroop bead.

Brother Quirk was appointed manuductor. Suddenly he was everywhere, making announcements, reminding his brothers about changes in the schedule, posting a new *de more* notice. It was the same old schedule but elaborately printed to resemble an illuminated manuscript and translated, unnecessarily, as "Regular order."

Finn stood before the noticeboard doing his rabbit imitation.

5.30	rise
6	visit chapel
6.15–7	meditation
7–7.45	Mass
7.45–8	breakfast
8–8.30	free time

He drew a deep breath. The rest of the day was divided into blocks of time for conference, Rosary, class, examination of conscience, lunch, two hours of assigned work, study, more meditation, dinner, chores, spiritual reading, a second examination of conscience, and finally, at nine thirty, following a last visit to chapel, bedtime.

"At least they give you time to hit the toilet," Finn said to anybody listening and, as God would have it, that happened to be Brother Reilly, who looked at him as if he were an insect.

———

Finn's rabbit imitation had come to him during a visit to chapel. He was wondering what made Brother Quirk so annoying and, with no shame at all, he stared at him. He looked like Bugs Bunny. His front teeth stuck out a little and he had a nervous tic that sometimes made his lips twitch just like a rabbit's. A pious rabbit. With a pronounced Dorchester accent.

Finn pushed his upper lip forward and exposed his front teeth, and for an awful moment he became Brother Quirk. It was unkind. He wouldn't do it again. But later, alone in a toilet stall, he tried it one more time. Just for practice.

"Grace is God's free gift. We can't earn it. We can't deserve it. God gives it to whom he wills."

Finn knew this well and he found it depressing.

"We can open ourselves to grace by constant prayer, but we can't merit it. It's given gratuitously."

Finn's mind wandered. Was novitiate life making him infantile? Other men his age were fighting in Korea, and here he was on his knees, confessing to uncharitable thoughts. What ever happened to making his life a sacrifice?

It was visiting day. On the great south lawn, guests gathered in groups, anxious to greet the new Jesuit in the family, with his new black habit and his new air of holiness.

Finn's group included just his parents and himself. They had brought him presents—a black sweater, winter gloves, a huge box of chocolates—and Finn thanked them lavishly. But he was proud of his new poverty and couldn't resist telling them that gifts of any kind became common stock.

"We don't own anything. Isn't that wonderful? If somebody needs a sweater, he just asks, and they'll give him this one."

"Oh, but we got it for you."

"There isn't any me anymore, Mother. Not like that."

Her eyes filled and she said, "Don't."

"He's just being dramatic, Claire," his father said. "Let it go."

Finn bristled at "dramatic," but he knew his father was right and found himself blushing.

"I love the sweater," he said. "Maybe they'll let me keep it."

"You don't want to ask for exceptions," his father said. "A rule is a rule."

It was the old family dynamic: his mother hurt and his father stepping in to lighten her disappointment and shift the blame to Finn. This was how it would go. She would be depressed tonight and need her tranquilizers. And his father would lie awake beside her, talking until she could finally get to sleep. And the unspoken blame would be laid on guess who.

Finn leaned over and kissed her on the cheek. "My sweet old *Mutti*," he said. "She's the best." She raised a hand to protect herself, but Finn was determined to salvage their day. "Come on, Momoo," he said and, pretending to twist her ears, he made motor sounds. "Start your engine! Come on! Lift off!" until she pushed him away, saying, "People will see!" But she laughed and his father laughed and so the visit was saved.

The afternoon was made easier by brief visits from the young priest, Father Lomax, who taught the novices Latin, and by Father Spalding, the old priest who taught them Greek. They said hello and welcome and goodbye, smiling and nodding as they moved on to the next group.

"They're all so nice," Finn's mother said. "What about that young man, the one who showed us around last time? He was very nice."

"Brother Reilly has fits."

"Oh, no."

Finn thought, Here's a good story, but he knew it was a story he had no right to tell.

"He has screaming fits in the night," he said.

"That's awful."

"He had one a few weeks ago. He started screaming, and I mean major full-on screaming, it was the middle of the night, and we all woke up, we were terrified, you can imagine. Reilly, of all people! Then he stopped and everything went quiet and he said—calm as could be—he said, 'Everything's fine. There's nothing the matter. Just go back to sleep.' And he left the dorm and went down to the infirmary and he was there for days. It was incredible." Finn paused. This was all wrong. He added, lamely, "He had a fit."

"Poor man. Isn't there anything they can do for him?"

"It's shell shock or something."

They were quiet for a while, thinking.

Finn broke the silence. "I probably shouldn't have told you that."

"It's sad. It's a sad story."

"I shouldn't have told it," he said again.

Toward the end of the afternoon, when they all seemed talked out, his father said—and it was obvious they had planned this—that if ever Finn wanted to leave, they would completely understand, that what they cared about was his happiness, that's all. They wanted him to be happy. Finn assured them he was happy.

Finally it was over.

Visiting day had been a great success. Finn, however, felt sick. He had squandered what little progress he had made in the spiritual life. He had trivialized it. He had talked it away.

De more for months now. Mass and meditation, spiritual conference, and on and on until litanies in chapel, and so to bed.

Then Father Larsen arrived. He appeared one day at noon, silent, forbidding, entering the refectory behind everyone else. He looked ancient. His back was crooked and he walked slowly, bent over. His habit hung on him like a shroud. But it was his face that was shocking. A thick scar ran from his left eyebrow down to his chin, pulling his mouth a little to the side so that he appeared to be sneering.

The novices, observing custody of the eyes, pretended not to see him. They stood for the prayers before meals and when they sat down

Father Superior declared "*Deo gratias*," which meant they were free to talk. Finn, who was waiting on the faculty table, noted that although the priests spoke quietly among themselves, Father Larsen spoke hardly at all.

Later, as he gave out *laborandum* assignments, Brother Quirk explained—in English—that Father Larsen was ill. He was here for a rest and he was completely off-limits. No confessions and no spiritual advice. These were orders from Father Superior. Father Larsen had been a prisoner on the Bataan death march. He had survived torture and starvation, but he had never really recovered. So he was here to rest. Period. The other novices had many questions about the death march and about the torture—what had happened to his face?—but it was work time and Brother Quirk sent them on their way.

So Finn felt deeply betrayed the next day when, coming out of chapel, he saw Brother Reilly leave the line of novices and join Father Larsen, who was waiting for him on the veranda. They exchanged a few words and then, like old chums, took the path down to the lake. Finn went off to *laborandum* to dig more goddamn potatoes and wrestle with his jealousy of that fucking Reilly.

Winter was long and cold, but at last the snow melted and Lent began and Finn was a changed man. He no longer imitated Brother Quirk or broke the rule of silence or said witty things at the expense of his brothers. Moreover, he was content. He felt no need to perform. He merely listened while Brother Haberman told his stories about life in Dorchester, and he dutifully learned the names of Irish parishes in Southie, and when he and Brother Reilly were assigned to the same work crew, Finn did his best to draw him out. They were planting those everlasting potatoes.

The day was cool, but Finn felt uncomfortably hot, except for his hands, which were freezing. He was tempted to complain, but he concentrated on Brother Reilly instead.

Finn scooped out a hole and buried a chunk of potato, the eye facing up. "I guess this isn't much like the marines," he said.

"It is, as a matter of fact. Mindless tasks and no women."

Finn pondered that, shocked. How about that! "I notice you walk with Father Larsen. What is it like?"

"It was an order from Father Superior. For my mental health."

"Oh." And then, "What do you talk about? I mean, what does he talk about?"

"Baseball. Sports."

"Sports? But he must talk sometimes about… well… about being a prisoner."

Brother Reilly punched a hole in the dirt and said nothing. He was pale with anger.

"Or about the death march."

"Cut it! Would you just cut it out! All this shit! Honest to God."

Finn fell silent, and at the end of *laborandum*, when Brother Reilly said, "I apologize, Brother Finn," Finn resisted the urge to tell him to shove it and merely said, "I shouldn't have pried. My fault."

Later that day he learned that Brother Reilly had been told he would have to wait another year before taking vows. Poor Brother Reilly. Finn went to chapel to pray for him. He didn't feel well. He had a pain in his chest and his breathing was strained. He was coming down with a cold. Never mind. It was another thing he could offer up.

SEMPER FIDELIS

Brother Infirmarian was old and he was tired. Over the years, he had given pills to countless novices who were dealing with doubts about their vocation by working themselves up into a fever. Finn's temperature was 101, nothing surprising. So Brother gave him the strongest cold pills he had—the yellow and black ones—and told him to take a lie-down instead of *laborandum* for the next few days. A day passed and then another and, though Finn took the yellow and black pills, he was racked by a constant cough and dizzy with fever. His coughing distracted everybody during meditation so he was sent back to the infirmarian for a second round of pills. But his fever was now 103 and he was badly dehydrated so, against his instincts and principles, Brother Infirmarian admitted him as a patient deserving of

antibiotics and his own devoted attention. Finn began to feel better at
once, and after his second day he began to hope for visitors. Maybe
someone interesting might get ill, Finn thought—just slightly ill—
and he'd have a roommate to talk with. He should have guessed it
would be Brother Reilly.

Brother Reilly had had another fit, even worse than the others.
He woke, raging in the night, loud and obscene, with a soaring fever
and a compulsion to talk. He was brought straight to the infirmary.

Far from being company for Finn, Brother Reilly continued
on with his fit, mumbling angrily about whores and gooks and dead
marines. This called for Seconal, Brother Infirmarian decided, along
with his own private concoction of honey and water, and a little whiskey,
for the love of God. Brother Reilly slept through the entire day and
then through the night, muttering the whole time. By the following
morning, he had quieted down and showed signs of returning to his old
self. Around noon, he growled something unpleasant to the infirmarian
and toward evening, with a grunt and a moan, he acknowledged the
presence of Finn. At ten o'clock, lights out for the Great Silence,
Brother Reilly had recovered sufficiently to attempt a chat. He was
groggy but plainspoken.

"I disliked you from the day you arrived," he said.

"I know you did. I disliked you too. But I prayed about it."

"Did it work?"

"Not really. I'm sorry about your vows."

"Fuck the vows."

This was too much for Finn. "We're not supposed to be talking
during the Great Silence. I'm not going to talk."

"Fuck the Great Silence."

Brother Reilly fell asleep then, and when he woke in the middle
of the night, he was shaking with fever and his teeth were chattering.
He called out to Finn.

"I'm sorry for what I said, Finn. Finn?"

"Thank you for calling me Finn."

"I'm having a fit. How are you?"

"We're not supposed to talk during the Great Silence."

"We could say the Rosary together."

Finn got out of bed and padded, barefoot, across the dark room to kneel beside Brother Reilly's bed. They said the Glorious Mysteries, with Finn starting the prayers and Brother Reilly responding. Finn was eager to finish and prayed fast. "Amen," Finn said finally, and Brother Reilly said, "Amen."

Finn knelt in silence, in the dark, unsure what to do now.

Brother Reilly made a choking sound, as if he was trying not to sob.

"Are you all right?" Finn couldn't bear the silence.

"I wanted to be a Jesuit to make up for my life."

"To sacrifice it."

"No. To make up for it. To atone for all I've done."

"I wanted to make my life a sacrifice. Self-obliteration. For God."

"You gotta be careful what you ask for. Sometimes you get it."

Another long silence.

"It's late," Finn said.

"Do you want to get in bed with me?"

"Yes." Finn astonished himself because that was indeed what he wanted. "But I don't think it's a good idea."

"It wouldn't be anything sexual. We'd just hold each other."

Finn felt himself getting hard.

"I just want to hold you," Brother Reilly said.

"Yes."

"I need to hold you."

"I don't think I can do it."

"The truth is," and Brother Reilly paused, his voice shaking, "the truth is I need to be held."

Finn thought about this and shook his head no. "I can't," he said and then, determined, "I won't."

He padded back to his bed and tried to sleep. He could hear Brother Reilly moaning, perhaps crying. Finn blocked his ears and turned from side to side. Finally he got up and took one of the two Seconals from Brother Reilly's nightstand and in minutes he fell soundly asleep.

Finn woke the next morning, groggy and numb, barely aware that something was happening around him. Brother Infirmarian and Father Superior were wheeling Brother Reilly out to the corridor where an ambulance was waiting to take him to the hospital. Finn turned his face to the wall, guilty. What had he done? But he had no time to consider what he had done or, more importantly, what he had not done, because Brother Infirmarian had decided it was time for Finn to go. He wanted his infirmary back the way it should be: empty.

In no time at all Finn was standing at the *de more* bulletin board, where a notice from Father Superior suggested that to prepare for the feast of Saint Ignatius, they should all meditate on the vows.

Finn's meditation was distracted by thoughts of Brother Reilly. Do you want to get in bed with me? He had wanted to and he had nearly done it. He felt his face burn. He would go to confession during this evening's examination of conscience.

But when the time came, Finn couldn't bear to tell all this to Father Superior, so he went to old Father Spalding, the Greek teacher, who had taught at several different Jesuit colleges and had heard everything. Besides, he was a little deaf.

Finn confessed that in the infirmary one of his brother novices had asked him to get in bed with him. "He just wanted to be held, but I knew it was clearly an occasion of sin," Finn said, "and I knew it was my own fault." Father Spalding belched softly. "That's all, Father."

Father Spalding sighed and said, "I know." He gave Finn a long talk about loneliness in religious life and the importance of chastity and the danger of friendships that became emotional. He paused and, as if he were merely distracted, he said, "Religious life is not for everyone. But be of good cheer and pray for a peaceful heart."

Vow day came and went while Brother Reilly remained in the local hospital. After two weeks he was transferred to Shrewsbury Mental and then was released to his family.

On his first day home he shot and killed himself with his marine service pistol, but not before writing a letter to Finn saying, "My death happened years ago and has nothing to do with you. Have a happy, holy life." It was signed, "Love, Brother Reilly."

Father Superior opened the letter, as he opened all novice mail, and after he had considered the matter at prayer, he called in Brother Finn and told him of Brother Reilly's death. Finn went white and slumped in the chair but said nothing. He put the letter in his inside pocket next to his scroop beads and went downstairs to chapel. He sat in the back pew and tried to think. But he didn't know how to think any longer and old words kept circulating in his brain. Finally it came to him that he was to blame. For everything.

Finn knocked at Father Larsen's door and waited. He knocked again and heard a kind of grunt, so he pushed the door open and entered. The room was thick with smoke and smelled of cigarettes and whiskey. Father Larsen was at his desk. He looked annoyed. He pushed his drink aside.

"I don't hear confessions."

"I know, Father."

"Or give spiritual advice. Or listen to novices' sob stories."

"No."

Father Larsen turned his scarred face toward Finn so that he seemed to be sneering. "Well, what then? I'm not able to help you, whatever it is."

"It's about Brother Reilly."

Father Larsen pushed aside the book he had been reading, the New Testament in Latin and Greek. He lit a cigarette and told Finn to sit down.

"What's this about Reilly?"

"It's about his death."

"Who told you he's dead?"

"He wrote me a letter before he did it."

"Reilly was a good man. A good marine."

An awkward silence, and then Finn blurted out, "It was all my fault." He began to sob, softly at first, then louder. He choked finally and blew his nose. He said, "I'm a mess. I'm sorry."

Father Larsen pulled deeply on his cigarette and waited.

Finn told him of their instant mutual dislike, Brother Reilly and himself. "Mostly my fault," Finn said. He searched for the least offensive words and told Father Larsen about the encounter in the infirmary and his refusal to get in bed with Reilly. "He wanted to be held," Finn said, "and I refused." He looked at Father Larsen and the scar running from his brow to his chin and said, "It's all my fault."

"Is it?" Father Larsen said. "That would make you more important than you are." This caught Finn's attention.

Father Larsen tapped the ash from his cigarette and looked at him. As if that were an invitation to tell him everything, Finn began with wanting to be an actor and exchanging that for scroop beads and his struggle with the rules and on and on until he reached that desperate scene with Brother Reilly.

"He wanted to be held. What he said was he *needed* to be held. And I refused."

Father Larsen sat back in his chair. He said to Finn, "Would it have been so bad to get in bed with Reilly? Would there have been terrible harm to anyone?"

"Do you mean I should have? Is that what you're saying?"

Father Larsen hesitated and then said, "I would have, poor shit that I am. Sometimes we have to risk our soul to save somebody else."

"But it would have been a mortal sin." Finn blushed. "Because I wanted it." He paused. "I wanted to get in bed with him. I was aroused. I had an erection. So I walked away and left him there." He paused again. "I stole one of his pills and went to bed, trying not to think of Reilly or my erection. The next morning they took him to the hospital. I'm to blame. I blame myself."

"A man kills himself. A sick man. And you—in a monstrous act of proprietary guilt—you blame yourself." He lowered his voice to a whisper. "You. You. You. It's all about you. I really think you should go. I think you should leave now before it's too late."

Finn made a choking sound.

"Leave. Before you turn totally inward… and rot."

"Leave," Finn said.

"Everything you've told me is about you. Your guilt. Your blame. Your pitiful erection."

"But I was following the Jesuit rule. Or trying to."

"You've turned it inside out. You're supposed to be growing in Christ and instead you've been growing in self-satisfaction."

The clock ticked on Father Larsen's desk and from the chapel came the sound of the bell for litanies. Then there was silence in the room and it was terrifying.

"Is this because of Reilly?" Finn asked.

"Reilly has nothing to do with it."

Father Larsen lowered his voice to a near whisper. He made as if to wash his hands. "You should go. You should leave the Jesuits. That's the only help I can offer. That's it. *Finis*. The end."

Father Larsen sat back in his chair. He was done with Finn. He had said the hard and necessary thing and now they both had to live with it. He lit a cigarette. He was exhausted. It was Bataan again, every day of his life. He said, "This is why they don't want me dealing with novices."

Finn thought, So this is despair.

Reading his mind, Father Larsen said in a hard voice, "Don't despair, kiddo. There are plenty of other ways to sacrifice your life."

Two days went by. Finn found he could not pray. He went through the motions of meditation, Mass, and thanksgiving, but he was not conscious of praying. He was existing, merely, a testament to shame and disgrace. And then on the third day, he woke at five thirty, *de more*, yawned, and before going back to sleep—at that precise moment and with a joyful heart—he decided to leave the Jesuits, admit his failure, and let sacrifice find him when he was ready for it. He slept until nearly eight and got up just in time for breakfast.

It was Friday, which meant pancakes, and he had three of them with extra syrup. He looked frankly around the refectory at his brother

Jesuits. He admired them this morning, men who had made a free choice and, at great cost, were trying to disappear into the long back line. Finn did not want to disappear.

"I'm free," he said aloud. The other novices continued to concentrate on breakfast. Everyone knew Brother Finn was impossible.

Finn left that afternoon in a burst of freedom. He had Father Superior's blessing and he made a last visit to chapel with no feeling of regret. He felt comfortable in his jacket and tie.

As he stood alone at the train station, he was visited suddenly by feelings of remorse. He wouldn't have it. "I'm free," he said aloud, just to hear it. And then he shouted it—the platform was empty—and it felt good and true. But with a year's grace behind him—unearned, undeserved—he recognized that this new freedom was only temporary and the words he shouted to the empty air would in time come back to him, and back, in a pale echo: Brother Reilly, Father Larsen. But for now life was good and Finn chose it.

The train arrived and Finn got on and left.

DEPARTURES

The priest is arriving on the train. He is not really a priest, because he is only twenty-five and still a seminarian, but he wears a Roman collar, and everyone thinks he is a priest, and he thinks of himself as a priest. It is six years since he has visited his parents in their home. They have visited him at the seminary, of course, but this is his first visit to them, and he is very anxious about it.

There is a crazy couple across the aisle, and as the train pulls into the station their anger and excitement come near to hysteria; they have just had—as they keep saying—a scrape with death. "We could have been killed," she says, her voice sharp, abused. "We've had a terrible scrape with death." She only pretends to speak to her husband; actually she is addressing the priest and the couple in front of him and the whole car. Her eyes are glassy and wild and she goes on talking with small gasps and shrieks while her husband—glassy eyed too and in shock—says, "You're right, you're right," and wrestles a red plastic suitcase from the rack overhead. They are still exclaiming as they forge down the aisle, important and proud at being almost dead.

The priest waits. He does not want to be near those crazy people when he greets his parents. This will be a special moment and he wants it to be perfect. These six years have made him ill at ease in public. He cannot stand the noise, the rudeness, the urgency in voices. Emotions spill out of people, they shout in public; anger bristles everywhere, in everyone, in the street, the train station, the train. People chew gum.

They belch. They push. He is revolted by the vulgarity, the nakedness of it all. In the seminary there is no emotion, no anger, no urgency—at least not visibly. Everyone keeps inside himself whatever it is he feels.

So the priest stays in his seat until the crazy people have disappeared from the car. Then he gets up, sets his face in a smile—a half smile—and prepares to meet his parents. As he climbs down the steep iron steps, he is conscious of people on the platform looking. At him? Or just for somebody they are here to meet? Suddenly a woman shrieks and the priest turns to help her, thinking she must be hurt, thinking of Anna Karenina beneath the train wheels. But no. The woman is merely excited and the scream is only delight at seeing a boy, her son probably. "Billy," she says, "Billy baby." She hugs him, kisses him, screams again. The boy is embarrassed and the priest, embarrassed too, turns away. Mother and son, he thinks, a travesty. He has told his parents he will meet them in the waiting room, on the east side, and he joins the crowd moving toward the stairs. Ahead of him he sees another priest, about his own age, red haired and stout. Sanity, he thinks, an oasis. But as they reach the bottom of the stairs a woman lunges at the red-haired priest, hugging him once and then again, while a man—his father, with the same red hair and fat—slaps him on the back over and over. "Father Joe," they call him, though, by their ages, he has to be their son. The woman puts her arm under Father Joe's and leans into him, her possession.

There is a disturbance now; somebody is shouting, somebody touches his arm. It is the crazy couple, even more hysterical than before, asking him something, insisting he explain to another couple what happened on the train. A little crowd is gathering and the priest, confused, turns from person to person. He is not listening, he merely wants to get away. And then suddenly he sees his mother smiling from beyond the crowd and his father behind her, his hands on her shoulders, smiling. They are a picture of order in all this chaos. The crazy woman tugs at his arm, but he pulls away from her and, moving blindly through the crowd, walks toward his mother and father. Yes, the priest thinks, I will bring order out of chaos.

His mother is beautiful, radiant, and she will not be dead for another fifteen years. She smiles and comes to meet him and he will remember her this way always. He will wake in the night remembering how she is now, what he does to her. Because as she goes to put her arms around him, as she lifts her face to kiss him, he says to her, with a smile made icy by his self-control, "I'll just kiss you on the cheek—don't touch me—and I'll shake hands with Dad, and then we'll turn and walk out of here." And he bends to kiss her on the cheek but stops because she has pulled slightly away; she has gone white, and the look of panic on her face is not nearly so terrible as the look of drowning in her eyes.

The priest's father has been dead for five years and now the priest sits by his mother's bedside waiting for her to die. Fifteen years have passed since his train came in and he did not kiss her and she turned her face away. His mother has Parkinson's disease and the benign effects of L-dopa have worn off, so that she is bent now and trembles violently whenever she tries to do anything for herself. She drools sometimes and sometimes she cannot control her bowels. But the priest has been told it is not Parkinson's that is killing her; it is cancer. The priest thinks a great deal about death and about the things that kill us. He is not surprised, being forty and having seen many people to their deaths, that dying is not only an agony, it is boredom. He has been waiting by her bedside for months now, an hour or two each day, and still she has not died.

His mother is unconscious much of the time. Or barely conscious; it is hard for him to tell. On the occasions when she turns to him and says something, he is astonished that very often it is something he has been thinking himself. A month before he had been remembering his father's death, a quick and merciful heart attack—how it had been the death his father would have chosen if he were given choices.

"Your father died well," she said, and the priest leaned forward in surprise. He thought she had been unconscious.

"Father?" he asked.

"He died the way he would have wanted," she said.

"Yes," he said, "I was thinking that."

She sighed and shook her head, and a tear showed in the corner of her eye.

"What?" he asked.

"This is not the way I would have chosen," she said.

And though he did not say them he thought the words he hated most: *self-pity*. So he bit the inside of his lip and said, "Try to sleep, Mother."

Again, a week or so later, he was thinking how he had always taken from them, his mother and father; he had never given them anything. He looked at her lying there, her eyes closed, sweating, and he thought, I'll wet the washcloth and put it on her forehead. But before he could reach the washcloth she said to him, "You've always given to us. You've given us everything." And she looked at him with the drowning look.

This sort of thing has happened several times. He has begun to wonder if he causes her to think of what he is thinking: the exercise of the stronger mind on the weaker. No, it can't be that. And so he sits by her bed reading his Shakespeare—he is studying for his PhD in English—and sometimes he adjusts her pillows or wipes her forehead, and when she is able, he talks to her. But more and more now it is a matter of waiting for the end. Her medication has been increased; even when she is not unconscious she is so heavily doped against the pain that conversation is impossible. He waits.

The priest's mother is living and the priest is waiting for her to die. He is wanting her to die now that the pain is so bad, now that he cannot bear any longer the suffering, the boredom. But she does not die.

And then finally she does die. But before she dies she wakes and talks to him one last time. He has been thinking of the train, that terrible day when he destroyed everything, when he tried to bring some order out of chaos and said "Don't touch me," and she turned away from him. He has been thinking of that all day.

She wakes now and drugged, confused, she says to him, "You're not to worry. When the train comes in, I won't kiss you. I won't touch you."

"No!" the priest cries out sharply. "Mother, no." He leans over the bed to kiss her, but as he does, she turns from him and says, "I'll be good, I promise. I'll be good."

With her dying breath, her face still turned from him, she says, "I will."

It is the same day. It is always the same day, except that now he remembers it differently. The priest is leaving on the train, Boston to Springfield, a three-hour trip. He is not really a priest, because he is only twenty-five and is still a seminarian, but he thinks of himself as a priest and so do his parents. His father will not die for another ten years, his mother for fifteen. They will both live to see him ordained.

The train pulls out of the station and the priest begins to read his book, Sartre's *L'existentialisme est un humanisme*. It is boring but good for him. Existentialism is good and humanism is good, and he feels that boredom is just something that goes along with the package. He reads half a page before he realizes he has no idea what he is reading. He is upset about something. What? He doesn't know. Was it getting on the train? Seeing all those people elbowing one another to get ahead, that old woman chewing gum, the man who belched? Partly that. He felt so alien, so removed from them—inhuman. All that pushing and shoving, and there are plenty of empty seats. It makes no sense.

The door between the cars opens and a middle-aged couple come in. She is carrying two shopping bags, one full of presents, wrapped in metallic papers, the other full of something the priest cannot see, because there is a sweater over the top. The man drags an enormous red suitcase, which bumps his leg at every step. It is a warm day and they are both perspiring.

"How about here?" she says, pointing to the seat directly in front of the priest, but then she sees him and says, "No, over here instead," and she backs up, bumping into her husband, who drops the suitcase and curses. "Here," she says. "Yes, this is nice. This side is better. This is fine. Sit down, Freddie. No, let me get next to the window." The man groans and says nothing, giving all his attention to getting the suitcase up onto the luggage rack. "This, too," she says, giving him the bag with the presents. "No, I'll keep it at my feet," she says, and takes the bag back. Finally they are settled. The priest has watched them from where he sits, on the other side of the aisle, one seat back, and he continues to watch them. He is surprised to find the taste of acid in his mouth. He wants to spit; he doesn't know why.

Where he has felt uneasy before, he now feels anger. At himself, perhaps. He returns to his book. He is more than a seminarian, he is a Jesuit seminarian, and so he has an obligation to theology and to culture. But after another two pages he decides he does not have an obligation to Sartre and he puts the book in his briefcase. He decides to meditate. Jesuits meditate for at least an hour each day, usually on some episode, some moment, in the life of Christ, and he has never missed meditation once, not even when he lay for a week in the infirmary with a temperature of 103.

In fact, the infirmary meditation is the nearest he has come to a kind of mystical experience. He had been meditating on the Crucifixion, lying in bed with his scalding temperature, watching what was happening. He saw them drive the nails through the wrists, through the bent feet, saw them lift the heavy cross to the correct angle, until the base thudded into the stone notch that would hold it upright. There was a groan and some blood splattered onto the seamless white tunic they had stripped from him and which now lay at the base of the cross. And then there was blackness. He fell asleep, he supposed, and when he woke, his body soaked with sweat from the fever, he tried to see that white tunic beneath the cross. But he could not see it, he could see only the broad back of a soldier and he could hear the rattle of dice. Then the soldier moved and he could see the others, three of them, taking their turns with the dice, gambling for the tunic and the sandals. And when the last had thrown, one of the soldiers scooped up the dice and held them out to the priest. His hand hung there, offering the dice in his open palm, and while they all stared the priest put out his own hand and slowly, tentatively, took the dice. And then, with the small strength he could muster, he closed his fist around them.

The priest was fevered for three days more, and what he remembered after was that for those three days he held the dice in his hands. It is a meditation he can call back at will. He can and he does now, though he does not know why. Not because of the way it makes him feel— because feeling, he knows, has nothing to do with anything. No, he calls it back because it has something to do with not feeling, with the reason he is a priest in the first place.

At college his roommate had said to him one day, "Seeing as how you're a Catholic, and the best thing a Catholic can do with his life is be a priest, don't you feel obliged to be a priest?" He laughed, seeing he had struck deep. "I mean, you're smart enough, and you're moral enough—you don't screw or anything—so why not? I mean, aren't you obliged to?" The words were insignificant; it was what they did to him at that particular moment that mattered. Because he had been thinking of the priesthood and wanting, but fearing to ask for, a sign. His roommate's words seemed some kind of sign—no miraculous intervention, just the intervention of pure reason. And the meditation on the dice seemed somehow a confirmation of this sign.

The priest opens his eyes. The train has been stopped for some time, new people have got on, and now it is pulling slowly away from the platform. They are near Worcester somewhere. The priest looks out the window opposite him and can see up ahead a grassy hill where three small boys are waving to the train. On the other side of the aisle the woman is rummaging through her shopping bag, totally absorbed with whatever she has in there. The man is gone; he is at the far end of the car getting a drink of water. The train pulls alongside the little boys and the priest waves to them, but they do not wave back. They throw stones, which fall short of the train—all except one, which strikes the window next to the woman with the shopping bag. It makes a sharp sound and at once there appears on the window a white spot the size of a nickel and, radiating from it, a sunburst of silver cracks.

The priest sits forward, prepared to do something, but there is nothing to be done. Despite the noise, like a door slamming, the woman does not seem to hear; she continues plunging her hand into the bag and bringing out things he cannot see. The other people around are either sleeping or absorbed in their reading. No one has noticed except him.

The man returns with a cup of water for his wife. She drinks it and they sit in silence looking out the window.

"Was that window like that before?" he asks.

"Of course," she says. And then she looks at it. "Well, I'm not sure," she says. She puts her finger on the spot of white and traces one of the cracks that radiate from it. "It looks like it's been broken," she says.

"Somebody must have thrown a stone," he says and settles back in his seat.

"Well, if it happened while I was sitting here, I could have been hurt—if the glass broke," she says.

"It was probably just a stone," he says.

"The window could have broken. I could have been hurt," she says, "if it was a bullet. It could have been a bullet...."

She is excited now and leans forward to the couple in front of her. "Did you see this happen? Did you see this window get broken? Right by my head?" But they have seen nothing. She turns to the man across the aisle, to the couple in front of him, to the empty seats behind her. Nobody has seen.

The conductor appears and she waves at him, calling, "Look at this, there's been an accident. Somebody broke this window right while I was sitting here."

The conductor looks at the window and at the woman and at the window again. "What?" he says. He looks at the people in front of the couple and across the aisle from them; he looks at the priest.

The priest says, "A little boy threw a stone and it hit the window."

"Do you see? Do you hear?" the woman says. And she turns to the priest. "Was it a stone? Was I sitting here? Right by the window?"

"Yes," the priest says.

"I could have been killed," the woman says to the conductor. "Do you hear what that priest said? Would a priest lie? It could have been a bullet."

"Damned kids," the conductor says and moves down the aisle.

"We've had a narrow escape from death, Freddie," she says, and from here to Springfield her anger and her enthusiasm grow.

The priest is sick. The chaos of life, the chaos of mind. It is all hopeless. Look at that crazy couple. The boredom of lives lived so purposelessly depresses him, sickens him. The emotion, the anger, the public displays.

The train is in Springfield but he waits until the crazy couple gets off. He does not want to be near them when he meets his parents. Getting off the train, he hears a woman shriek as she descends upon her son; he sees a fat priest with red hair; he is overwhelmed by the noise, the vulgarity. And then there is a disturbance of some sort. It is the crazy couple. Her husband is tugging at the priest's arm, the woman is trying to draw him into a group that has gathered around her.

"The priest saw it all," she is saying. "See that priest? He's living proof. If it wasn't for that priest, we wouldn't be here now."

But the priest does not hear what she says because suddenly beyond the crowd he sees his mother, looking beautiful and composed, smiling, and behind her his father. She will not be dead for fifteen years. They will live to see him ordained, his life fulfilled.

He goes to meet them, conscious that he is in public, conscious of a small circle of order in this chaos. And as his mother opens her arms to him, he says, "I'll just kiss you on the cheek—don't touch me—then..."

But already she has begun to turn away.

The priest is arriving on the train, New York to Boston, a five-hour trip. He has been a priest for many years and he sometimes thinks he is a good priest. But what is *good*? He thinks he does not know that. Sometimes he thinks he does not care. Thinking is his life now and that is enough. Thinking and seeming. He is fifty-five and will not be dead for another fifteen years. But dying is a moment he does not care to think about.

The priest is returning from New York, where he attended the wake of his last living relative. There is a peculiar satisfaction in that, a finality he does not fully understand but which he recognizes all the same. He would have said the burial Mass for his aunt but she died on Good Friday, which means the burial cannot take place until Monday, so the priest is coming back to Boston where he can be used at midnight tonight in the Easter Vigil service. And then tomorrow the Mass of the Resurrection... whoopee! He is irreverent sometimes in the way he thinks; it is his psyche's accommodation to absurdity; or perhaps pain, or bitterness. Anyway he will be back in Boston in no time, and then he will go to his room and have a good belt of scotch, and then a couple of hours in bed to recover for the Easter Vigil.

Trains mean nothing to him anymore. He does not see the people who chew gum, who push, who carry on angrily over nothing. He does not care. That is simply how they are, that is how life is, and what can anyone do about it?

His drinking is not a problem, he thinks. It might have become one if he had not, at forty, finished his PhD in English. That has stabilized him somehow; teaching English is more human than teaching theology. He is grateful for the diversions provided by his PhD. He has seen too many priests hit forty and realize nothing else is ever going to happen to them, and he has seen the dodges they take—running off with the school nurse, having affairs with their students' mothers, hitting the bottle. His dodge would have been—would be—hitting the bottle. But it will not happen to him. He is careful, for now. He drinks a fifth of scotch each week, and if he runs out before the week is over, then he goes without. Of course he does, on occasion, stop by somebody else's room and have a drink from his scotch. But that is social drinking. That is different. He is handling his after-forty problem very well. He has no regrets, he thinks.

The train pulls into the station and he pushes his way to the front of the car. He is eager to get off and get home. He does not hear the woman who shrieks with pleasure as she descends upon her teenage son. He does not notice the demonstrations of anger and frustration and delight. He does not even smell the rank odor of cigarette butts and urine. He just keeps his eyes cast down and makes his way through the waiting room to the cabstand. Leave the dead to bury the dead, he used to think as he left these depressing public places, but now he does not think about them at all. He is a priest who has left the world to itself, truly.

He is home in his little room and he pours himself a scotch and drinks it. He showers and stands in front of the long mirror examining the evidence of too much food, too much drink. He will have to cut down. He puts on his yellow pajamas and sets the clock. He has four hours before he must put on vestments for the Easter liturgy. He stretches out on the bed and closes his eyes, ready for sleep. But the trip to New York and the aunt's wake and the trip back to Boston swim through his mind and he cannot sleep. He feels good, and he feels guilty for feeling good. The boredom is over, those long hours on trains, the unpleasantness of all those strangers at the wake. Over is good, he thinks. Finality is good. But what is *good*. Well, he feels good and that's something.

The priest wakes from a nightmare. His head aches and he has trouble getting his breath. He is shivering. What was he dreaming? He cannot remember. He is late. He hurries through his shower, shaves, dresses, his mind going back and back to the dream. But always it eludes him. Perhaps it was the soldier dream again. He no longer meditates but often in his sleep he sees the soldier's back and hears the rattle of dice. The soldier shifts position and the priest sees the others, three of them, taking their turns with the dice. Finally, as always, the last one scoops up the dice and hands them to the priest, who takes them and closes his fist on them and when he looks down—this is the new part, the awful part—he sees that blood is oozing from between his fingers. And then he wakes up. The old meditation, which for years gave him some kind of abstract comfort, has turned from dream to nightmare. But it was not the soldier dream tonight, it was... And again the dream eludes him.

The priest is vested now and says a brief prayer before leading the procession to the rear of the chapel. The vigil is a long and complicated ritual and in his mind he ticks off the major sections. There is the striking of the new fire—a tricky business, because all the lights are out and you have to fumble around with the flint device. Then the blessing of the new fire, the blessing of the Easter candle, the solemn procession. The singing will be tough, because he has a weak voice. The readings. Then the blessing of the baptismal water... Death by drowning, he thinks, and for a second his mind veers to "The Waste Land," but then he comes back to the vigil. The baptism of the baby— he must check the baby's name before that part of the ceremony— and then the litany and finally, at midnight, Mass. Fire and water. Burning and drowning. Light in the darkness. The water that gives rebirth. It is a symbolism so ancient, so basic, that it must guarantee a reality, he thinks.

And so the ceremony has begun and the priest stands in the vestibule surrounded by the entire community. The lights have been extinguished in the chapel and now the light over the door goes out and they are plunged into complete blackness. They are waiting, all of them, for him to strike flint against flint and start that spark that will be the light shining in the darkness. The flint grates and grates again, and just as he has begun to think he will never get it to work right, there is a flicker and a dot of light, and then a flame. The flame catches in the little pot of wax and by its light the priest begins the blessing of the new fire.

"The Lord be with you," he says. And the community responds, "And with your spirit." He breathes easy, because the rest of the prayer he knows by heart. He stares into the fire, reciting the blessing. "Let us pray. O God, through your son, Jesus Christ, you bestowed the light of your glory upon the faithful. Sanctify..."

But then, in the fire, he recognizes his nightmare. He sees the soldier's back and hears the rattle of dice; the soldier moves and the priest sees not the three other soldiers but his mother; her drowning face is turned away from him and her hand is held out. In her hand are those dice, bloody, eyeless.

"Sanctify..." the priest says once more, and now it is time to raise his hand in blessing, but for the moment he cannot, and he continues to stare into the fire. "Sanctify..." he says again, staring and staring, still unable to bless, unable to go on or turn away.

"Sanctify..."

The word echoes in the darkness and the light flickers until with his bare hand the priest reaches forward and puts the fire out.

CLOTHING

Damien had been a Jesuit for sixteen years now and an ordained priest for three of those years. He was a member of the long black line; he had faded into the woodwork; he was a minor cog in a vast machine. This is how he thought of himself, in images not his own but drawn from the rules of the Society of Jesus, from conversations in the rec room, from admonitions of superiors. Life was bland, uneventful, with few successes and no dangers to speak of. The habit does finally make the man, he told himself.

There were sources of anxiety, to be sure, but not really dangers, not terrible temptations. A drink too many, perhaps, or imprudence in speech (telling sophomores in a high school English class that "Cardinal Spellman, quite simply, is a fascist"), or undue intimacy with the mother of one of his students (Mrs. Butler and that funny business at the pool). But nothing serious, nothing to worry about. Still, habit or no habit, there was something very wrong. Something— he searched for the word—hopeless.

And then, in the spring of his fourth year as a priest, he was officially transferred from the prep school where he taught in Connecticut to the retreat house in downtown Boston, the transfer to be effective in summer. Suddenly it all seemed impossible to him: the vow of obedience, the awful loneliness, the waste of his talent as a poet. He had published two books, and they had been well received by reviewers, but what was he doing—as a priest—writing poems at all? And why?

He went into a prolonged depression. He prayed. He drank too much. He flirted, deep in his subconscious, with the idea of suicide. Finally, while there was still a week to go before his transfer to Boston, it came to him that he did not have to die to get out, he just had to get out.

Damien went to his major superior, the provincial, and said he wanted some time to consider his vocation, he had come to a point where he had to do this one thing for himself. It was the 1960s and in the aftermath of Vatican II half his priest friends had already left, but Damien did not want to just leave, he said. He wanted to make a decision at least as rational and prayerful as the decision he had made when he entered. Damien paused in his declamation and appraised the provincial, who looked bored, and so he took a deep breath and said that while he was thinking through this problem, he did not want to work in, did not even want to live in, the retreat house.

"I see," the provincial said. "How's your drinking?"

Damien thought about that for a while, rejected the idea of a smart aleck response, and said, "Well, the drinking will always be a problem... for any of us, I suppose, but I think I've got it under control. What I'm talking about, Father, isn't a crisis of booze, or even a crisis of faith. It's a crisis of hope. I don't hope anymore."

"Hope, schmope," the provincial said. "Look. You're just one of over a thousand men we have to deal with, Damien. Things are changing. In the old days I'd have simply told you to go to the retreat house or get the hell out, but we can't do that anymore. Superiors have to *confer* with a subject now, we have to consult his *needs*, we have to *adapt*. So look, I'm short on time; I've conferred and I've consulted and I've adapted. What do you want?"

"Well, I thought..."

"Where are you going to live, first of all?"

"Well, I thought I'd stay right where I am."

"And do what?"

"Well, I thought I'd continue to write my poetry and reviews. And give readings. I thought I'd... pray."

"And who's supporting you, please, while you're writing this poetry?"

"Well, I thought, the Jesuits. I've given almost seventeen years of my life, after all, and... well, I thought..."

"Well, you thought. Well, you thought. Think again, my friend, and when you do, be very clear on one thing." The provincial leaned across the desk to make his point. "The Society of Jesus owes you... nothing. Got it? Nothing."

Damien felt hot and dizzy. The provincial seemed to come in very close to him, their faces almost touching, and then he pulled away, far back, far, far back. Damien was isolated suddenly, lost, a small ridiculous figure in a world that in seconds had become distant from him. He saw himself as he was: self-absorbed, pretentious, deluded. As if, in this huge organization of brilliant and holy men, he could possibly matter: ridiculous. He had deceived himself with this self-important talk about hope. The room tipped away from him and he wanted to hide.

Then all at once, something inside him said no, and at that instant the room righted itself. Words came to him and Damien leaned forward to say, But I want my life. I have a right to my life. It's my only hope.

But instead, he heard himself saying in a strange voice, a child's voice, "Of course you're right, Father. I'll go to the retreat house. I'll try harder."

And in the long silence that followed, he said, "Hope isn't that important anyway."

A year later—after seventeen weekend retreats to laymen and laywomen, after thirty talks to high school students on sex and marriage, after five Cana conferences and many baptisms and innumerable confessions, after a brief love affair with a divorcée (Mrs. Butler, who left her husband and family and came to Boston to find herself; she found herself, eventually, in AA), and a long love affair with a former nun (Alicia, whom he intended to marry as soon as he got his walking papers from the Jesuits)—a year later, Damien made formal application to leave the Jesuits and be reduced to the lay state. He was assigned an interrogator, Father Casey, a man in his seventies with a perpetual cough and a bad cigarette habit.

"*Interrogator*?" Damien asked. "*Reduced* to the lay state?"

"Just technical terms, boy," Father Casey said. "Don't get jumpy now; they told me you're the jumpy type. Poetry."

Damien said nothing. He was doing this not for himself but for Alicia, who had her own code of morality. She would have sex with him, she would even live with him, but she would not marry him except in the Catholic Church. Love is fine, she said, and so is sex as long as there is love, but marriage outside the church was unthinkable; it did violence to her integrity. And so he was doing this for her, submitting himself to a final humiliation so that they could be married as Catholics.

For over an hour Damien sat with his right hand on the little blue book that enshrined the rules of the Society of Jesus, the blue book itself resting on a Douay version of the holy Bible, while he answered questions about whether his parents had married for love or obligation, whether he was a wanted or unwanted baby, whether they had urged the priesthood on him or he had come upon the idea himself. Damien answered and contradicted himself and then answered again. Father Casey dutifully wrote down everything he said.

Telling himself he had only to hang on and eventually this nightmare would be over, Damien concentrated on the priest's handwriting: perfect little letters of the same height and slant, perfectly controlled, perfectly legible. Perfection in even the smallest things. Would this never end? Finally Damien's patience gave out.

"Why are you writing down every word I say? This is going to take forever!"

Father Casey looked up, amused. He had all eternity ahead of him. "I have to," he said. "This is a legal document. It will be sent to Rome. You've been in the Jesuits for seventeen years; it doesn't seem to me unreasonable to ask you to spend a few hours getting out."

"But who could answer these questions?" Damien said, exasperated. "This whole process is designed to prove that I never really had a vocation, that somehow I was forced into this. But you're not going to make me say that. I was not forced into the priesthood. I did not enter the Jesuits under any misconceptions. I did understand fully what I was doing."

There was a long silence in the room. Damien was about to apologize, but said instead: "I entered the priesthood of my own free will and now it's because of my own free will that I want out. I want to be my own man. I want to make my own mistakes. I want to be free."

"Free," Father Casey said, the word loaded with meaning.

"To make my own mistakes," Damien said.

Another long silence. "We'll try again." Father Casey lit a new cigarette and said, "This is going to take hours, son, so I'd suggest you cool down. Now, as to the question of your vocation: to what do you attribute it; to what exact person or event or moment? It's very important, so I want you to think. Are you thinking?"

Damien thought and said nothing. It was as if the priest had not heard a word he'd said.

An hour later Father Casey had moved on to other topics. How often did Damien masturbate? Never. Very good, but when did you stop? I never began. Never? Never at all? No, never. Why? What was the matter? A long pause, and then another cigarette, and more irritation on Damien's part, but no explosion this time.

"And has there been any sexual congress with others during the past years?"

"Yes," Damien said; an unequivocal answer.

"Frequently?"

"Sometimes."

"Women? More than one?"

"Two."

"Men?"

"No men."

"Ah." Father Casey took out his handkerchief and mopped his brow. Damien laughed, thinking the priest meant to be funny.

"Yes?" Father Casey was puzzled.

"No. I mean, we're nervous. Or at least I am."

"Now, about these women." Father Casey paused, significantly.

"The first was an affair. It was just sex. I broke it off after two weeks.

Confessed it, of course. The other is love; a love affair, if you want; but it's permanent. We're going to marry as soon as my papers come through."

"If they come through."

"When they come through."

"Be careful." Father Casey held his pen suspended for a moment in the air.

"Father, I've been careful and I'm all done. I've given seventeen years of honest service to God, and one year of very muddled service that was meant to be for God but that ended up being for me, I guess, because it's getting me out. And I don't particularly care what you think of me or what Rome thinks of me, because it's myself I've got to live with. And all I want from you is *out*. I'm done. Like it or not, I'm free."

"You go too far." Father Casey's voice was suddenly the voice of God. "You go too far."

I'll do it for Alicia, Damien told himself and bowed his head as if he were sorry for his outburst.

"You are dealing with Mother Church, and she is a very indulgent mother indeed. But even mothers can be pushed too far. Do you understand me?"

Later, hours later, when Damien was leaving Father Casey's room, he turned and said with a kind of innocent surprise: "I suddenly remembered. Your question about my vocation, about when exactly I knew I had one? It's just come back to me: I was a child, about five or six, and I had a terrible quarrel with my mother about something or other. It was shortly after that quarrel that I began thinking I'd be a priest; not because I wanted to, but because it just seemed inevitable."

"It doesn't matter now," Father Casey said. "I've finished taking notes."

Months went by and Damien moved from the retreat house into a studio apartment. At last a letter arrived asking that he come to the provincial's office to sign and receive his decree of laicization. He signed and, with that signature, he was reduced to the lay state.

But when he moved from his studio into Alicia's apartment just before the wedding, Damien discovered that—for some reason he could not explain—he still had in his possession his Jesuit habit: the cassock, the cincture, the Roman collar.

What was he to do with them? Obviously he couldn't keep them. Nor could he just throw them out.

The awful session with Father Casey came back to him, and then the scene in the provincial's office where he had signed away his Jesuit allegiance, surrendered the practice of his priesthood. No, he did not want to see those men again. Anger, resentment, shame; none of these described what he felt, but he knew he could not face them again for a long, long time.

"Betrayal," he said aloud, and though there was no connection in his mind between the word he said and the idea that came to him, he realized at once what he would do.

He folded the habit carefully and laid it on the bed. He folded the cincture in halves, and then in halves again, and then once more. He laid the white plastic collar on top of the habit and cincture.

He stared at the clothes for a moment and then, with purpose, he picked them up and draped them over his left arm.

He walked the five blocks to the retreat house and went in the door to the public chapel. Though it was early afternoon, the chapel was very dark, and it was a moment or two before Damien was certain that no one was there.

He knelt and said an Act of Contrition. Then he stood and placed the cassock carefully in the pew in front of him. He laid the cincture on the cassock, crossways, with the white plastic collar on top.

He turned to go, hesitated, and then quite deliberately turned back. He picked up the collar and, with no thought that it was sentimental or melodramatic to do so, he lifted it to his lips for the ritual kiss that custom and devotion had required of him for so many years.

He genuflected and walked out of the chapel, hopeful, free.

Damien sat in the rocking chair reading *Swiss Family Robinson* while his mother peeled carrots for the stew. They often spent Saturday mornings like this, Damien reading in the big rocker while his mother watered her plants or prepared meals or did the baking.

Damien was eight years old and there was nobody his age in this new neighborhood; his mother, trapped here by marriage and the Depression, missed her old chums in the city; and so they were friends, really, more like companions than mother and son.

But she was cross this morning, Damien could see, and she was not going to keep her promise.

"You should be outside, playing," she said.

"But what about the shoes?" Damien said, not looking up from his book. "We've got to go buy the shoes."

"I'm busy," she said, and tossed the last of the carrots into the pot.

Damien had been invited to Marianne Clair's birthday party that afternoon, and he had a present for her (one of his Thornton Burgess books; you couldn't tell it wasn't new), and so he was all set to go. Except for one thing. He had to have a new pair of shoes. He had only a single pair that he wore for school and for best, and somehow he must have scuffed the top of the toe on his right shoe because the leather had worn away and when he stood in front of the class to read, everybody could see his sock showing through.

Damien had not been able to tell his mother this, or tell her what had happened yesterday in school when Miss Moriarty made him stop reading and insisted that Marianne share with the whole class whatever it was that she found so funny. "You can see his sock through the hole in his shoe," Marianne said, and everyone had laughed. Damien could never tell her this; he could never tell anyone. But last night he had prayed over and over that he would get the new shoes soon.

Two weeks ago his mother had said that maybe next Saturday they would take a bus downtown and buy him a new pair of shoes. A week later she had said the same thing again. But this morning she had already mentioned several times how busy she was, how many things she had to do. It would be only a while longer—he could tell—before she said he would just have to wait another week for the shoes.

She finished preparing the stew and in no time spread the kitchen table with newspaper, got out her bag of soil and her pots, and was busy transferring the first of the window plants from a small pot to a larger one.

Damien looked over at her without raising his head; this way he could watch without her knowing it. She rapped the plant out of its pot and held it upside down in her left hand while she scooped soil into the new pot with her right. She was quick and certain, juggling the plant and the pot, pressing down the new soil with her knuckles, making it all come out right. Everything she touched grew.

She looked up at him suddenly. "You should be outside, in the nice sun," she said. "It's too nice a day not to be outside."

"But when are we going to buy the shoes?" he asked.

She said nothing.

"Mother? What about the shoes?"

"They'll have to wait," she said, her hands busier than ever with her potting.

"But you promised. You said."

She started on another plant, ignoring him.

"You promised. You never keep your promises."

"That's enough. Now stop, or you won't go to the party at all."

"What a cheater you are!"

"Damien!" she said, the last warning.

"You lied to me. You never intended to buy the shoes."

"That's it. That does it," she said. "You're spoiled and you're fresh and you're selfish, and you are not going to that party. Period."

"You just don't want to take me, that's all. You just don't want to buy me shoes."

"Go to your room! Now!"

"I hate you," Damien said, and headed—fast—for the door. "Besides, you're as homely as Mrs. Dressel."

It had popped into his head from nowhere. He had heard Mrs. Waters from next door say she thought Emily Dressel was the homeliest woman in town, and he had heard his mother repeat the comment to his father. He had heard them laugh and agree that it was probably true. His mother had said, "That poor woman; if I looked like that, I'd wear a hat with a veil."

So now he sat in his bedroom wondering why his mother had said nothing back to him. He had wanted to make her angry, to hurt her, badly, because she had ruined everything. Even if he said he was sorry and they were friends again, it wouldn't be the same. Even if she took him to get the shoes now, it wouldn't be the same. It was too late.

He would ignore her. He would be nice to her from now on, but never again the way he used to be. That was what she deserved. She had earned her punishment.

He tried to go back to *Swiss Family Robinson*, which, despite the speed of his escape from the kitchen, he had had the sense to take with him, but he couldn't concentrate on the words.

He wondered if she knew. Did she know that he was punishing her? And did she suspect that, in a way, he was relieved not to have to go to the party with all new kids?

She probably did. She probably knew, as he himself knew, that in a day or so, after he'd been punished for being fresh and after they'd gone without talking for a while, it would all be the same, and that next Saturday he would read some new book and she would bake cookies and all of this would count for nothing. He wanted to hurt her back, now, for good.

Instantly he realized how to do it.

He marched out to the kitchen and stood beside her at the sink. She was holding one of the repotted plants near the faucet, getting it wet but not too wet. She said nothing and so he waited. He would give her one more chance. But when she still remained silent, he said, "Do you want to know something? You really are as homely as Mrs. Dressel. And tomorrow or the next day when we're not mad at each other anymore, I'll tell you I didn't really mean it. I'll tell you I just said it to pay you back. But I do mean it, and you know what? I'll mean it then, too, even when I say I don't. Because it's the truth."

His mother said nothing, but her face got hard-looking, and she shook. Suddenly the plant fell from her hands. The fresh soil spilled into the sink and the water from the faucet drilled hard on the plant until even the old soil fell away and the roots were exposed, but still she did nothing to save it. She only stared straight ahead.

Damien turned smartly and walked down the hall to his room. He shut the door behind him.

His face was hot and he felt dizzy, but not sick dizzy. He was dizzy with a kind of power, a strange sense of who he was and what he could do. He looked around the room and everything seemed different. His bed was so small, and the chair too, and his bureau. Not exactly small, but distant; as if he had moved away from them, as if he had nothing to do with them anymore. Even his books looked different; they looked old, ancient; he knew everything that was in them. With one finger, with a single word from his mouth, he could dismiss them from existence. He was capable of anything now.

And at once he knew he must hide. But where? He went to his closet and climbed in among the slippers and boots and old toys, but that was not enough.

He took his bathrobe down from its hook and put it over his head. No. He was still not hidden.

He pulled down his shirts from the shelves, his pajamas, his underwear; in a frenzy he tore everything from the hangers, heaped the clothes in a mound on the closet floor. It was not enough.

He stripped himself then, adding his shirt and trousers to the pile on the floor, and, pulling the door tight behind him, crawled beneath the heavy pile of clothing and lay, for a time, hidden.

Hours later his mother found him there, still shaking with power and terror.

Alicia was dying of metastatic liver cancer.

Hers was the typical case. While shaving beneath her arms one evening, she had noticed an odd little lump near the nipple of her left breast. The next morning she phoned her gynecologist, and almost before she had time to realize what was happening, she was recuperating from a radical mastectomy. At her third-month checkup she seemed fine, but three months later a tumor appeared in her right breast and she had to undergo another mastectomy.

Two years passed, filled for Alicia and Damien with a kind of desperate hope, and then the hoping was over. Alicia developed a nagging cough, she began to lose weight, her fine white skin began to turn sallow. Even before the doctor examined her, he pronounced it cancer of the liver—final and fatal. Alicia had been in the hospital for over a month now, with the promise of days to live, or hours. And still she had not complained.

Whenever he had a cold, Damien always said—by way of apology to her and acknowledgment to himself—that on his tombstone he wanted carved this simple inscription: He suffered no pain without complaint.

What he could never understand, therefore, was how Alicia could suffer so much and complain so little. Or rather, not at all.

He had sat by her bed each day, telling her about his classes (he taught English at Sacred Heart College), about her friends from school who had phoned to inquire how she was doing (she taught English at Sacred Heart Prep), about their German shepherd, Heidi. She had smiled, her hand resting lightly on his, and in her new voice—husky, strained, exhausted—she had done her best to cheer him up.

But now she slept all the time, or perhaps she was unconscious. Damien sat beside her bed, forcing himself to look at her emaciated hand or at the small mound her feet made beneath the covers, or at the reproduction of the *Madonna della Strada* on the wall opposite. Anywhere but at her face.

Because the last time he had looked at her sleeping face, he had thought, Go. Please go. I have never known you anyway. And he could not bear to think that again.

Damien had known her since that last terrible year in the priesthood, when he had prayed and drank and made love to her and then gone to confession, promising he would end this affair, and he had meant it. Then he would start all over again. How had she endured it? Endured him?

He shot a quick glance at her face. Her skin was smooth, taut to her skull, and with the advance of the disease, the color had darkened from its natural white to a pale yellow and then to a deep tan; now it was reddish brown, thin and hard to the touch. Her face was a death mask made of copper.

This was not Alicia.

He tried to summon some image of her, some proof that he had known her after all. He saw them walking on the beach with the dog; he saw them fighting, spitting out the angry words they would take back later; he saw them making love. But that was not it; that was not what he was looking for. He thought of her as she had been for the past two years, broken with cancer, and he remembered kissing the pink flesh where her breast used to be and looking up to see the single tear on her cheek. He thought of her in bed with him, her head twisting on the pillow, the sounds of her pleasure in his ear. But that was not the right image either. It was hopeless.

Then, just when he had given up, it came to him: the photo of Alicia on the swing. She was five years old and she was wearing a birthday dress. She sat on the swing with both feet planted on the ground; her hands gripped the ropes solidly; she looked straight into the camera. There was a smile on her face, a look of confidence, a sureness about everything in her world. Her eyes saw, and liked what they saw, and she was perfectly content. Hope was not even a question.

Damien fixed the picture firmly in his mind, smiled at the freshness, the inviolability of that child, and then he turned to look at Alicia.

"The relentless compassion of God," he said aloud, and as if she had been waiting for him to say that, Alicia opened her eyes and looked at him.

"Never," she said, and then something else that Damien could not make out.

He leaned over her to catch the words, and at once her eyes tipped upward in her head and she began to push away the sheets. "Help me," she said. "Oh, help me with these." She sat up somehow and managed to kick the sheets free of her body. She clawed at the johnny tied loosely at her back; the string broke and she flung the thing on the floor. She was sitting up in the bed now, naked, staring, her eyes empty in her copper face. "Help me," she said once more. "I never loved."

"No," Damien said, taking her by the shoulders, turning her to look into his face. "No, that's not true," he said, desperate this time. "You loved me. You always loved me."

She focused on Damien then and something came into her empty eyes, a kind of promise.

"And I loved you," he said, but already her eyes had begun to close. He lay her back on the bed, slowly, gently, and she seemed finally to be without life altogether. "No," Damien sobbed. "Oh, God, no. No." And then he thought he heard her echo him, "No. No."

He did not cover her dead body but left it as it was, naked, decent. He stood by her bed and prayed, hoping against hope.

A KIND OF HAPPINESS

"Happy?" Alison said and leaned back a little in her chair.

She was after him, constantly, to be happy. Or at least to say he was.

"There's happy and happy," he said. He rattled on with distinctions in major and minor modes of happiness and she turned it off. She would not let herself be antagonized by this. She watched a bee circling her glass.

He was Russ Lenehan, professor of Latin literature at Newton College of the Sacred Heart. He had been a Catholic priest with a so-so degree in classics, and then he had made a bad marriage that ended—badly—and now he was sitting at a sidewalk café in Assisi with his wife of one month, Alison Rodgers. She had married him because he was so unhappy and she wanted to change that. He had married her because he understood she needed him—she was forty, not married, not beautiful—and he wanted to do it right this time. They had already discovered that their marriage was a mistake and they worried now, on their honeymoon in Italy, that they might end up hating one another.

"Happiness aside," Alison said, brushing the bee away from her glass, "it's lovely to sit in the shade of this lovely umbrella and watch all these people go by and drink a lovely gin and tonic."

"Loverly," he said. And then, repentant, "Being here—with you, with *you*, that is—should make anyone happy."

He took her hand. They smiled, newlyweds, and clinked their

glasses so that he felt kind and generous again, and she felt patient and tough.

"To us."

"To us."

The bee settled for a moment on Russ's wrist, but he flicked it away, and it lit upon the crimson vine flaming the wall behind them. They sat in comfortable silence, holding hands as they watched the exhausted tourists make their way—gasping, most of them—to the town piazza at the top of the hill. The air was thick with a sweet honeyed smell. A bird called, a short, high sound. And then a fat gray cat poked its head out of the café door, looked around judgmentally, and curled up in the shade beneath their table. Silence.

It was high summer in Assisi, and hot, hot, hot. Tourists, pilgrims, penitents, priests and nuns, busy Franciscans in their brown habits: the sidewalks were packed with people who overflowed into the sweltering streets and onto the terraces and into the cool, dark interiors of bars and restaurants. There was no carnival atmosphere; a kind of churchy hush hung over conversations in the street. Even at the tables where people sat drinking, there was a certain solemnity, as if the air of Assisi obliged them to show respect for the poverty and humility of Saint Francis.

"There's something truly spiritual about this place," Alison had said that morning, early, before the heat set in. "You betcha," Russ had said, and that took care of that. Russ was suspicious of piety in any form.

They had started their day in the basilica at the foot of the steep hill. They had paused inside the great church just long enough to be aware of the Cimabues in the cross transept and the endless row of Giottos that lined the walls, looking somehow illuminated from within, and then they descended to the lower church where they heard Mass in Italian. Only a dozen or so people attended the Mass but all of them received Communion from the hands of the nervous young priest who had the looks of a movie star and a rather unfortunate lisp. "He'll never survive the gay purge," Russ whispered, and Alison made a point of not hearing him.

After Mass they idled in the basilica, marveling at the Cimabues and trying to identify the narrative in the Giotto frescoes. There were twenty-eight of them, so simple and powerful they were almost embarrassing, and they told the story of improbable wonders in the life of Saint Francis. After an hour of strained looking, when they had reached number twelve—Francis in ecstasy, lifted up on a little pink cloud—Russ declared museum fatigue and they left to get a cup of coffee.

Crowds had begun to gather by now in the huge piazza outside the church. Suddenly a little space cleared in front of them—people stepped aside for some reason—and Alison said, "My God, look at that poor woman." Russ followed her gaze. The woman was human wreckage, a spindly thing of fifty or sixty, with sticks for legs—rigid in steel braces—and she hunched over crutches as she inched her way from the basilica toward the long, punishing incline of the Via San Francesco. She wore a cotton hat to shield her from the sun, but she seemed nakedly exposed nonetheless. Russ looked, quickly. Tears sprang to his eyes. He muttered "Christ!" as if he were angry, and said, "Let's get something to eat." Alison saw that he was shaken and, patient as always, said nothing. They found a coffee bar with a couple tables and settled in. They ate croissants and drank a cappuccino, then another cappuccino.

The sun was strong and getting stronger; it was going to be a very hot day. They chatted about life back at the college—Alison taught in the philosophy department—they were concerned about their salaries, the coming year, the new dean. They talked about Rome. They talked about Florence. They dallied in the coffee bar until Alison decided Russ had finally put the woman on crutches out of his mind. They went back to the basilica to examine the sixteen remaining frescoes. Eventually they took another break. Overload struck them at about the same time. They went outside and sat on the wall and gazed down on the magnificent church that housed the Porziuncola, the doll-size chapel where Francis himself had prayed, and beyond it the valley of Spoleto with its lemon groves and cypresses and tidy patches of green fields. The view was breathtaking even in this heat. "There's something truly spiritual about this place," Alison said, and Russ replied, brusquely, "You betcha." Later he said, "There is. You're right. Let's go back in." They spent the better part of the morning this way, in and out of the basilica.

Finally they began the trek up the endless, exhausting, vertiginous Via San Francesco, the arterial street that led straight up and up and opened finally into the broad flat piazza at the top of the town. On the way up they stopped for lunch. They stopped to look at the museum shops. They stopped for a drink. Anything for a little rest.

Now, in midafternoon, they were seated on the patio of a small café, having a gin and tonic. Behind them a crimson vine poured down the wall and before them was the street, alive with tourists. They sat beneath an umbrella, holding hands, watching the rest of the searching world pass by.

"To us," they said, clinking their gin and tonic glasses.

"It's been a good day," Alison said.

"It's been an exhausting day. That hill! It's excruciating!"

"It's killing."

"In fact, I think I'll skip Mass tomorrow. The walk down that hill is bad enough, but by the time you get back up you're too exhausted to do anything but lie down. Right?"

"Right," she said. "In this heat." She detached her hand from his, sensing he'd had enough.

The bee returned, circling their drinks for a moment, and then flew off to a neighboring table. They sat in silence, Russ gazing into his drink, thinking, and Alison gazing down the hill at the wilting tourists as they struggled upward.

Their silence was interrupted by a little commotion up above, near the piazza. Russ raised his head in time to see the crowd part to

let a man in a wheelchair make his way through. Behind him came
a much younger man with a deformed leg, moving one foot slowly
forward and dragging the other in its high boot to meet it. Russ looked
away, quickly, and then looked back. The crowd parted again for a
woman on crutches.

"Good God," Russ said, and Alison turned in her chair to stare
frankly at the approach of this tiny pilgrimage. "That's her," he said.
"It's that same woman from down at the basilica!"

"Don't stare."

"Do you realize what this means? She's spent the entire day getting
up that hill! In this heat! My God!" He turned away from Alison as
tears came to his eyes.

"Don't."

"I can't bear it."

"Then don't look."

"I'm not looking," he snapped at her, his voice cracking. "And
how could you not look anyway? How can God... ?"

The woman was advancing down the hill toward the table where
they sat. Russ looked up at her. She was short and morbidly thin; both
of her spindly legs were supported by steel braces, and the crutches
pressed hard beneath her arms. She had on a sleeveless shirt and blue
shorts. On her feet she wore brown laced-up shoes that seemed as
inflexible as the braces themselves and the sinews in her arms and legs
stood out horribly against the flesh. He had thought she was fifty or
sixty but he could see now that she was not old, not young; she was
no age at all. When you looked at her, you saw first a mass of metal
apparatus coming at you and then, more awful still, you saw the face,
raddled with pain, distorted. It was terrible to see. Unable to take his
eyes off her, Russ watched as she dragged herself along.

She moved her left crutch forward a few inches and then leaned
heavily to her left side—he could see how the crutch cut into her
armpit—and then she moved her left foot forward an inch, then two,
then a little more. She paused and drew a breath, slowly.

She moved the right crutch forward and threw the weight of her small body against it, urging her right foot forward an inch, then a little more. Her shoulders shook with the effort, there was a ripple of thin muscle across her back, and her hip slumped hard against the crutch as the pain shook her. She drew another breath and repeated the motions, moving inches at a time, relentless.

Russ turned away from her as she neared their table. Only a few feet separated them.

Suddenly she paused, and Russ, recognizing that she had paused, turned slowly to face her. She gazed hard at him, long and slow. The sun seemed to stop in the sky as she fixed him with a look, and held him, and to Russ that look said she had known him forever and, having found him at last, would never let him go.

They left Assisi sooner than they had planned and went on to Venice where it seemed that everybody walked about holding hands and every church claimed at least one Tintoretto and even a plate of spaghetti turned into a feast. Gondolas drifted by on the canals, the gondoliers singing their corny Neapolitan songs to Japanese tourists who crouched, grim, among the stained velvet cushions. The weather was perfect—warm but breezy—and though they had been warned that the canals stank, it was not true. In the morning there was the smell of damp sidewalks and fresh bread; in the evening the delicious smell of seafood cooking. And there was the surprise of birdsong late in the night.

Russ grew more calm. They made love again, and they had not made love since Assisi. Alison remained wary nonetheless.

By the time they reached Paris, Russ was his old self. He was witty, ironic, bemused at the outlandish superiority of Parisians. The cabdrivers were maniacs. The traffic police were gestapo. The waiters mocked his French and he tipped them anyway. Russ was entertained and entertaining, so Alison was tempted to put aside her worry that this marriage was a vast, glittering mistake. That was a relief. She did not intend to sacrifice her tough mind and acid tongue to be an emotional slave to anybody. A servant, a handmaid, fine. But a slave, thank you, no. She drew a deep breath and plunged into the French part of their honeymoon.

They had rented, from the friend of a friend, a small apartment in the Latin Quarter. It looked directly onto the back of Notre-Dame—the flying buttresses were framed in their living room window—and from their bed they could look out on the booksellers and the instant portrait artists and the odd pickpocket busy at work on the banks of the Seine.

Alison knew Paris well from her time studying philosophy at the Sorbonne, and so she planned their daily itinerary. They visited the Panthéon because it was practically next door. They took the metro to Sacré-Cœur, they took the train to Versailles, they took walking tours of the Louvre. They spent a day in bed making love and eating miniature pastries.

It was the Paris she had known and loved. She had been happy there and she was happy now. And Russ seemed happy too, more or less. At least he had stopped complaining about God.

They left Paris and returned to Boston in time for fall semester at Newton College of the Sacred Heart.

September faded into October, with the deep red and gold of maples all around them and cold light silvering the gravel paths. There was the racket of squirrels everywhere—in the eaves, on the front steps, on the road dashing between cars.

"Inviting instant death as they prepare for winter," Russ remarked.

"Lighten up," Alison said. "We all die."

Russ was deeply troubled. He didn't love her? Could that be true? So why were they playing out this farce? At the same time he was terrified she would leave him. Because then what would he do? Who would he be? There was nothing waiting for him but fate and he knew he could not face it. And how had he come to believe in fate in the first place?

Alison was troubled as well. In the few months since their marriage, she had become a different woman—more like her old self, in fact.

What had brought them together was their odd notion of Catholicism. Alison, who had never been married and was not interested in being a priest, was nonetheless very much in favor of women in the priesthood, gay marriage, and abortion on demand. No one in the administration questioned her right to think or speak about these enthusiasms but she was made to understand that this was, after all, a Catholic college and Catholicism did not embrace gay marriage, female clergy, or a woman's right to kill her unborn child.

"Ahem," she said. "I'm Catholic too and you can't stop me being a Catholic just because you hold unreasonable opinions."

Word of this exchange got around campus and Russ looked her up to say how much he liked her attitude.

"It's not attitude," she said, "it's conviction."

"Exactly," he said, lowering his voice an octave and giving her what used to be his roguish smile.

So they started off together as renegades, and within no time they were—philosophically—in love. That is, Alison saw how unhappy he was by himself and how much less unhappy he was with her, and she could see no real distinction between happiness and love. Russ, responding, could see how much she needed him. He was a fifty-year-old man who had failed at everything—as a priest, as a scholar, as a husband—but here was a chance for him to do it right, to be there for somebody who needed him, and maybe even to be happy, whatever that meant. And so they had married in spring.

And in summer they had honeymooned in Europe.

Now it was fall.

Alison decided that she and Russ needed a serious marital chat. She had come to the conclusion—despite Aquinas—that love should not be confused with wishing someone well and, further, to wish someone well was not enough to build a marriage on. She had more thinking to do, but she felt it best to put Russ on notice.

"I'm a patient woman," Alison told him. "I'm a patient woman but patience, like everything else, has its limits."

Russ waited for her to go on, but she chose not to. She would have to think some more, she said, because patience was not the real issue. Love was the issue.

Russ, terrified, lapsed into silence.

Later that day—it was night, actually, and they were in bed— he asked, "Is it our marriage? Are you reconsidering our marriage?"

"It just has to be thought upon," she said.

Cold had begun to settle in. It was going to be an early winter and a frigid one. The grass was thick with frost each morning and there was that tang in the air that signaled the end of football weather and the arrival of snow. In her graduate seminar Alison was teaching Sartre and de Beauvoir, two people who annoyed her extremely. What annoyed her most was the way de Beauvoir facilitated Sartre's affairs with other women, pretending they were all in the interest of freedom and honesty, when the whole time she was eaten up with rage and despair. What misery. What self-deception. She found herself annoyed with Russ. What did he want, finally, from life?

And then a remarkable thing occurred. Russ's last living relative, an aunt by marriage, a woman of great wealth and austerity, suddenly died and left all her money to the Salvation Army, except for a million and a half that she left to Russ. Russ had met the aunt only twice, once as a boy when he made his First Communion and then much later when he was ordained a priest, so there was very little emotion expended on the news of her death. Why she had left him so much money remained mysterious. Russ reread the lawyer's letter informing him that he was now, by Newton College standards, a rich man.

"We should go out to dinner," he said. "Celebrate."

"Living the high life," Alison said, "in Newton, Mass."

That same evening Alison decided she had had enough of caretaking Russ. He had money now. He could be free. And, more important, she could be free. She would tell him tomorrow.

They had just left Beauséjour after a superb dinner. They had reached the little park in downtown Newton and paused at the corner when suddenly Russ—happy and grateful—put his arms around her and pulled her close. He gave her a small kiss on the forehead and another, softly, on the lips and he lingered there. He folded her deeper in his arms, happy, warm. Then suddenly a car full of teenagers appeared from nowhere. It roared along the street in front of them—the kids greeting them with shouts and wolf whistles—and turned sharply, with a shriek of brakes and screaming tires as it approached the corner. Russ and Alison pulled away from each other, startled. At that moment a squirrel dashed suicidally toward the car, there was a short thunking sound, and it was over. The squirrel was crushed, dying. It all happened in a matter of seconds and the kids were still laughing and shouting as they drove away.

"Oh, no!" Alison said, as she pulled away from Russ. Then, with a soft moaning sound, she moved toward the dying thing in the street. The squirrel lay there twitching, its back crushed, blood at its mouth. "Oh, God!" Alison said. She bent over it and tried not to think about what she was doing. Horrified, determined, she took its tail between her thumb and forefingers and half-lifted, half-dragged it from the street and across the sidewalk into the bushes. "Poor thing," she said. "Poor sweet thing." She took a handkerchief from her purse and wiped her fingers, rubbing them hard, shaking the smell of death from them. "All right," she said, "okay. I'll wash as soon as I get home." She looked back at the bushes where she'd left the squirrel. She could see its front paws curling against the shock. "Poor thing."

Russ stood on the sidewalk exactly where he had been standing when the car struck the squirrel. His face was white, he was paralyzed, he could say nothing.

"Come on," she said. "I know how you feel. It's just awful."

Russ began to tremble slightly. He clasped his arms around his chest and tried to stop the trembling. "Russ?" Alison said. "Come on, sweetheart, let me take you home." He stared at her blindly until she gave him a hard shake. He stopped then, white in the face and speechless, and she led him across the street to the car and drove him home.

As soon as they entered the house, Alison went to the kitchen and poured him a stiff scotch. "Here," she said. "It's not the solution, but it'll make you feel less awful. Or at least make you feel less."

"The problem isn't feeling," Russ said. "The problem…"

"Drink it," she said. "For God's sake, drink it."

"God! Ha!" he said. "God is the problem."

He drank the scotch.

"High drama," she said, unable to stop herself. "Grand passion."

A week passed before Alison decided she was ready to talk about ending all this. "Not the squirrel," she said, "that isn't it. It's a much larger problem. It's two problems, actually." She paused to see how he was taking this. "We're very lucky people. We have good jobs, we've paid off this house, and—thanks to your auntie—we have lots of money socked away in Merrill Lynch. On the personal level, we're smart, we're honest, and we meant to love each other."

"Meant to?"

"I want this to be nice," she said. She smiled a little and he smiled in return. "The problem, I thought at first, was that I wasn't able to make you happy. Loving you didn't seem to make any difference. But now I've come to the conclusion that it's not my fault. You can't be happy. It's just a fact of your nature. You're not able to be happy." She paused. "And you blame God for it."

Russ nodded in agreement.

"I can't live with that."

"I could change!" He had blurted it out. "I could try."

"You've been trying all along. You can't. That's the first problem. The second problem makes the first one even sadder. You feel too much." He looked away. "To outsiders at least, you don't seem to feel anything. They all think you're a cold fish, and of course you are in most respects, but that's the public you. You've crushed feeling down so deep that when something awful really reaches you, like the squirrel, you come apart, you're a mess."

She sat there looking at him sadly.

"Russ, listen. Why can't you just accept the facts? People suffer. Squirrels suffer. God allows it, or maybe he just doesn't give a damn, but there's nothing you can do about it. It's how things are. You can't make your life into a battle with God."

Russ had stopped listening some time ago.

"So what does this mean? You're leaving me?"

And still she held back what she believed to be the truth: his misery was self-indulgent and sentimental. He preferred it to happiness.

"Alison?"

She had said enough for now.

He thought of that crippled woman in Assisi, and not for the first time. She was happy, if you could call it that. She had recognized him. And he knew he had been recognized.

Spring now. The semester was almost over.

In the middle of a class on Ovid's *Metamorphoses*, he was explaining that passion in Ovid led invariably to transformation—a visit from the gods, an extinction of the former self, the emergence of a new and scary creature—when suddenly he got a piercing pain in the right side of his head as if someone had launched a javelin through his skull. "God!" he said sharply, and the students looked up to see what was happening. Russ had his hands to his head and his face was crimson— he was obviously in pain—but he didn't say anything so they presumed it was just one of those things classics professors sometimes did.

Later that afternoon he went to bed with the worst headache of his life. He got up for dinner, and after dinner they watched highlights of that day's Olympic competitions, the women's gymnastics and then the men's.

"They do this perfect routine, it's just fantastic," Alison said, "and then they carry on about sticking the landing. As if performance is nothing and only the landing matters."

"Maybe they're right," Russ said, his mind half on the performance, half on the pulsing in his head. "Want a Coke?"

Alison said, "Watch!" pointing to the young man from China who was the favorite for the floor competition.

Russ hauled himself from the couch and suddenly his left leg gave way and—slowly, almost idly—he fell onto Alison, who pushed him gently aside, saying half to herself, "Stick that landing!" She ducked her head around him so that she wouldn't miss the performance.

He limped off to bed.

Alison watched the rest of the competition alone.

When Russ awoke the next morning, the pain was gone but he could not get out of bed. Alison took one look at him and went white. "Let's not panic," she said, "it's probably not very serious. You just lie there." But he made movements as if he wanted to stand—"No, no," she said—but he persisted, so she helped him to his feet where he stood wobbling upright for a moment and then he collapsed to the floor. He tried to say, "I can't stick that landing," but it came out a sort of gargle. Alison, thoroughly panicked by now, dialed 911.

It was a stroke but, as the doctors informed him later, a relatively benign one. There had been a blood clot in the brain, and it had burst, but fortunately the hemorrhage had been slight and he had a good chance of recovery. His speech was gone, but not completely, and there was some feeling in his left side, and it seemed likely that the facial paralysis—the left side again—might lessen in time, might even disappear completely. The first month would be pivotal. Meanwhile he should get a lot of rest and not worry about a thing.

Alison took care of everything: nurses, physical therapy, enforced rest; she bathed him and she massaged his crippled left arm and leg, and she sat with him while he did his speech exercises. His speech returned, blurred and jerky, but he was able to say "Thank you" and "I'm sorry," the required speech of the invalid, and eventually he had access to "son of a bitch" and other useful phrases. As his speech improved, the paralysis left his face and he looked almost like the old Russ. Some movement in his arms and legs came back, very slowly and very little, but within two months he could stand with the aid of crutches and could shove his right side forward enough to allow his left side to fall in line beside it, and thus to simulate walking of a kind. This was all on the outside. Inside, he was undergoing a process of clarification that daily astonished him. He did not know where it was taking him, but he knew it was taking him forward and he knew it was right. The process took many months and it was their first wedding anniversary before it all became clear.

The day passed with no sudden illumination; they read, they had friends over for an early dinner, they watched the late news. It was a long, slow, and very tiring day. Alison, exhausted, bathed and massaged him and tucked him up in bed, and by then he felt he couldn't wait any longer. He put his good hand on her arm, indicating he wanted to speak.

"Now?" Alison said. "It's our anniversary."

"Listen," Russ said. "I've got it now. I understand. The problem isn't the marriage. The problem is God."

She tried to hold back, to say nothing, but she couldn't help herself. "Can't you—just for one night—forget about God!"

"I can't accept God's inhumanity." He was trying to be very clear.

"God has nothing to do with it. God doesn't give a damn. The fact is that you're just feeling sorry for yourself."

"Not for me. For that woman. That awful woman in Assisi."

Alison took a deep breath. She'd been wrong about so many things.

"I've given up on God," he said.

Finally it was too much. The self-importance of the man! The self-delusion!

"Oh, for Chrissake," she said. "Why don't you face it! The problem is your obsession with a God who's a monster. Why don't you marry him! Find out what love is really like!"

Russ lay there, stunned.

"You've got God in you like a stinger!"

Alison said this because she was exhausted and impatient and she had no idea what she meant. But Russ—in a flash of understanding— knew exactly what they meant. He had had a stroke, a sit-down with death, and got nothing out of it. But now, illuminated by her anger, he understood: he had God in him like a stinger. Of course. Suddenly, with blinding clarity, he saw his fate and he accepted it.

Alison remained furious. In the night she woke and said to him, still furious, "God! Is there no end to you!"

But Russ was asleep, resigned, determined. Happy, more or less.

They parted as friends. They were civilized and partings mattered. Russ flew from Boston to Florence, and from Florence he took the train to Assisi. The walk from the train station to the Porziuncola was excruciating—the crutches cut into his arms, the brace on his leg weighed a ton—but he wanted to begin his new life in the tiny church where Francis himself had prayed. He sat in the church for a good part of an hour, afraid to pray, afraid—as always—of everything. It was a sweltering summer day and he had before him the long climb up the hill to the basilica and then, if he was able to go on, the merciless climb from the basilica up and up and up to the town piazza. And, in time, down again. And then up.

Alison was at home in Newton teaching her courses and thinking about what she should do for Russ, if indeed anything was called for. He knew who he was now, she thought. He knew what he wanted.

She remained this way, thinking, and two years passed. Then, because her thinking gradually turned to what seemed like love, she flew from Boston to Florence and took the train to Assisi and a cab by the back route—not the pilgrim route—to the very top of the hill and the broad, open piazza. She had lunch, and afterward, leisurely, she started down the hill toward the basilica until she came upon their little café with its patio and the wall behind it covered with that crimson, flaming vine. She ordered a gin and tonic and sat there to wait.

In time, as she expected, Russ appeared, hunched over his crutches, moving forward. He was hideously thin. His jaw was hard and his face was distorted with the effort, but he shoved his right foot forward and let his left fall in to meet it, and in this way he moved ahead, slowly, painfully. He paused for breath. He continued on.

Behind him came the woman with the leg braces and crutches, looking like vengeance on life support. How could she still be alive? It was excruciating to watch her as she moved beneath her own light. She looked straight ahead at Russ and Russ looked straight ahead at the long road down to the basilica.

It was worse than she had imagined. It was hideous, obscene. They were a terrible sight, a cruel parody of pilgrimage. Alison turned away in revulsion.

Later, alone in her hotel, she found she understood—at some deep level in the blood where thought and feeling could not reach—that Russ had done what was right. He had not surrendered to this fate, he had chosen it out of love. He was happy. In his way.

She watched Russ slowly disappear, and as he went she turned over and over in her mind the mysterious, cruel, and terrifying manifestations of God's love.

THE EXPERT ON GOD

From the start faith had been a problem for him, and his recent ordination had changed almost nothing. His doubts were simply more appropriate to the priesthood now. That was the only difference.

As a child of ten he was saying his evening prayers when it suddenly struck him that Catholics believed in three gods, God the Father, God the Son, and God the Holy Ghost. He blushed and covered his face. What if the kids at school found out? They were Protestants, and therefore wrong, but at least they had only one God. Instantly it came to him that there were three persons in one God. It was a mystery. He was very embarrassed but very relieved, and he actually looked around to see if anyone had heard his thoughts, and for the rest of his life it remained for him a moment of great shame. At eighteen, when he entered the Jesuits, he got up his courage and told this story to his confessor, who laughed. Matters of faith, he decided then, were better kept secret.

There were other doubts. He doubted Christ's presence in the Eucharist. He prayed for faith, and some kind of faith came to him, because he left off doubting about the Eucharist and moved on to doubt other matters: the virginity of Mary, the divinity of Christ, and then later the humanity of Christ. At one time or another, he doubted every article of belief, but only for a while, and only one at a time. Faith demanded a different response to each mystery, he discovered, but doubt was always the same. The initial onslaught of doubt lasted for only a moment, a quick and breathtaking conviction that none of it was true, and then that conviction itself surrendered to doubt, leaving an awful lingering unspeakable ache.

In the end he doubted the love of God, and that doubt did not pass.

He was a popular priest but he had no friends. He kept other Jesuits at a distance, he forced them away. He had no time for the intimacies of his own kind, caught up as he was in his assault on God. He prayed for faith. And when that did not come, he prayed for hope. And when that did not come, he went on anyway, teaching, preaching, saying Mass at the odd parish whenever he was asked. That is how things stood with him on the day of the accident.

It was Christmas Day, not because Christmas is symbolic, but because that is when it happened. Snow had fallen for nearly a week, and then on Christmas Eve there had been hail and then rain and then a sudden freeze. The streets were ready.

He had said Mass at Our Lady of Victories and was driving back to the Jesuit house. It was almost noon and the sun was high. "It doesn't matter," he said. The air was clear and the day was bright after all that snow, and as he drove through the vast open countryside, he marveled again at the absence of God. "It doesn't matter anymore."

He had very nearly achieved a kind of trance, staring at the sun on the ice, trying to obliterate all thought. Suddenly, off to the side of the road, he saw a dark-blue car turned half on its side and three boys huddled near it, looking at him as if he might be bringing help. He braked quickly, skidded in a half turn, and came to a stop. It was then that he noticed the tiny red sports car in the field on the opposite side of the road. It was crumpled nearly in two. The priest looked at the boys, but they only looked back, stunned. Finally one of them pointed to the red sports car.

He scrabbled through the glove compartment until he found the little vial of holy oils. He sprinted toward the car, following the wild track it had made as it spun through the snow, and when he got to it, he was not surprised to see the front end was completely demolished. He stooped and looked through the shattered window. The driver had been thrown to the side. The dashboard, crumpled back into the car, had pinned him, head down, in the passenger seat. The door hung on a single hinge, open a few inches but not wide enough for the priest to get in. The door would not give and he could not force it to open wider. He looked around a moment for help and saw that of course there was none; the boys huddling together across the road were too stupefied to help—or maybe they were injured, for all he knew.

He put the vial of oils in his pocket and jogged rapidly around the car. There was no way in. Somebody was inside, dying perhaps, and though he was only a few inches away, he could not reach him. It was maddening. He struck the car with his fist and sobbed suddenly in anger and frustration. Desperate then, he braced his back against the side of the car, pushing outward on the broken door and twisting, half-crazy, until the hinge gave way. He squeezed himself into the car behind the driver's seat. He could hear a kind of gurgling sound from the man trapped beneath the dashboard. He edged across until he was behind the passenger seat and, with what strength he could muster, he pulled back on it until it snapped and broke loose. He climbed onto it so that he was behind the body. He squatted, doubled up, hunched over, scarcely able to breathe, but at last he got his arms around the body and eased it free of the dashboard.

It was a boy, in his new car, and he was still alive, or nearly. He made a sound that might have been a sigh or a groan. Blood trickled from his mouth. But he did not die.

The priest held him in his arms. Crushed himself, he nonetheless managed to get the oils from his pocket and to wet his thumb with them and to place his thumb on the boy's bloody forehead, saying, "I absolve you from all your sins. In the name of the Father and of the Son and of the Holy Ghost. Amen." Then he was silent.

There was no sound from outside the car, no ambulance wail, no curious viewers. They were in the middle of nowhere, he and this dying boy he held in his arms. He had touched the boy with the holy oils and he had offered him absolution for his sins, and something should have happened by now. Someone should have come to help.

The boy should have died. Something. But there was silence only, and the boy's harsh, half-choked breathing.

He began to pray, aloud, which struck him as foolish: to be holding a dying boy in his arms and reciting rote prayers about our Father in heaven, about holy Mary, mother of God. What could he do? What could he say at such a moment? What would God do at such a moment, if there were a God?

"Well, do it," he said aloud, and heard the fury in his voice. "Say something." But there was silence from heaven.

His doubts became certainty and he said, "It doesn't matter," but it did matter and he knew it. What could anyone say to this crushed, dying thing, he wondered. What would God say if he cared as much as I?

He shook with an involuntary sob then, and as he did, the boy shuddered in agony and choked on the blood that had begun to pour from his mouth. The priest could see death beginning to ease across the boy's face. And still he could say nothing.

The boy turned—some dying reflex—and his head tilted in the priest's arms, trusting, like a lover. And at once the priest, faithless, unrepentant, gave up his prayers and bent to him and whispered, fierce and burning, "I love you," and continued till there was no breath, "I love you, I love you, I love you."

CERTAINTIES

ROMAN ORDINARY

His Holiness Pope Paul VI is an ordinary saint. All day long he does what he has to do, and at night he dances.

First thing in the morning, after meditation and Mass, he has a little orange juice and a sweet roll with butter. Some days coffee. Some not. It depends on what Romagnoli brings. And then His Holiness goes to the toilet, but not very much. Afterward, he makes his bed.

Then it's business, business, business without a letup. Cardinals are in and out all day: Vatican finances, the pill, a paternity suit against some bishop. Cardinals Bagnio and Konig present in outline their report on Opus Dei, a suspect lay order in Spain; it turns out that Opus Dei is allied with the right wing of the curia and it turns out too that its influence in Spain, and even in Italy, is benign. Not only tolerable, but benign. *Floreat* Opus Dei. A decision must be made on the secret archives of the Vatican Library. And what about that Benedictine nun who said Mass in Chicago? Is His Holiness thinking of—how can we put it—retirement? Perhaps when he is eighty? No? Pilgrims are lined up and waiting for the papal blessing, a sea of believers awash in their saris and double knits and platform shoes. So much ugliness and hope. Did Christ have all of this in mind? The thought flickers for a second through the papal consciousness, but His Holiness extinguishes it with the single bat of an eyelash. He smiles distantly. He speaks a few words of welcome in German, in French, in Greek, in English. A cardinal whispers to him and then he welcomes the Indians and the Slavs. People dear to our heart. All one in the love of our Lord and Savior Jesus Christ. Some damn fool snaps a picture even though cameras are forbidden. After a while they all let His Holiness go and he trails his long white robes behind him to the papal apartment. Time for a lie-down.

The papal apartment consists of a sitting room, a bedroom, and a bath. The sitting room has four little chairs, designed to be uncomfortable, and a big desk where His Holiness sits during private audiences; lots of faded tapestries cover the walls. The bedroom is huge, with a glistening parquet floor and almost no furniture. A wooden bed of no special design stands over near the windows; at its head there is a small armoire that holds the pope's robes, and next to that a bureau for his socks and underwear and hankies. Against the opposite wall stands the great armoire to which Pope Paul VI alone has the key.

His Holiness lies down on the narrow bed, but the quiet doesn't last long. That little priest Romagnoli is banging around in the sitting room, laying out the tea. Cold tongue of lamb, three caramels, a piping cup of Constant Comment. His Holiness bolts the lamb tongue because he is always famished in midafternoon. Then he sits back and tucks a caramel into the side of his jaw and sucks at his tea. This is his private time, with the shoes kicked off and the old feet up, just enjoying his caramels and tea. Life is good. When he was younger, he used to meditate on the transitoriness of all things mortal during this teatime, but now that he is in his late seventies, he makes his mind a blank. Nothing. Nothing is happening.

His fifteen minutes are up now and the little priestypoo is chapping at the door, ostensibly to take away the tray, but really to edge His Holiness into the next round of duties.

Delegations are waiting from Russia, from Persepolis, from Houston. The mistress of a South American dictator demands, for the twentieth time, a private interview. Cardinal Wright is waiting to talk about Joan of Arc and about election procedures for choosing the next pope. A monsignor from *L'Osservatore Romano* is owed a private word because of his ringing defense of the personal lives of two curial members—kinky, both of them—and perhaps after the private word, His Holiness could pose for a quick photograph? Investments in obsolescent housing must be liquidated, now, while prices are still adequate. A bishop is waiting, a cardinal has a special report, three monsignors have brought money in dollars. Can Henry Ford remarry? Can President Ford? His Holiness attends to all these matters, his frail yellow hands pressed hard against the white breviary he carries everywhere, his mind only occasionally wandering to the night and to the great armoire in his bedroom.

Finally the work is done and he is free. He goes to his private chapel and prays, sometimes for only twenty minutes, sometimes for an hour. He goes out of himself during this time, looking back wistfully at his own kneeling figure, or looking down from the stations of the cross high on the gilded wall, or—more and more, lately—looking off to nothing, nothing at all.

Dinner is laid in the papal sitting room: a large bowl of granola, an apple or an orange or some exotic fruit in season, a single glass of wine. It is ten o'clock by now and Rome is beginning to come fully alive. His Holiness toasts the city and its twenty layers of civilization, roof built upon ruined roof, bone upon bone.

Everything is in the process of decay. While the number of Catholics has continued to increase, the number of priests has dropped: last year from 344,342 to 339,635. The Vatican deficit is about $6.4 million. The Americans don't give a damn. What to do? His Holiness shakes his head slowly, wisely, from side to side. Again he raises his glass to Rome, to the Via Veneto with its Ferraris and movie stars and Anita Ekberg, and beneath it all to the catacombs with their still unexplored chambers of whitened bones.

After dinner it is canasta time, or blackjack, or honeymoon bridge, whichever Romagnoli prefers. Monsignors, bishops, cardinals, indeed all ecclesiastical Rome dreams of someday playing canasta with His Holiness, but those dreams will never be realized. His Holiness plays only with Romagnoli, the young priest who brings his meals and tidies up around the place. A Sicilian, hot tempered, Romagnoli plays to win and usually does.

At eleven that Dominican, private confessor to the pope, appears at the door; at eleven thirty, his soul washed clean, His Holiness takes to his bath so that by twelve he will be fully prepared.

It is a few minutes to twelve now and almost time. His Holiness puts on his pajamas of some rough cloth, immaculately white. The trousers balloon out shapelessly, but they are tied at the ankles with thin brown ribbons. The top slips over his head and is gathered at the waist by a brown sash. The sleeves are wide and loose. His white slippers turn up at the toe like a medieval jester's. He is almost ready. He goes quickly to the small bureau near the head of the bed and, reaching far back into the top drawer, he withdraws a large square of white cloth embroidered with brown. In the center of the cloth there is a circle of leather that will protect his skull from the knife blade. He folds the cloth carefully and then places it on his head, the circle of leather directly on the crown. He tucks the folds of cloth back from his face, arranging it like an Arab burnoose, and then binds the headdress firmly into position with a brown silk circlet. In the mirror he adjusts the silk cord across his forehead and smooths out any wrinkles in the cloth. Is this some sort of Jewish rite? Is this some compromise with Muhammad? The embroidery along the edge of the white cloth could tell us something, surely, but we cannot examine it closely enough because there is no time.

The bells of Rome have begun to proclaim midnight. While they toll on and on, His Holiness walks to the great armoire and turns the little key smoothly in the lock. The carved double doors swing open.

His Holiness genuflects and then stands with his palms together in the attitude of prayer. But he is not praying. He is marveling yet again at his wonderful bones.

The armoire before which he stands contains a tier of thirteen shelves, each of which, at the mere touch of the papal finger, slides out to provide ready access to its contents. Pope Paul VI presses one of the lower shelves where his large bones lie on a ground of purple silk; gently, soundlessly, it moves toward him until it touches his folded hands, and then it stops. Spread out there before him in perfect order are his femur, his tibia, his fibula. Next to them lie clavicle, humerus, radius, ulna; on the shelf above, the metacarpal and the phalanges. Light from the ceiling casts a violet shadow on the bones and they glow almost with a life, with a soul, of their own. He presses gently on the shelf above this one and out slides a display of his corpus, his tarsus, his patellae. And then the special shelf, the one with his skull intact, the bones very nearly articulate. His Holiness runs his fingers lightly over the forehead and his pale hand tingles. The eye sockets are smooth round holes, yellowing at the edges; he pokes his thumb into that strange aperture, no eye there, no vile jelly left. The pope catches his breath. This is how it will be, later, when at last he lies dead: his bones will wait in some dark vault for something, for anything. And yet they lie here now, put away out of sight, out of use, while he goes on each day living the life of an ordinary saint. His breath comes quicker, lighter. He presses the shelf above, and the shelf above that, and then rapidly, one after another, all the shelves but the top one, each with its cargo of white and glistening bones. His bones.

The double doors stand open, the shelves of the armoire expose their treasure to the empty room and to the pope, who has begun to back away. Facing the huge armoire, he bows deeply and then, thumb and middle finger pressed together, he raises his arms out from his sides until he stands cruciform. Is it a flamenco dance? He extends one leg to the side and brings it forward suddenly in a kind of crouch, spins on his forward foot in a sweeping circle, and then repeats the motion with his other leg. No, it is not flamenco. He is dancing slowly, ritually, like a harem dancer, like some small Persian boy trained to do this and this alone. His headdress flutters behind him and the full sleeves flow and dip to the fluid motions of his arms. He is losing himself, his eyes have taken on a distant look, as if he sees beyond this room and these bones he honors with his dancing.

Now the pope approaches the armoire in a formal hesitation step. He bows low for several measures and then he presses the topmost shelf, which slides toward him bearing the long curved sword with which he must dance. Tenderly he lifts the sword in his two hands and holds it up, a presentation, before the armoire. And then he moves to the other side of the room and makes his presentation, and then to the next and the next. In the center of the room he stops. His head is bowed. He summons his considerable powers of concentration and then, decisively, he places the sword squarely on the crown of his head, the curved blade poised on the circular leather patch, the tip hanging to the left side of his head, the handle to the right. He adjusts the sword for balance, but it continues to teeter. A fraction of an inch to the left and then it rests motionless. His Holiness takes a tentative step or two. Perfect. The blade whispers against the leather but remains in balance.

His Holiness is smiling as his body moves about the room. The small feet glide soundlessly on the parquet floor. The muscles in his back and belly ripple like water. As his frail torso lurches forward and back, his buttocks respond and his thighs follow through. He dances slowly and with grace. On their exposed shelves, his bones are radiant. He dances on and on, though the bells of Rome have struck one o'clock and then two. It seems he must stop now, surely he must, he has danced so long. But he continues.

And now he kneels, the blade on his head dipping from right to left. Slowly, so slowly he can feel the blood pulsing in his thighs and temple, slowly he sits back upon his heels. He slides somehow to his hip and then his buttocks until, incredibly, he is lying on the floor at full length, but with his head erect and the sword in calm and easy balance across his crown. Ecstatically, all the muscles of his body ripple, for he has completed this impossible thing. On their shelves his bones clatter. It is done.

With a sudden twist of his entire body, His Holiness is on his feet once more, free now of the most exacting part of his dance; the rest is sheer jubilation. He dances gladly, arms swinging out and away from his body, legs twining and untwining as he moves in arcs and arabesques undreamed of. On and on he goes, though the minutes slip by, though the clocks strike again and again. His flesh ripples and flows. The garments that surround his flesh seem to float free of it. There is nothing beneath those garments but water or air. No flesh is there, surely.

Pope Paul VI's bones have rested in the armoire for how long now, attended nightly by this ritual dance. And now the flesh is gone as well. Yet His Holiness dances on, his eyes glazed and all-seeing, his body and bones reduced to pure spirit.

Later, unfleshed, His Holiness will kneel at the window to watch dawn break and later still he will crawl to bed for an exhausted hour of sleep before the rest of his world awakes and Romagnoli comes to announce time for meditation and Mass. He will take up again his make-believe life of interviews and reports and decisions, pretending. But now it is the dance that matters.

The dance winds on faster and faster and the sword too moves with an independent life. His Holiness twists endlessly clockwise and the sword, its curved silver blade glimmering in the light of the bones, twists counterclockwise, faster and faster as His Holiness Pope Paul VI, that ordinary saint, dances out of his flesh and bones, and dances.

SINS OF THOUGHT, SINS OF DESIRE

Until she was twenty-six, Beezie Connors had never thought of murdering anyone, and by that time she was Sister Mary Thekla, a teacher of English in the Sisters of Divine Prudence.

"I only thought of it, Father. I'm not certain I desired it, but I know I thought of it."

"I see." The words came out "I shee," because Father Rolfe spoke through jaws clenched tight on a yawn. He was tired, and he knew that that young Turk, Snee or Snay or something, had already cozied the ice for drinks.

"I didn't do it, of course."

"No, yes, that's just as well." He gathered himself for speech. "In the spiritual life, Sister, these thoughts come to us—murder, adultery, oh, terrible things—and we resist, Sister, because we are soldiers of Christ, fighting his battles, and he it is who gives us the strength. He is the commander; we are the foot soldiers. He is the chief; we the followers. He is the five-star general; we, uh, you see the point. And so it is, too, in the spiritual life."

What had happened? He'd come full circle. Well, no matter, they were all good girls.

"So never be discouraged, Sister, keep up the fine work for Jesus. Remember, he gives and he takes away." Oh dear, that was another speech. "Grace is everything, Sister; follow the promptings. Always follow the promptings."

For a moment he wondered if this was the best advice.

"Now for your penance say three Hail Marys and a Glory Be."

Here he shifted his generous bulk to the left and freed his shorts, which were stuck. He was sweaty all over from that damned leather cushion.

"Ah, yes. May almighty God have mercy on you, forgive you your sins, and..."

The monotone mutter began, and Father's right hand swung into action and Sister Thekla left the confessional absolved. The little window rattled shut behind her.

Sister Thekla had thought of murdering Mother Humiliata, an intransigent nun who bore a startling resemblance to Bette Midler and who combined in herself the power of convent superior and high school principal. She was held in awe by her community not because of her virtue or wisdom but because for eighteen years she had managed always to hold some kind of superior's position: sister treasurer, minister of material needs, principal. "Your money, your food, or your life," Sister Thekla said, reminding herself not to be uncharitable. That was in January. By October, Mother had become openly hostile, and by November Sister Thekla in a rage, if only for a second, had thought of murdering Big Mama, as she called the reverend mother.

She had thought of it. And despite her tentative confession, she had certainly desired it. But she had not done it. Though in fact she was capable of it. Hers was a character that finds its natural home in wars and in pure politics and in religious life. She was one of those single-minded persons who are able to live for an ideal and to die for it. And who are able also to kill for it. In this she resembled Mother Humiliata herself and a fair proportion of the Sisters of Divine Prudence.

Stupid of me even to confess it, Sister Thekla thought. As if I could do such a thing. And she went off to Sister Aelred's room for tea, which was forbidden by Holy Rule.

Murder, imagine, Father Rolfe said to himself and dismissed the matter from his mind. Good old Snee would have the scotch ready, thanks be to God and his Holy Mother.

And so a month later, when Mother Humiliata was found dead, pinioned to her seat by the steering wheel of house car number two, it surprised Father Sneigh—age twenty-nine and nervous by nature— to learn in confession that Father Rolfe felt himself guilty of criminal negligence in the matter of Mother's death and that Sister Thekla, normally a sensible girl, suspected Mother might have committed suicide.

But that was a month in the future, and at the moment Sister Thekla, newly absolved, was saying to Sister Aelred, "You know, Aelred, I think old Rolfe's going gaga."

"But he's always been gaga. That's how he is."

"I know, but this is different. Tonight he started giving me the 'so too in the spiritual life' speech, and then he got off onto the five-star general and then, of all things, the death of a relative, and then back to 'so too in the spiritual life.'"

"You put your own sugar in. You always want something different when I do it."

"Big Mama."

"Big Mama."

They toasted Mother Humiliata, clinked their teacups together, and drank, glad that theirs was a holy conspiracy.

In the newest section of the convent Father Sneigh gave his watch an angry glance. Five to nine; old Rolfe would be hulking in any minute for his two or three nightcaps and his predictions of evil days to come. Father Sneigh did not mind the nightly visits—it was company of a sort—but they always fell right in the middle of his studies. For years he had been working on exegesis of the Kurios passage from Philippians, but how could you ever get going if you were being interrupted all the time. How could you sift your notes. How…

There was a knock, and in hulked Father Rolfe.

"Another day, another dolor, ho ho ho."

That again, he thought, and filled the glasses, responding

automatically, "Ho ho ho." It was not laughter but gentle self-mockery; it passed for a sense of humor in Father Rolfe.

"Your health, Snay."

"Sneigh. As in sky."

"Your health all the same."

Drop dead, Father Sneigh thought, and surprised himself. He did not have a whimsical turn of mind.

In the oldest section of the convent Mother Humiliata sat holding the autobiography of the Little Flower, a saint to whom she had special devotion. She held the book tilted toward the lamp, with its 60-watt bulb. Though the other nuns were allowed only 40-watt bulbs, Mother justified her extra 20 watts on the grounds that as a superior she could not afford to risk eyestrain. At the moment there was no danger of eyestrain, since Mother had fallen gently asleep just as the Little Flower was receiving "the miracle of the snows" she had requested, a snowfall Mother would have found less remarkable had she known that the miracle occurred in the dead of winter.

Relations between Sister Thekla and Mother Humiliata had been strained from the start. On her way from her previous assignment at the rather too liberal Saint Rigobert's, Sister Thekla had stopped to visit her parents, and while visiting was not actually forbidden, it required special permission that Sister Thekla had not requested and that was rarely granted before final vows. Her arrival at Our Lady of Prudence High coincided with an epic downpour, and Sister Thekla, shrouded in a flamboyant yellow slicker, dashed back and forth between the car and the portico carrying more books than any nun was allowed to possess. Mother had noted these things and would note others.

Sister Thekla's real troubles began during the time for manifestation of conscience, a twice annual event in which each sister was summoned by Mother Superior, so Holy Rule said, "for the purpose of revealing herself with all her shortcomings and failures honestly and completely numbered, so that the superior may command whatever measures she thinks good for the spiritual amelioration of the sister and the edification of the community."

"It means you get what's coming to you," Thekla said.

"If only things didn't upset her so much."

"What things?"

"You can never tell till after she's upset."

"It's when her face goes puce that I worry."

Mother Humiliata looked upon manifestations as the most trying time of a life spent in unremitting trial. Someone always said something disconcerting. This time it was Sister Annunciata who, cross-examined for the third time, admitted that when she made the rounds with the morning Deo gratias, Sister Thekla was nearly an hour late rising. Her testimony was made worse by Sister Maudita's admission, again under examination, that she frequently had evening tea in Sister Aelred's room along with Sister Thekla. The three of them, the unholy trinity, Mother thought. Nor did it help Sister Thekla's case that on the day before her interview she drove house car number two into an evergreen on the front lawn for the sum of four hundred dollars' damage.

The accident had happened, so Sister Thekla claimed, because the steering wheel had locked in place and something funny had gone wrong with the accelerator. Moreover, when she tried to turn off the ignition, the key had simply stuck where it was. Whatever the facts, Mother Humiliata was not pleased.

Sister Thekla's manifestation at first went smoothly enough. She managed to confess faults that were genuine—moodiness, distractions in prayer, occasional negligence in preparing classes—without having to get onto more uncomfortable ground. She had steered clear of the sleeping business and the tea. Manifestation seemed to be gliding to a penance, a blessing, and a dismissal, when suddenly Mother Humiliata smacked her meaty palm against the desktop.

"And these books? What about these books?"

"Books, Reverend Mother?"

"Reports have been made, Sister. Charges have been brought."

"I'm afraid I don't understand."

"Tennessee Williams, Sister; does that ring a bell? Graham

Greene? Faulkner?" Her voice rose in volume and pitch as she ticked off the offending names. "*Catcher in the Rye*, Sister? Evelyn Waugh? Steinbeck?" On *Steinbeck*, Mother's face began to turn puce.

"Of those writers, Reverend Mother, I've taught only Steinbeck's *The Pearl*, and that's absolutely harmless."

"You admit it!"

"It's on the required reading list."

"I thought you'd have some sort of explanation like that, Sister. Well, let me tell you right now…"

Mother Humiliata told her right then, and proceeded for a half hour to tell her a great deal more, about books and tea and sleeping late. She was furious with a holy fury, not at Sister Thekla herself, but at the very idea that there were always people in this world who made the smooth ordering of existence impossible. Her rage was impersonal; Sister Thekla merely provided the occasion.

"You are preparing for final vows, Sister Thekla. I want you in the coming months to think hard about whether or not you belong in religious life. I raise the question. And I promise you, unless you rise at the appointed hour and not a minute later, you will last in the Sisters of Divine Prudence just as long as it takes me to write a letter to Rome. Now if you will, please, get out."

And Sister Thekla got out, murder in her mind.

At once she went looking for Sister Aelred and found her with Sister Maudita, who was crying because Mother had threatened to postpone her final vows for a year.

"Why?"

"The tea. The damned tea."

"How many years did you get, Aelred?"

"None. I told her I was thinking of leaving, and that broke her stride."

"She said she would throw me out." Sister Thekla was surprised to hear her voice crack.

"For tea? She can't throw you out just for tea."

"For not getting up on time."

They all cried for a little while about that, because not getting up would be grounds for dismissal. Then it was time for Sisters Aelred and Maudita to help with preparing dinner, their weekly extra. Left alone, Sister Thekla's fighting spirits collapsed, and she spent the rest of the afternoon in chapel wondering if Mother was right and praying she was not. That night in confession she mentioned to old Father Rolfe that for a minute she had thought of committing murder and perhaps had even desired it. But she had not done it.

Mother Humiliata was killed on December 6, two weeks after the death of President Kennedy. Though deeply moved by the assassination, Mother said that life was for the living and must go on. Accordingly she refused to close school during the days of mourning and permitted her community to watch for only an hour each evening the vast television coverage of the wake and burial of the president. Classes were held, duties were performed, life went on.

Sister Thekla, according to holy obedience, met with her regular classes but refused to teach them; nor could she have done so even if she wanted, overwhelmed as she was by the tangible grief and moral inertia that seemed to be everywhere. When she went to meet her Adult Christian Doctrine group on Tuesday evening, she was not surprised to find that only two people had come. And when they proposed driving into Washington to stand with that endless line filing past the casket, this struck her as the only sensible action to take.

And so it happened that much of the world and most of the Sisters of Divine Prudence saw on television the Sisters Thekla and Aelred and Maudita, who should have been within the convent walls at work or at prayer. Mother Humiliata, puce colored before the screen, vowed instant vengeance, a vow she retracted within the next few minutes when three of the school's most generous benefactors phoned to congratulate her on sending a delegation of sisters to the president's wake.

"I felt I must," she said. "I felt I had no choice," and her voice was sad as she spoke half the truth. But to herself she said, "Well, there's still her final vows, and she'll take those over my dead body."

Her dead body was found in house car number two. The blame for her death was officially laid to the car—the steering wheel and accelerator, to be exact—though Father Rolfe felt he was more than partly to blame, and Sister Thekla harbored suspicions about Mother herself. The cause of greatest wonder in the convent, however, was how Mother Humiliata came to be in a house car in the first place.

Our Lady of Prudence High was the legal owner of three cars: two 1960 Chevrolets, which were known as house car number one and house car number two, and a 1963 Oldsmobile, Mother's favorite, known as the Prisoner of Love. Black and slightly battered, the house cars were kept in the small garage behind the school while the Prisoner of Love, polished daily by old Ralph the handyman, stood gleaming in the oval drive directly beneath Mother's window.

The thirty teaching sisters in the convent kept the two cars in almost constant use for courses at Catholic University, lectures at Loyola and Woodstock, dentist appointments, doctor appointments, and one daily trip to the psychiatrist. Mother Humiliata approved of none of this, agreeing with the Fates—as her three sister consultants were known—that a sister without final vows should not be allowed outside the convent walls, whatever the reason. But though she did not approve, she could do nothing to prevent these excursions, since they had the approval of Mother General, who was too much influenced, she felt, by those Jesuits now at the council. And so to make the cars available to all and to guarantee that no one but herself drove the Oldsmobile, Mother Humiliata ruled that anyone might use either car provided she signed up for it ahead of time.

There were only two forbidden periods when a car was not available: every Friday evening house car number two had to pick up Father Rolfe at Saint Ursula's, where he heard the confessions of the retired nuns; every morning from seven till ten house car number one was out, reason unspecified. The reason was not specified because nobody was supposed to know that Sister Dymphna was packed off each morning to a psychiatrist, where she made up for her years of convent silence with a marathon hour of talk to Dr. Conroy, whom she loved and feared, and once, shamefully, dreamed about. All the sisters knew about poor crazy Dymphna, of course, but because it was supposed to be secret, everyone pretended not to.

Mother Humiliata often explained to the Fates that her own car was always available for emergencies. The only emergency that had ever arisen, however, was during the annual visitation of Mother General, who had insisted on driving one of her Jesuits to the airport in the Oldsmobile. Its other use was for Mother Humiliata's daily trip to the post office, an act of humility she combined with a pleasant drive through the Maryland farm country, and for her Saturday morning visit to her doctor.

For the past eighteen years Mother had risen each Saturday morning, meditated for an hour, attended Mass, breakfasted, and driven off for her treatment. She had found this ritual unpleasant at first, but over the years she had come to enjoy it. The embarrassing part lasted only a minute or two, and then there was the long, pleasant talk with the doctor, little Tommy Murphy, who lisped and pouted like an old woman, but who over the years had shown great understanding of the burdens she had to bear as a religious superior. She never mentioned even to the Fates the nature of her illness, nor did they ask, because they knew it was a delicate matter and they knew too that Mother often had trouble sitting for very long.

On the final morning of her life Mother Humiliata happened to be in house car number two because on the previous evening she had succumbed for a moment to her ancient vice of eavesdropping. She had been passing by the study room after recreation when she heard Sister Maudita's complaining voice and, telling herself she was not going to eavesdrop, not really, she walked back to the door and stood there listening.

"Yes, with Porkers," she heard Maudita say. "Can you imagine driving all the way to Boston with Porkers? And in that death trap too."

Though Mother Humiliata was ignorant of most of the convent nicknames—her own, Big Mama, would have brought on monumental rage—she knew at once that Maudita was talking about the unfortunate Sister Porcella. She knew, because she herself had told Sister Maudita she might drive to Boston on Saturday for her uncle's funeral. She might also deliver to Mother General the written reports on the manifestations of conscience. And she might also drive Sister Porcella, who was deaf, to the Lahey Clinic, where a number of fine doctors were waiting to look into her ears. And in a way she sympathized with Maudita because Sister Porcella, besides being deaf, was a deadly bore who talked endlessly about her brother the priest who had gone mad from giving his food to starving children during World War I, when in fact everyone knew that he had run off with a floozy who was reported to be a nightclub singer and was probably something worse.

Having eavesdropped, Mother went to her room furious, not at what she had heard but at what she had done. None of her other failings distressed her in the least, but this one was so beneath her, so embarrassing to confess, that remorse descended on her almost at once. She prescribed for herself a stinging penance, one the Little Flower would have approved. She sent for Sister Thekla.

"You will tell Sister Maudita that you, not she, will pick up Father Rolfe at Saint Ursula's tonight; she has my permission to retire early."

"But Reverend Mother…"

"And you will tell her that tomorrow she may drive the Oldsmobile to Boston. I will use a house car for my doctor's appointment."

"But Reverend Mother…"

"That will be all, Sister Thekla."

As obedience required, Sister Thekla picked up Father Rolfe. Together they drove down the road and eventually drove off the road and across an open field, the car gathering momentum and shooting straight ahead as once again the steering wheel locked. In a panic Sister Thekla thumped at the brake with no effect whatsoever and then, confused, pressed heavily on the accelerator. Perversely, that gave her control of the car once more, and she was able to stop it and then turn it so that once more it pointed toward the road. Only when she had done this, after much fiddling with the gas pedal and the steering wheel, did she allow herself to get hysterical. For five minutes she screamed and cried, making a great deal of noise in the wintry countryside and making Father Rolfe far more upset than he had been by the wild drive through the field.

She stopped crying finally when Father leaped out of the car and, frantic, began to call for help. She got him back into the car and, having coaxed from him the promise that he personally would explain to Mother what had happened, she drove very slowly along the narrow winding road that brought them, after almost an hour, to the convent.

Father Rolfe was too unnerved to see Mother immediately, so he stopped to have a drink with Father Sneigh, who was not in. Father helped himself to some scotch anyway, thinking that Sneigh would be along shortly, and then some more scotch, because Sneigh had not come, and after another—a nightcap—he went to bed, still unnerved but no longer recalling why.

Sister Thekla lay sleepless for over an hour, and then decided to write Reverend Mother a note about the car. Mother Humiliata was convinced that there was nothing wrong with it, having twice been assured by old Ralph that the car was in perfect condition, and Thekla feared that, with her heavy foot and mighty self-confidence, Mother would drive off and kill herself. She slipped the note under Mother's door and returned to bed.

After another sleepless hour, this one spent thinking about Tess of the D'Urbervilles and the inherent perils of putting notes under doors, Sister Thekla threw her coat over her nightgown and trudged down to the garage, where she slipped another note under the windshield wiper. "And that takes care of Big Mama," she said. Sister Thekla slept very late the next morning.

Early the next morning Mother Humiliata woke, appalled to think that her car had gone off to Boston, alone, so to speak. She was consoled, however, that it was the kind of generous action that wiped her slate clean, and that she was once again squared away with her Maker, slates and squares being much to the fore when she contemplated her relations with God. As she dressed, she turned over in her mind the topic of this morning's meditation, a tranquil spirit in a troubled world. Before she left for chapel she picked up the note at her door and, with a glance at Thekla's bold handwriting, placed it in the center of her desk. Nothing was so important that it could not wait until after prayer.

Later, when Sister Thekla heard about the accident, she went to Mother's room and found her note, unfolded, in the center of the desk. Wondering, she checked the garage and then the car, but could not find the second note. It turned up in Mother's coat pocket. Sister Thekla went off to confer with Father Rolfe, but he had come completely undone, and she could not make him understand that Mother had been warned about the dangerous steering wheel, warned not once but twice, and in writing. It was futile trying to talk sense to him. She spent the rest of the day in prayer, and that night under the seal of confession discussed the matter with Father Sneigh.

How could Mother possibly have driven that car after reading the two notes unless, God forbid, the accident was not an accident? How, she wanted to know.

Father Sneigh, reeling from an hour's session with the distraught Father Rolfe, was confused by Sister Thekla's curious story. He was a scripture scholar, not a detective. Why did these people torture themselves over nothing? The woman was dead, let her rest in peace. She was a dreadful woman anyway.

And so, as soon as he was decently able, Father Sneigh raised his hand in blessing and dismissed Sister Thekla, who would simply have to get along as best she could, relying, like Rolfe and in Rolfe's own formula, on the tender mercies of God and his Holy Mother.

Never having grasped her question, Father Sneigh could offer Sister Thekla no answer. The answer was simple: Mother Humiliata had not read either note.

Like any inveterate eavesdropper, Mother was possessed of an insatiable curiosity. But she was curious about only those things she was not supposed to know. Letters from Mother General, official papers that came across her desk, the notes beneath her door held no interest whatsoever for her. If anything, she regarded them with fear and suspicion. A letter from a superior meant another departure from ancient custom, and a note from a subject meant a request for some exception to the Rule. Either way, the serene order of convent life was interrupted, so when she saw the note beneath the windshield wiper, she plucked it out and, with a glance at the handwriting, thrust the bit of paper into her pocket.

"So much for Thekla," she said, and, a tranquil spirit in a troubled world, she backed the car smoothly out of the garage.

The morning was cold and clear, and Mother Humiliata drove along the winding road humming "O Sacrament Most Holy." Despite the recent snowfall there was very little snow on the ground, and with the clear air it was a perfect day for driving. Mother began to plan a little excursion for the afternoon, a drive up the Potomac perhaps. When she came to the stretch of road that had been newly paved in late summer, she sped up a bit. She was not strictly within the speed limit, but there was no traffic on a Saturday morning and, besides, the road was wider here and not nearly so winding.

Her thinking was quite correct. The road was not winding. It was in fact so very nearly straight that she was unaware the steering wheel had locked until she tried to turn the car around a slight bend. Mother slammed her foot on the brake, which did no good at all, and the car shot off the road and into a long gully. It lurched a little and tore off in a new direction. Mother's foot crunched the brake pedal and her eyes bugged as the car gathered more speed, flattening several rows of icy cornstalks and making a neat passage between two enormous oak trees.

It was exhilarating, actually. Beyond the trees another gully and then another field. And in the middle of the field, a cow.

Crazily, Mother Humiliata found herself thinking about the cow. What was it doing in the middle of the field? In December. With snow on the ground. And then it was over. The last thing the cow saw was a huge black car bearing down on it, a nun at the wheel, grinning, as if she had intended this all along.

Mother Humiliata took the cow at sixty miles an hour, accelerating even as she struck it.

Leonora started out pretty and bright.

"She could be a movie star," her mother said, "but I would never do that to my child. I would never allow a child of mine to be in the limelight. I want Leonora to be just normal."

So Leonora took ballet and tap and piano.

"Perhaps she has other gifts," the dance teacher said. "Perhaps she has a gift for music."

The piano teacher was more to the point. "She has nothing," he said. "And she's driving me crazy."

"You could be a movie star," her mother said.

In junior high Leonora was one of the first to grow breasts; the other girls resented her for that. But in high school her breasts made her popular with the boys, so she didn't care about the girls. She became a cheerleader and after every game she and the other cheerleaders crowded into the booths at Dante's and waited for the team to arrive. Then they all drank Cokes and ate cheeseburgers and grabbed at one another in the booths—nothing serious, just good fun—and made out on the way home.

In November of her senior year Leonora was parked in front of her house in Chuckie's car.

"Why won't you do it?" Chuckie asked. "Everybody does."

"I don't know," she said, miserable. "I want to, but I can't. I just can't."

"Nobody saves themselves for marriage anymore. Is that what you think you're doing?"

"I think I was meant for better things," she said, not really knowing what she meant. "I mean, I get straight As and Bs."

"Ah shit," Chuckie said. "Just put your hand here. Feel this."

"No, I was meant for better things."

"But you've got to start sometime," Chuckie said. "Hell, I'm captain of the team."

But Leonora was already getting out of the car, feeling chosen, feeling—she searched for the word—exalted. Yes, that was it. She was meant for better things.

In the admissions office at Stanford, Leonora was a floater, somebody who hadn't yet sunk to the bottom but somebody who wouldn't get picked out of the pool unless a real Stanford freshman decided to go to Yale or somewhere. That year a lot of freshmen went to Yale and so Leonora, floating almost to the end, was admitted to Stanford.

"You could be a college professor," her mother said. "Or a famous writer. You could win the Nobel Prize, maybe."

"Dry up," Leonora said. "What do you know about it? You never even went to college."

"Oh baby," she said. "Oh sweetheart, don't be mean to your mother, Leonora. I only want what's best for you. I only want you to be happy."

"Then dry up," Leonora said.

The worst part about Stanford was that they made her take freshman English. She had been among the top thirty in high school and now she was back to writing compositions. At first she had just been a little nasty to the teacher in class, to let him know how she felt about being there. But after she had written the first assigned paper, she decided to go see him and demand an explanation. He gave it to her. He explained that it was a requirement of the university that every student demonstrate a basic competence in expository writing and that she had not, in the qualifying tests, demonstrated that. And then he handed her the corrected paper.

It was covered with little red marks—Diction? Antecedent? Obscure, no no no—and there was a large black C at the bottom of the page.

"You gave me a C," Leonora said. "I've never had a C in my life."

"There's nothing wrong with a C," he said. "It's a perfectly acceptable grade. It's average, maybe even above average."

"You gave me a C," she said and, choking on her tears, ran from his office.

Her next two papers came back with Cs on them also, so she knew he was out to get her. His name was Lockhardt and he had written a couple of novels and thought he was hot shit.

Leonora went to the ombudsman and complained that she was being discriminated against. She should not have to take freshman English in the first place, and in the second place Lockhardt was guilty of unprofessional conduct in browbeating her and making her feel inferior.

The ombudsman went to the chairman of the English Department, who called in Lockhardt and then called in Leonora and finally checked her papers himself. The next day he told Leonora that yes, she would have to take freshman English like all the others, that the grades Professor Lockhardt had given her seemed fair enough, that he was sorry Professor Lockhardt had made her feel inferior. He told Lockhardt for God's sake go easy on the girl, she's half-crazy, and whatever you do don't be alone with her in your office. He told the ombudsman that the problem had been settled to everyone's satisfaction and there was no need to take all this to the provost. So everyone was miserable and satisfied.

Leonora's final grade was a C, all because of that bastard Lockhardt.

Patty Hearst was wrestled, struggling, into the trunk of a car in Berkeley and the next day she was a headline in all the papers. Leonora narrowed her thin eyes and thought, Why couldn't they have taken me?

In her junior year she moved in with Horst Kammer. He was clearly one of the better things that she was meant for. He was very smart and spent a lot of time with the housemaster, so that in Horst she had not only a roommate, she had instant acceptance as well. Horst was too intellectual to be much interested in sex, but he didn't mind occasional sex with Leonora and that was enough for her.

Horst dressed in army fatigues and spent a lot of his time protesting Stanford's investments in South Africa. Leonora protested along with him and they were arrested together during the spring sit-in at Old Union. Leonora felt proud to be involved in something historical, something that mattered. There were over a hundred students arrested and they were each fined nearly two hundred dollars. Leonora's mother sent the money, and with it a note saying, "You're like Vanessa Redgrave or Jane Fonda. You're doing your part."

"God, that woman is hopeless," Leonora said.

Two photographs.

One. Leonora is home from college and all the relatives have come over for dinner. Afterward somebody snaps an Instamatic of Leonora and her mother and father sitting on the floor in front of the Christmas tree, surrounded by gifts. The mother and father each have an arm around Leonora and they are smiling directly into the camera. Leonora is smiling too, but she is looking off to the right of the camera, as if at the very last minute she decided the picture is not what she wants; she wants something else.

"She could be a photographer's model," her mother says, examining the picture. "She could be on all the covers."

Two. Leonora has just crested the hill on Campus Drive and is about to make the long clear descent on her new ten-speed bike. She passes two professors who are taking a noon walk, looking like anybody else, just enjoying the California spring. Leonora does not notice them, does not see that one of them is Lockhardt. She sees only the long, long hill before her, and she feels the warm wind blowing through her hair. She sits high on the seat, no hands, and lifts her arms straight out from the shoulders, surrendering completely to the sun and the wind and being young and pretty, with everything, every wonderful thing ahead of her.

"Look at that girl," Lockhardt says. "God, somebody should photograph that."

In her senior year, her second year with Horst, Leonora was all showered and getting ready to go to a frat party when Horst said, "Come on, let's do it."

He wasn't interested in doing it that often, so she said, "I'm all dressed for the party, but if you're sure you want to…"

"I want to," he said. "I'm up for it. Look." And so he chased her from the bedroom into the living room and then back into the bedroom, where she collapsed on the bed, laughing and tickling him, and they made love.

"Was it wonderful?" she said. "Was it better?"

"You're terrific," he said, "you're great. Where the hell is my deodorant?"

At the party everybody drank a lot of beer and tequila sunrises and after a while they got to the subject of how often you ball your roommate. When Horst's turn came, he gave a long and funny speech about the primacy of the intellect and the transitory nature of sexuality. He described the postures you get into and he made them sound new and funny, and he said the real problem is that an hour later you're still hungry for more. He had everybody with him and he was feeling really good about his performance, you could tell, and then he paused and said, anticlimactically, "Let's face it folks, what we're dealing with here is just two mucous membranes rubbing together."

Everybody laughed and applauded and spilled beer. Horst shook his head and smiled sneakily at Leonora.

But then somebody added, "They're sebaceous membranes, actually. Get your membranes straight, Horst."

Everybody laughed even louder and Leonora laughed too and Horst saw her do it.

So he was furious and, on the way home, when Leonora leaned against his side, her head on his shoulder, Horst put his hand on her breast. He felt for the nipple and when he had it firmly between his thumb and forefinger, he twisted it suddenly and violently, pressing down with his thumbnail. Leonora screamed in pain.

"You bitch," he said. "You fucking whore. Why don't you get out of my life? You're just a nothing. You're a noose around my neck."

"No," Leonora said. "No."

Patty Hearst was arrested in an apartment in San Francisco. Her picture appeared in all the papers, laughing like crazy, her fist clenched in the revolutionary salute. She gave her occupation as "urban guerrilla." Leonora was done with all that now that she was done with Horst. And who cared about Patty Hearst anyhow?

Leonora got her diploma in June, but she had to take one more course that summer before she had enough credits to officially graduate. She signed up for creative writing, taught by "staff." But staff turned out to be that bastard Lockhardt. He didn't seem to remember her, and everybody said he was a really good teacher, and she wanted to write a novel someday, so she decided to give him another chance.

Lockhardt wasn't interested in the things that interested her. She wanted to write something different, but Lockhardt kept talking about the initiating incident and the conflict and the characters. Old stuff. She wrote a story about a shoplifter named Horst, following him from the moment he picked up a tie until the moment he got out of the store, and she wrote it completely from within his mind, what he was thinking. Lockhardt said that the reader had no way of knowing that Horst was shoplifting and that she should simply say so. But she explained that she was trying to be more subtle than that. She explained that the reader was supposed to find out Horst was stealing only after the fact, after he was outside the shop, otherwise the story would be just like any other story. They argued back and forth for a long time and then Lockhardt just shrugged his shoulders and said, "Well, I guess you've accomplished what you set out to do. Congratulations." The same thing happened with her next two stories. He didn't like them, so he said the reader couldn't follow them. He couldn't seem to understand that she was doing something different from the old stuff.

And then in August she got her grade. A flat C. She went straight from the registrar's office to Lockhardt.

"I have to speak to you," she said.

"Sit down," he said. "Have a seat. But I've got to see the dean in five minutes, so if you're going to need more than that…"

"You gave me a C."

"Right. I hope you weren't too disappointed."

"You," she said. "You," but the words wouldn't come out.

"Well, your work was not really extraordinary, was it. I mean, I think you'll agree that it wasn't A work."

"It was C work, I suppose. It was only average."

"There's nothing wrong with being average. Most of us are. Most of our work is average."

She stood up and walked to the door. "What do I care," she said. "I can live with a C." And she slammed the door behind her.

She came back late the next afternoon, she was not sure why, but she knew she had to tell him something. Lockhardt was at his desk, typing, his back to the open door, and Leonora stood there in the corridor watching him. Nobody else was around. She could kill him and no one would know she had done it. If she had a knife or a gun, she could do it. That bastard.

He kept on typing and she just stood there watching him, thinking. And then suddenly he turned around and gave a little shout. "My God, you scared me half to death."

Leonora just stared at him, and he stared back, looking confused or maybe frightened. Then she turned and walked away.

She had not told him what he had done to her, but she would someday. She'd let him know. She'd let him know.

Leonora moved to San Francisco to be on her own. She got a studio apartment with a fire escape that looked down onto the roof of the Jack Tar Hotel and she applied for jobs at Gump's and at the Saint

Francis—they asked her "doing what?"—and she shrugged and said to hell with them, she had a Stanford education. But her money ran out eventually and she took a job at Dalton's selling books.

Nothing interesting ever happened at Dalton's, and besides you had to press sixty buttons on the computerized register every time you rang up a sale. The worst part was that everybody kept buying a novel called *The Love Hostage*, written by that bastard Lockhardt. After the first four sales, she refused to sell any more. "I'm on my break," she'd say and make the customer go to another register.

Leonora hated her job, hated the people she worked with, hated books. Somewhere there must be something different happening. Even Patty Hearst, who was a zilch, a nothing, even she had things happen to her. With a name like Patty.

One night when she had worked late, Leonora decided to take a walk. She would make something happen. She moped along Polk Street to Geary and then back, but nothing happened. There were a million or so faggots eyeing each other, but nobody eyed Leonora. She went up to her studio and had a beer and then came down again and set off deliberately in the direction of Golden Gate Park. She knew what she was doing. She could be raped. She could be murdered. Lockhardt used to talk all the time about Joyce Carol Oates's characters, how they set up situations for themselves, getting trapped, getting murdered, having their pink and gray brains spilled out on the sidewalk. She liked Joyce Carol Oates. She got as far as the Panhandle and was about to turn around and go home when she realized somebody was following her. For a block, then for a second block. She could hear the heels go faster when she went faster, slow down when she did. Her heart began to beat very fast and she could feel the vein in her forehead pulsing. She wanted it to happen, whatever it was. She turned around suddenly, hands on hips, her head thrown back, ready. At once the man following her crossed the street and headed in the opposite direction. Leonora walked for another hour and then went home. Would nothing happen to her, ever?

The next day she quit her job at Dalton's. They were limiting her. They were worse than Stanford.

The women's support group was having a terrible time with Leonora.

"You've got to open up to your feelings as a woman," they said. "Men have done this to you. They've refused to let you get in touch with your feelings," they said.

"What is it you feel? What is it you want?" they said.

"I want," Leonora said, "I don't know, but I think I want to die."

"No, what do you really want?" they said.

Leonora bought a gun and a copy of *The Love Hostage* on the same day. There was no connection she could see. She wanted them, that was all. It was time.

She loaded the gun with six bullets and hid it in a Kleenex box under a lot of tissues. It was for protection in this crazy city. It was a safeguard. It was just something nice to have around.

And then she sat down to read *The Love Hostage*. From the first page she was fascinated and appalled. The dust jacket said it was a novel about a young heiress who is kidnapped and brainwashed and all the other stuff that would make you think it was about Patty Hearst. But it wasn't about Patty at all; it was about her, it was about Leonora. Lockhardt had changed things to make it look as if it was about Patty, but she knew he meant her. He described her as an ordinary girl, a normal girl, average in every way. So now he had finally done it. He had killed her.

Leonora put the gun to the side of her head and pulled the trigger. There was an awful noise and the gun leaped from her hand and she felt something wet on the side of her face. She had only grazed her scalp, but inside she was dead just the same.

On the night she was committed to Agnews Mental, Leonora had forced down the beef stew her mother served for dinner and then she had gone back to her room to lie down. Almost at once she threw up into the wastebasket by her bed and then she went to the bathroom and threw up again. Back in her room she put on Phoebe Snow's

"Poetry Man." She played the album through twice, though she was not listening. She was thinking—as she had been for these last three weeks—of Lockhardt and how he had ruined everything and how someday she would let him know. But not now. Someday.

And then, as if it were somebody else doing it, she got up and got dressed and drove to the Stanford campus. She found Lockhardt's house with no trouble at all, and it was only when she had rang the doorbell that she realized she didn't know what she was going to say. But it didn't matter; somehow she would just tell him, calmly, with no tears, that he had degraded her, humiliated her, he had ruined her life.

"Yes?"

"I want to talk to you. I want to tell you something."

"Are you a student of mine? A former student?"

And then she realized that this was not Lockhardt at all, this was a much older man with a beard and glasses. The Lockhardts, it turned out, had moved to San Francisco.

Leonora got back into her car. She was frantic now, she would have to find a phone booth and get his address. She drove to Town and Country Shopping Center and found a booth, but there was no San Francisco directory. She drove to Stanford Shopping Center, and again there was no directory. Never mind. She would drive straight to the city, she would find him, he wouldn't get away from her now. She would let him know.

Traffic on 101 was heavy and it had begun to rain. Leonora passed cars that were already doing sixty. She had to get there. She had to tell him. The words were piling up in her brain, like stones, like bullets. Bullets, yes, she should have brought the gun. She should kill the bastard. A car pulled into her lane and then began slowly to brake. Leonora braked too, but not fast enough. Her car fishtailed and, with a short crunching sound, it smashed the side of a Volkswagen. She tore on ahead, though she could see in her mirror that the Volkswagen had ground to a halt, that its lights were blinking on and off. Tough shit. Yes, she should kill him, she thought, and she pressed her foot harder on the accelerator.

She couldn't find a parking space and so she left the car in a tow zone a block from the Jack Tar Hotel and ran back in the rain. She found the phone booth, the directory, she opened it to the Ls. Lockhardt lived in North Beach. Of course he would, with all that money from *The Love Hostage*. She ran back to her car. A tow truck was backed up to it and a little bald man was kneeling down trying to attach a bar under the front bumper. "No!" she shouted. "Stop it. Stop it. Stop." He stood up and looked at her, a screaming woman with her wet hair flying all around, a real crazy. "Okay, lady, okay," he said. "Okay." And then she was in her car again, tearing up Van Ness, running yellow lights, turning right on Pacific. In a few minutes she was there, at Lockhardt's blue and gray Victorian.

Leonora's head was pounding now and her back ached. She wanted to throw up, but there was nothing left to throw up. She wanted a drink. She wanted a pill. She wanted to take Lockhardt by the hair and tear the scalp off him, to expose the pink and gray brain that had written those things, that had done this to her.

She put her finger up to ring the bell, but she was shaking so much she couldn't do it. She began to beat the doorbell with her palm and then with her fist. Still the bell made no sound. She struck the door itself, with her hand, and then with her foot, and then she leaned her entire body against it, beating the door rhythmically with her fist and then with both fists, the rhythm growing faster and faster, the blows harder and harder, until there was blood on her hands and blood on the door and she heard a voice screaming that sounded like her own.

The door opened and Lockhardt, with a book in his hand, stood there looking at the young woman whose wet hair was streaked across her face, a face distorted beyond recognition by hysteria, and he listened to the screaming, which made no sense to him until her voice broke and he could make out the words. "I am not average," she sobbed. "I am not average. I am not average."

It was nearly a half hour before the orderlies came and took her away.

The world had gone crazy, that's just the way it was. Leonora's mother stared at the television where for days she had been watching pictures of the 911 corpses in Guyana. They had taken poison mixed with grape Kool-Aid and in five minutes they were dead. Every one of them. And Patty Hearst was still in prison. And Charles Manson had been denied parole. And her own Leonora in that loony bin. Leonora could have been something once. She could have been... but nothing came to mind. It was Lockhardt's fault, Leonora was right. It was all Lockhardt's fault. Leonora's mother turned up the volume on the TV. And now somebody had shot Mayor Moscone and that Harvey Milk character. It was the way you expressed yourself today, you shot somebody.

She thought of the gun hidden in the Kleenex box and suddenly it was all clear to her. She got in the car and drove to North Beach. She had no trouble finding Lockhardt's house; she had been there three times since Leonora was taken away. She had just parked opposite the house and sat there and watched. But this time she went up the steep wooden stairs and rang the bell. She rang again and as she was about to ring a third time Lockhardt opened the door, laughing. She could hear other people laughing too; he must be having a party. Over his left shoulder, in the entrance hall, she could see a chandelier, a deep green wall, the corner of a picture. She couldn't make out what it was a picture of, but she could see that he was rich. He had everything. "Yes?" he said, and there was more laughter from that other room. "Yes?" he said again.

"Leonora," she said. "She could have been something."

She took the gun from her purse and leveled it at his chest. There were three loud shots and when his body slumped to the floor, Leonora's mother could see that the painting on the green wall was one of those newfangled things with little blocks of color, all different sizes, that really aren't a picture of anything.

CONSOLATIONS OF PHILOSOPHY

Mr. Kirko was taking his time dying in bed number seven. He just kept lying there week after week.

"Not even getting any worst. At least not to the naked eye," said his daughter Shelley. "Look, I've got obligations, the children," she said.

"Obligations we've all got," her brother, Mervin, said. "You've got obligations. Angel's got obligations. And my obligations you know. I'm the son. So forget your obligations sometime. It's Papa."

"It's too true. It's Papa," said Angel, who was unmarried and had nothing. "He's all I've got," Angel said.

"And he's dying," Shelley said.

The orderlies came, hollering, "Beds number seven and eight!" and pulled the curtains around to make tents. Then they staggered off with Mr. Kirko and bed number eight to give them baths. These were old orderlies and their backs didn't straighten much anymore, so they just put Mr. Kirko and bed number eight in the water and let them sit there. Then these orderlies broke out the old Camels and smoked while the sick people sat in hot water till their behinds shriveled.

"This is how it is when you're one of the masses," one said.

"Rome wasn't built in a day," the other said.

Then one said a lot and the other said a lot and they checked to see if Mr. Kirko's behind was shriveled, and it was, so they got their hooks under his armpits and dragged him out of the tub. He groaned and his eyes rolled up, but at least he didn't die on them. They sat him on a three-legged stool to dry him. The stool scraped on the tile floor.

"Hear that noise?" Mr. Kirko asked.

They stopped toweling him because he never spoke and now he was speaking.

"That's the springs in my ass, breaking."

He threw up then, yellows and browns, and most of it went into his slipper.

"Goddamned pigs when they get old."

"There's no fool like an old fool."

These orderlies slammed his foot into the slipper and propped him against the wall. His face was all red from his bath and his foot was yellow and brown.

They checked to see if bed number eight's behind was shriveled, and it was, so they got their hooks into him and started to drag, but he wouldn't give. They let him have a little punch in the head to show they meant business, but it didn't do any good because he only gave a moan or two and died.

"Well, naught is certain save death and taxes."

"We'll let this sleeping dog lie."

They staggered back to bed number seven with Mr. Kirko. The son, Mervin Kirko, was pacing up and down outside the room, looking at his watch. Angel Kirko, who had nothing, was standing in the corner, twisting her handkerchief. Shelley Kamm was looking through her purse and sighing a lot.

"Did we have a nice bathie-poo?" Shelley said to her father as these orderlies pulled the curtains.

"It's little enough to have," Angel said.

Inside the tent the orderlies rested for a while and then they each took an arm and counted down. "Three, two, one, *go!*" And Mr. Kirko went thundering up onto the bed, headfirst. His head went shlunk into the wall. He wailed for a minute and then tuned down to whine.

They threw back the curtains and approached the weeping women.

"It's an ill wind that blows no good," one said.

"It's too true," Angel said.

"It's a mercy some of them go when their time has come," the other said.

"I know you're doing everything you can," Shelley said.

On the way out these orderlies nodded at good old Mervin. "You can just pace around," they said, "up and down, back and forth, you name it."

Angel and Shelley didn't know what to do next.

"He doesn't look any worst to me," Shelley said.

"Not to the naked eye, he doesn't," Angel said.

"Oh, nurse, nurse," Shelley said, calling Nurse Jane. "He doesn't look any worse, does he?"

"Well, he's going to," Nurse Jane said. "They don't just go in and out of here unless they're seriously, you know. What he needs is some needles and bottles, some pickies and pokies, and a tube up his nose."

Nurse Jane returned with everything she had promised.

"Bed number eight," she said to Angel. "Where is he?"

"Personally, I don't know," Angel said. "I haven't the slightest."

"She hasn't the slightest," Shelley said. "She's never had anything and now she's losing her papa."

"It's a matter of professionalism," Nurse Jane said. "There are lists to be filled out, tags, markers, numbers, identity bands, indicators, thingamabobs, you have no idea. So you can't just have bed numbers disappearing. Now you, Miss Kirko, when did you last see bed number eight?"

"Well, I'll do my best," Angel said. "He was last seen by me personally when they staggered him off for his bath."

"Bath," Nurse Jane said and stalked away, kachung, kachung. "Very good," she said a few minutes later. "Very good, Miss Kirko. We found him dead in the bath and so he's accounted for." She leaned across Shelley and put her hand gently on Angel's bosom. "It's just so we know," she said tenderly. "We have to know."

"It can't be easy," Angel said.

"It's the children I worry about," Shelley said.

"When the doctor comes, you'll see," Nurse Jane said, and wheeled the empty bed out of the room.

The doctor appeared at seven o'clock on the bonker. He had a clipboard in his hand and he kept looking from it to the place where bed eight used to be.

"I see they've dispatched bed eight," he said. "You must be the Kirkos. You belong to bed seven."

"Yes, we're the Kirkos," Mervin said. "I'm the son and these are the two daughters, Angel Kirko and Shelley Kamm. Shelley was a Kirko before she was a Kamm."

"How do you do," they all said, shaking everything.

"I'm Dr. Robbins," Dr. Robbins said.

"Dr. Robbins," they all said, grateful as anything.

Angel and Shelley took a good long look at Dr. Robbins while he took a good long look at Mr. Kirko. In each arm old Kirko had needles that ran down from bottles full of white and bottles full of yellow, and there was a tube up his nose that went somewhere and another tube that ran from his winkler into a bottle under the bed. Mr. Kirko was getting the full treatment.

"You're very young for a doctor," Shelley said, taking in the little bulge in his white pants.

"But competent," Dr. Robbins said.

"Oh, I didn't mean," Shelley said.

"We never meant," Angel said.

"Of course, of course," Dr. Robbins said, and he bit the inside of his face so they'd know. "I'll wait outside," Mervin said.

"You can pace up and down," Dr. Robbins said. "Or back and forth. You name it."

The doctor stood for a while looking at Mr. Kirko. He plucked at his leg; it looked like turkey.

"I think that leg's going to have to come off," the doctor said.

"Oh no!" Angel said, fainting.

"Oh, God in heaven!" Shelley said.

Angel kept on fainting.

"Mervin! Mervin! We've got to make a decision. This Dr. Robbins here says the leg has got to come off. It's our duty to decide," Shelley said.

Mervin came back in from his corridor.

"These are the moments one dreads, Doctor," Mervin said.

"Oh, no!" Angel said, fainting some more.

"Before we decide," Shelley said, "I think I should have a word with the doctor in private."

"I've never had anything," Angel said as Mervin dragged her from the room.

Shelley shut the door and leaned against it, her head thrown back. Outside she could hear them pacing up and down, back and forth.

"I thought we should have a word alone," Shelley said.

"Most understandable at a time like this, Mrs. Kamm," he said, reaching for his zipper.

"Yes, it's difficult for all of us, Doctor. It's the children I worry about." She slipped off her panties and in one graceful motion scooped them up from the floor and tucked them into her purse.

They stood for a moment looking at bed number seven. "We could put him on the floor, Doctor. He wouldn't mind."

"It's better the patient not be disturbed," he said and gave a little tweak to a tube here and a tube there.

"Oh, dear," Shelley said.

"Now if you will please step over to the door and lean your back against it, so," the doctor said. "Very good. And now we'll lift this skirt and—yes, you'll have to bend your knees as if you were sliding down the wall, that's right—and then I'll just slip this in here. Um, we need a little wiggly, then oomph, there we are."

"Yes, that does do nicely, Dr. Robbins," Shelley said.

They stood there like a Rorschach.

"Perhaps, Mrs. Kamm, you'd prefer to put your purse on the floor."

"Oh, silly of me."

"Just drop it. That's right. And then you can put your hands right here."

"Oh," she said. "Oh."

"I think you'll find, Mrs. Kamm, that once your father's leg comes off, you'll be more than pleased you agreed to it."

"Oh, I'm sure you're right, Dr. Robbins. It's just that, you know, we've known him so long, Doctor, and always with the leg."

"Yes, yes, of course. These feelings are natural. There would be something wrong if you didn't feel them."

"Oh, yes," she said.

"Could you move that knee out a little, and away?"

"Like this?"

"Fine," he said. "Well, we're having marvelous weather… for this time of year."

"Marvelous," she said. "Doctor, I want to thank you sincerely for giving us your valuable time. We truly appreciate it."

"A doctor does his best," he said. "Comfortable?"

"Mmm, yes. Doctor, I hope you won't think me overly personal, but I couldn't help noticing when you took it out what an enormous jumjum you have."

"Oh, I don't know," he said, shrugging modestly.

"Oh, you do, you do. Truly."

He gave her a little jab to the left.

"Thuth thuth thuth," they laughed.

"You must have gone to a wonderful medical school," she said.

"Harvard," he said. "They teach you everything."

"It must be wonderful," she said.

"Philosophy," he said. "'Every proposition is true or false.' Langer."

"That's deep," she said.

"Heidegger," he said. "'Listen to what is not being said.'"

"That's deep too," she said.

"Bucky Fuller," he said. "'Everything that goes up must come down.'"

"I've heard that one," she said.

"Human behavior is a language," he said.

"Yes," she said.

"If the material of thought is symbolism, then the mind must be forever furnishing symbolic versions of its experiences," he said. "Otherwise thinking could not proceed."

"Ooh," she said, moving her right hip forward and backward in a new way.

"Perhaps I'm being too technical, Mrs. Kamm?"

"Oh no, Doctor, no. Those are beautiful thoughts," she said.

"Very well," he said. "Now, Mrs. Kamm, if you would just move this foot forward and in a bit."

"Oh!"

"You see."

There was a banging outside the door, bonka bonka bonk.

"It's Angel," Shelley said.

"If you'll concentrate, please," he said.

"Oom, oom," she said, and her feet rose from the floor.

Their bodies began to shake like dustrags, and then she bit his neck, and then he punched her ribs to make her stop. Finally she shook uncontrollably and he tore at her hair.

Bonka bonka bonk at the door.

"Hungh," he said, pulling her loose and dropping her in the corner. "Hungh," he said again and stood looking down at his ruined jumjum.

Bonka bonka bonk at the door again.

"It's me," Angel's voice said. "I want to come in."

"I'm just pacing," Mervin said from down the corridor.

Shelley brushed off her dress and patted her hair into place. "It's not bad enough about Papa," she said. "They have to make a scene in the corridor."

"It's the tension," Dr. Robbins said, all zipped and polished. He opened the door. "Come in," he said. "Your sister has reached her decision."

"The leg has got to come off," Shelley said. "Dr. Robbins is right."

"What's all this?" Angel said, pointing to the chunks of Shelley's hair with blood on the ends.

"That's my hair," Shelley said. "These decisions are never easy, Angel."

"Whatever the doctor says," Mervin said.

"I'll tell Nurse Jane," Dr. Robbins said.

In a moment the two orderlies came hollering, "Bed number seven!" and wheeled out the last of Mr. Kirko. It was a sad noise going.

"Man proposes, God disposes," one said.

"Every cloud has a silver lining," the other said.

Angel and Shelley and Mervin stood in the empty room looking at one another.

"Once that leg is gone it will be different."

"That leg was the trouble."

"He never looked any worst. Not to the naked eye."

"He looked worst with tubes and needles."

"And the thing in his winkler."

"There's nothing left to do but pray."

A storm broke outside the window. They all went and looked at it. Rain fell like swords.

"Well, at least he's not out in that storm."

"Yes, that's a mercy."

"It's the children I worry about."

THEMSELVES

Harriet and Margaret. Margaret and Harriet. Oh, there were two. Wide winged and passionate, they swooped down on a banquet table like goddesses of chaos, turning conversations inside out, exposing fools, worshipping folly, whipping up an intellectual revolution. You know. There they were; and utterly at home in any dining room anywhere, in Paris at the George V or in some run-down apartment in East LA. *Chez eux*, wherever they happened to be. Themselves.

When I knew them, they were in their seventies. Beautiful still, with those fine bones and the inner calm that comes from knowing right at the start that you belong, you have a place in it all. But deep beneath the inner calm lay something else, something fine and problematic, but that doesn't come in until later. So.

Margaret and Harriet. Margaret first.

Margaret had no fear but quite a bit of craziness. It was Margaret who decided one night that she was in love with the man next door and right away, dressed only in her nightgown, she went and stood on his lawn in the moonlight, waiting for him to look out and see her there. She knew that this was crazy. They were both in their forties at the time and she already had a perfectly good husband. Nonetheless she had decided that this was the great passion of her middle life and she'd be a fool not to risk everything for passion, so she did. Every night for two weeks, then, she stood out there on the lawn, risking pneumonia, risking discovery by the neighbor's wife, risking arrest, when you think of it. The pneumonia got her first and, after that, she decided she wasn't interested in this neighbor after all. Also, she liked to stand up in canoes, she drank the water in Mexico, and she refused to comprehend money. And she always, whatever the situation, said what she was thinking.

There are other examples of Margaret's folly, as you can imagine from what you know already.

Now for Harriet. Harriet had some fear, and a little craziness, but no folly at all. Harriet was afraid of offending anybody except mean people. She was afraid of other people dying, because she had known about her brother and her other sister before they died, and she knew about Margaret. There was nothing she could alter about other people dying and that was why she was afraid of that. Of her own dying she was less afraid; still, she didn't like the idea of not being, and she didn't like the process, because it would be such a mess disintegrating in front of people who had known her whole. But she wasn't afraid of spiders or giving a speech or rapers and murderers or entering a strange room full of people or any of the ordinary things. Moreover, her craziness was merely verbal, no baying at the moon for Harriet, and her folly was nonexistent.

What Harriet and Margaret had in common was this: they were sisters and they were dervishes. They spun. They were a firestorm in the living room.

That's how it was when they had dinner at my place the night I died.

What Harriet and Margaret have in common now is: me.

Well, get on with it. The dinner, as I've said, was my last. Ron was there, and Stephanie and Michael, P. Fish of course, and *moi*. They all arrived in a bunch and then, before they even had drinks in their hands, in came Harriet and Margaret. Talking and laughing and taking off coats and handing around drinks: that's how it was. "What a wonderful apartment, I've never seen so many books, how do you keep it so nice." And so forth. Margaret and Harriet, Harriet and Margaret, making a party. "What a delicious dinner, I think this is the best dinner I've ever had in my life." But you've all been to busy dinners, so you know.

And, in fact, I didn't really have that many books and the dinner was just JJ & F's chicken cordon bleu that I bought already layered and rolled and tucked up and then just heated in my oven, but it was nice in the roar of the firestorm to hear such a generous acknowledgment of my efforts. Nobody mentioned the flowers, it's true, but then again the flowers had already put on a wilty look before anybody arrived. False economy. Be advised.

But none of this is the point. The point is that Margaret was gaggling away, being a party, with her life already hostage to cancer and with the promise of a year at most. And Harriet too, because she was seventysomething and frenzied with too much caring and too much being responsible for the world, dear kind mad Harriet, the dervish of Dartmouth Street, she must have known what lay around the next dark corner. I, however, was the only one to go. Death had been ticking in my head for such a long time and I had never heard it. And then, ping!, after the guests had gone but before I even finished washing the dishes, I had the stroke, and my brain simply burst with the effort of accommodating all the new things that were going on, and, well, here I am.

But really that is not the point either. The point is the conversation we had. Margaret, like everybody, is an atheist, but like all atheists she's fascinated that some people believe in God. She can't imagine why. So she asks them all the time. In this crowd, Ron and I are Catholics of a sort, Stephanie was married to a Catholic once, and Michael was raised a Catholic but he doesn't care for Catholicism anymore. I should add that I used to be a priest and now I'm not. Or rather, to be absolutely accurate, I am still a priest—because you can't stop being a priest any more than you can stop being a Christian or a Jew—but I don't do priest things any longer. So, with a crowd like this, it was inevitable that Margaret would ask lots of questions, and she did, and so there were lots of answers.

But mostly she wanted to know how I could believe, and I tried to explain that faith isn't something you choose, it's something you're given, except that in a way you have to want to choose it. But how can you want it, Margaret said, if you don't even know what it is. In fact why would you want it? Well, it's all too confusing, and she was done with it, she thought.

Well, it was confusing, because right across the table Stephanie was telling Ron and P. Fish how she had married her first husband in a Catholic ceremony on a beach in Hawaii, but it was all perfectly legal even though it was exotic, and P. Fish was saying he'd had no idea Catholics were so broad-minded, and Ron was trying to say they weren't and they shouldn't be and that Stephanie was undoubtedly mistaken in thinking it was a Roman Catholic ceremony, it was probably something else. Harriet volunteered to the Stephanie conversation that she preferred Catholics to Baptists because the Catholics at least promised you something in the next life even if it might only be hell, whereas the Baptists didn't promise you anything here or there. And she volunteered to the Margaret conversation that faith was impossible because you couldn't believe in what you didn't know about, and what you did know about was so appalling that it was better not to even think about it, and anyhow did I prefer Jesus to God? Or who? And why did Catholics have to have so many?

So many gods? I tried to change the subject to poor nations or to folly or fear, to just anything, but Margaret would not let go of the question of faith and Harriet kept wanting to know faith in whom? Or in what? And then they moved on to grace, or rather Harriet did, because she kept hearing about grace in Flannery O'Connor and had never been able to figure out what it was. And so once again I tried to explain. "Oh, I see," Harriet said at last, "grace is just exactly like nothing… except it hurts."

Well, what was the use. I cleared away the dishes and brought out the fruit and brie and lots more wine. The noise level continued to rise, and the fun, and all of a sudden Margaret just sort of wailed, "Gosh, I'm so tired of Jesus and God."

And that's how we got to where we are now. Something happened in my skull then, factually as well as figuratively, and though I didn't realize it, at that moment the definitive step had been taken: for Margaret, for Harriet, for me.

This is the point: God is absolutely ironic. When you hear someone say, But why me? How could God let this happen to me?, you can be sure you are listening to a person who doesn't know about irony. And when you read in the *Enquirer* about how some desirable actress withered away and died of sheer loneliness, or when you read in the *Lives of the Saints* that somebody who was proud got the pride kicked out of him before he could become a saint, or when you're dead and comfortable and can look into secret hearts and discover that the only way God can get to some people is by treating them to a good long look at their alcoholism or by helping them to discover beneath their arrogant defensive armor of virility, guess what? yes, the thin strong thread of homosexuality, well, to round this out and wrap it up, when you see somebody destroyed by his virtues and, ironically, rescued by his weaknesses or what he thinks are weaknesses, then you see the point about irony. Except that with God, as you know, irony is absolute.

So there we were at the dinner table, all of us tired of God and Jesus, but especially Margaret and Harriet, who were not used to giving either of them that much time, when something happened in my skull, a tick so quiet I didn't even notice, just God calling. The definitive step had been taken. Oh Margaret. Oh Harriet.

Then there were exclamations, how late it is, what a wonderful dinner, everyone deranged and interesting, and finally the coats and kisses and goodbye.

Goodbye. Goodbye.

Before I'd even closed the door, death slipped into my life, barely breathing, tenebrous, loitering beside me while I rinsed glasses and sorted silverware and put the dishes in the sink.

In good time, it was over. A bloody flower bloomed inside my head and my eyes seemed to want to get out and all I could think of was Harriet and Margaret, obsessed by other people's faith, besieged by grace, not wanting—they thought—what they could not know. The flower bloomed, and burst, and faded.

Irony is absolute and faith is absolute. And so I go now, all ways, with Harriet and Margaret, trailing in the wake of their laughter and perfume, noting fear, noting folly, noting how all things labor unto good.

Harriet and Margaret. Margaret and Harriet. Oh!

THE ANATOMY OF DESIRE

Because Hanley's skin had been stripped off by the enemy, he could find no one who was willing to be with him for long. The nurses were obligated to see him now and then, and sometimes the doctor, but certainly not the other patients and certainly not his wife and children. He was raw, he was meat, and he would never be any better. He had a great and natural desire, therefore, to be possessed by someone.

He would walk around on his skinned feet, leaving bloody footprints up and down the corridors, looking for someone to love him.

"You're not supposed to be out here," the nurse said. And she added, somehow making it sound kind, "You untidy the floor, Hanley."

"I want to be loved by someone," he said. "I'm human too. I'm like you."

But he knew he was not like her. Everybody called her the saint.

"Why couldn't it be you?" he said.

She was swabbing his legs with blood retardant, a new discovery that kept Hanley going. It was one of those miracle medications that just grew out of the war.

"I wasn't chosen," she said. "I have my skin."

"No," he said. "I mean why couldn't it be you who will love me, possess me? I have desires too," he said.

She considered this as she swabbed his shins and the soles of his feet. "I have no desires," she said. "Or only one. It's the same thing."

He looked at her loving face. It was not a pretty face, but it was saintly.

"Then you will?" he said.

"If I come to know sometime that I must," she said.

The enemy had not chosen Hanley, they had just lucked upon him sleeping in his trench. They were a raid party of four, terrified and obedient, and they had been told to bring back an enemy to serve as an example of what is done to infiltrators.

They dragged Hanley back across the line and ran him, with his hands tied behind his back, the two kilometers to the general's tent.

The general dismissed the guards because he was very taken with Hanley. He untied the cords that bound Hanley's wrists and let his arms hang free. Then slowly, ritually, he tipped Hanley's face toward the light and examined it carefully. He kissed him on the brow and on the cheek and finally on the mouth. He gazed deep and long into Hanley's eyes until he saw his own reflection there looking back. He traced the lines of Hanley's eyebrows, gently, with the tip of his index finger. "Such a beautiful face," he said in his own language. He pressed his palms lightly against Hanley's forehead, against his cheekbones, his jaw. With his little finger he memorized the shape of Hanley's lips, the laugh lines at his eyes, the chin. The general did Hanley's face very thoroughly. Afterward he did some things down below, and so just before sunrise, when the time came to lead Hanley out to the stripping post, he told the soldiers with the knives: "This young man could be my own son; so spare him here and here."

The stripping post stood dead center in the line of barbed wire only a few meters beyond the range of gunfire. A loudspeaker was set up and began to blare the day's message. "This is what happens to infiltrators. No infiltrators will be spared." And then as troops from both sides watched through binoculars, the enemy cut the skin from Hanley's body, sparing—as the general had insisted—his face and his genitals. They were skilled men and the skin was stripped off expeditiously and they hung it, headless, on the barbed wire as an

THE ANATOMY OF DESIRE

example. They lay Hanley himself on the ground where he could die.

He was rescued a little after noon when the enemy, for no good reason, went into sudden retreat.

Hanley was given emergency treatment at the field unit, and when they had done what they could for him, they sent him on to the vets' hospital. At least there, they told each other, he will be attended by the saint.

It was quite some time before the saint said yes, she would love him.

"Not just love me. Possess me."

"There are natural reluctancies," she said. "There are personal peculiarities," she said. "You will have to have patience with me."

"You're supposed to be a saint," he said.

So she lay down with him in his bloody bed and he found great satisfaction in holding this small woman in his arms. He kissed her and caressed her and felt young and whole again. He did not miss his wife and children. He did not miss his skin.

The saint did everything she must. She told him how handsome he was and what pleasure he gave her. She touched him in the way he liked best. She said he was her whole life, her fate. And at night when he woke her to staunch the blood, she whispered how she needed him, how she could not live without him.

This went on for some time.

The war was over and the occupying forces had made the general mayor of the capital city. He was about to run for senator and wanted his past to be beyond the reproach of any investigative committee. He wrote Hanley a letter that he sent through the International Red Cross.

"You could have been my own son," he said. "What we do in war is what we have to do. We do not choose cruelty or violence. I did only what was my duty."

"I am in love and I am loved," Hanley said. "Why isn't that enough?"

The saint was swabbing his chest and belly with blood retardant.

"Nothing is ever enough," she said.

"I love, but I am not possessed by love," he said. "I want to be surrounded by you. I want to be enclosed. I want to be enveloped. I don't have the words for it. But do you understand?"

"You want to be possessed," she said.

"I want to be inside you."

And so they made love, but afterward he said, "That is not enough. That is only a metaphor for what I want."

The general was elected senator and was made a trustee of three nuclear-arms conglomerates. But he was not well. And he was not sleeping well.

He wrote to Hanley, "I wake in the night and see your face before mine. I feel your forehead pressing against my palms. I taste your breath. I did only what I had to do. You could have been my son."

"I know what I want," Hanley said.

"If I can do it, I will," the saint said.

"I want your skin."

And so she lay down on the long white table, shuddering, while Hanley made his first incision. He cut along the shoulders and then down the arms and back up, then down the sides and the legs to the feet. It took him longer than he had expected. The saint shivered at the cold touch of the knife and she sobbed once at the sight of the blood, but by the time Hanley lifted the shroud of skin from her crimson body, she was resigned, satisfied, even.

Hanley had spared her face and her genitals.

He spread the skin out to dry and, while he waited, he swabbed her raw body carefully with blood retardant. He whispered little words of love and thanks and desire to her.

A smile played about her lips but she said nothing. It would be a week before he could put on her skin.

The general wrote to Hanley one last letter. "I can endure no more. I am possessed by you."

———

Hanley put on the skin of the saint. His genitals fitted nicely through the gap he had left and the skin at his neck matched hers exactly. He walked the corridors and for once left no bloody tracks behind. He stood before mirrors and admired himself. He touched his breasts and his belly and his thighs and there was no blood on his hands.

"Thank you," he said to her. "It is my heart's desire, fulfilled. I am inside you. I am possessed by you."

And then, in the night, he kissed her on the brow and on the cheek and finally on the mouth. He gazed deep and long into her eyes. He traced the lines of her eyebrows gently, with the tip of his index finger. "Such a beautiful face," he said. He pressed his palms lightly against her forehead, her cheekbones, her jaw. With his little finger he memorized the shape of her lips.

And then it was that Hanley, loved, desperate to possess and be possessed, staring deep into the green and loving eyes of the saint, saw that there can be no possession, there is only desire. He plucked at his empty skin and wept.

THREE SHORT MOMENTS IN A LONG LIFE

I.   THE SPY

Beverly LaPlante and I were second graders at the New Carew Street School and we both hated recess. She hated recess and she cried the whole time and nobody knew why so everybody made fun of her. I hated recess because it wasn't really school and we weren't learning anything. It was a waste of time. I knew Beverly only by name and by what I could tell from spying on her. Her last name was LaPlante, which was strange and therefore wrong, and she was famous for being a crybaby. She was not even pretty. Her crying all the time frightened me so I never spoke to her. Besides, I didn't want anybody to think I was her friend.

She didn't belong. And, secretly, I feared I didn't belong.

The nice thing about Beverly LaPlante was that she disappeared sometime during the winter. One day Miss Williams was taking attendance and, after a little pause, she skipped over Beverly's name. We all looked at where she was supposed to be sitting and her seat was empty. I remember thinking, Yes, good, she didn't belong and now she's gone. I wondered if she was still crying in her new place, wherever that was. I wondered how she managed to disappear or if her mother and father had done it to her. I wondered, for the first time, why she cried.

Second grade came to a dull close without any further thought about Beverly LaPlante.

Third grade started with a bang. We had a new teacher, Miss Connolly, who loved me because I was smart and clean, and I loved her back because she was beautiful. At dinner my mother said to my father, "She's very nice, but dear God, those teeth."

"What's with her teeth?" my father said.

"She's got buck teeth. Like a horse." It was only conversation, but it was against Miss Connolly and therefore wrong. I hated them both until I went to bed.

We had a new reading book, a thick one with a brown-and-orange cover, and during recess I hid in the bathroom and read ahead in the stories. On my third day of hiding in the bathroom the janitor caught me and told Miss Connolly, who gave me a lecture about good citizenship. She didn't look beautiful. She looked like an angry horse and that made me cry. She gave me a hug then and told me she understood but I couldn't skip recess anymore. I had to do what everybody else did. So I promised. But I still read ahead in the brown-and-orange book.

In third grade we played dodgeball during recess. I liked dodgeball because I was good at it. I was skinny and quick and I could see ahead of time where they were going to throw the ball and I'd get out of the way so the ball hit someone else, someone who was fat or slow. My friend Billy Muir was fat and slow, but he was an exception. He managed to avoid getting hit most of the time. Billy Muir's father always wore a suit. He was successful in business so he was transferred to the Chicago branch, where he continued to be successful until they discovered he was embezzling money from the company, and he hanged himself. With his belt around his neck. That was later. In third grade Billy Muir had no idea his father would end up famous. Billy was fat and slow but he could dodge the ball anyway, so that was something to think about. But the big thing to think about was the new girl. Her name was Beverly, just like the LaPlante girl who had disappeared last winter, but this new Beverly was pretty and she laughed all the time and she talked a lot.

I was the best at dodgeball, but on the day the new girl arrived I was the first one out, which made me miserable. It was fair but it was wrong because I wasn't paying attention and the ball hit me while I was thinking about "The Little Mermaid," the story I was in the middle of. Hans Andersen, with an *e* instead of an *o*. Now that I was out, I began to pay attention to the game. Standing at the edge of the circle, I could get a good look at everybody, and that was when I recognized the new girl. Her hair was short now and she was a different Beverly LaPlante, but she was Beverly LaPlante all the same. How was this possible? She was wearing a Girl Scout outfit with clumsy Girl Scout shoes. She was laughing and making noise, and when Billy Muir got hit and had to go outside the circle, she noticed the angry face he made and she said, "Jesus Christ! Your face would sour the milk!" Nobody seemed to hear her but I did and I looked at Miss Connolly, who made a horse face that meant she had heard her too. But she didn't say anything. Taking the Lord's name in vain was wrong and therefore Miss Connolly was wrong in pretending she hadn't heard. But then Joycie Adams got hit by the ball and just stood there like a dummy until everyone yelled at her that she had to leave the circle. She said that wasn't fair because the ball had barely hit her, and Beverly said, "What the hell! Don't be such a damn crybaby." Everybody heard her this time and they all turned toward Miss Connolly, who finally said, "Now, now! Language, please!" The kids all went quiet, waiting to see what would happen, but Beverly laughed into the silence and said, "Shit, piss, fuck!"

Miss Connolly said very loudly, "Time for class, people. Everybody to the stairs now. Now! Not tomorrow!" She said "People!" in that special voice so we all ran to the front stairs and waited. Miss Connolly took Beverly aside and we couldn't hear what she said but Beverly just laughed and said something back. Miss Connolly took Beverly's arm and shook it hard, but Beverly pulled away and ran to the center of the dodgeball circle, where she did a little dance in her Girl Scout shoes, shouting over and over, "Jesus Christ and shit, piss, fuck! Jesus Christ and shit, piss, fuck!" She shouted as if she had finally found out the truth and couldn't wait to tell the world. Miss Connolly herded us up the front stairs and into the classroom, where she gave us private reading time until lunch period.

I tried to figure out what had happened at dodgeball but it just made my head hurt. It was wrong, but I didn't know how. The bad words were wrong, of course, and taking the Lord's name in vain was wrong, but it was more complicated than that. It was something about Beverly herself. I wondered what had happened to her that made her happy now but with dirty words, when a year ago she had just cried all the time. Then, she had disappeared. Now, she was back and laughing. She wasn't like any of us, she didn't belong, she didn't fit in. I tried all the time to fit in and no one noticed that I didn't, but now I wondered, secretly, if I was like Beverly LaPlante.

I began to think of her when I was supposed to be doing arithmetic and geography, which were no fun anyway. I began to think of her on the walk to school each day and again on the walk home. Then one night when I said my prayers before bed, I finished up with the sign of the cross and, trying not to say it, I said, "Please God, let Beverly LaPlante die." It was a real prayer and I knew it was wrong and I would go to hell. I said, "I take it back," but you can't take back prayers. I said a lot of Our Fathers and after a while I felt maybe I wouldn't go to hell and I should stop thinking about Beverly. She was just one of the things I was afraid of. I wasn't sure what all the others were but I knew for certain that I was afraid of Beverly LaPlante.

When the summer came the LaPlantes moved away. Nobody knew why. I wondered what would happen to Beverly and how she would be now that I didn't know her anymore. I wondered if she would change back to being a crybaby but without the dirty words. That would be wrong, I thought. And then I thought, maybe not. She had been one person and then she was another. But at least she wasn't dead.

Beverly died that summer of polio. My mother said, "No more swimming at the pond. That's how you get polio. That's how your little friend died, the LaPlante girl, swimming in the pond." So I didn't swim that summer, but I knew then that I would have Beverly LaPlante stuck in my mind forever.

In fourth grade everything was different. There were new people and some of the old people were gone. I began to realize that people disappeared and changed and then sometimes they hanged themselves or came back different and they still didn't fit. They were a mystery, I decided, like the Resurrection at Sunday school. Jesus died and was buried and then he rose from the dead. He said hello to Mary Magdalene—she was the first to see him because she had washed his feet and dried them with her hair—and later he made breakfast for his disciples to prove he had died and then came back real. There was no crying involved with Jesus. And no dirty words. Then he disappeared for good, just like Beverly LaPlante.

2. THE WRITER

I was working on my novel—don't even ask—when I heard the doorbell ring. My wife was out teaching school so I'd have to answer it myself. I got up from my computer, went downstairs slowly because I had turned my ankle the other day, and just as I got to the door I tripped on the new carpet and heard myself saying, "Jesus Christ!" I opened the door and it was him.

"Hey," he said.

"Hey," I said.

I recognized him immediately from his pictures. He had long blond hair and those eyes that follow you around the room.

My head had been bothering me lately—I figured it was the asthma medications I've been taking—but I couldn't believe they were powerful enough to conjure up a lithograph Jesus at my front door. I'd been meaning for some time to read one of the Gospels straight through, to get the story straight from the approved source, so maybe that was it. He was always on my mind these days, and now he was standing on my porch. He really did look like those pictures.

"Right," he said.

At first I was embarrassed, but after a minute I got over the blond hair and the eyes and I could see he was nothing special, just another guy trying to get along. Maybe he was a vet. Iraq? Afghanistan? Anyway he had on grungy jeans and an orange sweatshirt and he could have used a shower.

"How's it going?" he said.

I was tempted to tell him how it was going. I had written all these books and nobody gave a shit and I was in the middle of another one that nobody would give a shit about either. My subject this time was guilt, I suppose, if novels can be said to have a subject. It was the story of a high school teacher who was guilty of lots of things—infidelity, verbal cruelty, petty theft, the usual lying and cheating—but he was not guilty of molesting one of his students, and that's what he was accused of. I was trying to use this poor chump to explore the infinite variety of guilt and justice and injustice. At the moment I was trying to do a scene in which a harmless conversation between this teacher and a student would be overheard by another teacher, a troublemaker, who would later testify he had witnessed what sounded like a seduction. The scene was too complicated as I had written it, but I was trying to make it simpler without lessening the tension and without giving away what would happen later. The problem was that I didn't really understand the teacher or his guilt. It seemed that he just didn't fit in. He didn't belong and I didn't understand why. Meanwhile I was staring at this guy in an orange sweatshirt who was standing on my porch.

"You okay?" he said.

"So," I said.

He got down to business. He asked if he could help me out in exchange for a meal and I explained that wouldn't be possible because I was a writer with an obsession and there wasn't much help anybody could give me. I nudged the door a little, sort of a hint. He said his father was a writer, and I said is that so? And he said he never published though, and I said yes, publishing is hard. I shifted my weight off my sore ankle to let him know we were all done talking. I gave him a hard look and he looked back. It crossed my mind for a second that he could rob me or kill me and nobody would ever know. I tried not to show what I was thinking. Finally he asked could I spare a dollar. There was something proud—or maybe humble—in the way he asked, as if he was owed it, as if I had no choice in the matter. I thought what the hell and gave him a five. He could get a latte and a morning bun at Starbucks, I figured, though he didn't look the latte type. I thought of what my wife would do and I gave him another five.

"Have a good day, man," he said and waved his hand, sort of a combination salute and blessing.

"You too," I said and closed the door.

I was halfway up the stairs when I knew I had done the wrong thing. He was the breakthrough that would have made all the difference in my life. I should have invited him in and given him some coffee and then simply confessed everything. Everything. But what, exactly? Was it confession I wanted, or some kind of exoneration? I sat down on the stairs to give this some thought. Jesus Christ and shit, piss, fuck. After a while I went back down and opened the door and looked around. Of course he was long gone.

I went back up to my computer and looked at what I had been writing. The scene was no good because it was just a bunch of ideas. I could see that clearly now. The fact is that I was that most useless of creatures: a writer obsessed with Jesus. And suspicious of him. I don't mean like Flannery O'Connor. She was obsessed with writing good stories—and Jesus often turned up in them. I was just obsessed with Jesus. Period. Jesus and guilt. And to what end? I wouldn't know Jesus if he knocked at my front door and I had never faced guilt in my entire life, except that once when I prayed Beverly LaPlante to death. Otherwise I was an innocent, really. My wife would understand.

What the scene in my novel dramatized was my own obsession and my failure to understand. It was all meaningless. Life too. It was all hopeless.

Perhaps I had begun to fit in after all.

For a long time I sat in front of my computer, lying to myself. Then I highlighted the whole manuscript and pressed Delete.

3.   THE SUBSTANCE OF THINGS HOPED FOR
"Here's another one," the EMT said. "White male, eighty."

C'est moi, I thought. *Eccomi qua*. I was full of thoughts, some of them rational.

My wife had called 911 because I was stuck lying crossways on the bed, my head and shoulders hanging off one side and my legs— from the knees down—hanging off the other. I was unable to move and she was unable to move me. You're burning up, she said, her hand on my forehead. I asked her to give me a couple hours and I'd figure it out but she said, This is a mess, This has gone too far, We can't exist like this, and she called 911. A bunch of EMTs came and said, Where is he and It's a good thing you called and Everything's gonna be fine. The youngest one looked around and said, I've never seen so many books. What was he, a professor or something? What is he, I mean. My wife led the way upstairs and said, Lift him carefully. He's got Parkinson's. How ya doing, the young one asked and I told him, Fabulous! And so they put me in the ambulance and drove me to the hospital, three miles exactly, at a cost of seventeen hundred dollars. But that came later. Right now the ambulance was pulling into the loading dock.

"Here's another one," the EMT said. "White male, eighty."

"What's his story?"

"Pneumonia, most likely. High fever. Trouble breathing. Can't really move."

"I can move."

"But you couldn't when we picked you up."

"Where's my wife?"

"White male, eighty." They passed me down the line and parked me against a wall in a big room. There were a lot of other people on gurneys and I was happy to see them but somebody pulled a curtain around me and that was that.

So. I was a thing labeled male, white, eighty. A nameless commodity that had something wrong with it. I was not me.

Outside someone was crying quietly and someone else, a doctor maybe, was saying, It's all right, it's going to be all right.

I was back in third grade, thinking, This was wrong, it was untrue, nothing was going to be all right. Still, I understood that, like Miss Connolly, the doctor meant well.

Doctors were interesting now that they had decided to go by their first names. Humility. Very nice.

Then there was some time I can't account for. Maybe things happened. Maybe I failed to imagine them. I was aware only that my hands were freezing and my head was on fire. My wife was there and then she was not there.

Tiffany pulled the curtains open and said, "I'm your nurse. I'm Tiffany." She was in her early twenties and she wore her hair pulled back tight against her skull and she bristled with efficiency. "Name?" she said. "Date of birth?" And then, rapidly, "Residence? What day is it? What is the date?" I passed the first tests easily: I knew who I was and when I was born and where I lived but I couldn't remember the day or the date. She seemed to take it personally.

"You don't know the *day*?"

I briefly considered mentioning the hippopotami.

"Where's my wife?"

"She can't see you now."

"Why not? Is she here?"

"You're here for pneumonia," she said, "so there'll be an x-ray and a CT scan."

"I have Parkinson's," I said.

"Whatever," she said. She went away, clickety-clack.

Now that I'm retired and just read all day, I'm not good on time. When she asked me what day it was I thought of that cartoon, the one with the two hippopotami up to their chins in water and one says to the other, "I keep thinking it's Tuesday." Of course if I had said that, they'd have put me in the crazy ward. I'd been there five or six years ago after I made an attempt at suicide. Thirty-six Ambiens and a handful of Xanax and the effect the next day was not death but a bad headache and a very sore throat. Plus two weeks locked up with my kind of people. Like me, they thought they wanted to cease being a burden on someone they loved.

I had fallen getting out of the bathtub. Zip, slip, and I was down. Three broken ribs. When they healed I could no longer draw a deep breath. And I couldn't stop trying. It was like being smothered slowly, over and over and over. For three weeks I went around gasping. Exhaustion. Panic attacks. Once in the middle of the night when I was pretending to sleep I heard my wife sobbing quietly and I realized I was driving her crazy. I was killing her. So, without a thought for Jesus or even for Beverly LaPlante, I decided to kill myself instead. Hence the Ambien and the Xanax. And then lockdown in the company of my fellow suicides. Like me, they each had some personal obsession and they had come to confuse obsession with love and, again like me, they had tried the easy way out. Afterward, I told my wife I was sorry, and she said, "If you ever try that again, I'll kill you myself."

My wife. You have to know her to understand. She's a genuine saint, the real thing without any pious crap, so she's not always easy to live with.

She was not a saint when we first married. She had her faults—plenty of them, I thought at the time—but she was beautiful and smart and funny, and she considered me interesting, so who could resist? Later, after she had rubbed some of the rough edges off me, I began to see her differently. Or maybe she changed. I don't know. But I became aware of that glow from inside her that nothing could dim, not even sickness or frustration or my occasional rage and jealousy, things that made her sad, not angry. Hers was an everyday kind of sanctity. She had an unnerving fondness for the truth and knowing her made you want to be a better person. Saints are not the easiest companions.

After my suicide attempt—immediately after—I lost my obsessions and began to enjoy life. It was as if I had died and come back a different person, free of all that nonsense. I had always been afraid of living, but

I wasn't any longer and I wasn't afraid of Jesus. Moreover, if she had still been around, I wouldn't have been afraid of Beverly LaPlante: I was that self-confident.

My wife and I grew closer and closer. We joked that we were becoming a single person, not even guessing that it was true.

So life was good and its nasty surprises didn't seem so nasty anymore. Not even the Parkinson's. It happened slowly. My left hand began to shake when I was typing, but I was in the final draft of a new book and until it was done I just ignored the shakes, corrected the errors, and finished my work. Then I took my shaky hand to Dr. Burn. A familial tremor, he said. Not Parkinson's. Familial tremor, my wife said, at least it's not the dread disease itself. A year later I was shaking more and walking in a half-assed kind of stumble so we went to Dr. Burn who said, Let's see a neurologist. The neurologist was Dr. Gershfield and he knew everything. Gershfield said, It's not, strictly speaking, Parkinson's. It's parkinsonism. Ism? Yes, parkinsonism. Well, my wife said, I'm glad we cleared that up. Then we all had a friendly Parkinson laugh. We saw him again in a month, and then every month for a year. By this time I was half in love with him and so was my wife. After all, like Jesus he had the power to dispense life or death. I was half in love with Jesus too.

There was a long night when they woke me every hour to draw blood. Toward morning they took another chest x-ray and a fresh CT scan of my lungs. I fell back asleep and in no time it was wakies. Tiffany stood by my bed at the ready. I said, "Good morning," but she was too busy for that. She nodded yes and went about taking my vitals.

"I keep thinking it's Tuesday," I said.

"It is Tuesday," she said. "Very good."

"One hippopotamus says to the other, 'I keep thinking it's Tuesday.'"

"It is Tuesday," she said. "Stop worrying."

The ceiling was spinning again.

"I thought I couldn't move because of the Parkinson's."

"We'll get that pneumonia under control by tomorrow. You can take that to the bank."

I laughed and said, "Take that to the bank!"

"It's a saying," she said. And off she went, kachung, kachung.

My wife came every day, morning and afternoon. She read a book while I slept and tried to make conversation when I woke but I wasn't making a lot of sense and naturally she was bored to death. Even saints get bored waiting. Maybe saints especially.

A doctor with a clipboard poked his head around the door.

"Just checking," he said.

"It's Tuesday," I said.

"Are you in great pain?"

"I'm not in any pain at all. I'm a male, white, eighty."

"I can see that," he said.

"You look about fourteen," I said.

He wrote something on his clipboard.

I was hot and drowsy and a little dizzy.

"No pain?" he said. "You sure?"

I couldn't find the words and I needed to explain to him about the limitations of being just a white male etcetera. I was feeling light-headed and the ceiling kept spinning as if I were drunk.

"I'm not drunk," I said.

"You're a riot," he said. "Hold on to that sense of humor."

Some time went by, maybe an hour or maybe a day, and another doctor appeared, a woman this time. She said, "Tiffany says you're concerned about Parkinson's, but your problem at present is pneumonia. You're on two antibiotics—that's the drip bag on your left—and your fever should be under control in another day. Maybe two. Then you can go home. Do you have any questions?"

"So I'm being cured of pneumonia?"

"Well, we can't cure Parkinson's. Yet."

"But the paralysis was caused by pneumonia? I've never heard of that."

"Nevertheless."

"What's your name?" I said. "Just so I know."

"Janet," she said.

"I mean what's your last name. Doctor what?"

There was a long pause. "We're here to make you well, not to make new friends." And she took off.

So it was pneumonia and not Parkinson's that had me momentarily paralyzed. Talk about downers! I would never have come here if I'd thought it was pneumonia.

My wife shouldn't have called 911. The plan had been to let pneumonia carry me off before Parkinson's had its final fling with me. If you're going to die anyway, we had agreed, better to do it before you begin to shake all day and your voice melts and maybe your mind as well. I had had three bouts of pneumonia in the past year, so we planned on having one ready when the time came. Or at least that's what we hoped. One night as we were winding up a long chat about whether we could count on pneumonia to do it or if we'd have to face the horrors of death by Parkinson's, my wife yawned and said, "Maybe you'll be lucky, sweetheart. Maybe you'll get run over by a truck."

I've always been lucky and I just knew I'd be lucky at the end. *La fin. Finito.*

My fever was gone and I was feeling terrific. The fourteen-year-old turned up after breakfast to say the x-ray and the CT scan were fine but they had revealed an unexplained mass in my left lung.

"A mass of what?" I said.

"Very funny," he said. "But this is a serious matter and you ought to take it up with your primary physician."

"A mass of stuff?" I said. "What kind of stuff?"

"At the least, you'll be prone to frequent bouts of pneumonia. Deep pneumonia."

I said, "I knew it! I've always been lucky."

"Do you have any other questions?" he said.

"How old are you?" I said.

"Keep up the good work," he said. "Keep smiling."

He left the room without saying goodbye.

So. A mass in my lungs. He hadn't used the *C* word but what else could a mass be? Lung cancer. Consider it. Cancer of the lungs. It didn't sound so bad, really. Maybe this was the truck that would run me down before Parkinson's had its final fling. Before the drooling set in. So now we had two possibilities of escape: pneumonia and cancer. Which would be first, I wondered? Which would be less painful? And then a surge of relief as I realized that, cancer or pneumonia, my wife would be there. And good old Dr. Burn would refer me to palliative care. Maybe with my own little bottle of morphine. I was looking forward to a choice of death and I couldn't wait to tell my wife.

A momentary pause. A catch in my breath.

Was I just kidding myself or had our constant talk about escaping Parkinson's done the trick, and any escape seemed good?

"What happened to that boy doctor?" I said to the empty room. "And what about Tiffany?"

Nobody answered. A bell rang. A door slammed.

Tiffany appeared and said, "You're being discharged today. You'll sign papers at the desk. Your wife is here. Still." She pushed my bed tray into a corner and pushed the visitor's chair out of her way and marched off to bring order and efficiency to other lives. Her heels clacked annoyance as she went.

A year passed and my balance grew more shaky, my walk became a stagger, and my voice was reduced to an unsympathetic whine. My wife took all this to heart and, just for companionship, she whined along with me now and then. But mostly she took care of me as if attendance on a half-dead white male, eighty, was real fun and just what she had been hoping for in life.

Over the past year we had gradually become one person, or maybe two persons in one being, as Aquinas might say. We had transubstantiated and become a problem in philosophy. Or theology.

It was getting late and where was the pneumonia, we wanted to know, where was the cancer? The cancer had turned out to be a benign tumor with little promise, though we tried to hurry it along by prayer and good works. So for now pneumonia had become our only hope.

We saw friends and went out to dinner and carried on with our crooked life. All around us people were coughing and wheezing and saying they couldn't stand this flu, they wished they were dead, and here we were waiting on just one little pneumonia bug to do its work.

Then, there it was. We were watching television—*Judge Judy*, to be exact—when suddenly I went cold. Not all over, just in my hands and feet. My head was hot and grew hotter and my hands grew colder and I tried to stand but I couldn't move. This is it, I said, or at least I think so. My wife said, Oh God, no! She tried to help me off the couch but, paralyzed, I weighed a ton and she had to give up. Never mind, I said, but don't call 911. So we just sat together on the couch. Two old people wrapped in each other's arms.

Everything comes to an end.

Mobility returns and you help me to my bed. A day goes by and then another. You pray to know what to do but we have long since agreed to do nothing and that's what we do.

I say, I'll miss you when I'm dead. And in a while there comes the final moment: the earth stops turning and a luminous silence descends. And then, as we draw one last breath together, I snatch your hand. And hold it. Holding it, and holding it, and still holding it. I breathe out.

Still, I'll miss you when I'm dead.

ACKNOWLEDGMENTS

I want to offer my profound gratitude to Deborah Treisman, Fiction Editor of the *New Yorker*, for her editorial expertise and her unique generosity of mind and spirit. Her assistance, offered unconditionally and without limit, has made this collection possible.

Many of these stories originally appeared in three collections: *Family Affairs*, *Desires*, and *Comedians*. Most of these stories were first published in magazines, to whose editors I offer my thanks: the *New Yorker*, the *Atlantic*, *Epoch*, *Harper's*, *Esquire*, *Penthouse*, *Village Voice*, *Catholic World*, *Story*, *Sequoia*, *Tendril*, *Fiction*, *Granta*, and *Zyzzyva*.